Praise for the charming Regency romances of

Stephanie Laurens

"All I need is her name on the cover
to make me buy the book."
—bestselling author Linda Howard

"Her lush sensuality takes my breath away."
—author Lisa Kleypas

"Coulter and Quick, look out!"
—*Affaire de Coeur*

STEPHANIE LAURENS

was born in Sri Lanka, but has lived mostly in Australia. After qualifying as a scientist, she and her husband traveled extensively through the Far and Middle East, as well as throughout Europe and England. Four years in London gave her the settings for her Regency romances. Now settled once more in Australia, she lives in a comfortable suburban house with her husband, two children, a mindless but lovable dog and a cat with a crooked leg.

A Season for Scandal

Stephanie Laurens

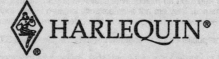

HARLEQUIN®

TORONTO • NEW YORK • LONDON
AMSTERDAM • PARIS • SYDNEY • HAMBURG
STOCKHOLM • ATHENS • TOKYO • MILAN • MADRID
PRAGUE • WARSAW • BUDAPEST • AUCKLAND

ISBN 0-373-83479-9

A SEASON FOR SCANDAL

Copyright © 2001 by Harlequin Books S.A.

The publisher acknowledges the copyright holder of the individual titles as follows:

TANGLED REINS
Copyright © 1992 by Stephanie Laurens

FAIR JUNO
Copyright © 1994 by Stephanie Laurens

CONTENTS

Tangled Reins

CHAPTER ONE

'Mmmm.' Dorothea closed her eyes, savouring the taste of sun-warmed wild blackberry. Surely the most delicious of summer's delights. She surveyed the huge bush. Burgeoning with ripe fruit, it stretched across one side of the small clearing. More than enough to fill tonight's pie, with plenty left over to make jam. She settled her basket on the ground and set to. Working methodically over the bush, she selected the best berries and dropped them into the basket in a fluid stream. While her hands laboured, her mind went tripping. How childlike her sister still was, for all her sixteen years. It was at her suggestion Dorothea was here, deep in the woods of the neighbouring estate. Cecily craved blackberries for supper. So, brown eyes sparkling, golden ringlets dancing, she had begged her elder sister, about to depart for a ramble to gather herbs, to make a detour to the blackberry bush.

Her elder sister sighed. Would London erase that dazzling spontaneity? More importantly, would their projected trip to the capital free Cecily of this humdrum existence? Six months had passed since their mother, Cynthia, Lady Darent, had succumbed to a chill, leaving her two daughters to the guardianship of their cousin, Herbert, Lord Darent. Five interminable months spent at Darent Hall in Northamptonshire while the lawyers picked over the will had convinced Dorothea that no help and much hindrance could be expected from that quarter. Herbert, not to put too fine a point on it, was an indefatigable bore. And Marjorie, his wife, prim, prosy and hopelessly inelegant in every way, was worse than useless. If their grandmother had not appeared, exactly like the proverbial fairy godmother, goodness only knew what they would have done.

Suddenly unable to move, she paused to gaze, unperturbed, at a bramble hooked about the hem of her dress. Just as well it was her old dimity! Despite Aunt Agnes's bleats about mourning clothes, she had insisted on her practice of wearing the outmoded green dress for her foraging expeditions. The square-cut neckline and bodice fitted to the waist belonged to another time; the full skirts, without the support of the voluminous petticoats they were intended to cover, clung to her willowy figure. She examined the tiny tears the briar thorns had left in the material.

As she straightened, the warmth of the clearing, hemmed in by undergrowth and trees and lit by the sun slanting through the high branches, struck her anew. On impulse, her hands went to her hair, hanging heavy in a bun on her neck. With the restricting pins removed, it fell in a cascade of rich mahogany brown to her waist. Cooler, she resumed her picking.

At least she was confident of what lay in store for herself in London. No amount of effort from her grandmother would be sufficient to win *her* a husband! Green flashes ran like emeralds through her huge eyes. Her eyes, of course, were her major, and only, asset. All her other points, innocuous in themselves, were disastrously unfashionable. Her hair was dark, not the favoured blonde; her face pale as alabaster and not peaches and cream like Cecily's. Her nose was well enough but her mouth was too large and her lips too full. Rosebud lips were the craze. And she was too tall and her figure slim against the prevailing trend to voluptuous curves. To cap it all, she was twenty-two, with a strong streak of independence to boot! Hardly the type of female to attract the attention of the fashionable male. With a deep chuckle she popped another ripe berry between her too full lips.

Her relegation to the ranks of the old maids disturbed her not at all. She had enough to live comfortably for the rest of her days and looked forward to years of country pursuits at the Grange with equanimity. She had received considerable attention from the local gentlemen, yet no man had awoken in her the slightest desire to trade her independent existence for the respectable state of matrimony. While her peers plotted and schemed to get that all-important ring on their finger, she saw no reason to follow their lead. Only love, that strange and compelling emotion that, she freely admitted, had yet to touch her heart would, she suspected, be strong enough to tempt her from her comfortable ways. In truth, she had difficulty envisaging the gentleman whose attraction would prove sufficient to seduce her from her established life. For too long now she had been her own mistress. Free to do as she wished, busy and secure—she was content. Cecily was a different matter.

Bright as a button, Cecily yearned for a more glittering lifestyle. Although so young, she had a burning interest in people, and the horizons of the Grange were far too limited for her satisfaction. Sweet, young and fashionably beautiful, she would surely find some elegant and personable young man to give her all her heart desired. Which was the primary reason they were going to London.

Dorothea had been absently regarding a particularly large berry, almost out of her reach. With a sudden smile she stretched one white hand high to the tempting fruit. Her smile dissolved into stunned surprise as a strong arm slipped around her waist. The fact barely registered before a deft movement delivered her into a crushing embrace. She caught a glimpse of a dark face. The next instant she was being ruthlessly, expertly and very comprehensively kissed.

For one long moment her mind remained blank. Then consciousness flooded back. She was not inexperienced. Lack of response would see her released faster than any action. Prosaic and practical, she willed herself to frigidity.

She had seriously misjudged the threat. Despite perfectly clear instructions, her body refused to comply. Horrified, she felt a sudden warmth rush through her, followed by an almost overwhelming urge to lean into that embrace, clearly poised to become even more passionate if she succumbed. No country admirer had dared kiss her like this! The desire to respond to the demanding lips crushing her own grew second by second, beyond her control. Thoroughly unnerved, she tried to break free. Long fingers slid into her hair, holding her head still, and the arm around her waist tightened ruthlessly. The strength of the body she was now crushed against confirmed her help-lessness. From a disjointed jumble of thoughts, rapidly becom-ing less coherent, emerged the conclusion that her captor was neither gypsy nor vagabond. He was certainly no local! That first fleeting glimpse had left an impression of negligent ele-gance. As she was drawn inexorably beyond thought, senses reeling, a strange turbulence threatened to engulf her. Then, abruptly, as if a door were slammed shut, the kiss was skilfully brought to an end.

Her mind awhirl, senses scorched, she looked up · into a dark-browed face. Hazel eyes, distinctly amused, gazed into her own green orbs. Sheer fury erupted within her. She aimed a stinging slap at the laughing face. It never landed. Although the action was not betrayed by a flicker of an eyelid, her hand was caught in mid-air in a firm grip and gently drawn down to her side.

Her assailant smiled provokingly, thoroughly appreciative of her beautifully outraged countenance. 'No, I don't think I will let you hit me. How was I to know you weren't the black-smith's daughter?'

The voice was light and gentle, definitely that of an edu-cated man. Recollecting how she must look in her old green dimity with her hair about her shoulders, she bit her lip, feeling ridiculously young as the betraying flush rose to her cheeks.

'So,' continued the soft voice, 'if not the blacksmith's daughter, who, then?'

At the gently mocking tone, she raised her chin defiantly. 'I'm Dorothea Darent. Now will you please release me?'

The arm around her moved not one whit. A slight frown creased her captor's brow. 'Ah…Darent. Of the Grange?'

A slight nod was all she could manage. Conversation was a major effort while held so closely against him. Who on earth was he?

'I'm Hazelmere.'

A blunt statement of fact. For a moment she thought she had not heard aright. But that face, arrogant amusement deeply etched in the lines about the strong mouth, surely belonged to no one else?

She had heard the rumours. Their old friend, Lady Moreton, whose estate encompassed these woods, had died while they were at Darent Hall. Her great-nephew, the Marquis of Hazelmere, had reputedly inherited Moreton Park. The news had set the district abuzz. In a small county backwater the possibility that one of the acknowledged leaders of the ton might be the new owner of a major local estate was, in any circumstances, likely to generate a certain amount of curiosity. When the person in question was the Marquis of Hazelmere the curiosity was frankly rampant.

The rector's wife had primmed up her mouth in a most disparaging way. 'My dear! Nothing on earth would induce me to acknowledge such a man! Such a shocking reputation! *So* notorious!' When Dorothea had, not unnaturally, asked how this reputation had been gained, Mrs Matthews had suddenly recalled to whom she was speaking and rapidly excused herself on the pretext of passing around the scones. At Mrs Mannerim's she had heard such charges as gambling, womanising and general licentiousness laid at the Marquis's door. Although she was inexperienced in wider society, common sense was her forte. As Lord Hazelmere continued to grace the ton presumably the gossip, as usual, was exaggerated. Besides, she could not imagine the eminently respectable Lady Moreton having a licentious great-nephew.

Dragging her mind from contemplation of his mesmeric hazel eyes and long sculpted lips, she rapidly revised her opinion of the Marquis of Hazelmere. Put simply, the man was even more dangerous than his reputation indicated.

Her thoughts had flowed across her face, a clear procession from initial bewilderment, through dawning realisation, to awed and scandalised comprehension. The hazel eyes glinted. To a palate jaded by an unremitting diet of society's beauties, on whose simpering faces no trace of genuine emotion was ever permitted, the beautiful and expressive countenance was infinitely attractive.

'Precisely.' He said it to see if she would blush so delightfully again and was amply rewarded.

Dorothea indignantly transferred her gaze to contemplation

of his left shoulder. She was hardly short, but her topmost curls barely reached his chin. Which left his chest, very close, at eye-level. Nothing in her limited experience had taught her how to deal with a situation like this. She had never felt so helpless in her life!

With her attention elsewhere, she missed the deepening curve of the severe lips which had so recently claimed hers. 'And precisely what is Miss Dorothea Darent doing, trespassing in my woods?'

The proprietorial tone brought her head up again, as he had known it would. 'Oh! You *have* inherited the Park from Lady Moreton!'

He nodded, reluctantly releasing her and almost imperceptibly moving aside. The hazel eyes did not leave her face.

Relieved of the distracting intimacy, she paused to gather her wits. In a manner as imperious as she could muster she replied, 'Lady Moreton always gave her permission for us to gather whatever we wished from her woods. However, now that *you* own the Park—'

'You will, of course,' Hazelmere interposed smoothly, 'continue to gather whatever you wish, whenever you wish.' He smiled. 'I will even undertake not to mistake you for the blacksmith's daughter next time.'

Dorothea swept him a contemptuous curtsy, green eyes flashing. 'Thank you, Lord Hazelmere! I'll be sure to warn Hetty.'

The comment stumped him, as she had intended. She turned to pick up her basket. Still mentally adrift from the after-effects of that kiss, she hastily concluded that in this instance retreat was the better part of valour. She had reckoned without Lord Hazelmere. 'And who, exactly, is Hetty?'

Arrested in the act of ignominious flight, she gathered together the shreds of her composure to reply acidly, 'Why, the blacksmith's daughter, of course!'

Under her fascinated gaze the striking, almost harsh-featured face relaxed, the satirical amusement replaced by genuine delight. Laughing openly, he put out a hand to grasp the basket, preventing her from leaving. 'I think we're quits, Miss

Darent, so don't run away. Your basket is only half full and there are plenty of berries left on this bush.' The hazel eyes were quizzing her, his smile disarming. Sensing her hesitation, he continued, 'Yes, I know you can't reach them, but I can. If you'll just stand there, and hold your basket so, we'll soon have it full.'

It dawned on Dorothea that her qualifications to deal with the gentleman before her were inadequate. Unwise in the ways of the world, she had no idea what she should do. On the one hand, the rector's wife would expect her to withdraw immediately; on the other, curiosity urged her to remain. And, even if she did make up her mind to go, it was doubtful whether this masterful creature would allow her to leave. Besides, as he had positioned her here with the basket in her hands and was even now filling it with the choicest berries from the top of the bush, it would hardly be polite to walk away. Thus reasoning, she remained where she was, taking the opportunity to more closely inspect her tormentor.

Her initial impression of quiet elegance owed much, she decided, to the excellent cut of his shooting jacket. Honesty then forced her to acknowledge that broad shoulders set atop a lean and muscular frame significantly contributed to the overall effect of masculine power only superficially cloaked. His black hair was cut short in the prevailing mode and curled gently over his brow. The hazel eyes, so appropriate, she thought, in the Marquis of Hazelmere, were disconcertingly direct. The decidedly patrician nose and firm mouth and chin declared that here was a man used to dominating his world. But she had seen both eyes and mouth soften with humour, making him appear much more approachable. In fact, she decided, his smile would be utterly devastating to young ladies more impressionable than herself. Then, too, there was that subtly attractive aura, which fell into the category of subjects no well-bred lady ever discussed. Remembering his reputation, she could find no trace of dissipation. His actions, however, left little doubt of the existence of the fire that had given rise to the smoke.

Correctly guessing most of the jumble of thoughts going

through her head, Hazelmere surreptitiously watched her face from the corner of his eyes. What a jewel she was! The classically moulded face framed by luxuriant dark hair was arresting in itself. But those eyes! Like enormous twin emeralds, clear and bright, they mirrored her thoughts in a thoroughly beguiling way. Her lips he had already sampled—soft and yielding, deliciously sensual—and he could readily imagine developing a fascination for them. The rest of the package was equally enticing. Nevertheless, if he was to further their acquaintance he would have to go carefully.

Removing the loaded basket from her hands, he retrieved his hunting rifle from the opposite side of the clearing. Correctly interpreting the question clearly written on her uncertain face, he said, 'I'm now going to escort you home, Miss Darent.' Inwardly grinning at the mutinous expression that greeted this calm pronouncement, he continued before she could speak. 'No! Don't argue. In the social circle to which I belong, no young lady would ever be found out of doors alone.'

The pious tone made Dorothea's eyes blaze. Lord Hazelmere's tactics were proving extremely difficult to combat. As she could find no ready answer nor see any way of altering his resolve, she reluctantly fell into step beside him as he started down the path.

'Incidentally,' he continued conversationally, pursuing a subject guaranteed to keep her on the defensive, 'satisfy my curiosity. Just why *are* you wandering alone in the woods, without the presence of even a nitwit maid?'

She had suspected this question might come, precisely because she had no good answer. The reprehensible creature was undoubtedly teasing her! Swallowing her irritation, she calmly replied, 'I'm well known in this neighbourhood, and at my age can hardly be considered a young miss in need of constant chaperoning.' Even to her ears it sounded lame.

The reprehensible creature chuckled. 'My dear child, you're not *that* old! And quite clearly you do need the protection of an attendant.'

As he had just proved the truth of that, she could hardly argue the point. But, her temper flying and caution disappearing with it, her unruly tongue marched ahead unheeding. 'In future, Lord Hazelmere, whenever I'm tempted to walk *your* woods I'll most certainly take an attendant!'

'Very wise,' he murmured, voice low.

Unattuned to the nuance of his tone, she did not stop to think before pointing out, in her most reasonable voice, 'But I really can't see the necessity. You said you would not mistake me for a village girl next time.'

'Which merely means,' he said in tones provocative enough to send a tingling shiver down her spine, 'that next time I'll know whose lips I'm kissing.'

'Oh!' She gasped and stopped to look up at him, outrage in every line.

Halting beside her, Hazelmere laughed and gently touched her cheek with one long finger, further increasing her ire. 'I repeat, Miss Darent—you need an attendant. Don't risk walking in my woods or anywhere else without one. In case the country beaux haven't told you, you're by far too lovely to wander alone, *despite* your advancing years.'

The amused hazel eyes held hers throughout this speech. Dorothea, seeing something behind the laughter which made her feel distinctly odd, could find nothing to say in reply. Irritated, furious and light-headed all at once, she turned abruptly and continued along the path, skirts swishing angrily.

Glancing at the troubled face beside him, Hazelmere's smile deepened. He sought for a suitably innocuous topic from the tangle of information poured into his ears by his great-aunt before her death. 'I understand you have recently lost your mother, Miss Darent. I believe my great-aunt told me you were staying with relatives in the north.'

This promising sally fell wide. Dorothea turned her wide green eyes on him and, ignoring the dictum that ladies should not answer a gentleman's question with another question, asked breathlessly, 'Did you see her, then, before she died?'

The marked degree of disbelief, for some reason, stung him. 'Believe it or not, Miss Darent, I frequently visited my great-aunt, of whom I was very fond. However, as I rarely stayed longer than a day, it's hardly surprising that neither you, nor

in all probability the rest of the county, were aware of that
fact. I was with her for the three days prior to her death and,
as I was her heir, she endeavoured to instruct me in the families of the area.'

This speech, not unnaturally, brought the colour to her
cheeks, but instead of turning away in confusion, as he expected, she met his eyes unflinchingly. 'You see, we were such
good friends that I was most unhappy not to have seen her
again.'

The hazel eyes held hers for a pregnant second. Then he
relented. 'The end was quite painless. She died in her sleep
and, considering the pain she'd been in over the past years,
that can only be viewed as a relief.'

She nodded, eyes downcast.

In an attempt to lighten the mood he tried again. 'Do you
and your sister plan to remain at the Grange indefinitely?'

This time he had more success. Her face cleared. 'Oh, no!
We're to go to our grandmother, Lady Merion, early next
year.'

Hermione, Lady Merion, previously the Dowager Lady Darent, had swept through the chilly corridors of Darent Hall like
a summer breeze, warm from the glamour of London. And
had taken undisputed charge. The sisters, together with Aunt
Agnes, the elderly spinster who acted as their nominal chaperon, had been dispatched home to the Grange, buried deep in
Hampshire, there to wait out their year of mourning. They
were to present themselves to her ladyship in Cavendish
Square in February, six months from now. And what was to
happen from that point on was, they all had been given to
understand, very definitely in her ladyship's competent hands.
Reminiscing, Dorothea grinned. 'She intends to present us.'
Noticing the sudden lift of the dark brows, she continued defensively, 'Cecily is considered very beautiful and, I believe,
should make a good match.'

'And yourself?'

Suddenly inexplicably sensitive on this point, she believed
she detected a derisive note in the smooth voice. She answered
more categorically than she intended. 'I am hardly ware for

the marriage mart. I intend to enjoy my days in London seeing all the sights, and, if truth be known, watching those about me.'

She glanced up and was surprised by the intensity of the hazel gaze fixed unswervingly on her face. Then he smiled in such an enigmatic way that she was unsure whether it was intended for her or was purely introspective. A thought occurred. 'Do you know Lady Merion?'

The smile deepened. 'I should think all fashionable London knows Lady Merion. However, in my case, she's a particularly close friend of my mother's.'

'Please, tell me what she's like?' It was his turn to be surprised. Seeing it, she rushed on, 'You see, I've not met her since I was a child, except for the one night she spent at Darent Hall earlier this year, when she came to tell us we were to come to London.'

Hazelmere, reflecting that this conversation was undoubtedly the strangest he had ever conducted with a personable young lady, helped her over the stile and into the lane, then fell to considering Lady Merion. 'Well, your grandmother has always been a leader of fashion, and is well connected with all the old tabbies who matter in London. She's thick as thieves with Lady Jersey and Princess Esterhazy. Both are patronesses of Almack's, to which you must gain entry if you wish to belong to the ton. In your case, that hurdle will not be a problem. Lady Merion is independently wealthy and lives in a mansion on Cavendish Square, left her by her second husband, George, Lord Merion. She married him some years after your grandfather's death and he died about five years ago, I think. She's something of a tartar, and a high stickler, so I would advise you not to attempt to wander London unattended! On the other hand, she has an excellent sense of humour and is known as being kind and generous to her friends. She's in some ways eccentric and rarely leaves London except to visit friends in the country. All in all, I doubt you could find a lady more capable of launching you and your sister successfully into the ton.'

Dorothea pondered this potted biography, finally remarking in a pensive tone, 'She did seem very fashionable.'

'She is certainly that,' he agreed.

They had reached a gate in the high stone wall that had bordered the lane for the last hundred yards. Dorothea stopped and reached for the basket. 'These are the gardens of the Grange.'

'Then I'll leave you here,' Hazelmere promptly replied. He had escorted her home purely to prolong his time in her company but had no wish to be seen with her. He knew too well the gossip and speculation which would inevitably spring from such a sighting. Expertly capturing her hand, he carried it to his lips, enjoying the spark of anger that flared in the green eyes and the blush that rose in response to his understanding smile. 'But remember my warning! If you wish to keep in your grandmama's good graces, don't go about London unattended. Young ladies who venture the London streets alone won't remain alone for long. Farewell, Miss Darent.'

Released, Dorothea opened the gate and made good her escape.

She hurried through the garden, for once unconscious of the heady scents rising from the rioting flowers. The long shadows cast by the ancient roof of the Grange fell across the path, heralding the end of the day. She stopped in the garden hall; the coolness of the dim, stone-flagged room brought relief to her burning cheeks. The clattering steps of the housemaid sounded in the passageway. Moving to the door, she called her in.

'Take these berries to Cook, please, Doris. And after that you can lay out the meadowsweet on the drying racks.' With a wave of her hand she indicated the wooden frames covered with tightly stretched muslin lying on the bench along one side of the room.

As an afterthought, she added, 'And please tell my aunt I've gone to lie on my bed until dinner. I think I must have a touch of the sun.' More accurately, a touch of the Marquis of Hazelmere! she thought furiously. Successfully negotiating the passageway and stairs undetected, she closed her bedchamber door and sank on to the window-seat.

Gazing over the now deeply shadowed garden, she struggled to bring some order to a mind still seething. Ridiculous! She had left the Grange a serenely confident twenty-two-year-old, entirely secure in her independent world. Yet here she was, a scant hour later, feeling, she suspected, as Cecily might if the Squire's son had made eyes at her! It was not as if she had never been kissed before. It shouldn't make the slightest difference who was doing the kissing. The fact that it had made a great deal of difference exacerbated a temper already tried by a pair of hazel eyes. A pair of all too perceptive hazel eyes. She spent the next ten minutes reading herself a determined lecture on the inadvisability of forming an attachment for a rake.

Fortified, she forced herself to consider the matter in a more reasoning light. Undoubtedly she should feel outraged, ready to decry the Marquis as a licentious scoundrel. Yet, despite her irritation, she was too honest not to admit that her inappropriate attire was partly to blame. Moreover, she suspected that the response of a young lady on finding herself in the arms of the Marquis of Hazelmere should have been quite different from the way she had behaved. In her defence, she felt it should be noted that had she swooned in his arms he would have had little choice but to wait with her until she recovered. Then the situation would have been, if anything, worse. By following this train of thought, she convinced herself there had been nothing particularly reprehensible about the proceedings after Lord Hazelmere had released her. In fact, he had proved a valuable informant on the subject of her grandmother.

What continued to bother her were the events preceding her release from that far too familiar embrace. Her fingers strayed to her lips, which, despite his expertise, were slightly bruised. The memory of his hard body against hers was still a physical sensation. The clock on the landing struck the quarter-hour. She determinedly put her thoughts on the afternoon's events aside, resolutely consigning the Marquis and all his works to

the remotest corner of her mind. Nothing was more certain
than that *he* would forget all about *her* by tomorrow.

Changing out of her old gown and into the freshly pressed
sprigged muslin laid out for the warm evening, she gauged
her chances of unwittingly running into him again. Well
versed in the ways of the local gentry, she knew it would be
all but impossible for him to meet her socially in the country.
And, by his own admission, he was not in the habit of remaining over-long at Moreton Park. She told herself she was
relieved. To make doubly sure her relief remained undisturbed,
she resolved that, in future, she would ensure that her reluctant
sister joined her on her rambles.

Picking up a brush, she attacked her long tresses vigorously
before winding them up in a simple knot. She glanced quickly
at her reflection in the mirror perched on her tallboy. Satisfied
she had dealt sufficiently with the potential ramifications of
the advent of the Marquis of Hazelmere into her life, she went
downstairs to her dinner.

A fortnight later, returning to Hazelmere House, his mansion in Cavendish Square, situated almost directly opposite
Merion House, the Marquis found a large pile of letters and
invitations awaiting him. Sorting through them, he strolled into
his library. Extracting an envelope of a particularly virulent
shade of purple from the bundle, he held it at arm's length to
escape the cloying perfume emanating from it and groped for
his quizzing glass. Recognising the flowery script of his latest
mistress, a dazzling creature abundantly well endowed for her
station in life, his black brows drew together. He opened the
letter and scanned the few lines within. The black brows rose.
A smile of a kind Dorothea Darent would not have recognised
twisted the mobile lips. Throwing both letter and envelope into
the fire, he turned to his desk.

The footman who answered the summons of the library bell
ten minutes later found his master fixing his seal to a letter.
Glancing up as the door opened, Hazelmere waved the envelope to cool the wax, then held it out. 'Deliver this by hand
immediately.'

'Yes, m'lord.'

Watching the retreating back of the footman, Hazelmere considered the probable reception of his politely savage missive. Thus ended yet another *affaire*. Stretching his long legs to the fire, he fell to considering the constantly changing parade of his high-flying mistresses. While providing the ton with a stream of *on-dits*, he felt that the inevitability of the game was beginning to bore him. After more than ten years on the town, there were few fashionable vices he had not sampled and the pattern of his activities was becoming wearyingly predictable.

Thinking again of the discarded Cerise, he compared her ripe beauty with that of the green-eyed girl whose face had proved disturbingly haunting. His dissatisfaction with his present lot stemmed in large part from that encounter in Moreton Park woods. Entirely his own fault, of course.

Marc St John Ralton Henry, at thirty-one years of age the fifth Marquis of Hazelmere and one of the wealthiest peers of the realm, let his mind wander back to the first time he had heard Miss Darent's name, during a conversation he had had with his great-aunt the night before she died. A remarkably forthright old lady, she had fixed him with a steely look and embarked on an inquisition as to his marital intentions. This had been prefaced by the remark, 'I know your mother won't mention this, so I'm takin' advantage of the fact that, as I'm dying, you can't very well tell me to go to the devil!'

Appreciative of the ploy and having admitted he had no present plans in the matter, he had settled down to listen with good grace to the subsequent dissertation, something he would not have done had it been anyone else.

'Can't say I blame you for not wanting to marry any of these namby-pamby misses presented every year,' she'd snorted derisively. 'Can't abide such ninny-hammers myself! But why not look to wider fields? There's plenty of suitable chits who for one reason or another have never made it to London.'

Catching sight of his sceptical face, she had continued, 'Oh, you needn't think that just because they're country misses they

couldn't handle life in the ton. There's Dorothea Darent, for
one. Young, beautiful, well dowered and as well born as yourself. The only reason *she* hasn't been presented is that she's
spent the last six years running her widowed mother's household. Cynthia Darent should be *kicked* for not bringing her out
years ago!' Here Great-Aunt Etta had paused, musing on the
sins of the late Lady Darent. 'Well, it's too late for that now,
'cause she's dead.'

'Who? The beautiful Dorothea?' had asked Hazelmere, all
at sea.

'No, fool! Cynthia! She died a few months ago and the girls
have gone to Darent Hall for a while. Pity. I should have liked
to see Dorothea again. No namby-pamby miss, that one!'

'How is it that, despite never having been presented, this
paragon is not yet wed? Surely the country gentlemen are not
such slowtops?'

Great-Aunt Etta had chuckled. 'I rather suspect that's because no gentleman has yet shown her any good reason to
marry! Look at it from her point of view. She's got position
enough, wealth enough and her independence to boot. Why
get married?'

He had grinned back, responding to the laughter in the old
lady's eyes. 'I dare say I could make a few suggestions.'

'Yes, I dare say *you* could! But that's neither here nor there,
for you're not likely to meet her. Unless Hermione Merion
takes an interest. I've written to her, so she may do. There's
Cecily too. The younger sister, and another beauty, though of
a different style. She'll have to be brought out, too. But Cecily
would try the patience of a saint. And, as you definitely ain't
one, she won't do for you. But enough of the Darent sisters.
I merely give them as examples.' And so the conversation had
moved on.

The idea that Great-Aunt Etta had, in fact, been trying to
make him look at Dorothea Darent as a potential wife had
occurred to him shortly after he met that remarkable young
lady.

Over the past ten years he had steadfastly refused to seriously consider any of the flighty young females paraded for

his approval at Almack's and the ton parties. This had caused considerable consternation among other family members, notably his two older sisters, Maria and Susan, who were constantly pushing one or other of their favoured aspirants in his way. His stance had been fully supported by his mother and Great-Aunt Etta, both of whom seemed to understand the almost suffocating boredom he felt within minutes of attempting to converse with the latest simpering and apparently witless offerings. He knew his mother longed for him to marry but had reputedly told an acquaintance that unless they changed the prevailing fashion in débutantes she never expected to see it. As for Great-Aunt Etta, she had never said a word to him on the subject until that night.

Given that Great-Aunt Etta had known him every bit as well as his mother, it was perfectly possible that she had intended to draw his attention to Miss Darent. She would never have been so gauche as to approach the matter directly, knowing that the most likely outcome by that route was polite and chilly refusal to have anything to do with the chit. Instead she had introduced her name in a roundabout fashion, merely telling him that the girl was in every way suitable, but leaving him to make his own ground. *Very* like Great-Aunt Etta! Well, Great-Aunt Etta, he mused with a smile, I've met your Dorothea, and in a more effective way than I think even you would have dreamt of!

CHAPTER TWO

A low moan brought Dorothea's head around sharply to peer through the dim light at her sister, curled in the opposite corner of the carriage. Cecily's eyes were shut but the line between her fair brows showed clearly that she was far from sleep. She moved her head restlessly on the squabs. The coach lurched into a rut as the horses' hoofs skidded on the icy road. Dorothea caught the swinging strap to stop herself from being thrown. As the coach ponderously righted itself and resumed its steady progress she saw that Cecily had drawn herself up into a tight ball and wedged herself firmly into the corner, her face turned away.

Dorothea returned her attention to the dreary landscape, glimpsed fitfully through the bare branches of the trees and hedges lining the road. The grey February afternoon was closing in. The patter of drizzle on the coach windows punctuated the stillness within. Then, rising like a castle through the gathering gloom, standing on a crest surrounded by the dark shadows of its windbreaks, loomed the Three Feathers Inn. As it was just over halfway to London from the Grange, situated on the Bath Road, she had chosen it as their overnight stop. If it had been only herself travelling to London she would have made the journey in a single day. But Cecily was a poor traveller. With luck, their slow pace broken by a night's rest would allow her to arrive in Cavendish Square in a fit state to greet their grandmother.

The only other occupant of the carriage was their middle-aged maid, Betsy, who had tended them from the cradle. She dozed lightly, enveloped in woollen shawls on the seat facing Dorothea. After much consideration, Aunt Agnes had been left behind. There had been nothing specific in Lady Merion's letter summoning them to London, but the discussions at Darent Hall had clearly been on the unspoken understanding that Aunt Agnes would continue to do her duty and escort her charges to Cavendish Square. However, Aunt Agnes's rheumatism was legendary, and Dorothea had no wish to saddle herself with the querulous, though much loved old lady, either on the road to London or once they were arrived, supposedly to enjoy themselves. Furthermore, Aunt Agnes's opinions on men, of whatever station, were dampening in the extreme. Dorothea thought it unlikely that her presence would aid in the push to find Cecily a husband. Nevertheless, her polite note to Lady Merion, informing her of their expected date of arrival, had made no reference whatever to Aunt Agnes.

The coach lumbered on through the steadily thickening mists. It had been overcast all day, but for the most part the rain had held off, much to the relief of their coachman, Lang. The journey to London with the roads only just cleared was always a risky business. Wrapped in his thick frieze coat, he was deeply relieved to turn his team in under the arch of the inn. It was a large establishment, one of the busiest posting houses in the district. The main yard was devoted primarily to travellers changing horses or temporarily halting. The large travelling carriage rumbled through and on under another archway into the coachyard. Ostlers ran to free the steaming horses, and the landlord came forward to assist the sisters into the inn.

Here, however, a problem lay waiting.

While they warmed themselves before the roaring fire in a snug, low-ceilinged parlour Mr Simms apologised profusely. 'There's a prize-fight on in the village, miss. We're booked out. I've kept a bedchamber for you, but I'm afraid there's no hope of a private parlour.' The rubicund landlord, middle-aged, with daughters of his own, eyed the young ladies anxiously.

Dorothea drew a deep breath. After travelling at a snail's pace all day she did not really care what was going forward in the neighbourhood, as long as she and Cecily were ade-

quately housed for the night. She automatically appraised the
neat and spotlessly clean room. At least there would be no
danger of damp sheets or poorly cooked food in this house.
There was no point in being overly distressed by the lack of
a parlour. Drawing herself to her full height, she nodded to
the clearly worried Simms. 'Very well. I see it can't be helped.
Will you please show us to our bedchamber?'

Mr Simms had correctly guessed the Darent sisters' station
from Dorothea's letter requesting bedchambers and parlour.
While he rarely criticised the ways of his clients, he thought
it a crying shame that two such pretty young ladies were travelling escorted only by servants. He led them up to the bedchamber he had had prepared for them. Experience of the go-
ings-on likely to occur within his house before the night was
through had led him to house them in the large bedchamber
on the north side of the inn. This was the oldest part of the
rambling building, isolated from the rest, and reached only by
a separate stairway close to his private domain.

Arriving, puffing, on the landing, he threw open a stout
door. 'I've put you in this bedchamber here, miss, because it's
out of the way, like. The inn will soon be fair to burstin' with
all the young gentlemen been to see the fight. My missus says
to tell ye to stay put in your chamber and lock the door and
she'll see to it that only she and my daughter come up with
your meals and suchlike. That road, we'll all like as not avoid
any unpleasantness. I'll have your bags brought up in a jiffy,
miss.' With these words Simms bowed and retreated, leaving
Dorothea, brows flying, and Cecily, pathetically pale, staring
at each other in consternation.

'Oh, my!' said Betsy, sinking down on one of the chairs by
the fire, eyes round with dismay. 'Maybe we should travel on,
Miss Dorothea. I'm sure your grandma wouldn't like you staying at an inn with all these rowdy, boisterous, ramshackle lads,
miss!'

'I don't believe there's any other inn near, Betsy. And after
all, as the landlord says, if we keep the door locked and stay
in our room, surely we'll come to no harm?' Dorothea spoke
in her normal calm tones, drawing off her gloves and dropping

her travelling cloak over a chair. After her momentary dismay, undoubtedly due to tiredness, she was inclined to dismiss the situation.

'Well, if it's all the same to you, Thea, I would much rather stay here than try to go on,' said Cecily.

The thin, reedy voice clearly conveyed to Dorothea just how unwell her sister was feeling. She walked briskly to the bed and turned down the coverlet. The sheets were dry and clean. She plumped up the pillows invitingly. 'And so we shall, my love! Why not curl up on the bed until dinner arrives? I must confess, I'm not convinced that removing from here wouldn't land us in a worse pickle than the one we're in at present.'

A tentative knock came at the door. 'Who is it?' said Betsy, rising.

'It's only me, ma'am. Hannah, the landlord's daughter.'

Betsy opened the door to reveal a stout damsel with a mob-cap perched above a comely face. 'My mum will have the dinner ready shortly, but she was wanting to know if you needed anything else, ma'am?' Hannah hefted the sisters' bags into the room and stood looking enquiringly at Dorothea.

'Why, yes! We'd like some warm water, and could a truckle-bed be put up in here for our maid? I'd rather she spent the night with us.'

The girl nodded. 'I'll be back in two shakes, ma'am.'

Five minutes later Hannah was back with a jug of steaming water and a truckle-bed in bits. While she and Betsy struggled with this contraption Dorothea and Cecily washed the dust of the road from their faces and felt considerably better. Finally conquering the recalcitrant truckle-bed, Hannah wiped her hands on her apron and addressed Dorothea. 'I'll be back in half'n hour with your dinner, miss. Be you sure to lock the door after me.'

Dorothea murmured her thanks as the bolts slid to behind the helpful Hannah. Cecily, drowsy, curled up on the bed. Betsy sat by the fire, working on some sewing she had brought with her to while away the time.

Now that her immediate needs were satisfied, Dorothea prowled the room, restless and cramped. After a day spent in

the carriage, she longed to get just one breath of fresh air
before a night spent within the airless cocoon of the bedchamber. Suddenly she remembered Lang. With Cecily as passen-
ger, they would normally leave mid-morning. However, her
limited knowledge of prize-fights and their aftermath suggested that an early departure might be preferable. She looked
out of the window, but this faced the back of the inn. She
could hear no noise or ruckus to suggest that the audience
from the fight had arrived.

Quickly she crossed to Betsy's side. 'I'm just going down
to see Lang. We should make an early start tomorrow to avoid
the crush.' She had lowered her voice. 'You stay here and
watch over Cecily. I'll only be a moment.'

Before Betsy could protest she picked up her old travelling
cloak and whisked herself out of the door. She paused on the
landing to fasten the cloak. Sounds of ribald laughter came,
muted, from where she supposed the taproom to be. She made
her way quietly down the stairs and along the corridor in the
opposite direction, eventually reaching the door giving on to
the coaching yard. Here she found a mêlée of ostlers and
horses. Pausing in the shadows, she scanned the area, trying
to locate Lang. He was nowhere to be seen. Remembering that
private grooms often helped the ostlers at times like these, she
ventured to the archway and peeked into the main stableyard.

'My, my! What have we here? A pretty young thing, come
to help us celebrate!'

She gasped. The sensation of an arm slipping around her
waist made her heart stand still, but instead of hazel eyes lazily
regarding her she found herself looking into a vacuous face
with cherubic blue eyes that seemed to have trouble focusing.
The man holding her had been drinking but he was not altogether drunk.

He dragged her, struggling furiously, around the corner to
fetch up within a riotous group of seven semi-drunk gentlemen, intent on a night of carousing, having watched their favourite win the fight. Dorothea realised her mistake too late.
The main yard of the inn was full to overflowing. One of the
men reached out and flicked her hood back, and the light from

the inn's main door fell full on her face. She tried desperately to pull free, but the young man had a good grip on her arm. She winced as it tightened.

Immediately a drawling voice cut through the clamour. 'Do let the lady go, Tremlow. She is known to me and I really cannot let you embarrass her further.'

Recognising the voice, Dorothea wished the ground would open up and swallow her.

The effect of the statement was instantaneous. The hold on her arm was immediately withdrawn as the dark shadow of the Marquis of Hazelmere materialised at the edge of the group.

'Oh! Sorry, Hazelmere! No idea she was a lady.'

This last sentence, uttered *sotto voce*, made Dorothea's cheeks burn. She pulled up her hood as the men in the group peered to see which lady could thus claim Hazelmere's protection.

The Marquis, unhurriedly strolling across the group to her side, largely obscured her from view. Arriving beside her, he turned to the group and continued in the same languid tone, 'I feel sure you would all like to offer your apologies for any embarrassment you have, however unwittingly, caused the lady.'

A chorus of, 'Oh, yes! Definitely! Apologies, ma'am! No offence intended, y'know!' greeted this bald statement.

Simms, having noticed the problem rather late in the day, now hung on the fringe of the group, waiting to render any assistance at all to one of his most valued customers. The Marquis's eye alighted on him. 'Ah, Simms! A round of ale for these gentlemen after this slight misunderstanding, don't you think?'

Simms took the hint. 'Yes, m'lord! Certainly! If you gentlemen would like to come this way I've a hogshead of a new brew I'd much appreciate your comments on.' With this treat on offer, he had little difficulty in herding the group towards the taproom.

As they moved away Anthony, Lord Fanshawe appeared at his friend's side, a questioning lift to his brows. One moment he had been walking across the stableyard beside Hazelmere, heading towards a hot dinner, when Marc had suddenly stopped, uttered one furious oath and then plunged through the crowd towards a small group of revellers near the coach-yard. Although nearly as tall as his friend, with Marc ahead of him, he had had no chance to see what had attracted his attention. As he drew closer he heard Marc at his most languid. He assumed there was a lady in it somewhere, but it was only when Hazelmere turned to address some remark behind him that he realised he was effectively protecting her from the eyes of the stableyard.

Hazelmere turned to him. 'Check they're all in, will you, Tony? I'll join you in the parlour in a few minutes.'

Fanshawe nodded and without a word turned back towards the inn. The languid tones had disappeared entirely, replaced by Hazelmere's normal speech with the consonants somewhat clipped. That single glimpse of his childhood friend's face had confirmed his suspicion. The Marquis of Hazelmere was in a towering rage.

As he had reached her side Hazelmere had unobtrusively taken Dorothea's arm, initially holding her beside him. When the group had made their apologies and moved away he drew her back so that she was shielded by his height and the vo-luminous driving cloak which hung in many tiers of capes from his broad shoulders. Conscious only of a desperate need to quit the scene, she tried to retreat into the coachyard. He turned but did not release her. With the light behind him, his face was unreadable. 'One moment and I'll escort you indoors. I'd like a word with you.'

Even to Dorothea, unwise in the ways of the Marquis, the words had an ominous ring. She was furious with herself for falling into this scrape and mortified that, of all men, it should be Hazelmere who had rescued her from it. *And* in such a way!

He turned back to speak briefly with another tall man who came up. Then, much to her relief, as her legs felt strangely weak, he ushered her into the coachyard.

Once in the comparative privacy of the rapidly clearing inner yard, he stopped and drew her around to face him. She almost gasped as the light from the inn door lit his face. The hazel eyes were hard and reflected the light from the inn; his lips were set in an uncompromising line. It was obvious to the meanest intelligence that he was furious, and equally obvious that she was the object of his wrath. 'And what, may I ask, were you attempting to accomplish out there?' The sarcastic tones stung like a whip.

Far from being cowed, Dorothea immediately took umbrage. She flung up her head and her eyes snapped back. 'I was seeking my coachman, if you must know, to tell him I wish to leave this inn very early tomorrow, to avoid precisely the sort of attention that I was most regrettably unable to avoid tonight!' She was slightly breathless by the end of this speech, but continued to give the odious Marquis back look for look.

His eyes narrowed. After a slight pause he continued in less harsh tones, 'It seems very remiss of Simms not to have warned you to keep to your chamber with your door locked.'

She had to swallow before she was able to answer, but she managed to return his hard gaze. 'He did tell me.'

The expression on his face became even stonier. 'I can only marvel at your lack of care for your own reputation. I've already warned you that your hoydenish ways will not do in wider society.' He had grasped both her arms just above the elbow in a far from gentle grip. For one appalled moment she thought he was going to shake her. Instead, after a pause heavy with tension, he spoke again, his tone a study in suppressed fury. 'I can only repeat what I've said before: under no circumstances *whatever* should you venture outside unattended! And add a rider to the effect that if I *ever* find you alone like that again I will personally ensure that you won't sit down for a sennight!'

She gasped, green eyes wide in utter disbelief, whereupon he continued, his tone savage, 'Oh, yes! I'm quite capable of doing so.'

Looking up into the implacable face, the hazel eyes almost black, she realised that the threat was no bluff. But by now she was every bit as angry as he was. By what right did this imperious man order her around and threaten her? Imperious, arrogant and totally *insufferable*! Normally the most collected of women, she struggled to shackle her anger and direct it specifically towards its source.

But Hazelmere gave her no time to vent her fury. Becoming aware that he was still holding her in full view of the coach-yard, thankfully almost deserted, he abruptly turned her towards the inn and, one hand hard at her elbow, swept her indoors. 'Which chamber has Simms put you in?'

Unable as yet to command her tongue, Dorothea indicated the door at the top of the small stairway.

'Very wise! That's probably the safest chamber in the inn tonight. You may not have a peaceful night, but with luck it should be free of unwelcome interruptions.'

Glancing at her furious white face and over-bright eyes, Hazelmere drew her on to the stairs. On the second step she swung around, thinking to give him a piece of her mind while he was on the lower step and not towering over her. But, correctly guessing her intention, he had slipped past her and continued to draw her upwards on to the small landing.

The landlord suddenly appeared in the corridor, heading for the back of the inn.

'Simms!'

'Yes, m'lord?'

'A glass of your best brandy. At once.'

'Yes, m'lord!'

Dorothea thought the request extremely odd, but dismissed it as yet another example of his lordship's vagaries. She was more concerned with giving voice to her frustrations. Turning to face him across the small landing, she was disturbingly aware of his presence so close, and disliked having to look up such a long way to meet his eyes.

'Lord Hazelmere! I must tell you that I find your manner of addressing me quite unacceptable! I do not at all accept your strictures on my conduct. Indeed, I do not know by what right you make them. Tonight was an unfortunate accident, that's all. I'm quite capable of looking after myself—'

'Would you really rather I had left you in the hands of

Tremlow and company? You wouldn't have found it entertaining, I assure you.' Hazelmere, deciding that she could not be allowed to talk herself into hysterics, broke in smoothly over her diatribe. His words, uttered in a stonily bored tone, acted like a cold douche, effectively stopping her in mid-sentence.

He was again afforded a view of her thoughts as they passed clearly over her face. He watched the realisation that it was, in fact, due to him that she was not at this moment in quite desperate straits finally sink in. He had not thought it possible, but she paled even further. Watching her closely, he saw Simms approaching. He took the proffered glass, dismissing the landlord with a curt nod and the words, 'I'll want to speak to you in a few minutes, Simms.' Turning, he held out the glass to her. 'Drink it.'

'No. I don't drink brandy.'

'There is always a first time.'

When she continued to look rebelliously at him he sighed and explained. 'Whether you know it or not, you're exhibiting all the symptoms of shock. You're white as a sheet and your eyes look like green diamonds. Soon you'll start to shake, and feel faint and very cold. The brandy will help. So be a good girl and drink it. If you won't, you know perfectly well I'm quite capable of forcing you to.'

The glittering green eyes widened slightly. There had been no change in his tone and she felt no direct menace, as she had before. Then, looking into his eyes, she gave up the unequal struggle. She took the glass and, shivering slightly, raised it to her lips and sipped. Hazelmere waited patiently until she drained the glass, then removed it from her hands and dropped it into one of his cloak pockets.

As she looked up he remembered her unfinished errand. 'I take it you're travelling to London?'

She nodded. His face had softened, the harshly arrogant lines of ten minutes before had receded, leaving the charmingly polite mask she suspected he showed the world. She felt as if he had, in some subtle way, withdrawn from her.

'What's the name of your coachman?'

'Lang. I'd thought to leave at eight.'

'Very sensible. I'll see he gets the message. I suggest you enter your chamber, lock the door and don't open it to anyone other than the landlord's people.' The tone was calm, with no hint of any emotion whatever.

'Yes. Very well.' She was completely bemused. Her head was whirling—shock, fury, brandy and the Marquis of Hazelmere combining to make her distinctly befuddled. She pressed the fingers of one hand to her temple, forcing her mind to concentrate on what he was saying.

'Good! Try to get some sleep. And one more thing: tell Lady Merion I'll call on her the day after tomorrow.'

She nodded and moved to the door, then turned back. Still angry, she knew she was beholden to him, and pride forbade her to leave without thanking him, however little inclined she was to do so. She drew a deep breath and, head held high, began. 'My lord, I must thank you for your help in releasing me from those gentlemen.' Lifting her eyes to his, she found that this bland statement had brought the most devastatingly attractive smile to his face.

Wholly appreciative of the effort the words had cost, he replied, his voice light, 'Yes, you must, I'm afraid. But never mind. Once you're in London, I'm sure you'll find opportunities aplenty to make me sorry for my subsequent odiously overbearing behaviour.' One dark brow rose at the end of this outrageous speech, the hazel eyes, gently and not unkindly, quizzing her. The answering blaze of green fire made him laugh. Hearing voices below, he reached out a finger to caress her cheek gently, saying more pointedly, 'Goodnight, Miss Darent!'

Speechless, she whirled away from him and knocked on the door. 'Betsy, it's me. Dorothea.'

Hazelmere, lips curving in a smile that, had she seen it, would have reduced Dorothea to a state of quivering uncertainty, drew back into the shadows as the door opened with an alacrity which spoke louder than words of the fears of those inside.

'Heavens, miss! Come you in quick; you look white as a

sheet, you do!' Dorothea was drawn into the room and the door shut.

Hazelmere waited until he heard the bolts shot home, then made his way, pensively, downstairs. At the back door, he encountered Simms.

'Simms, I have a problem.'

'M'lord?'

'I want to make sure those ladies are not disturbed tonight. You don't perchance have a large burly cousin lying about, who could take up sentry duty on that stair?'

Simms grinned as he saw the gold sovereign in his lordship's long fingers. 'Well, as it happens, m'lord, my oldest boy has the most dreadful toothache. He's been mooning about in the kitchen all day. I'm sure he could do sentry duty, seeing as you ask.'

'Excellent.' The coin changed hands. 'And Simms?'

'Yes, m'lord?'

'I'd like to be sure those ladies get the very best of treatment.'

'Of course, m'lord. My wife's about to take their supper up to them now.'

Hazelmere nodded and wandered out to the middle of the coachyard, looking up at the stars, twinkling now that the clouds had cleared. He paused, apparently lost in thought. Jim Hitchin, his groom, stood a few yards away, waiting until his master acknowledged him. He had been Hazelmere's personal groom ever since the young Lord had required one. Well acquainted with his employer's foibles, he waited patiently. Hazelmere stretched and turned. 'Jim?'

'M'lord?'

'I want you to find a coachman staying here, name of Lang, coachman to the Misses Darent. Miss Darent wishes to leave at eight tomorrow, to avoid the inevitable action around here. She obviously cannot deliver the message in person.'

'Yes, m'lord.'

'And Jim?'

'Yes, m'lord?'

'Tomorrow morning the Darent party is to leave here by

eight. If there's any difficulty in achieving that departure I want you to see I'm summoned. Is that clear?'

'Yes, m'lord.'

'Wonderful. Goodnight, Jim.'

Jim departed, not the least averse to an early morning if it led to a clear sight of this Miss Darent. He had witnessed, distantly, the exchange in the coachyard. To his mind, his lordship was not behaving in his usual manner. Losing his temper with young ladies was definitely not his style. Jim was burning to see what the lady who could throw his master off balance looked like.

Hazelmere, fortunately oblivious to the speculations of his underling, strolled back through the main entrance of the inn and paused outside the open taproom door. Noise, like a cloud, rolled out over the threshold to greet him. Through a bluish haze of tobacco smoke he saw the group of young blades from whom he had rescued Dorothea standing at the end of the bar. It took him longer to locate the last of their number, seated at a small table in the corner, deep in conversation with Sir Barnaby Ruscombe. After considering the scene for a moment, he walked on to the private parlour he always had when staying at the Feathers. Entering, he saw Fanshawe, feet up on the table, carefully peeling an apple.

Fanshawe looked up with a grin. 'Ho! So there you are! I was wondering whether it'd be prudent to come and rescue you.'

A ghost of a smile greeted this sally. 'I had a few errands to attend to after returning Miss Darent to her room.' Hazelmere removed his driving cloak, remembering to extract the glass from the pocket before he threw it on a chair. He moved to the sideboard and poured himself a glass of wine.

'And who the hell is this mysterious Miss Darent?'

The Marquis raised his black brows. 'No mystery. She lives at the Grange, which borders Moreton Park. She and her sister are travelling to London to stay with their grandmother, Lady Merion.'

'I see. How is it, I ask myself, that I've never heard of the girl, much less set eyes on her?'

'Simple. She's lived all her life in the country and hasn't moved in the circles we frequent.'

Fanshawe finished his apple and swung his feet down from the table as the door opened to admit Simms, bearing trays loaded with food. 'At last!' he cried. 'I'm famished.'

Simms placed the platters on the table and, checking that all was in order, turned to Hazelmere.

'Everything's taken care of, m'lord, as you requested.'

Hazelmere nodded his thanks, and Simms retired. Fanshawe looked up from heaping his plate, but said nothing.

The friends took their meal in companionable silence. They had quite literally grown up together, being born on neighbouring estates within a month of each other, and had shared their schooldays at Eton and, later, Oxford. During their past ten years on the town the bond between the Lords Hazelmere and Fanshawe had become almost a byword. Over the years there had been few secrets between them, yet, for reasons he did not care to examine, Hazelmere had omitted to mention his acquaintance with Dorothea Darent to his closest friend.

Once the platters were cleared and they had pushed their chairs back from the table, savouring the special claret brought up from the depths of Simms's cellar, Fanshawe, dishevelled brown locks falling picturesquely over his brow, returned to the offensive. 'It's all too smoky by half.'

Resigned to the inevitable, Hazelmere nevertheless countered with an innocent, 'What's too smoky by half?'

'You and this Miss Darent.'

'But why?' The clear hazel eyes, apparently guileless, were opened wide, but the thin lips twitched.

Fanshawe frowned direfully but agreed to play the game. 'Well, for a start, as she doesn't move in the circles we frequent, tell me how *you* met her.'

'We met only once, informally.'

'When?'

'Some time last August, when I was at Moreton Park.'

The brown eyes narrowed. 'But I visited you at Moreton Park last August, and I distinctly remember you telling me such game was very scarce.'

'Ah, yes,' mused Hazelmere, long fingers caressing the stem of the goblet. 'I do recall saying some such thing.'

'And I suppose Miss Darent just happened to slip your mind at the time?'

The Marquis smiled provokingly. 'As you say, Tony.'

'No, dash it all! You can't possibly expect me to swallow that. And if I won't swallow it no one else will either. And, as that fellow Ruscombe's about somewhere, you're going to have to come up with a better explanation. Unless,' he concluded sarcastically, 'you want all London agog?'

At that the dark brows rose. Hazelmere drew a long breath. 'Unfortunately you're quite right.' He still seemed absorbed in his study of the goblet. Fanshawe, who knew him better than anyone, waited patiently.

Sir Barnaby Ruscombe was a man tolerated by society's hostesses purely on account of his trade in malicious gossip. There was no chance that he would abstain from telling the story of how Hazelmere had rescued a lady from a prize-fight crowd in an inn yard. The fact that Hazelmere was sure to dislike having his name bandied about in such context would ensure its dissemination throughout the ton. Although not in itself of much import, the story would reveal the interesting fact that the Marquis had some previous acquaintance with Miss Darent. And that, as Fanshawe was so eager to point out, would lead to complications.

After some minutes had passed in silence Hazelmere raised his eyes. 'Confessions of a rake, I'm afraid,' he said, both voice and features gently self-mocking. Seeing the surprise in Fanshawe's brown eyes, he continued, 'This time the truth will definitely not do. The details of my only previous meeting with Miss Darent would keep the scandalmongers in alt for weeks.'

Tony Fanshawe was amazed. Whatever he had expected, it was not that. He knew, none better, that, while Hazelmere's *affaires* among the *demi-monde* might be legion, his behaviour with women of his own class was rigidly correct. Then he thought he saw the light. 'I take it you mean that when you met her in the country she was unchaperoned?'

The curious smile on Hazelmere's lips deepened. The hazel eyes held Fanshawe's for a moment, before dropping to the goblet once more. 'I am, naturally, devastated to contradict you. You're right in assuming we were unchaperoned. But what I meant is, if the truth ever became public property Miss Darent would be hopelessly compromised and I, in all honour, would be forced to marry her.'

It was not possible to misinterpret that. 'Good lord!' said Fanshawe, thoroughly intrigued. 'Whatever did you do?'

Hazelmere, sensing the wild speculations running through his mind, hastened to bring him back to earth. 'Control your satyric imaginings! I kissed her, if you must know.'

'Oh?' Fanshawe was positively agog.

Feeling horrendously like a schoolboy describing to his more backward friends the details of his first encounter with a wench, Hazelmere regarded him with amusement tinged with irritation. Correctly interpreting the slightly awed expression in the brown eyes, he nodded. 'Precisely. *Not* a peck on the cheek.'

Fanshawe stared at Hazelmere for a full minute before saying, his voice quavering with suppressed incredulity, 'Do you mean to say you kissed her as you would one of your mistresses?' Hazelmere's brows merely rose. 'No! Dash it all! You can't go around kissing young ladies as if they were bordello misses!'

'Perfectly true. The fact, however, remains, that in Miss Darent's case I did.'

Fanshawe blinked. It was on the tip of his tongue to ask why. But he could not quite bring himself to enquire. Instead he asked, 'How long did she take to come out of her faint?'

'Oh, she didn't faint,' replied Hazelmere, the smile in his eyes pronounced. 'She tried to slap me.'

Fanshawe was fascinated. 'I must meet this Miss Darent for myself. She sounds a remarkable young lady.'

'You can meet her in London shortly. Just remember who met her first.'

And that, thought Tony Fanshawe, is a very revealing comment. He sighed, exasperated. 'If that's not just like you, to find all the choicest morsels before anyone else has laid eyes on 'em. I don't suppose she has a sister?'

'She does, as it happens. Just turned seventeen and a stunning blonde.'

'So there's hope for the rest of us yet.' Abruptly eschewing their light banter, he returned to the serious side of the affair. 'How are you going to account for your knowing Miss Darent?'

'She's Lady Merion's granddaughter, remember? I'll call at Merion House as soon as we get back to town and, figuratively speaking, throw myself on her ladyship's mercy.' He paused to sip his wine. 'It shouldn't be beyond us to concoct some believable tale.'

'Provided she's willing to overlook your behaviour with her granddaughter,' Fanshawe pointed out.

'I rather think,' said Hazelmere, his gaze abstracted, 'that it's more likely to be a case of Miss Darent being willing to overlook my behaviour.'

'You mean, she might try and use it against you?'

The hazel gaze abruptly focused. Then, understanding his reasoning, Hazelmere gave the ghost of a laugh. 'No. What I mean is that, although she was furious with me, I'm not sure she'll tell Lady Merion the full story.'

Fanshawe mulled this over, then shook his head. 'Can't see it, myself. You know what the young ones are like. Paint you in all sorts of romantic shades. The chit will probably have blabbed it all to at least three of her bosom bows before you even get to see Lady Merion!'

The strangely elusive smile that kept appearing on Hazelmere's face was again in evidence. 'In this case, I think it unlikely.'

A thought struck Fanshawe. 'The girl's not an antidote, is she?'

'No. Not beautiful, but she'd be strikingly attractive if properly gowned.'

'You mean, she wasn't properly gowned when you met her?'

A soft laugh escaped Hazelmere. 'Not exactly.'

Reluctantly Fanshawe decided not to pursue it. He was consumed by curiosity but slightly scandalised by the revelations thus far. He had never known Hazelmere in this sort of fix, nor in this sort of mood. For the first time in his life he was sure that Marc was hiding something.

Hazelmere volunteered a few more pieces of the puzzle. 'She's twenty-two, and sensible and practical. She didn't faint, nor did she enact me any scenes. If I'd allowed it she would have terminated our interview a great deal sooner. Tonight, instead of falling on my chest and thanking me for deliverance from the hands of Tremlow and company, she very nearly told me to go to the devil. In short, I doubt that Miss Darent is in the least danger of succumbing to the Marquis of Hazelmere's wicked charms.'

Fanshawe gaped. 'Oh. I see.' But he did not see at all.

Unfortunately he had no more time to pursue the matter. A sharp knock on the door heralded the arrival of a group of their friends, come late from the field. More wine was called for and the conversation took a decidedly sporting turn. It was not until much later that Tony Fanshawe recalled his conviction that Marc Henry was concealing something from his childhood friend.

CHAPTER THREE

Early next morning, before the appointed time and without further incident, the Grange party set off from the Three Feathers, watched, appreciatively, by Jim Hitchin.

The day was cool but the thaw had set in. The roads improved as they neared the capital, so the motion of the coach was more even and their progress noticeably more rapid. Dorothea was in a subdued frame of mind. On her return to their chamber the evening before she had been subjected to a barrage of questions from Cecily and Betsy. Her head still swimming, she had let the tide flow over her, knowing from experience that silence would more effectively stop the inquisition than any argument. This time, her normal stratagem had failed. The questions had continued until she lost her temper. 'Oh, do stop fussing, both of you! If you must know, I had an encounter with an extremely impertinent gentleman on my way back from the coachyard, and I'm quite vexed!'

Cecily, piqued at her subsequent refusal to recount the incident, had only been diverted by the appearance of their meal. In August, in a moment of ill-judged candour, Dorothea had told her sister of her impromptu meeting with Lord Hazelmere in the woods. The memory of the tortuous explanations she had had to fabricate to conceal from Cecily's avid interest the full tale of that encounter had ensured that this time she easily refrained from blurting out the name of the gentleman involved. In no circumstances could she have endured another such ordeal. Not when she was feeling so unusually exhausted.

She had had little appetite, but to admit this would only have reopened the discussion. So she had forced herself to eat some pigeon pie. After the brandy she had not dared to touch the wine. The meal completed, she had pointedly prepared for bed. Cecily, thankfully without comment, had done likewise.

A light sleeper, Dorothea had found it impossible to even doze until dawn, when the racket in the inn finally abated. She therefore had had ample time to reflect on her second encounter with the Marquis of Hazelmere. His calm assumption of authority irritated her deeply. His arrogant conviction that she would do exactly as he wished irked her beyond measure. The knowledge that, despite this, he possessed a strange attraction for her she resolutely pushed to the furthest corner of her mind. The last thing she felt inclined to do, she had sternly told herself, was to develop a *tendre* for the odious man! In all probability he would spend the night enjoying the favours of some doxy elsewhere in the inn. For some reason she found this thought absurdly depressing and, thoroughly annoyed with herself, had tried to compose her mind for sleep. Even then, when sleep finally came, it was haunted by a pair of hazel eyes.

Once they were under way, the swaying of the chaise quickly lulled her into slumber. She woke when they paused for lunch at a pretty little inn on the banks of the Thames. Only partially refreshed, she forced herself to consider how she was going to handle the coming interview with her grandmother. How, exactly, was she to broach the subject of Hazelmere and his promised visit? Back in the carriage, she dozed fitfully while her problems revolved like clockwork in her mind. She came fully awake when the wheels hit the cobbled streets. Gazing about, she was astonished by the hustle and bustle of life in the capital. As the carriage moved into the areas inhabited by the wealthier citizens the clamour was left behind, and both sisters were soon engaged in examining and pronouncing sentence on the elegant outfits they saw.

After asking directions, Lang finally drew up outside an imposing mansion on one side of a square in what was clearly one of the more fashionable areas. In the centre was an enclosed garden in which children and nursemaids were taking the late-afternoon air. The sun's last rays were gilding the bare branches of the cherry trees there as the sisters were assisted

from the carriage by the stately butler who had answered
Lang's knock.

Relieved of their cloaks and escorted to the upstairs drawing-room, the sisters made their curtsy to their fashionable
grandmother. Lady Merion surged towards them, enveloping
them in a mist of gauzes and perfume. Her blonde wig was
perfectly set above a face still graced by traces of the pale
beauty she had once been. Sharp blue eyes watched her world,
set above a long straight nose and a mouth only too ready to
laugh at what she saw.

'My dears! I'm so glad to see you safely arrived! Now sit
down and let me give you some tea. My chef, Henri, has sent
up these delicacies to tempt you after your journey.'

Drawing them to sit around the fire, already burning
brightly, Lady Merion noted that neither sister was looking
her best. 'Tonight we'll have a very quiet time. You must both
retire immediately after dinner. Tomorrow morning we've an
appointment with Celestine, the most fashionable modiste in
London. You must have recovered from your journey by then.'

As soon as they had eaten the delicious pastries and drunk
their tea, Lady Merion rang the bell. It was answered by
Witchett, a tall, angular woman with sparse grey hair whose
peculiar talent in life lay in being able to turn out her elderly
mistress in the most suitable of the currently fashionable
styles. She was burning with curiosity to view the latest chal-
lenges to her skill. A quick glance at the Misses Darent told
her that Mellow, the butler, had not exaggerated. In spite of
their tiredness, their potential was apparent. The younger,
properly dressed, would be a hit. And Miss Darent had that
certain something that Witchett, a veteran campaigner, instantly recognised. The sisters were therefore favoured with a
thin smile.

'Ah, there you are, Witchett. Please conduct Miss Darent
and Miss Cecily to their rooms. I suggest, my dears, that you
rest before dinner. Witchett will see your things are unpacked,
and she'll take charge of your dressing until we can find suitable maids. Off with you, now.' She dismissed them with a
wave of one heavily beringed white hand.

They followed Witchett to two pretty bedchambers, obviously newly refurbished, Dorothea's in a soft pastel green and Cecily's in a delicate blue. Everything was already unpacked, and Witchett helped them undress. 'I'll return to assist you to dress for dinner, Miss Darent.'

Dorothea sank thankfully into the soft feather bed and immediately fell asleep.

Lady Merion had instructed her chef that a light and simple meal was all they required that evening. Consequently there were only three courses, each of some half a dozen dishes. Luckily both Dorothea and Cecily had recovered their appetites and were able to do justice to their first experience of the culinary delights of London.

Their grandmother was pleasantly surprised to find them considerably restored. Throughout dinner she monopolised the conversation. 'First and by far the most important task is to have you both suitably gowned. For that, Celestine's is first on our list. She's the best known of Bruton Street's modistes for good reason.'

Lady Merion had paid a visit to Celestine as soon as she had decided to launch her granddaughters into the ton. She had made it clear that she required that lady's best efforts. Celestine had built her highly successful business through shrewd assessment of her clients' abilities to display her creations in ton circles. Lady Merion's granddaughters would be paraded at all the most exclusive venues. Having extracted a description of the young ladies, she had graciously agreed to do all possible to ensure their success.

'Celestine's talents are truly stupendous. After that, we'll have to get your hair seen to, and I've organised a dancing master as well. I don't expect you know the waltz?' She paused to help herself to some buttered crab. 'Once you're presentable, our first outing will be a drive in the Park. We'll go about three, which at this time of year is the right time to meet people. I'll introduce you to a number of the leaders of the ton, and hopefully we can find some of the younger generation for you to make friends with. In particular, I hope we'll meet Lady Jersey. Her nickname is "Silence", because she chatters all the time. Don't be put out if what she says seems rather odd. Princess Esterhazy should also be there. Both these ladies are patronesses of Almack's. You need vouchers from them to attend. If you're not admitted to Almack's you may as well give up the Season and go home.'

'Good heavens!' said Dorothea. 'I'd no idea it was that important.'

'Well, it is,' answered her grandmother with absolute conviction. She continued in this style, pouring forth an abundance of information. Dorothea and Cecily listened avidly. Possessing a fair degree of common sense, they needed no urging to learn all they could of the mores and practices of the fashionable from their experienced grandmama before their first venture into the critical world of the ton.

At nine o'clock, seeing Cecily stifle a yawn, her ladyship brought her lecture to an end. 'It's time both of you were in bed. Ring for Witchett, Dorothea. She'll help you change. Go along, now. You've had enough for one day.'

As the door shut behind the sleepy girls Lady Merion settled herself more comfortably in the corner of her elegant sofa. She was going to enjoy this Season. Lately, her accustomed routine of fashionable pleasures had been sadly lacking in excitement.

She had not spent over sixty years at the hub of aristocratic life without learning to gauge the qualities of those around her. Every bit as shrewd as she was fashionable, she had been agreeably impressed by her rustic granddaughters when she had met them, for the first time in many years, at Darent Hall. On the basis of one afternoon's reacquaintance she had decided it would be highly diverting to unleash them on the ton. While she had little doubt she would become sincerely fond of them, her main purpose had been purely selfish. Now, having re-examined their fresh faces and charmingly assured manners, she wryly wondered whether she would be able to cope.

Thinking again of the girls, she frowned. Dorothea had seemed strangely preoccupied. Hopefully she had not conceived a *tendre* for some country gentleman. Still, even if she had, the delights of a London Season would soon distract her from her sleepy country past.

Her cogitations were interrupted by a knock on the door. Dorothea, clad in a delicate pink wrapper with her dark hair swirling over her shoulders, put her head around the door. Seeing her grandmother, she entered.

The fair brows over the sharp blue eyes rose to improbable heights. 'Why, child, what's the matter?'

'Grandmama, there's something I must tell you.'

Ah-ha! thought her ladyship. Now I'm going to find out what's bothering her. She motioned Dorothea to sit next to her.

Sinking gracefully down, Dorothea fixed her eyes on the fire and calmly let fall her bombshell. 'Well, for a start I have to tell you that the Marquis of Hazelmere will call on you tomorrow.'

'Good gracious!' The exclamation was forced from Lady Merion as she jerked bolt upright, her fascinated blue gaze riveted on her grandchild. 'My dear, how on *earth* did you meet a man of Hazelmere's stamp? I didn't know your mother was acquainted with the Henrys.'

Hermione was conscious of a dreadful sinking feeling at the mere mention of Hazelmere's name. Drat the boy! He'd been the bane of many a hopeful mother's life, proving so fascinating to their impressionable daughters that there was no doing anything with the silly chits. As he had proved impervious to the charms of all but certain delectable members of the *demi-monde*, careful mothers were wont to advise their daughters that, in spite of his undoubted eligibility, Lord Hazelmere did not feature on their lists of likely suitors. Dorothea's words had started all sorts of hares racing in her mind, but why Hazelmere would want an interview with herself was more than she could imagine. She settled herself so that she had an uninterrupted view of her granddaughter's face. 'Start at the beginning, child, or I'll never understand.'

Conscious of the steady scrutiny, Dorothea nodded and carefully began. 'Well, the first time I met Lord Hazelmere was while I was berrying in Moreton Park woods last August.

He had recently inherited the estate from his great-aunt, Lady Moreton.'

'Yes, I know about that,' said her ladyship. 'I knew Etta Moreton quite well. In fact, she wrote to me after your mother's death, urging me to take a hand in your lives.'

'Did she?' That was news to Dorothea.

'Mmm. But what happened when you met Hazelmere? I presume he made himself charming, as usual?'

Dorothea reminded herself that she had no idea how charming Hazelmere might be expected to be. She stuck to her edited story. 'He introduced himself. Then, because I was unattended, he insisted on walking me home.'

Lady Merion, reading into her granddaughter's careful tones rather more than Dorothea would have wished, leapt to a conclusion. 'My dear, you needn't be shy about telling me he made love to you shamelessly. He does it all the time. That devil can be utterly undeniable when the mood takes him.'

Her gaze wildly incredulous, Dorothea saw the crevasse yawning at her feet only just in time. Lady Merion had used the term 'made love' in the sense in which it was used in her heyday, to denote suggestive flirtation. Swallowing the words she had so nearly uttered, she forced her voice to calmness. 'Charming? Actually, I found him rather arrogant.'

Her ladyship blinked at this cold assessment of one of society's lions.

Dorothea hurried on. 'I met Lord Hazelmere again at the inn last night.'

Lady Merion would have described herself as being inured to the ways of those around her. It was consequently with some surprise that she realised that her granddaughter, having been in the house for only a few hours, had managed to seriously shake her calm. She repeated weakly, 'The Marquis was at the inn last night?'

'Yes. And so were a large number of other gentlemen, because there'd been a prize-fight on near by.'

Lady Merion closed her eyes, asking herself what next this outrageous child would reveal. She received Dorothea's carefully censored version of events at the inn in silence. She was, in fact, more than a little puzzled. While Hazelmere had acted most properly in rescuing Dorothea, his subsequent actions were much harder to understand. She could not see why he had been so angry. Highly unlike him to lose his temper at all, let alone with a chit he hardly knew.

Aware that Dorothea was waiting for her verdict, she put the puzzle of Hazelmere's behaviour aside. 'Well, my dear, I cannot see anything in your conduct which should cause you undue concern. I would not wish you to go about anywhere unattended, that's true. But I know your life at the Grange lacked the formality it might have had. The happenings at the inn were highly regrettable, but you could not have known how it would be and thankfully Hazelmere was there to rescue you.' She paused, suddenly thoughtful. 'Do you have any idea why he wishes to see me tomorrow?'

Dorothea had given that particular question a great deal of thought. 'I wonder whether it was because of the other gentlemen in the stableyard. He knew them, and they now know he has met me previously. I assume we'll have to agree on some acceptable tale to account for that?'

Lady Merion considered this, then nodded. 'Yes, that's a likely explanation.' Hazelmere would be well aware of the possible consequences of that public acknowledgement of their acquaintance, and it was quite in character that he should seek to minimise any damage. Whatever else he might be, Hazelmere would always behave as he ought.

Relieved of the nagging worry that she had committed some heinous social sin, Dorothea enjoyed a blissful night's sleep. Cecily, too, slept the sleep of the innocent and was fully recovered from their travelling. Arriving in Bruton Street, they were met by the great Celestine herself. One look sufficed to tell that sharp-witted modiste that in the Misses Darent she had models equal to her talents. Five minutes in their company convinced her that, with their charmingly open manners and that unconscious air of the truly well bred, they were destined to be among the foremost hits of the Season.

The last thing needed to make her throw all her most prized

designs at the Darent feet was provided when, on their arrival, Lady Merion took her aside. 'My granddaughters' affairs are moving apace, *madame*. Miss Darent has made the acquaintance of one of the unmarried peers. I can't, of course, reveal his name, but he is *most* eligible. Lord H is definitely behaving with very much less than his usual sang-froid. I have every hope to see her creditably established before the Season ends.'

No mean player of society's games, Lady Merion was confident of the response her indiscretion would elicit. At the very least, Hazelmere's intrusion into her granddaughter's life should be put to good use. She had no illusions about her elder granddaughter. Cecily would take very well; she was virtually the epitome of the current craze for blonde beauties. Dorothea was striking, but would, she was sure, pale into insignificance in her sister's company. And, on top of that, she was far too much in command of herself to appeal to any gentleman's chivalrous instincts. Although a brilliant match was wishful thinking, a good match was still well within her reach. Particularly with Celestine's help.

On the matter of style, Celestine, a superbly gowned dark-haired woman of indeterminate age, made her pronouncements with a slight French accent. 'Miss Cecily is so young and so fair that she *must* be dressed *à la jeune fille*! For Miss Darent, however, I would recommend a more sophisticated style. With your permission, my lady?' She glanced speculatively at Lady Merion.

'We are entirely in your hands, *madame*,' responded her ladyship.

Celestine nodded. If that was so, she would seize this opportunity with both hands. Dressing the simpering daughters of the ton rarely gave her scope for her genius. To be presented with a client of the quality of Miss Darent was a God-given chance to display her true skill. Good bone-structure, perfect poise, regal deportment, striking and unusual colouring, a truly elegant figure and an arrestingly classical face—what more could a first-class modiste desire in her client? When she had finished with her Dorothea Darent would stand out in any crowd and, thank the lord, had the confidence to carry it off.

Her black eyes sparkled. '*Bon*! Miss Darent's colouring is sufficiently unusual. Also her deportment…so much more—how should I say?—elegant, poised. We will use daring colours and severe styling to make best use of what God has created.'

The next two hours were spent in a haze of gauzes and silks, muslins and cambrics as the relative merits of the various designs, materials and finishes were discussed and measurements taken.

After giving an order for a staggering number of gowns, some to be delivered later that evening for their first promenade in the park the next day, Lady Merion triumphantly led her granddaughters back to their carriage.

Returning to their rooms after a light luncheon, the girls found that in their absence Witchett had been shopping too. Opening their drawers, they found them fully stocked with underwear liberally edged with lace, stockings of the finest silk, ribbons of every hue, together with gloves, reticules, scarves, fans—in short, everything else they could possibly need. Witchett, coming up to see if they needed any assistance, found them exclaiming over their finds.

Seeing her at her bedchamber door, Dorothea beamed. 'Oh, thank you, Witchett! I'm sure we would have forgotten all these things until we were about to go out!'

Witchett found herself, uncharacteristically, returning the smile. 'Well, miss, I'm sure you've got plenty of other things to think about.' Really, it was very hard not to fall under the spell of these happy young things. 'Now, Miss Cecily! I see you've crushed that pretty dress of yours terribly. You'll have to be more careful with your new London gowns. Betsy can press it while you rest. She's waiting in your chamber to help you undress.'

'Oh, but I don't want to rest!'

The querulous tone alerted Dorothea. Cecily could wilt rapidly when over-tired, and it was only the day before that they had been travelling. Catching Witchett's eye to enjoin her silence, Dorothea, examining a lace collar by the window, calmly said, 'If you don't wish to rest then no one shall make you. Of course, we'll have to pay attention this evening while Grandmama teaches us about society's ways, but as long as you're sure you'll be awake I see no point in resting. It's such a beautiful day that I think I'll take a stroll in the park in the square. Why don't you come with me?'

Witchett held herself aloof.

The expression on Cecily's face turned thoughtful. On consideration, she was not so sure she could sustain another evening of dos and don'ts without fortification. 'Oh, maybe Witchett's right and I should rest. I always find it so difficult to remember things when I'm tired. Enjoy your walk!' With an airy wave she drifted across the corridor.

Dorothea remained at the window, looking at the cherry trees swelling into bud and the children playing on the lawns underneath. 'Witchett, I'm not perfectly sure, but is it acceptable for me to walk in that park?'

'Yes, miss. Provided you have an attendant.'

'Who would be an appropriate attendant should I wish to go for a walk now?'

'I'll accompany you, miss, as is right and proper. If you'll wait for me in the hall I'll just get my coat and join you there.'

Witchett was as prompt as her word and within five minutes Dorothea was strolling under the cherry trees, enjoying the sensation of sunlight on her face. Her pelisse kept out the cold breeze as she wended her way around the paths past beds of bright daffodils and early crocus. A child's ball suddenly landed at her feet. Stooping to pick it up, she looked around for the owner. A fair lad about six years old stood uncertainly on the lawn on the other side of the daffodil bed. Smiling, she walked around to him, holding out the ball.

'Say thank you, Peter,' came a voice from a seat under one of the trees. Dorothea saw a nursemaid rocking a baby in her arms, smiling and nodding at her.

She turned back to find the child bowing from the waist, saying, 'Thank you, miss,' in a small gruff voice.

Impulsively she asked, 'Would you like me to play catch with you for a while? I've just come out to enjoy the sunshine, so why don't we enjoy it together?'

The wide smile that greeted this was answer enough, and, after glancing at his nursemaid to see she approved, young Peter settled down to a game of catch with his new-found acquaintance.

So the Marquis of Hazelmere, strolling around Cavendish Square on his way to Merion House, found the object of his thoughts playing ball in the square. Leaning on the railings surrounding the park, he watched as Dorothea taught Peter to throw. She was facing away from him, some distance away. Suddenly a particularly wild throw of Peter's, greeted with hoots of laughter from the players, sent the ball rolling across the lawn to land in a nearby flower-bed. Dorothea followed. As she bent to pick the ball up Hazelmere couldn't resist asking, 'Alone and unattended again, Miss Darent?'

She whirled to face him, an 'Oh!' of surprise dying on her lips. For one wild moment his threat to beat her if he found her unattended again took possession of her mind. The appreciative gleam in his eyes left her in little doubt that he had accurately guessed as much. As her equilibrium returned she mustered what dignity she could to reply, 'Why, no, Lord Hazelmere! I'm now too experienced in society's ways to make that mistake, I assure you.'

One black brow rose. Hazelmere, unused to having young ladies cross swords with him, noticed Witchett materialising at Dorothea's elbow. 'I'm about to call on Lady Merion,' he said. 'I think perhaps, Miss Darent, you should also be present.'

'Oh, yes. I'd forgotten.'

Unable to see her face as she bent down to take leave of the boy, Hazelmere could not be certain whether the comment had been artless or uttered on purpose to deflate his pretensions. Very little of Miss Darent's conversation was artless. Well, that was a pleasant game for two to play, and there were few more skilled in it than he. He continued his stroll along the railings to the gate, where he stood, negligently at ease, and openly watched her as she came towards him.

To herself Dorothea made a firm resolution. Henceforth she was not going to let the odious Marquis get the better of her!

She was a calm, cool, mature woman—even Celestine had commented on her poise. Why on earth she fell apart whenever Hazelmere was about was more than she could comprehend. She was heartily sick of the betraying flush that rose so readily in response to his taunts. Every second comment he made was designed purely to throw her into confusion and allow him to manage matters as he willed. Well, thought the determined Miss Darent, very conscious of that hazel gaze as she approached the street, that might work on the London misses but I'm not going to let him stage-manage me! With the sunniest of smiles, she met him at the gate.

If Hazelmere entertained any suspicions of this evident change of heart he kept them to himself. His experienced eye registered the countrified pelisse and the tangle of her hair, wind-blown and escaping from its pins. He wondered why such a combination should appear so attractive. In silence they crossed the street and were bowed into Merion House by Mellow. 'Lady Merion is expecting you, my lord.'

Surrendering her pelisse to Witchett, Dorothea caught sight of her reflection in the hall mirror. Arrested by the picture of her hair in such turmoil, she wondered whether she should keep her grandmother waiting while she set it to rights. She raised her glance to find herself looking into the Marquis's hazel eyes, reflected in the mirror. He smiled in complete comprehension. 'Yes, I would if I were you. I'll tell her ladyship you'll join us in a few moments.'

Realising she could not continually pull caps with him, particularly when he was being helpful, she confined herself to a curt nod before whisking herself up the stairs, Witchett trailing behind.

Hazelmere paused for a moment to flick a speck of dust from his sleeve before nodding to Mellow. 'You may announce me now.'

For this interview Lady Merion had arrayed herself in a gown she knew made her look particularly formidable. Instinct born of experience warned her that there was more to the encounters between the Marquis and her granddaughter than she had been told. She was unsure that Dorothea herself knew the full sum. On the other hand, Hazelmere would certainly be aware of every nuance. She was determined to extract a much more detailed explanation from him before she called Dorothea to attend them. As he strolled elegantly across the room to bow over her hand she fixed him with a basilisk stare which in years past had produced confessions from the most hardened of reprobates.

Hazelmere smiled lazily down at her.

With a jolt she realised that there was a large difference between demanding the reason for a cricket ball landing in her drawing-room from a ten-year-old boy and demanding an accounting of his behaviour from a thirty-one-year-old peer, who, aside from being a leader of the ton, was also one of the most dangerously handsome men in the kingdom. And, she fumed, noting the amused understanding in the hazel eyes, the jackanapes knows it!

Baulked, she motioned him to a seat and reluctantly gave her attention to the next item on her agenda. She waited until he was seated, admiring the way his immaculate morning coat sat across his shoulders. His long muscular thighs were encased in skin-tight buff knee-breeches, and his Hessians shone like the proverbial mirror. She might be old, but she still noticed such things. 'I understand I must thank you for rescuing my granddaughter, Dorothea, from an unfortunate incident at that inn the other evening.'

One well-manicured hand waved dismissively. 'Having recognised your granddaughter, even someone with a conscience as faulty as mine could hardly have left her there.' The gently mocking tone and the laughter in his face robbed this speech of any impropriety.

Accustomed to the subtleties of social conversation, Lady Merion thawed visibly. 'Very well! But why this meeting?'

'Unfortunately the crowd from which I extricated Miss Darent contained at least one member of the ton who cannot be trusted to forget the incident.'

'Dorothea mentioned Tremlow.'

'Oh, yes. Tremlow was there, and Botherwood and Lords Michaels and Downie. But they are relatively harmless, and, unless I'm much mistaken, would probably not recall the incident unless their memories were jogged, and perhaps not even then. I'm more concerned with Sir Barnaby Ruscombe.'

'Ugh! That repulsive man! He always dabbles in the most *malicious* scandalmongering.' She paused, then eyed the Marquis speculatively. 'I don't suppose there's anything you can do about him?'

'Alas, no. Anyone else, quite probably. But not Ruscombe. Scandal is his trade. Still, given that we can invent a plausible tale to account for my having previously met Miss Darent, I can't see there's any risk of serious damage to her reputation.'

'You're right, of course,' agreed Lady Merion. 'But it would be wise to have her here, I think. Ring that bell, if you will.'

'No need,' replied Hazelmere, 'I met her in the park on my way here. She went upstairs to tidy her hair before joining us.'

As if in answer to the comment, Dorothea entered. Languidly rising, Hazelmere acknowledged her curtsy by taking her hand and, after bowing over it, raised it to his lips, his eyes roaming appreciatively over her.

Lady Merion stiffened. Kissing a lady's hand was not the current practice. What on earth was going on?

Dorothea accepted the salute without a flicker of surprise. Seating herself in a chair on the other side of her grandmother, opposite Hazelmere, she turned an enquiring face to her ladyship.

'We were just discussing, my dear, what story to adopt to account for Lord Hazelmere recognising you at the inn.'

'Maybe Miss Darent has a suggestion?' put in his lordship, hazel eyes gently quizzing Dorothea.

'As a matter of fact, I do,' she replied smoothly. 'It would be safest, I imagine, to stick to occurrences no one else could dispute?' Her delicately arched brows rose as she gazed with unmarred calm into Hazelmere's eyes.

His expressive lips twitched. 'That might be wise,' he murmured.

Dorothea regally inclined her head. 'For instance, what if, on one of your visits to Lady Moreton, she'd been well enough to be taken for a ride in your curricle—not far, just around the surrounding lanes? I'm sure she would have liked to have done that if she'd been able.'

'You're quite right. My great-aunt did bemoan not being well enough for just such an outing as you propose.'

'Good! Only the outing did occur, and of course you didn't take your groom with you, did you?'

Hazelmere, entering into the spirit of the conversation, promptly replied, 'I feel sure I'd given Jim permission to relax in the kitchens that day.'

Dorothea nodded approvingly. 'Driving down the lane, you met my mother, Cynthia Darent, and myself, returning from paying a visit to...oh, Waverley Park, of course.'

'Your coachman?'

'I was driving the gig. And what could be more natural than that Lady Moreton and my mother should stop to chat? They were old friends, after all. And Lady Moreton presented you to Mama and me. After talking for a few minutes, we went our separate ways.'

'When, exactly, did this meeting occur?' he asked.

'Well, it would have had to be the summer before last, when both Lady Moreton and Mama were alive.'

'My congratulations, Miss Darent. We now have a most acceptable tale which accounts for our meeting and the only two witnesses who could say us nay are dead. Very neat.'

'Yes, but wait one moment!' interpolated Lady Merion. 'Why didn't your mother tell her other friends about this meeting? Surely such a novel encounter would have made an impression in the neighbourhood?'

'But, Grandmama, you know how scatterbrained Mama was. It would be quite possible for her to have forgotten all about it by the time we'd reached home, particularly if something else occurred to distract her on the way.'

Reminded of her daughter-in-law's vagueness, Lady Merion grudgingly agreed this was so. 'Well, then, why did you yourself not tell any of your friends about it?'

Dorothea opened her large green eyes to their fullest extent and, addressing her grandmother, asked, 'But why would I have done so? I've never been in the habit of discussing inconsequential occurrences with anyone.'

Lady Merion held her breath. She could not resist glancing at Hazelmere to see how he was taking being classed as 'inconsequential'. He appeared to be his usual urbane self, but she thought she caught a glint from those hazel eyes, presently fixed on Dorothea's face. Be careful, my girl! she mentally adjured her granddaughter.

'What a wonderfully useful trait, Miss Darent,' responded Hazelmere, deciding for the moment to ignore provocation. 'So now we have a believable and totally unexceptionable story to account for our previous meeting. Provided we stick to that, I foresee no difficulty in ignoring the inevitable tales of what happened at the Three Feathers.' He rose and with effortless grace bent over Lady Merion's hand. 'I gather you'll be attending all the ton crushes this Season?'

'Oh, yes,' responded her ladyship, reverting to her normal social manner. 'We'll be out around town just as soon as Celestine can clothe these children respectably.'

He crossed to Dorothea's side and she stood for him to take his leave. Again he raised her hand to his lips. Smiling down at her in a way she found oddly disconcerting, his hazel eyes trapping her own, he said, 'Then I will hope to further my acquaintance with you, Miss Darent. I do hope you'll not find me too inconsequential to remember?' The gently mocking tone was back.

Dorothea returned the provocative hazel glance without apparent concern, and, wide-eyed, remarked, 'Oh, I shouldn't think I'd forget you now, my lord.'

He only just succeeded in controlling his face but his eyes clearly registered the hit. He paused, looking down into her brilliant green eyes, his own brimful of laughter. Forever a sportsman, he could hardly complain, as he had set himself up for that one. Still, he had not expected her to have the courage to fling that back in his face, and with such ease. With one last enigmatic glance, he turned and, bowing again to the sorely afflicted Lady Merion, bid both ladies a good day and left.

As the door shut behind him Lady Merion turned a gaze equally made up of disbelief and conjecture on her granddaughter. However, 'Ring for tea, child,' was all she said.

CHAPTER FOUR

For the Darent sisters, the Season began in earnest the next day. The morning commenced with a visit from Lady Merion's hairdresser. The pert Frenchman no sooner clapped eyes on the girls than his loquacious soul knew no bounds. Celestine had insisted on being present, much to everyone's surprise. It transpired that she had decided to take complete control of the Misses Darents' appearance. Lady Merion was astonished at her unusual condescension and then even more surprised by the transformation wrought in her elder granddaughter. Wearing the first of Celestine's creations, delivered expressly for their promenade in the Park later that day, with her lovely dark hair lightly cropped and arranged in a variation of the fashionable *Sappho*, Dorothea had emerged much as the ugly duckling transformed into a veritable swan. The result, as Celestine confided in a whispered aside to her ladyship, could not be adequately described as beautiful—that was an epithet reserved more correctly for the youthful Cecily. She was attractive, stunning, and trailing a definite aura of sensuality, and the impact of the new Dorothea was unerringly directed at the more mature male. Lady Merion, with Hazelmere in mind, blinked and rapidly realigned her expectations.

The sisters were next introduced to their dancing master, hired for an hour every morning for a week, to ensure that they would not put a foot wrong in the more conventional dances, as well as to introduce them to the waltz. Both girls were naturally graceful, and country balls had made them familiar with all the current measures, save the waltz.

In the afternoon they set out in Lady Merion's barouche to see and be seen at the Park. The spectacle of the ton taking the air, meeting old acquaintances and making new ones, held both girls enthralled. Lady Merion, her eyes resting for the umpteenth time on the delightful spectacle on the carriage seat opposite, felt happier and more buoyed by expectation than she had in years.

They had barely commenced their first circuit when a tall and angular lady, dressed in the height of fashion and seated in a landau drawn up to the side of the carriageway, waved to Lady Merion, who immediately instructed her coachman to pull up.

'Sally, how delightful! Is Maria back yet?' Without waiting for an answer, Lady Merion continued, 'You must let me present my granddaughters. Dorothea, Cecily, this is Lady Jersey.'

After exchanging greetings with the girls, Sally Jersey fixed her ladyship with a penetrating stare. 'Hermione, you're going to cause a *riot* with these children. You *must* let me send you vouchers for Almack's *at once*! My dear, I had a *dreadful* premonition that the Season was going to be *so dull*, but with two such beauties around I can see there'll be *fireworks*!'

Both Dorothea and Cecily blushed.

Lady Merion remained chatting to Lady Jersey for some minutes, exchanging information on who had or had not returned to the capital. It became apparent to the two girls that they were attracting considerable attention, from the ogling stares of the soldiers and young bucks, which Lady Merion had instructed them to ignore, to the far more disconcerting stares of other mamas passing by in their carriages with their hopeful young daughters. Under the soporific effect of the drone of their grandmother's conversation, Cecily let her gaze wander to a group of elegant gentlemen chatting to two pretty young ladies on the nearby lawn. Dorothea, similarly abstracted, was abruptly brought back to earth by Lady Jersey. 'I hear, my dear, that you are already acquainted with Lord Hazelmere?'

Aware that to show the slightest hesitation would be fatal, Dorothea used her large eyes to great effect, lucently conveying an attitude of complete nonchalance. 'Yes. As luck would have it, I met him again recently. He was kind enough to assist me at an inn on our way to London.'

Her ladyship's prominent eyes did not waver. 'So you had met him before?'

Dorothea's composure held firm. Her brows rose slightly, as if the answer to that question should really be quite obvious. 'His great-aunt, Lady Moreton, introduced him to my mother and myself some time ago. She was a neighbour of ours in Hampshire.'

'Oh, I see.' Lady Jersey was clearly disappointed in this undeniably mundane explanation of Dorothea's acquaintance with one of society's more rakish bachelors. She returned her attention to Lady Merion.

After a further five minutes of acidly social intercourse the coachman was told to move on. As Lady Jersey fell behind, Lady Merion drew a deep breath and bestowed a look of definite approval on her elder granddaughter. 'Very well done, my dear. Now we just have to keep it up.'

What she meant by that became rapidly apparent as they engaged in conversation after conversation with dowagers and matrons and occasionally with mothers with unmarried daughters. Without fail, the incident at the inn would somehow find its way into the arena, in one version or another. After her success with Lady Jersey, undoubtedly society's most formidable inquisitor, Lady Merion let Dorothea deal with all these enquiries, only stepping in when some of the younger ladies seemed anxious to lead the description into areas too particular for her ladyship's sense of propriety. Cecily, absorbed in the Park and its patrons and too young for the matrons to waste much time over, largely ignored these conversations.

Almost an hour later they stopped to talk to the Princess Esterhazy. After the introductions were performed, the sweet-faced and distinctly plump Princess smiled sleepily at the girls. 'I saw you talking with Sally before, so I'm sure she must have promised you vouchers?'

Lady Merion nodded. 'She feels my girls will liven up proceedings.'

'Oh, undoubtedly, I should think,' agreed Princess Esterhazy.

At this point two elegant young gentlemen detached themselves from a group that had been eyeing the beautiful young things in the Merion carriage and approached. 'Your servant, Lady Merion,' said the first, raising his hat and sweeping a graceful bow, copied by his companion.

Lady Merion, turning to see who had addressed her, promptly exclaimed, 'Oh, Ferdie! Is your mother in town yet?'

Assured that Mrs Acheson-Smythe would be in the capital by the end of the week, Lady Merion introduced her granddaughters to the elegant pair.

Dorothea and Cecily looked down upon two stylishly correct gentlemen, both clearly of the first stare. Neither was tall or broad-shouldered, yet both contrived to give the impression of being well turned out, a perfect fit for whatever niche they occupied in the ton. Mr Acheson-Smythe was slim and fair, his pale face characterised by a pair of frank and guileless blue eyes. Mr Dermont, of similar build, was less confident than his friend, letting the knowledgeable Mr Acheson-Smythe lead the conversation. Knowing that Ferdie Acheson-Smythe could be trusted to keep the line, her ladyship returned to her gossip with the Princess.

Seeing the girls' attention claimed by the young men, Princess Esterhazy took the opportunity to satisfy her curiosity. 'But tell me, Hermione. What is the truth of this story that Hazelmere rescued one of these two from a prize-fight crowd at some inn?'

By this time Lady Merion had the answer by rote. 'Such a lucky thing he was passing, my dear. Dorothea had gone down to find her coachman, not realising that the gentlemen had already arrived.'

'I had not realised your granddaughters were acquainted with Hazelmere.'

'Most fortunately, Dorothea had been introduced to him by his great-aunt, Lady Moreton. You must remember, she died last year, and Hazelmere was her heir. The Grange borders Moreton Park, and Cynthia, my daughter-in-law, and Etta

Moreton were close friends. Dorothea! Where was it you first met Hazelmere?'

Dorothea, who had been trying to follow two conversations at once, turned to hear her grandmother's question repeated. She answered easily, 'Oh, out driving one day. He was taking Lady Moreton for a ride in his curricle.' She turned back to Ferdie Acheson-Smythe, as if the details of how she had met the Marquis could not be of any possible consequence to anyone.

Her lack of consciousness convinced Princess Esterhazy that the story was the truth. In her opinion, no young lady who had met Hazelmere in any ineligible way could possibly look as unconcerned as Dorothea Darent.

On their return to Merion House shortly afterwards, Lady Merion led the way upstairs to her private drawing-room. Throwing her elegant hat on a chair, she subsided in a cloud of stylish velvets and breathed a heartfelt sigh. 'Well! We did very well, my dears. That was an excellent start to your Season.' She settled into her chaise-longue and, supplied with tea by Dorothea, consented to answer their questions.

'Ferdie Acheson-Smythe?' she said in answer to one of these. 'Ferdie is the only son of the Hertfordshire Acheson-Smythes. Of very good family, first cousin to Hazelmere. Ferdie will have to marry some day, I dare say, but by and large he's not the marrying kind. However, he *is* an acknowledged authority on all matters of etiquette, so if Ferdie drops you a hint on anything to do with your behaviour or dress you'd be well advised to take heed! He's also completely trustworthy; he'll never go beyond the line of what is pleasing. Ferdie is an unexceptionable companion for a young lady, and a very useful cavalier. It wouldn't do you any harm to be seen with him.'

'And Mr Dermont?' asked Cecily.

'Anyone Ferdie introduces to you as a friend will be much the same style, though Ferdie himself is unquestionably at the head of that class.'

Lady Merion had accepted an invitation to a small party that evening, and both her granddaughters accompanied her.

Entirely satisfied with their appearance, she was pleased to see that they mixed easily with the other young people present, although Dorothea, with her stunning appearance and air of calm self-possession, was deferred to as senior to the débutantes and in something of a different category. This was true enough. In a larger gathering, with more mature gentlemen, such as Hazelmere, to claim her attention, her elder granddaughter would not lack for entertaining partners.

Watching Dorothea, she grinned, their words of that afternoon recurring in her head. Cecily had been resting when the rest of Celestine's creations had been delivered; she and Dorothea had been alone in her parlour.

'This is exquisite!' Dorothea had exclaimed, holding up a blue sarcenet ballgown of Cecily's.

'Your own are every bit as alluring,' she had returned.

Dorothea had laughed, turning her attention to yet another of Cecily's gowns. 'But it's Cecily who needs the husband, not I.'

The comment had stunned her to silence. Then, in one revealing instant, she had seen Dorothea through Dorothea's eyes. Despite her common sense and self-confidence, having lived in relative seclusion until now, her granddaughter had little idea how she appeared to others in the fashionable world. To men. Particularly to men like Hazelmere. It was hardly innocence, rather a lack of awareness. After all, she had never been exposed to such gentlemen before. Intrigued, she had folded her hands in her lap and calmly stated, 'My dear, if you have visions of becoming an ape-leader, I fear you'll be disappointed.'

The green eyes had lifted to hers in genuine surprise. 'Whatever do you mean, ma'am? I know I'm too old for the marriage mart and I hardly have the requisite looks for an acknowledged beauty. But I don't repine, I assure you.'

She had snorted her disbelief. 'You're two and twenty, girl—hardly at your last prayers! And if you think to be left on the shelf, well! All I can say is, you've another think coming.'

But her stubborn granddaughter had only smiled.

Now, as she saw the small but growing knot of young men around her elder granddaughter, a grin of unholy amusement lit her faded blue eyes. How long would it take for Dorothea to wake up and realise that she was likely to be pursued, if anything, with even more dedication than the vivacious Cecily?

The next morning brought the first of the invitations to the larger gatherings. Initially these arrived in a trickle, but by the end of the week, as Lady Merion's granddaughters became more widely known, the gilt-edged cards left at Merion House assumed the proportions of a flood. As Dorothea and Cecily were only too glad to share the limelight with their less well-endowed sisters, even the most jealous mother saw little reason to exclude them from her guest lists. Moreover, if the Darent sisters were to attend some rival party then half the eligible males would likely be there too.

Lady Merion insisted that they attend as many of the smaller parties held in these first weeks as possible. She was too experienced to discount the considerable advantage social confidence could give. So Dorothea and Cecily obediently promenaded every afternoon and were to be found at a soirée or party or musical evening every night, polishing their social skills and attracting no little interest. Within a short time, both had collected a circle of ardent admirers. While this was no more than her ladyship had expected, the band around Dorothea gave her endless amusement. In general not much older than Dorothea herself, these lovesick swains were continually vying one with the other for their goddess's attention, striking Byronesque poses at every turn. It was really too funny for words. Still, thought the very experienced Lady Merion, it was serving its turn. Dorothea was being bored witless, all her social ingenuity being required to keep her temper with her artless lovers. A very good thing indeed if her wilful granddaughter could be brought to an appreciative, not to say receptive, frame of mind before being exposed to the infinitely more subtle persuasions of Hazelmere and his set. Luckily these highly eligible but far more dangerous gentlemen were rarely if ever sighted at the preliminary gatherings.

Ferdie Acheson-Smythe was the most constant of Dorothea's cavaliers, rapidly attaining the position of cisisbeo-in-chief to the dark-haired beauty. His initial approach to Lady Merion's granddaughters had been prompted by a chance meeting with Hazelmere. His magnificent cousin had suggested that Ferdie might assist in the squashing of any rumours concerning himself and the lovely Dorothea. It was the sort of thing Ferdie, an adept at social intrigue, enjoyed. And, as the favour was asked by Hazelmere, Ferdie would have thrown himself into the breach had Dorothea been the most unprepossessing antidote. Finding Miss Darent to be far more attractive than Hazelmere had indicated, Ferdie took to his task with alacrity. The result was that within a week a friendship had been established, close to sibling in quality but without the attendant strains, much to the surprise of both participants.

It was at a musical evening at Lady Bressington's that Mr Edward Buchanan made his appearance. A solid country gentleman of thirty-odd years, he was mildly fair and slightly rotund, his pink face graced by soulful brown eyes at odds with the rest of his robust figure. For reasons Dorothea failed to divine, he made straight for her side, ousting a darkly handsome Romeo by the simple expedient of suggesting that Miss Darent had had enough mindless maunderings for one night.

Miss Darent was slightly stunned. The Romeo, shattered, took himself off, muttering dark and dire threats against unspecified unromantic elders. Mr Buchanan took his place.

'My dear Miss Darent. I hope you'll excuse my approaching you like this. I realise we haven't been properly introduced. My name is Edward Buchanan. My father was a friend of Sir Hugo Clere and I looked in on him on my way to town. He mentioned your name and asked me to convey his regards.'

Dorothea sat silent through this speech, delivered in a ponderous baritone. The excuse was hardly substantial; Sir Hugo was a distant neighbour and she could readily imagine the purely formal greetings he would have sent. However, Miss Julia Bressington, a vivacious brunette and one of Cecily's

closest confidantes, was about to start singing, accompanied
by Cecily herself on the pianoforte, so it was not the time to
make even the mildest scene. She inclined her head and pointedly gave her attention to the players.

Mr Buchanan had the sense to remain silent during the performance, but immediately the applause died he monopolised
the conversation, determinedly chatting to Dorothea on pas-
toral issues. This left the majority of her court, most of whom
had no knowledge of crops or livestock, stranded. Dorothea
herself was utterly bemused by his unstinting eloquence on
the subject. But as soon as the last of her admirers had drifted
away, defeated by his dogged discourse, he stopped. 'Ah-ha!
Thought that would do it!' Looking thoroughly pleased with
himself, he explained, 'I wanted to get rid of them. I knew
they wouldn't understand anything of moment. Sir Hugo gave
me the fullest description of you, my dear Miss Darent, but
he came far from doing justice to your beauty. You clearly
outshine all these other young misses, although I must say I
find the favoured style of dress for young ladies these days a
little too, shall we say, revealing for one of my years to countenance.' His eyes had dropped to the swell of her breasts
exposed above the scooped neckline of her stylishly simple
silk gown. 'I dare say you feel that in the circumstances,
placed as you are with your grandmother, who, I understand,
is a highly fashionable lady, you too must play the part. Still,
we can overlook such matters, I'm sure. You would feel far
different in country circles, where I'm sure you are much more
at home.'

Dorothea was rendered speechless by this monologue,
which had contrived to progress from over-full compliment to
insult in the space of two minutes. Aghast, unable to get a
word in edgeways, she was forced to listen to Mr Buchanan's
opinions of fashionable practices, which culminated in a description of his widowed mother's belief that, in her exposing
her only son to the wicked wiles of London society, he would
return to her, corrupted in body and mind. Mr Buchanan assured Miss Darent with jocular familiarity that such an outcome was highly unlikely. Dorothea, incensed and close to

losing her temper, bit back an acid rejoinder that if London society could teach Mr Buchanan his manners it would have achieved a laudable goal. Instead she said in frigid tones, 'Mr Buchanan, I must thank you for your conversation. If you'll excuse me, I must speak with some friends.' Which, she reflected, was as close to a verbal cut as made no difference. But even as she rose, and with a cool nod moved to Lady Merion's side, she saw that, far from his taking the hint, the dismissal had not pricked his ego in the least.

By the night of the first of Almack's subscription balls Lady Merion knew she had a major success on her hands. They were fully booked for at least a sennight and the invitations were still rolling in.

She had started preparations for the girls' coming-out ball, for which the ballroom at Merion House would be opened for the first time in years. Squads of cleaning women had already been in, and redecoration would soon begin. The invitations, gold-embossed, had arrived that afternoon, and tomorrow they could start sending them out. She had fixed the date for four weeks hence, at the beginning of April, just before the peak of the Season. By then all her acquaintances would have returned to Town and she could be assured of a full house.

As she watched her granddaughters descend the stairs dressed for their first ball, both apparently unconscious of the positively stunning picture they made, she admonished herself as an old fool. Of course, her ball would be the biggest crush of the Season, but its success would owe far more to these two lovely young things than to anything she herself could do.

Dorothea, a vision in pale sea-green silk, lightly touched with silver filigree work, moved to kiss her on the cheek. 'Grandmama, you look wonderful!'

Hermione unconsciously smoothed her purple satin. 'Well, my dears, you are both an enormous credit to me. I'm sure you'll create a considerable stir tonight!'

Cecily, shimmering in pale blue spangled gauze over a shift of cornflower-blue satin, impulsively hugged her. 'Yes, but do let's go!'

Laughing, Lady Merion called for their cloaks and then led
the way to the carriage.

As soon as they entered the plain and unassuming ballroom
that was Almack's it was apparent that the Darent sisters' arrival had been eagerly awaited. Within minutes their cards
were full, with the exception of the two waltzes. Lady Merion
had impressed on them that they were forbidden to waltz until
invited by one of the patronesses, who would introduce them
to a suitable partner.

The Season was now in full swing and the rooms were
crowded with mothers and their marriageable daughters and
gentlemen eager to view the new Season's débutantes. Dorothea was thoroughly enjoying herself, being partnered first by
Ferdie, with whom she was now on first-name terms, and then
by a host of politely attentive gentlemen. Her grandmother,
watching over her charges from the gilt-backed chairs arranged
around the walls to accommodate the chaperons, noted that
Dorothea had attracted far more than her fair share of attention
but none of the more undesirable blades had yet sought her
company. Talking to Lady Maria Sefton, she watched her elder
granddaughter go down the ballroom in the movement of the
dance, and then lost sight of her as the music ended and the
dancers dispersed.

At the end of the ballroom, on the arm of the charming
young man who had been her partner, Dorothea turned to
make her way back to her grandmother's side, knowing that
the next dance was the first of the forbidden waltzes. A well-
remembered voice halted her. 'Miss Darent.'

Turning to face the Marquis of Hazelmere, Dorothea swept
him the curtsy she had been taught was due to his rank and,
rising, found that he had taken her hand and was raising it to
his lips. The hazel eyes dared her to make a scene, so she
accepted the salute in the same unconcerned way she had previously. Then her eyes met his fully, and held.

There followed a curious hiatus in which time seemed suspended. Then Hazelmere, becoming aware of her awkward
young cavalier, nodded dismissal to this gentleman. 'I'll return

Miss Darent to Lady Merion.' Faced with a lion, the mouse retreated.

To Dorothea he continued, 'There's someone I'd like you to meet, Miss Darent.' He placed her hand on his arm and deftly steered her through the crowd.

She had seen him among the throng earlier in the evening. He was dressed, as always, with restrained elegance in the dark blue coat and black knee-breeches currently *de rigueur* for formal occasions, with a large diamond pin winking from the folds of his perfectly tied cravat. She had thought him attractive in his buckskin breeches and shooting jacket, and more so in his morning clothes. In full evening dress he was simply magnificent. She had little difficulty in understanding why he made so many cautious mothers distinctly nervous.

Strolling calmly by his side, her hand resting lightly on his arm, she tried to ignore the light-headedness that had nothing to do with the crowd or the dancing and everything to do with the expression in those hazel eyes. Oh, how very *dangerous* he was!

Their perambulation came to an end by the side of a dark-haired matron. This lady, turning towards them, exclaimed in a cold and bored voice, 'There you are, my lord!'

Hazelmere looked down at Dorothea. 'Allow me to present you, Miss Darent, to Mrs Drummond-Burrell.'

Unexpectedly faced with the most censorious of Almack's patronesses, Dorothea hastily curtsied.

Mrs Drummond-Burrell, on whom her surprise was not lost, was pleased to smile. 'I expect Lord Hazelmere did not tell you I wanted to meet you. It seems a vast pity such a lovely young lady should miss even one waltz tonight. So, as he has instructed me, I will give you permission to waltz in Almack's, my dear, and present Lord Hazelmere as a suitable partner.'

Although taken aback by the scale of his machinations, Dorothea had been expecting something of the sort since she had first realised he was present. She had sufficient presence of mind to thank Mrs Drummond-Burrell very prettily, bringing an unusually benign expression to that lady's face, before allowing the Marquis to lead her on to the floor as the first strains of the waltz filled the room.

As this was the first waltz of the Season and many débutantes had not yet been given permission to dance, the floor was relatively uncrowded and the assembled company had a clear view of the dancers. The sight of the beautiful Miss Darent in the arms of Lord Hazelmere made something of a stir, and Dorothea, gently twirling down the room, was well aware that many eyes were directed their way. She did not dare allow herself to be distracted, fearing that he would instantly ask her some outrageous question.

As it transpired, she need not have worried. Hazelmere was, uncharacteristically, lost for words. He had thought her quite lovely in an old dimity gown with her hair down her back. Now, in every way perfect in one of Celestine's most elegant creations, she was utterly stunning.

Within seconds of stepping on to the floor Dorothea realised that she was in the arms of an expert, and promptly ceased trying to mark time. She surprised herself by not feeling the least bit awkward at being once again in his arms, and responded to the movements of the dance with a confidence so transparent that it drew even more attention than her beauty.

As they moved gracefully around the ballroom Hazelmere finally remarked, 'Does it bother you to be the cynosure of so many eyes, Miss Darent?'

Considering this unexpected question, she looked up into the hazel eyes and with the most complete self-assurance answered, 'Not at all, my lord. Should it?'

He smiled and replied, 'By no means, my dear. But permit me to tell you that in that you are somewhat unusual.'

Misliking where this line of conversation might lead, she rapidly hunted for an alternative. She saw her sister also dancing, in the arms of a man almost as attractive as Hazelmere. 'Who is the gentleman dancing with my sister?'

Without glancing at the other couple, he replied, 'Anthony, Lord Fanshawe.'

Puzzled by a fleeting memory, she finally recognised the

man she had glimpsed in the inn yard. Her eyes came back to Hazelmere. 'Do you know him?'

He smiled down at her. 'Oh, yes.' After a pause he added provocatively, 'We grew up together, as it happens.'

Once again her face gave her away before she guiltily caught herself up. One glance at those amused hazel eyes told her that he had not missed her thoughts, and he promptly confirmed this by remarking, 'No, Miss Darent. We are not *that* much alike.'

She was pleased that she blushed only slightly.

Hazelmere, seeking to press his advantage, asked, 'Are you never thrown into maidenly confusion, Miss Darent? Or is it that, at twenty-two, you no longer feel the need to adopt such missish airs?'

This uncannily accurate reading of her behaviour was, most unfortunately, lost on Dorothea. Instead he came under the concentrated scrutiny of her clear green eyes as she promptly asked, 'How do you know my age?'

Mentally castigating himself for not being more careful, he was about to mendaciously attribute this information to his great-aunt. However, under the influence of that steady green gaze, he heard himself reply, 'Mr Matthews told me.'

'The rector?' Her disbelief was patent.

Highly amused, he could not resist continuing, 'He loves to talk, you know. And he knows so much of what is happening in his parish. I've formed the habit of inviting him to dinner whenever I'm at Moreton Park.'

Dorothea, knowing full well the rector's failing, immediately saw the implication of these remarks. Her suspicions were immediately confirmed.

'I know all about your visits to Newbury, and Aunt Agnes's rheumatism and the trouble Mrs Warburton had with the parish fair. Incidentally, that reminds me: your Aunt Agnes sends you her love.'

The wild incredulity in her face as she imagined his meeting her vague, shy and man-hating maiden aunt sorely tempted him to leave the subject as was. He finally relented sufficiently to add, 'Via the rector, you goose!'

Realising that he had accurately read her mind yet again, she found herself returning his smile. She was still smiling as they finished the dance with a flourish not far from her grandmother. Hazelmere drew her hand through his arm and led her back to Lady Merion's side.

Her ladyship had been staggered enough to see Dorothea in Hazelmere's arms, but the sight of Cecily chattering amiably to Lord Fanshawe as she circled the room had made her doubt her senses. It was unheard of for two débutante sisters to stand up with two of the most eligible peers for their first waltz. More importantly, this outcome could only have been achieved by skilful manipulation of the patronesses by the two gentlemen involved. She was not sure she approved of such rapid and direct attack.

However, she was not immune to the glory of the undoubted triumph. Sally Jersey had stopped on her peregrinations about the rooms and, nodding towards Hazelmere and Dorothea, had whispered in her ear, 'He'll have her, you know. Never known Hazelmere to stand up for a first waltz before!'

Lady Merion, watching the elegant couple as they drifted past, Dorothea laughing up at Hazelmere, both blithely unaware of the surrounding company, rather fancied that Sally, for once, was right.

Two glowing young ladies were very correctly returned to her side, from where they were claimed by their partners for the next dance. As both Hazelmere and Fanshawe had been acquainted with Lady Merion from birth, neither attempted to disappear without paying their respects. With the sweetly smiling Maria, Lady Sefton sitting at her ladyship's side, the conversation remained on a general plane until Lady Sefton claimed Fanshawe's arm to go in search of her daughter-in-law.

Lady Merion promptly seized the opportunity to remark to Hazelmere, 'Well, you certainly don't let the grass grow under your feet!'

He smiled in the thoroughly maddening way he had, then said, 'I take it you're not perturbed by my interest?'

'Don't be absurd! You know perfectly well you're one of

the biggest prizes on the marriage mart!' His question unsettled her. This was fast going, indeed! 'But you must by now know that my granddaughter is highly unlikely to ask my opinion on the matter.'

'True. Nevertheless, *I* would be bound to consider your opinion, even if she did not.'

'Very pretty talking, indeed!' she responded, not entirely displeased.

Seeing Fanshawe returning, she dismissed them both, adding with a laugh as they both bowed elegantly before her, 'I'm sure you can think of more exciting ways to spend your evening.'

Towards the end of the ball Mr Edward Buchanan appeared at Dorothea's side. She forced a smile to her lips as he bowed over her hand.

'My dear Miss Darent! A delightful pleasure! I'm afraid, my dear, that I'm not a dancing man. Perhaps you would care to walk about the rooms with me?'

Ferdie, standing beside her, goggled.

With the most heartfelt relief, Dorothea, cool regret in her tone, said, 'I'm afraid, Mr Buchanan, that I'm engaged for all the dances this evening.'

'Oh?' He was genuinely surprised.

Luckily young Lord Davidson approached at that moment to claim her for the cotillion just forming. With the barest nod to Mr Buchanan, she laid her hand on Lord Davidson's arm and moved away.

Ferdie stared at the strange Mr Buchanan. Feeling the scrutiny, Edward Buchanan blushed slightly. 'Friend of a friend, you know. In the country. Dare say Miss Darent could use some hints on how to go on in London. Not up to snuff and too many of these young blades about, y'know. But now I'm here I'll keep an eye on her, never fear.'

'Oh?' said the elegant Ferdie Acheson-Smythe in his chilliest voice. With the barest inclination of his fair head he walked away.

CHAPTER FIVE

After his waltz with Dorothea, Hazelmere, mindful of the eyes upon him, danced with three other young ladies newly presented to the ton. Of these, two were diamonds of the first water, but both lacked the fire and wit to attract him as the lovely Dorothea did. Feeling the familiar boredom rising, and being debarred by convention from waltzing with Miss Darent again, he looked for Fanshawe. Hearing the music for the second and last waltz of the night start up, he scanned the dancers and easily picked out Miss Darent in the arms of Lord Robert Markham. It was definitely time to leave. Spying his friend in a group by the door, he made his way to him, and together they left for White's.

The small hours of the morning saw them wending their way home through the deserted city streets. They had played Pharoah and Hazelmere had held the bank. Consequently he had risen from the table a cool five hundred guineas richer. However, his thoughts were not concerned with his customary luck with the cards, but with his potential luck with a certain green-eyed young lady. Fanshawe was similarly occupied in wondering which of her numerous qualities was most responsible for making Cecily Darent so attractive. Together they crossed Piccadilly and headed up Bond Street in companionable silence.

Hazelmere finally broke this to say, 'Well, Miss Darent appears to have successfully quashed all the rumours.'

Fanshawe glanced sideways under his lashes at his friend. 'Do you intend to have her?'

Hazelmere checked slightly in his stride. The hazel and

brown eyes met for an instant. Then he chuckled. 'Is it that obvious?'

'Frankly, yes.'

'I suppose, as it's virtually obligatory to play by the rules, given it's the start of the Season, my interest will hardly remain a secret for long.'

'No. You're right. We'll have to play by the rules.'

'We?' His friend's preoccupation since meeting Cecily Darent had not escaped Hazelmere. 'At the inn I mentioned Miss Darent's sister more in jest than design.'

'I know that! But she's a deuced taking young thing, all the same. Not in the class of your Dorothea, but attractive none the less.'

'Oh, granted! In the absence of Dorothea, Cecily would bear off the palm. But satisfy my curiosity. Does she, like her sister, engage in—er—a conversational style bordering on the improper?'

'Lord, yes! Asked me straight out how I'd jockeyed Countess Lieven into giving her permission to waltz, and then floored me by asking why!'

Entertained by this evidence that a predilection for such conversation was a Darent trait, Hazelmere asked, 'And what did you answer?'

'Told her 'twas on account of her beautiful eyes, of course!'

'At which she laughed?'

'Exactly. Lovely sound.' After a pause Fanshawe continued, 'You know, Marc, I can't understand why all these mamas turn their daughters into such simpering misses you can't exchange two sensible words with. Bores us all to tears and they wonder why. Well—look at the Tremlett girl! Dashed good-looking chit. But as soon as she opens her mouth I'm off! And just look at our set. Besides the two of us, there's Peterborough and Markham, Alvanley, Harcourt, Bassington, Aylsham, Walsingham, Desborough—oh, and a host of others! And they're just our set, let alone the younger ones. All of us are either titled or well connected, independently wealthy, and all of us have got to marry sooner or later. Yet here we all are, over thirty and still unattached, purely because there are so few chits with more wit than hair.'

'Which is exactly why,' concluded Hazelmere, grasping his erratic friend by the elbow to steer him around the railings of Hanover Square, 'we're going to assiduously attend all the ton crushes this Season.'

'Good God!' uttered his lordship, much struck by this logic. 'You mean they'll all be after the Darent girls?'

'You've just said it yourself. We're all on the lookout for suitable brides and we're all eligible. The Darent sisters are outstanding candidates on any man's terms. You and I, dear boy, have merely stolen a march on the rest. And I'll be much surprised if they don't try and make up lost ground very quickly. I rather think Markham has already made a start.'

'Yes, saw that too. And Walsingham was there as well.'

'I predict by tomorrow night the whole crew will have gathered. Which, if you're serious about the younger Miss Darent, is going to keep both of us on our toes.'

They had come to the corner of Cavendish Square and paused. 'What's on tomorrow night?' asked Fanshawe sleepily.

'The Bedlington rout. Why not come to dinner and we'll go on together?'

'Good idea.' He yawned. 'See you then.' And, with a nod and a wave, he headed off to his rooms in Wigmore Street, leaving Hazelmere to stroll the short distance to his house.

Entering with his latchkey, he made his way upstairs, to be greeted by his very correct gentleman's gentleman, who went by the totally unsuitable name of Murgatroyd. He had never managed to convince Murgatroyd, a dapper and decidedly top-lofty individual, that he need not wait up for him, and that he, Hazelmere, was perfectly capable of getting himself to bed. As by various subtle references Murgatroyd had made it plain that he considered his lordship's clothes required far greater care than his lordship was likely to bestow on them, he had finally capitulated, as in all other ways Murgatroyd suited him very well.

Snuffing out the candle and listening to the footsteps retreating down the carpeted corridor, Hazelmere crossed his arms behind his head and stretched luxuriously, smiling as he thought of a particular pair of brilliant green eyes. Tony had given voice to his own thoughts on their way home. There was going to be heavy competition for those young ladies' favours and most of it from highly experienced players. As things stood, he could certainly not be sure of winning the lady's heart. And, he admitted to himself, for reasons he was not entirely sure of, and quite definitely for the first time in his life, that was something he very much wanted to do.

Lady Bedlington's rout was a gala affair attended by everyone who was anyone. The eccentric hostess was gratified to receive Lords Hazelmere and Fanshawe, as well as a quite astonishing number of their associates. Not only were these gentlemen in attendance, but they also all arrived fairly early.

In the ballroom Hazelmere kept the head of the stairs in view. As Dorothea and Cecily appeared there he adroitly disengaged from the conversation around him and, without the least haste, made his way towards the stairs, his arrival at their foot coinciding with that of Miss Darent.

Seeing him coming towards her, Dorothea smiled and then curtsied as he bowed before her. She resolutely ignored the fluttering nervousness that made breathing strangely difficult.

Raising her hand to his lips, Hazelmere dropped a gentle kiss on her fingers, managing to turn the courtesy into a caress. He did not release her hand but turned it to flip up the dance card hanging from her wrist. These tiny cards with the order of dances listed with a place for each prospective partner to inscribe his name were much in vogue, and all the best hostesses invariably provided the débutantes with a copy, slung on a riband with a tiny silver-encased pencil attached.

'Miss Darent! You appear mysteriously free for all the dances tonight. However, I suppose I shall have to be content with just one waltz—the first, I think?'

As she laughingly assented he duly wrote his name in the appropriate spot, then, releasing her hand and turning to survey the descending multitudes of her admirers, continued in a voice lowered so that only she could hear, 'And, as a reward for being so early, I really think I should be allowed to escort you to supper, don't you?'

Dorothea did not reply, but her eyes met his in amused enquiry.

Correctly interpreting the glance, he answered, 'Quite proper, I assure you.' With a smile he moved away to make room for the hordes of gentlemen wishful of securing a dance with the lovely Miss Darent.

As he did so he noticed, as he had predicted, Markham, Peterborough, Alvanley and Desborough among the throng. In the crowd around Cecily Darent he could make out Lords Harcourt and Bassington, as well as Fanshawe, who had executed a similar tactic to his. This was not a matter for surprise; they had discussed it over dinner. Satisfied with their success, they both moved away to claim their partners for the first dance.

Dorothea had no chance to ponder the wiles of the Marquis, being claimed for every dance and attended assiduously by a coterie of admirers. She was thoroughly enjoying herself and consequently looked radiant in a bronze silk dress covered by transparently fine tissue faille, shimmering whenever she moved. The high-waisted style suited her slender figure, making her appear more startlingly beautiful than ever. More than one furious mama wondered why Celestine never suggested such designs for their daughters.

Unaware of this sartorial jealousy, Dorothea noticed a distinct and disturbing change in the quality of her partners. At Almack's, with the exception of the Marquis and Lord Markham, these had been charming young lads not much older than herself, who were in awe of the beautiful and self-possessed young lady and entirely amenable to allowing her to control both conversation and action. Tonight the majority of her partners were older, of the same vintage as Hazelmere, and with that came a great deal more difficulty. Some, like the gentle Alvanley, were no problem, and she quickly came to regard them as friends. Others, like wild Lord Peterborough and the rakish Walsingham, she was much more wary of. When, more than midway through the evening, Hazelmere came to claim her for the first waltz, rescuing her from Lord Walsingham's side, she went into his arms with a sensation much akin to relief.

Thoroughly appreciative of the situation, he could not resist remarking, 'Rather heavier weather tonight, Miss Darent?'

For an instant the hazel and green eyes met. Then Dorothea, in a voice every bit as languid as his, replied, 'Why, no, my lord! I find it all most entertaining.'

'Trying it on just a little too thick, my child,' he murmured.

Dorothea hit back, wide-eyed innocence writ large on her face. 'My lord! Such cant terms. How improper!'

Hazelmere laughed, then immediately returned to the attack. 'If we're to discuss impropriety, my dear, why is it that, try as I might, I cannot recall a conversation with you that has not been improper?'

She caught that up easily, murmuring with complete self-assurance, 'I should have thought the reason for that was obvious, Lord Hazelmere.'

As their glances once more caught and held, Hazelmere saw complete enjoyment of the moment reflected in her eyes. That was the second time he had walked himself into a trap with her. He must be slipping. Nevertheless, there was hay to be made yet. Trying for a sterner tone, he said, 'I'll have you know, my dear Miss Darent, that I'm not in the habit of conducting improper conversations with well-behaved young ladies.'

Not seeing where this was headed, she could do no more than show a politely surprised face. 'Oh?'

As the last strains of the waltz drifted across the ballroom, he whirled her to a halt. Smiling down into those glorious green eyes, he replied, 'Only with you.'

Eyes blazing in mock indignation, she could not keep a straight face. With a gurgle of laughter she allowed him to draw her hand through his arm and lead her back to Lady Merion's side. 'As I said, Lord Hazelmere, you are most improper.'

He promptly corrected her, raising her hand to his lips, his eyes fully on hers, 'We are both most improper, Miss Darent.'

Later he escorted her to supper, extricating her from the figurative clutches of Lord Peterborough. As he was well practised in the art of detaching young women from the attentions of his close acquaintances, these otherwise difficult tasks were accomplished with a minimum of fuss. They shared a supper table with Cecily and Lord Fanshawe and Julia Bressington, who had the punctilious Lord Harcourt in tow. The conversation was general and decidedly hilarious. Fanshawe, with Cecily interpolating the occasional observation, described the singular scene they had just witnessed between old Lady Melchett and Lord Walsingham, when that irascible old dame had taken his lordship to task for not dancing with her niece.

Realising that, with her limited experience of the ton, Dorothea could not be appreciating the half of the story, Hazelmere spent a pleasant five minutes filling in her knowledge, his head close to hers so as not to disturb the rest of the table.

For Dorothea and Cecily, the Bedlington rout was to provide a blueprint for the behaviour of the Marquis and Lord Fanshawe. Present at almost every major gathering they attended, their lordships were always among the first to write their names in the dance cards, usually for a waltz, and more often than not squired them to supper.

While considerable attention was initially focused on them, as the days lengthened to weeks the ton became accustomed to the sight of Miss Darent in Lord Hazelmere's arms and Cecily Darent in Lord Fanshawe's. Their lordships put up with a considerable degree of ribbing regarding their habit of being in everything together. This they bore with equanimity, surprising their associates and convincing those gentlemen that the affairs were indeed serious. By the first week of April, three weeks into the Season and the week preceding the girls' coming-out ball, the knowledgeable among the ton spoke of an understanding between the Darent girls and Lords Hazelmere and Fanshawe. Once this point was reached, their lordships knew that a far greater degree of licence would be permitted them in their dealings with their chosen ladies.

During those first weeks both were careful not to overstep

the line at any point. Hazelmere realised that Dorothea, for all her vaunted independence, turned to his arms as to a safe harbour, knowing that there she was protected from the likes of Lords Peterborough and Walsingham. Recognising the sterling service that these gentlemen were, however unwittingly, rendering him, he did not attempt to dissuade them from trying to cut him out. He found it ironic that in avoiding what she considered their dangerous attentions she should choose to seek shelter with him, where, had she but known it, she was in far greater danger.

He watched her carefully over the weeks of balls and parties and saw no sign of partiality for any other gentleman's company. He knew she enjoyed being with him; her eyes told him so every time he thought to gaze into them, which was often. What he did not know was whether she was in love with him. There was an elusive quality about her that for all his wide experience he had never before encountered.

Still, there was plenty of time. The rush of the coming-out balls would occur in the next few weeks. Afterwards the activities of the ton normally settled to a more comfortable pace, and such matters as marriage could be concluded in a more restful atmosphere.

As the Season progressed, Dorothea found herself in a curious quandary. Lord Hazelmere was the most fascinating man she had met. He was always attentive in a subtly understated manner that she appreciated far more than the suffocating endeavours of her younger admirers. He was, quite frankly, the only man she had ever, in the remotest recesses of her mind in the darkest hours of the night, considered marrying.

It had not needed Lady Merion's none too subtle hints to make her realise that the Marquis had singled her out, his continuing attentions making it clear that he was seriously courting her. But he had done nothing to further his interests beyond the tentative stage. She had a sneaking suspicion that, because she had not appeared to succumb to his quite considerable charm, he was laying siege to her susceptibilities, holding her tantalisingly at a distance until she acknowledged his attraction. She was a challenge and, as such, had to be conquered. Then his arrogant pride and imperious manner would, she felt, be quite insupportable.

There were even rumours of a bet being placed on the outcome of their contest of wills. Unwise in the ways of betting, she had no idea if this could be so, but she rather felt it rang true of the scandalous Marquis.

However, the questions that increasingly occupied her mind were concerned with his reasons for choosing her. They were starting to disturb her sleep. He had to marry some time, that much was obvious. But why her? Was he in love with her or was she merely convenient? How did he see her? A challenge to be overcome, a suitable connection, the granddaughter of one of his mother's closest friends, a woman of common sense, not so beautiful as to require constant vigilance? Or did he see something more? By all the tenets of her class, it should not matter one jot. But to her it mattered a great deal. She was in the enviable position of not having to wed unless she wished it. But, if their relationship continued to develop along its present course, refusing him if and when he offered might prove difficult. But when it came to ascertaining Hazelmere's motives she faced a problem—how could she tell? He was a man of considerable experience and ready charm. If he merely wanted a conformable wife, one who would interfere little with his established pursuits, then it would be, she reasoned, entirely in character for his arrogant lordship to choose, as the easiest route, to make a country miss fall in love with him and so more readily accept his suit.

Her inability to divine his motives was frustrating. Still, as things stood, there was little she could do. The reins were at present very much in his hands. With little scope for manoeuvre, the best she could do was enjoy his company and leave all difficult questions until they demanded an answer.

CHAPTER SIX

The Saturday before the Darent sisters' coming-out ball saw them riding in the Park, a daily treat organised by the enterprising Ferdie. He was now firmly established as their chief mentor and guide through the shoals of the Season, and had reached the position of being regarded by Dorothea, Cecily and even Lady Merion as part of their household.

The previous week he had decided that the Misses Darent would look well on horseback and had presented himself at Merion House with horses especially for them. Dorothea loved riding and even Cecily enjoyed a gentle canter, so he had not been disappointed with their reception of his idea. Within ten minutes both girls had changed into the elegant riding dresses Celestine had concocted and were on their way to the Park, escorted by the proud Ferdie and his shadow, Mr Dermont.

Attired in a severe sage-green outfit that showed off her figure to admiration, her glossy curls topped by a soft felt cloche with a beautiful peacock plume curling around her head, Dorothea had easily controlled a frisky bay mare. Cecily, quite happy with her docile palfrey, had been a picture, turned out in a pale blue tunic with fur trimming over a darker blue skirt with a matching fur hat. Their first excursion had been a resounding success.

This afternoon, riding easily beside Ferdie, Dorothea heard herself addressed in a familiar, gently mocking voice.

'What a very accomplished young lady you are, Miss Darent.'

Turning to meet the frankly admiring gaze of the Marquis of Hazelmere, Dorothea felt herself blushing. But, setting eyes on the beautiful black gelding he was riding, she involuntarily exclaimed, 'Oh! What a magnificent animal!'

The magnificent animal took exception to her tone but was effortlessly held. 'And with good taste, too! Which is more than can be said of this brute at present. He's not been out for three days and is in an evil temper.' The hazel eyes were fixed on her face. 'Why don't you come for a gallop, Miss Darent?'

Sorely tempted, she glanced around for her mentor, to find that Ferdie had unaccountably vanished.

'Afraid?' came that mocking voice again.

Dorothea threw caution to the winds. 'Very well. But which way?'

'Follow me.' The black leapt forward down a wide ride reaching into the depths of the Park. Although the gelding was the superior animal, Hazelmere rode a great deal heavier than Dorothea. She was an accomplished rider and so was not far behind as he drew up in a wide arc in the clearing at the end of the ride. Not as strong, she pulled up in a wider arc, closer to the trees. A low branch swept her hat from her head.

Both were laughing with exhilaration as Hazelmere rode to where her hat lay and dismounted to retrieve it. She rode back and waited as he picked it up and dusted off the plume. Curling the feather in his hand, he walked to her side, but instead of handing the hat to her he reached up to place his hands about her waist.

'Come down, Miss Darent.'

She considered refusing but had no idea how to without sounding missish or, worse, coquettish. Feeling the strength in the hands resting lightly at her waist and finding the hazel eyes amused as ever, she decided that boldness was her only answer. She slipped her feet free of her stirrups, and without effort he lifted her down to stand in front of him.

'Stand still,' he commanded and, freeing the long hat pin, expertly inserted it through her coiled hair to secure the hat in place. He ran his hand over the plume to settle it back around her face.

Dorothea found that she was looking into eyes which no longer laughed but glinted strangely. Mesmerised, she felt her own thoughts scatter to the four winds. She was acutely aware of the man before her and little else. She wondered for one moment if he was going to kiss her. But the next instant the mocking look returned and she was lifted back on to the mare.

'At least I'll return you to Ferdie in every way as immaculate as when I inveigled you away from his side.' The cynical tone sounded odd to her ears.

Deflatingly bewildered, she felt a spurt of anger that he should tantalise her, only to withdraw at the last moment. She frowned and then nearly gasped as the indelicacy of her thoughts struck her. She wheeled her mount, horrified that he would see her blushing and guess the cause.

Hazelmere remounted, and without comment they moved back along the ride, soon falling into an easy canter. He had seen her delicate brows draw together but attributed the response to anger at his actions rather than frustration at his reticence.

They emerged from the trees and by unspoken consent turned up a slight rise and halted, looking for the others. The rest of the party was not far distant. Lord Fanshawe had joined the group and was deep in conversation with Cecily. Even from her present distance, Dorothea could see that her sister was entirely captivated. Ferdie and Mr Dermont had been joined by two cronies and all four were aimlessly wandering further and further from the dallying couple. It suddenly dawned on her that Ferdie's judgement might not be infallible.

Assailed by sudden guilt, she realised that she, too, had been remiss. It would not be easy to explain why she had been alone with the Marquis of Hazelmere in a deserted ride. Thankfully she did not think they had been seen. But to leave Cecily virtually alone with Fanshawe in the middle of the Park! Really! Where had Ferdie's wits gone begging?

A deep chuckle from beside her brought her green eyes back to Hazelmere's face. The mocking gaze held hers steadily. 'You really can't blame Ferdie, you know. He would be as protective as you could wish were any others involved. But he would never see Fanshawe or myself as potentially threatening.'

She threw him an exasperated glance and headed off towards her sister. As she approached, Fanshawe looked up in surprise and lifted an enquiring eyebrow at Hazelmere, close behind. Dorothea did not need to see his answering laughing grimace to realise that, as far as her sister and herself were concerned, if Lords Hazelmere and Fanshawe were present the 'safety in numbers' maxim was unlikely to apply.

Seeing her quick frown, Cecily smiled sunnily, not the least bit discomfited, but she willingly brought her mount alongside as Dorothea turned towards the gate.

At that moment they were joined by Edward Buchanan, mounted on a showy cob. Hearing the news that the Darent sisters rode every day in the Park, he had conceived the happy notion that, while he might not shine in the ballroom, Miss Darent could not fail to be impressed by the vision of himself on a mettlesome steed. Unfortunately for him, his mettlesome steed, hired from a commercial stable, was far from elegant, being too long in the back and with a noticeable tendency to throw one leg.

Pulling up beside the group, he bowed to Dorothea. 'Well met, Miss Darent.'

Dorothea inclined her head, an action she managed to infuse with an arctic iciness. 'Mr Buchanan. I'm afraid we were on the point of returning to Cavendish Square.' Hazelmere's lips twitched.

'No matter, dear lady,' said Edward Buchanan, airily gesturing. 'I'll be only too happy to join your escort.'

Dorothea nearly choked. Short of refusing him point-blank, there was nothing she could do. Her face a mask, she was forced to introduce him to her companions. The Marquis merely raised one black brow in acknowledgement, and Lord Fanshawe was similarly reticent. Neither showed any inclination to surrender their positions flanking the Darent sisters to Mr Buchanan. Dorothea almost sighed in relief, then tensed as she saw the gleam in Edward Buchanan's eye. As they walked their horses towards the gate he launched into a discussion of harvesting techniques.

This time he had badly misjudged his victims. Hazelmere,

brought up from infancy to the management of the vast Henry family estates, and Fanshawe, not yet come into his patrimony but already involved in running the Eglemont acres, both knew more about that topic than he did. Between them they efficiently rolled up the subject, then turned an inquisitorial light on Mr Buchanan himself. Under a subtle pressure he had no defence against, he found himself admitting that he possessed a country holding in Dorset. No, not particularly large. How large? Well, actually, quite small. Livestock? Not a great number. No, he had not yet launched into breeding.

Her side aching from suppressed laughter, Dorothea glanced back at Ferdie, just behind, surprising a beatific grin on the guileless face. Mr Dermont, too, appeared strangely entertained. And Cecily, who had not previously encountered Mr Buchanan, was ecstatic. Her grin left no doubt that she understood their lordships' tactics. Dorothea returned to her sphinx-like contemplation of Mr Buchanan's difficulties, presently being added to by Fanshawe. Her eyes strayed to Hazelmere's face and, as if sensing her gaze, he looked down at her. The expression of unbridled hilarity that glowed for a moment in his eyes very nearly overset her.

Then Mr Buchanan, desperately seeking to change the subject, and by now conscious that his mettlesome mount could not hold a candle to any of the others in this group, said, 'I'm most impressed with the quality of your horses, Miss Darent. I take it they're hired?'

'Why, yes. Ferdie gets them for us.' She turned to Ferdie as she spoke and was surprised to see a peculiarly blank, not to say wooden, expression on his face.

'Ah. And which stable do they come from, Mr Acheson-Smythe, if I may make so bold as to enquire?' asked Edward Buchanan.

'You use the Titchfield Street stables, don't you, Ferdie?' said Hazelmere.

Ferdie started. 'Oh! That is, yes! Titchfield Street!' Dorothea wondered what on earth was the matter with him.

Hazelmere, well aware that there were no stables in Titchfield Street, and further, that, as far as he knew, there was no

Titchfield Street in the metropolis, smiled amiably on Mr Buchanan as they reached the gate.

Mr Buchanan, seeing the smile, decided that he had borne enough in the interests of his future for one day. Suddenly recalling a pressing engagement, he regretfully took his leave of the party.

His departure left them in stricken silence, which lasted until he was out of sight. Then they all dissolved into laughter.

Finally, still flanked by Lords Hazelmere and Fanshawe and with Ferdie and Mr Dermont bringing up the rear, the Misses Darent returned to Cavendish Square. On the way their lordships maintained a steady flow of general conversation, including both young ladies impartially. Dorothea suspected that this evidence of impeccable behaviour was a ploy to convince her there had been no impropriety in their actions in the Park. With a reasonable idea of what she and Cecily could expect on future rides, she realised that they would have to make plans to at least minimise the opportunities for such manoeuvres. She was not optimistic of their chances of eliminating such occurrences altogether; their lordships were simply too experienced in such matters.

Arriving in Cavendish Square, she moved to dismount but was forestalled by Hazelmere, who lifted her down. Holding her for a moment between his hands, he looked down at her lovely face, serious for once. The hazel eyes glinted, then Cecily laughed and the moment was gone. Releasing her, he swept her a bow and, with his usual amused air, said, '*Au revoir*, Miss Darent. I dare say we'll meet again tonight.'

Brought back to reality, Dorothea smiled her goodbyes and, finding Cecily at her elbow, entered Merion House.

Once inside, Mellow informed them that Lady Merion was resting before the ball and had insisted that her granddaughters do likewise. The Duchess of Richmond was entertaining tonight and her ball was one of the highlights of the Season. Held on the first Saturday of April, this was followed by all the coming-out balls. Traditionally the most important of these were held on the Wednesdays and Saturdays during the rest of April, sometimes stretching into May. While there were a number of lesser gatherings scheduled for the next Sunday, Monday and Tuesday, there was only one ball on the following Wednesday night—at Merion House. A few other mothers had originally planned to hold their daughters' balls on that night too, but, having taken stock of the Darent sisters, these ladies had wisely decided to change their dates. Better to be a bit thinner of company than to have no company at all.

Her interlude with Hazelmere had given Dorothea food for thought, so, thinking her grandmother's advice very timely, she and Cecily retired to their respective chambers, supposedly to rest.

Trimmer, her new maid, was waiting to help her change. Lady Merion and Witchett had decided that Betsy should stay with Cecily, as she was familiar with that young lady's occasional indispositions. Dorothea's style was more demanding of the attentions of a first-class dresser. When asked if she knew of any suitable candidate Witchett had eventually produced her niece, Trimmer. Luckily she and Dorothea had got on well, and Trimmer had, as her aunt before her, fallen under the spell of her lovely young mistress.

Pausing in the middle of the room to draw out the hat pin the Marquis had placed in her hair, Dorothea wished that Trimmer would go away, but did not have the heart to summarily dismiss her. She patiently waited while the attentive maid divested her of her outdoor clothes and left her enveloped in a green silk wrapper before letting her mind shut out the rest of the world and concentrate on the question of what she was to do about the Marquis of Hazelmere.

Sitting at her dressing-table, she loosened her hair and absent-mindedly brushed the gleaming tresses, staring unseeingly at her reflection in the mirror. From the moment she had first met him Hazelmere had made serious inroads against her heart's defences. That much, she admitted, was incontrovertible fact. But up until now she had avoided considering the natural outcome of that situation.

Staring intently into her own green eyes, reflected in the highly polished surface, she sighed. It had taken her some time to understand the novel emotions he aroused in her. But after

today she could no longer delude herself. Alone with him in
the clearing in the Park, she had been quite sure he would kiss
her. And she had wanted him to. Preferably as he had before
by the blackberry bush. Scandalous it might have been, but
she had been wishing for weeks that he would repeat the performance.

She laid the brush down and carefully rewound her hair.
She knew she looked forward to meeting him wherever they
went, and she derived much pleasure from his company, despite his high-handed ways, which still on occasion infuriated
her. The disconcerting habit he had of reading her mind merely
added spice to their encounters, and she thoroughly enjoyed
their highly irregular conversations. When he was not with her,
alternately mocking or provoking her, with that certain amused
expression in his hazel eyes, she felt sadly flat and found little
to please her. The inescapable conclusion was that he had captured her heart. That admitted, what exactly was she to do
about it?

Rising to cross the room, she lay on her bed, idly playing
with the tassels of the bedcurtain cord. While she was now
sure of her feelings, what had she learnt of his? He certainly
seemed genuinely attracted to her. But he was of an age when
he would be expected to marry. Maybe he had simply, in his
customary high-handed way, decided that she would do.
Surely, if that was the case, and his interest in her was illusory,
she would be able to tell? But he was a master at this game
and she was a novice. In the normal way of things, it seemed
certain that he would, at some point, offer for her hand. And,
by the same agreed code of behaviour, she would accept him.
The trouble was, she loved him. Did he love her?

She pondered that question for half an hour. Despite his
ability to guess most of her thoughts, she felt sure that she had
not yet betrayed the depth of her interest in him. It seemed
prudent to shield her heart until he gave her some indication
of his regard.

However, the present stage of innocuous dalliance could not
last; this afternoon's events proved that. Perhaps, during one
of their numerous interludes, she could find a way of encour-

aging him to declare himself? The idea of encouraging such a man as Hazelmere brought a grin of amusement to her face. That, at least, should not prove too difficult. Feeling, for no particular reason, more confident, she placed her head on her pillow and, worn out by her cogitations, slept until Trimmer came to dress her for the Duchess of Richmond's ball.

If she had looked out of her window instead of into her mirror Dorothea would have seen Hazelmere, Fanshawe and Ferdie entering Hazelmere House. They left their mounts in the mews behind the mansion and walked back to the front door, deep in discussion of horseflesh. Hazelmere opened the door with his key and crossed the threshold, only to come to an immediate halt. Ferdie, following, cannoned into him and, peering around his shoulders, remarked in wonder, 'Good lord!'

Hazelmere brought his quizzing glass to bear on the piles of band-boxes and trunks strewn about his hall. Seeing his butler attempting to approach through the welter of luggage, he enquired in a deceptively sweet voice, 'Mytton, what exactly is all this?'

Mytton, knowing that tone, promptly replied, 'Her ladyship has arrived, m'lord.'

'Which ladyship?' pursued Hazelmere, assailed by a sudden and revolting thought.

'Why, the Dowager, m'lord!' replied Mytton, at a loss to understand the strange question.

'Oh, of course!' said Hazelmere, relieved as enlightenment dawned. 'For one horrible moment I thought Maria and Susan had come back.'

This explanation made all clear to the assembled company. Hazelmere's antipathy towards his elder sisters was common knowledge. This stemmed from an attempt made some years previously by those rigid ladies to manage his matrimonial affairs for him. Their inevitable and ignoble defeat had culminated in their being *persona non grata* in his various establishments. As they were both married to men well able to provide for them, Hazelmere saw no reason for them to be cluttering up his houses with their meddling, strait-laced ways.

Absorbed in his own affairs, he had entirely forgotten that his mother, Anthea Henry, the Dowager Marchioness of Hazelmere, always came to town for a few weeks of the Season, and invariably attended the Duchess of Richmond's ball. Again surveying the scene, he asked, 'How is her ladyship, Mytton?'

'She has retired to rest, m'lord, but said she would join you for dinner.'

Hazelmere nodded absently and led the way in between the various trunks and boxes, down the corridor and through the double doors into the beautifully appointed library. Ferdie followed, with Fanshawe bringing up the rear. Closing the doors behind them, Fanshawe turned with a grin. 'They all seem to move with mountains of luggage, don't they? Can't think your mama will need the half of it, but mine's exactly the same.'

Hazelmere ruefully agreed. Realising that to dine alone with his sharp-eyed parent might not be all that soothing to his temper, already under strain, he decided to call in reinforcements. 'Tony, you'll come to dinner? And you too, Ferdie?'

Fanshawe nodded his acceptance, but Ferdie replied, 'Pleased to, but don't forget I'm to escort the Merion party to the ball, so I'll have to leave at seven.'

'Well, if you're leaving at seven we'll have to leave earlier,' said Fanshawe. 'Don't you dare leave Merion House until the carriage is away from this door!'

Hazelmere crossed to the bell pull and, when Mytton appeared, gave his orders. 'And my respects to her ladyship, but we dine at five and are to leave for the ball at seven. See that the carriage is waiting no later than seven.'

Mytton retreated to convey this unwelcome news to the culinary wizard downstairs. Hazelmere poured glasses of wine and, having handed these around, sank into one of the wing chairs gathered around the marble fireplace. Fanshawe had taken the chair opposite, and Ferdie was elegantly disposed on the chaise. Now that they were comfortably settled, a companionable silence descended. This was broken by Fanshawe.

'What on earth made you come back from that ride so quickly?'

Without looking up from his contemplation of the unlit fire, Hazelmere replied, 'Temptation.'

'What?'

With a sigh he explained. 'Remember we agreed we'd have to play by the rules?' Fanshawe nodded. 'Well, if we'd stayed any longer in that ride the rules would have flown with the wind. So we came back.'

Fanshawe nodded sympathetically. 'All this is turning out a dashed sight more complicated than I'd imagined.'

That brought Hazelmere's gaze to his face, but it was Ferdie, all at sea, who spoke. 'But why is it all so complicated? Would've thought it was all pretty much plain sailing, myself, especially for you two. Simply roll up and ask the girls' guardian, the horrible Herbert, for their hands. Simple! No problem at all.'

Seeing the expression of amused tolerance this speech elicited, Ferdie realised that he had missed some vital point and waited patiently to be set right. Hazelmere, eyes fixed on the delicate wine glass held in one white hand, eventually explained, 'The difficulty, Ferdie, lies in divining the true state of the Misses Darents' affections. To whit, I can't tell if Miss Darent is merely playing the game or whether her heart is at all engaged by your humble servant.'

Ferdie regarded him with absolute disbelief, utterly bereft of words. Finally regaining the use of his tongue, he exclaimed, 'No! Hang it all, Marc! Can't be true. You, of all people. Must be able to tell.'

'How?'

Ferdie opened his mouth to answer and then shut it again. He turned to Fanshawe. 'You too?'

Fanshawe, head sunk on his chest, merely nodded.

After a pause while he digested this astonishing intelligence, Ferdie said, 'But they both seem to enjoy your company.'

'Oh, we know that,' agreed Hazelmere dismissively. 'But beyond that, I, for one, can't tell.'

'True,' Fanshawe confirmed. 'Only need to look into those

eyes to see they like having us around. Like to talk to us, dance with us. Well, why wouldn't they, all things considered? Fact of the matter, Ferdie, m'lad, is it's a very long hop from that to love.'

The dilemma they were in was now clear to Ferdie. He was considering the possibility of helping them out, when he suddenly found himself the object of the Marquis's hazel gaze.

'Ferdie,' said Hazelmere softly, 'if you so much as breathe a word of this conversation outside this room—'

'We'll both make your life entirely unbearable,' finished Fanshawe. This was a standard threat between the three, and Ferdie made haste to assure them that such an idea had never entered his head. He faltered slightly under Hazelmere's sceptical gaze.

A dismal silence settled over them, until Fanshawe glanced at the clock on the mantelshelf and stirred. 'I'd best be off to change. Coming, Ferdie?'

All three rose. After seeing them out, Hazelmere went upstairs to find Murgatroyd already awaiting him. As Tony had said, it had become a lot more complicated than anticipated.

Over the light meal they sat down to before the Richmond House ball, Dorothea, prompted by Hazelmere's comments in the Park, drew out Lady Merion on the relationship between the Marquis, Lord Fanshawe and Ferdie Acheson-Smythe.

Lady Merion, thinking this a sensible question in the circumstances, was happy to describe the situation as fully as she could. 'Well, the principal seats of the Hazelmere and Eglemont peerages, held by the Henry and Fanshawe families respectively, lie in Surrey and adjoin each other. The families have always been close allies and friends. Hazelmere and Fanshawe were born only a few weeks apart; Hazelmere is the elder. Both have two older sisters and Hazelmere has a younger sister, too, but neither has any brothers. Consequently it was only natural that the boys grew up together. They went to Eton and Oxford together and have been on the town for…oh, over ten years now. The bond between them is very strong—stronger than if they had in fact been brothers, I suspect.'

'What about Ferdie?' asked Cecily.

'Ferdie is the son of Hazelmere's mother's sister, and so a first cousin to Hazelmere. He is about five years younger than Marc, but he was sent to spend most of his childhood summers at Hazelmere. I don't quite understand why, for in temperament they seem very dissimilar, and there's the age difference too, but Ferdie and Hazelmere and Tony Fanshawe are very firm friends indeed. They always help each other out and used to cover up for each other when they were younger and got into scrapes. Ferdie is very sincerely attached to the Marquis and Lord Fanshawe, and they always seem very protective and tolerant of him.'

By this time they had finished their meal and Lady Merion, glancing at the clock, shooed them off to put the finishing touches to their *toilettes*, saying, 'You know Ferdie will not be late and he hates to be kept waiting!'

Lady Merion was quite correct in telling her granddaughters that the bond between Ferdie and their lordships ran deep. It dated from Ferdie's first visit to Hazelmere, when, on his first morning there, the shy eleven-year-old had seen his magnificent sixteen-year-old cousin and his friend leave the stableyard for an early-morning ride. He had been in his bedchamber at the time, and had hurriedly dressed and gone down to the stables, thinking to get a horse and catch up with them. Instead, he had fallen victim to two young stable-lads, who, for a joke, had set him on a half-broken Arab stallion. The horse, very fresh, had broken away, Ferdie clinging for dear life to its back. Luckily it had headed in the direction taken by the older boys. In the ensuing chase, Marc and Tony Fanshawe had worked with Ferdie to save both him and the stallion. Sheer good luck and a deal of courage from them all had pulled it off. From that day onwards the three were, as far as their disparate ages and interests allowed, inseparable. Whenever other children had tried to bully Ferdie, they had very quickly learned they had to answer to either Tony or the even more formidable Marc.

Habits formed in childhood ran deep, and when Ferdie had got into trouble in the petticoat line at Oxford, it was to Marc, rather than to his own scholarly and eccentric father, that he had turned. And Marc had very efficiently sorted the problem out. On his coming on the town, those who belonged to the better of the gentlemen's clubs had quickly realised that if Ferdie Acheson-Smythe was threatened then Lord Fanshawe and the Marquis of Hazelmere had a habit of materialising behind him. When Ferdie got involved in controversy over another gentleman's efforts at fuzzing the cards and was challenged to a duel, illegal though that practice then was, it was Hazelmere who stepped in and ruthlessly put a stop to it.

In return, it must be said, their lordships had found that Ferdie possessed a rare talent: he was so very trustworthy that women tended to pour all their secrets into his ear. Thus Ferdie had proved more than useful to them over the past five years. However, as Hazelmere had truthfully told Dorothea, it was quite impossible for Ferdie to view either himself or Tony Fanshawe askance.

The Dowager Marchioness of Hazelmere descended the stairs of Hazelmere House, thinking how pleasant it would be to have a new Lady Hazelmere to make use of its beautifully proportioned salons. She had come up from Surrey, as was her custom, but this year she had much higher expectations of the Season.

At just over fifty, she was still a striking woman, tall and willowy, her abundant chestnut hair still retaining much of its glory, and the years had not robbed her face of its piquancy. She had contracted a bronchial complaint some years before and, as this was exacerbated by the fumes of the city, she usually spent only a week or so in London. Her expectations had been fuelled by the extraordinary intelligence conveyed to her by her London correspondents. As well as the carefully worded missive from Hermione Merion, detailing the history of her son's involvement with Dorothea Darent, she had received no less than six letters from other close friends, all comprehensively describing Hazelmere's infatuation with Miss Darent. Of these, the most informative had been the most recent, from the Countess of Eglemont. Tony's parents had returned to London a week earlier and Amelia Fanshawe had dutifully reported how things stood between both her son and Cecily Darent and Hazelmere and Miss Darent. More than anyone else, she would trust Amelia to correctly interpret Marc's behaviour. And what Amelia had written had been intriguing. Consequently she had been amused rather than surprised to find that her usually cool son had moved dinner forward so he could arrive at the ball ahead of his inamorata.

Entering the drawing-room, she was taken aback to find Tony Fanshawe and Ferdie in attendance. As her elegant son strolled across the room to plant an affectionate kiss on her cheek her eyes openly quizzed him. He was as immaculate as ever, in a perfectly cut black coat that looked as if it had been moulded to his broad shoulders, skin-tight knee-breeches encasing his powerful thighs. Diamonds winked amid the snowy folds of his cravat.

'Welcome to town, Mama! As always, you look quite ravishing.'

His eyes returned her regard with a bland and innocent air, which deceived her not at all. While Tony and Ferdie made their bows Mytton entered to announce dinner.

Throughout the meal Hazelmere, ably seconded by her nephew and Tony Fanshawe, kept her entertained, describing all that had occurred thus far in the Season, with two notable omissions. Amused by their strategy, she was even more entertained than they intended.

After the servants withdrew she seized the initiative. She fixed both her son and Fanshawe with a look that from long experience they knew meant that she intended to get to the bottom of whatever had excited her attention. 'Yes, that's all very well,' she said, breaking into yet another of Ferdie's anecdotes, 'but what I really want to know is why none of you has yet seen fit to mention Hermione Merion's granddaughters.

From everything I hear, you have all been somewhat preoccupied with them, have you not?'

She found herself looking into her son's hazel eyes as he
gently explained, 'But, Mama, you already know all about
them, and more, from all the letters you've been sent. We
didn't want to bore you.'

With the ground cut so masterfully from under her feet, she
could think of nothing to say. Instead she raised her glass in
mock salute. 'I trust they will be present tonight?'

'Most assuredly. Ferdie is to escort them there.'

'Then you must both promise to introduce them to me and
I'll promise to be silent on the subject all the way there.'

'And back?' asked Fanshawe, used to the Hazelmere conversations.

She laughed. 'All right. *And* back.'

'Under those conditions, I promise,' answered Hazelmere
with a grin.

'And I,' echoed Fanshawe.

'Good heavens!' ejaculated Ferdie, surprising them all. 'I'll
have to dash or I'll be late. Never do to keep them waiting!'

Amid laughter, he departed for the other side of Cavendish
Square, urging them to make haste if they wanted to get to
Richmond first.

Arriving on the doorstep of Merion House as the Merion
carriage rounded the corner, Ferdie had the forethought to ask
Mellow not to announce it until the Hazelmere carriage, already standing outside Hazelmere House and clearly visible
across the square, had departed. Mellow, accepting the golden
douceur Ferdie slipped him, understood perfectly.

Inside the drawing-room, Ferdie caught his breath at the
visions of loveliness that met his eyes. Even he had started to
wonder for how much longer the Darent sisters could dazzle
in elegant gowns that were quite unique.

Dorothea, standing by the marble mantel, was a stunning
picture in ivory satin, overlaid with lace around the neckline
and in a broad sweep down one side of the skirt. The pearls
at her throat shone warmly in the firelight, and her hair ap-

peared burnished by the flames. The simplicity of the gown was breathtaking. Thinking of the effect this creation would have on Hazelmere in his present mood, Ferdie almost felt sorry for the Marquis.

Cecily was adorned in pure white, with trimming of aquamarine ribbon set with tiny seed-pearls criss-crossed over the bodice and looped around her skirt. Again the effect was unique and quite lovely.

Lady Merion, satisfied with the effect her granddaughters' gowns had had on Ferdie, spoke up, telling him that they were now ready to depart.

Ferdie gulped and asked innocently, 'Oh, has Mellow announced the carriage?'

'No, Ferdie, he hasn't,' said Dorothea, suddenly suspicious.

'I don't know what's keeping them, then,' muttered her ladyship. 'We called for the carriage long ago.'

'Er—yes.' Ferdie decided that Lady Merion was the safest of the three to address. 'Just came from dinner at Hazelmere House. Lady Hazelmere was there, ma'am, and sent her regards. Said she'd see you at the ball.'

At this juncture, with Ferdie fervently searching for some topic to distract his three ladies, Mellow entered and solved the problem by announcing the carriage.

CHAPTER SEVEN

After an uneventful drive, the Merion carriage joined the long queue of coaches lining up to disgorge their fair burdens on the torch-lit steps of Richmond House. There had been little conversation on the journey, and Ferdie had had time to ponder what lay between the Darent sisters and his friends.

He recalled the look in Dorothea's eye that afternoon when he had hurried to catch up with them as they left the Park. He had been unable to interpret it at the time, imagining that the four of them had been together the whole time. But now, from what Marc and Tony themselves had said, it was clear that had not been the case. Ferdie's mind boggled when he tried to imagine what exactly had happened between Dorothea and Marc. And this while the Misses Darent were, after a fashion, in his care! If such a thing ever got out, his carefully nurtured reputation as a trustworthy ladies' companion would be ruined!

The carriage drew up and he helped his ladies to alight. Soon they were following the glittering line of arrivals up the grand staircase. At the top, they were greeted by the Duchess, and moved on into the ballroom as their names were proclaimed in stentorian accents by two massive footmen flanking the door.

Dorothea had only taken a few steps when she found Hazelmere at her elbow. Smiling up at him, she saw that his eyes were not laughing, but glinting at her in a way that made her heart stand still. All the other symptoms she now associated with his presence—breathlessness, confusion and a certain anticipation—immediately came to the fore. Then he smiled and the intense look dissolved into his usual warmly amused expression, dispelling her unease. His lips lightly brushed her gloved fingertips before he drew her hand through his arm.

'Come with me, Miss Darent; there's someone I'd like you to meet.'

'Oh? Who, pray tell?'

'Me.'

She chuckled. She was drawn out of the mainstream of the arriving guests, a tactic that confused the small army of gentlemen waiting patiently to greet her further along the ballroom. Hazelmere led her towards a corner, into the camouflage of earlier arrivals. He moved automatically through the crowd, not seeing them, not hearing them. His mind was awhirl with a heady sensation he had never experienced before. Whatever it was, it was exciting and uncomfortable at the same time, and its cause was the unutterably lovely creature walking so calmly beside him. The sight of her, encased in ivory, had taken his breath away. Then she had smiled at him with such open affection that he had had to fight an impulse to kiss her in the middle of the Duchess of Richmond's ballroom.

The temptation to continue their ambling stroll into the adjoining rooms was strong. He knew Richmond House fairly well. He was sure he could find a deserted ante-room where Miss Darent and he could analyse his strange response to her presence in more depth. He sighed inwardly. Unfortunately such intimate discussions were not listed among the acceptable ways of wooing young ladies during the Season.

Reluctantly pausing, he looked down at her again, drinking in the flawless symmetry of her face, drowning in her emerald eyes. He saw them widen, first in amused enquiry and then, as he remained silent, in increasing bewilderment. 'I'll have you know, Miss Darent, that I'm rapidly running out of ideas of how to whisk you away before your devoted admirers surround you.'

Smiling in response, Dorothea hoped that he couldn't hear the thudding of her heart. She was no longer sure of her ability to keep him from guessing her feelings—as he stood before her, magnificent as ever, the spell he cast was too potent. He had developed a certain way of looking at her, which made her feel deliciously warm and tingly and led her unruly thoughts into fields they had no business straying into. Well-brought-up young ladies weren't supposed to know of such things, let alone weave fantasies about them. Thinking that she could quite happily bask in that hazel gaze for the rest of forever, she forced herself to try for their usual conversational mode. 'Well, you seem to have succeeded to admiration this evening. I feel utterly deserted!'

'Do you, indeed?' he murmured, adding in a provocative undertone, 'Would that you were, my dear.'

In spite of her intentions, she was finding it harder and harder to meet his eyes with her customary cool unconcern.

Hazelmere finally looked down to examine her dance card. 'I don't suppose I should tell you that Lord Markham is presently making a cake of himself, searching through the place for you? No! Don't look around or he might see you. And the only reason Alvanley, Peterborough and Walsingham ain't doing the same is that they're watching Robert do it for them. Miss Darent, I notice there's a waltz immediately preceding supper, which is a very sensible innovation. I must remember to compliment the Duchess on her good sense. Will you do me the honour, my dear Miss Darent, of waltzing with me and then allowing me to take you into supper?'

Dorothea had managed to gain a firmer hold on her composure during this speech and was able to serenely reply, 'That will be delightful, Lord Hazelmere.'

One black brow rose. 'Will it?'

But she refused to be drawn with such an unanswerable question and simply smiled sweetly back. Hazelmere laughed and raised one finger to her cheek. 'Promise me you'll never put a rein on your tongue, my dear. Life would become so dull if you did.'

The caress and the even more provocative tones brought a familiar flash to her large green eyes.

'Ah! Miss Darent! Lord Hazelmere. Your servant, sir.' Sir Barnaby Ruscombe materialised at Hazelmere's elbow. Hazelmere suavely inclined his head, and Dorothea drummed up her best social smile for London's most notorious rattle. Sir

Barnaby, beaming as if delighted by these mild acknowledge-
ments, waved his hand towards the figure on his arm, a sharp-
featured woman of indeterminate years, dressed entirely in a
quite hideous shade of puce, clashing outrageously with her
improbable auburn locks. 'Permit me to introduce you. Miss
Darent, Lord Hazelmere. Mrs Dimchurch.'

The exchange of curtsies and bows was purely perfunctory.
'But I'm sure Miss Darent remembers me from the assemblies
at Newbury,' gushed Mrs Dimchurch. Hazelmere felt Dorothea stiffen. 'So sad about your dear mama! Lady Cynthia and
I always enjoyed a comfortable cose while we watched over
our daughters.' Her sharp eyes were fixed on the Marquis. 'I
must say, I was surprised to hear Lady Cynthia had made your
acquaintance, my lord. She never mentioned it. Strange, don't
you think?'

As an attempt to throw Hazelmere, it was so crude that
Dorothea only just managed to retain her composure.

His lordship, used to stiffer competition, made short work
of it. Regarding the offending Mrs Dimchurch with a coldly
gentle smile, he softly said, 'I very much doubt, my dear
ma'am, that Lady Darent was the type of lady who would
presume, on the basis of a single chance introduction, to claim
acquaintance with anyone. Don't you agree?'

Mrs Dimchurch turned brick-red, rendering her *toilette* even
more hideous.

Without waiting for a reply, Hazelmere nodded to Sir Barnaby and, bestowing a devilish smile on the unfortunate Mrs
Dimchurch, drew Dorothea's hand once more through his arm
and strolled back towards the milling crowds in the centre of
the large room.

Once out of earshot of the importunate couple, Hazelmere
glanced down. 'My dear Miss Darent, how many such mush-
rooms have you had to endure?' He sounded distinctly guilty.

She chuckled, then answered airily, 'Oh, hardly any since
the first week.' She looked up, confidently expecting him to
laugh with her and was surprised to see the hazel eyes reflecting real concern. Before she could do more than register the
fact they were spotted by her prospective partners.

The rooms were filled to overflowing and more people were arriving. Finding any lady in the crush was extremely difficult. Having totally lost Miss Darent, one of the crowd looking for her had asked if anyone had seen Hazelmere, as, knowing his lordship, Miss Darent was probably with him. This had led to a search for the Marquis who, because of his height, was a great deal easier to spot than Dorothea. With various comments, mostly in an uncomplimentary vein, being thrown at his head, Hazelmere good-humouredly surrendered Dorothea to her swains and was swallowed up in the crowds.

Dorothea was amazed that anyone could find anyone else in the throng of people filling the ballroom and spreading into the adjoining salons. She had no idea where her grandmother or Cecily were, but with so many acquaintances among the ton she was not in the least put out. Somehow her partners seemed to find her for their respective dances, when the ballroom would miraculously clear as the music began. As each dance finished, the floor would fill again with a shifting sea of gorgeously clad ladies, the gentlemen in their more sober clothes providing stark contrast. The evening passed in a whirl of conversation and dancing, and she had no time to ponder the subtle change she had detected in the Marquis.

The only cloud on her horizon was the persistent Mr Buchanan. He seemed to dog her erratic footsteps, continually appearing as if by some malignant magic wherever she chose to pause. Finally she appealed to Ferdie for advice. 'How on earth can I get rid of him?' she wailed as they trailed and dipped through a cotillion.

Although highly sympathetic, having already endured too much of Mr Buchanan's company and lacking Hazelmere's acid capacity to silence at will, Ferdie could find no magic formula to rid his protégée of this unexpected encumbrance. 'Hate to say it, but he's the sort who never takes the hint. You'll just have to be patient until he slopes off.' Then he was seized with inspiration. 'Why not ask Hazelmere to have a word with him?'

'Lord Hazelmere would probably laugh himself into stitches at the idea of Mr Buchanan pursuing me! He'd be more likely to encourage him!' returned Dorothea. They were separated by the movement of the dance, so she failed to see the effect her answer had on Ferdie. Retrieving his dropped jaw, he shook his head. Personally, he could not imagine Hazelmere encouraging anyone to pursue Dorothea, much less the importunate Mr Buchanan, who, unless he missed his guess, was a fortune-hunter of the most inept variety. Clearly a word in his cousin's ear would not go amiss.

No longer feeling the need to dance with other young ladies as a cover for his pursuit of Dorothea, Hazelmere spent much of the evening talking to friends, acquaintances and a not inconsiderable number of his relatives. He was not pleased when, turning in response to a tap on his arm, he looked down into the severe countenance of his eldest sister, Lady Maria Setford. Knowing that she would have heard of his interest in Dorothea, he persistently misunderstood every quizzing remark she made on that subject. Exasperated, she finally recommended he look out for his other older sister, Lady Susan Wilmot, who, she informed him, was also somewhere in the rooms and desirous of speech with him.

Her brother merely looked at her with an expression that very luckily she was incapable of interpreting, before excusing himself on the score of having seen their mother, with whom he required a few words.

He did, in fact, pass by Lady Hazelmere, deep in conversation with Sally Jersey, and paused to whisper, 'Mama, I know you've always sworn you were faithful to my father, but how on earth do you account for Maria and Susan?'

Lady Jersey, overhearing, burst into her twittering laugh. Lady Hazelmere made a face at him before asking, 'You don't mean they've started sermonising already?'

'I'm sure they would like to, only they haven't decided whether it's worthwhile yet,' returned her undutiful son, winking at her as he moved on.

Like Ferdie, Hazelmere had spent the journey to Richmond House sunk in thought. A despondent mood had overtaken him earlier in the day, when he had had to deny himself the pleasure of kissing Dorothea in the glade in the Park and had realised that would be his lot for some time to come. Since he was naturally autocratic and, as Dorothea had surmised, used to getting his own way in most things, the need to keep his passions on a very tight rein did not appeal in the least. He had already decided that he could not ask her to marry him until much later in the Season. This was not because he thought he needed more time to win her, nor that he feared to put his luck to the test. Rather it was because he, unlike Dorothea, was well versed in the ways of the ton. He could not be entirely sure of her answer, so he had to consider the possibility that she would refuse him. As their courtship had been carried out in full view of all the gossips and scandalmongers, such an outcome at the height of the Season would place them both in an intolerable situation. In addition, Lady Merion, Fanshawe and Cecily, and Ferdie too would be made to feel highly uncomfortable.

His mood had lightened when he learned that Fanshawe was in a similar position. A much more easygoing individual than himself, Tony would not find the enforced restrictions quite as hard to bear. Cecily, too, was as yet too young to do other than enjoy every moment as it came. Dorothea was another matter. While she never in any way encouraged him, she nevertheless accepted with complete self-assurance every attention he bestowed upon her. He shrewdly guessed that, being older, more mature and definitely more independent than the general run of débutantes, she was more ready and more able to savour the delights of sophisticated lovemaking, to which he was only too willing to introduce her. Her passionate nature, which he wryly suspected she did not yet realise she possessed, was not going to help matters. It was at this point in his mental ramblings that his sense of humour had come to his rescue. How very ironic it all was!

He had quit their carriage in a much lighter mood than he had entered it, and the last shreds of despondency had been wafted away when he had seen Dorothea enter the ballroom.

Moving through the salons, he saw Lady Merion ensconced in a corner, chatting amiably with Lady Bressington. He stopped to audaciously compliment them both on their dashing new *toilettes* and stayed to exchange the usual pleasantries.

Suddenly becoming aware they had been approached by some others, he turned to view the newcomers, surprising a look of annoyance on Lady Merion's face as he did so. The cause of this was immediately clear: the couple who approached were none other than Herbert and Marjorie, Lord and Lady Darent.

Hazelmere had been introduced to Herbert Darent years ago when that sober young man had first come on the town. Two years younger than the Marquis, Herbert was also a full head shorter and, in his ill-fitting coat, cut a poor figure in comparison.

After two minutes' conversation Hazelmere fully appreciated Lady Merion's decision to take the Darent girls under her wing. The idea that two such pearls could have made their début under the auspices of the present Lord and Lady Darent was too awful to contemplate. What a mess they would have made of it. To his experienced eye, Marjorie Darent lacked any degree of style or charm, and her austere observations on modern social customs, delivered for the benefit of the company without any invitation whatever, simply appalled him.

Lady Merion was so thunderstruck that she was literally speechless. When Herbert tried to engage Hazelmere in a discussion of rural commodities she was even more incensed. However, as she listened to Herbert, who had little real idea of what he was discussing, lecturing Hazelmere, who, as one of the major landowners in the country, had a more than academic interest in such matters, her sense of humour got the better of her. She rapidly hid her face behind her fan.

Looking up, her eyes met Hazelmere's, full of heartfelt sympathy as he adroitly extricated both himself and Lady Bressington, on the pretext of taking her ladyship to find her errant daughter.

As she moved off on his arm Augusta Bressington heaved a sigh of relief. 'Thank you, Marc. If you hadn't rescued me I would have been stuck. Poor Hermione! What a dreadful couple!'

'Definitely not one of the hits of the Season,' he agreed.

'And to think Herbert comes from the same stable as those two lovely girls,' she continued, quite forgetting his interest. As this came to mind, she blushed, but, glancing up at him, found he was laughing.

'Oh, no! I feel sure Herbert's mother must have played his father false, don't you?'

Lady Bressington gasped and then burst out laughing too. Drawing her hand from his arm, she bade him take himself off, adding that she now saw why all the girls fell to mooning over him.

Hearing the strains of the Roger de Clovely drifting from the ballroom and knowing it to be the dance before the supper waltz, Hazelmere accepted his dismissal with easy grace and moved back to the ballroom to find Dorothea. He had little difficulty in picking her out, whirling down the dance with Peterborough. Pausing for a moment to catch the tune and work out where they were likely to finish, he stationed himself near the end of the ballroom. As the dance concluded, Peterborough whirled Dorothea to a halt a few paces away. He strolled towards them. 'How obliging of you, Gerry, to bring Miss Darent to me.'

Peterborough whirled around, an entirely unacceptable oath on his lips. 'Hazelmere!' he groaned. 'I might have known!' As the Marquis possessed himself of Dorothea's hand he continued, 'I suppose you have the supper waltz?'

'Precisely,' said Hazelmere, his amused glance clearly baiting his friend.

Lord Peterborough turned to Dorothea and in a serious tone, belied by the expression on his face, said, 'I shouldn't have anything to do with Hazelmere if I were you, Miss Darent. Don't know if anyone's told you, but he's far too dangerous for young ladies to deal with. Much better to let me take you away.'

Dorothea laughed at this graceless speech. But Hazelmere's voice again drew Peterborough's attention. 'Oh, Miss Darent knows just how dangerous I am, Gerry.' At this outrageous statement Dorothea's eyes blazed. Looking up, she found the hazel eyes quizzing her as he continued smoothly, 'But she has agreed to overlook my dangerous tendencies. Haven't you, Miss Darent?'

Aware that to answer this provocative question in any way at all would be highly improper, Dorothea threw him a fulminating glance.

Smiling, he turned back to Peterborough and said, quite simply, 'Goodbye, Gerry.'

'Oh, I'm off, never fear. Take care, Miss Darent!' he added insouciantly as, sketching a bow to her, he disappeared into the crowd.

Turning to Dorothea, Hazelmere saw she had opened her fan. 'You're flushed, Miss Darent. Now I wonder if that's due to these overheated rooms, the Roger de Clovely, Peterborough's remarks or mine?'

Smiling up at him, she calmly answered, 'Why, a combination of all four, I should think.'

'Then, instead of waiting for the next dance, why don't we repair to the terrace, where I see quite a few others have already gone to enjoy the cool of the evening?'

Looking in the direction he indicated, Dorothea saw that the long windows at the end of the ballroom giving out on to the terrace had been thrown open. A number of couples were strolling in the moonlight. She had definite misgivings of the wisdom of venturing into such a fairy-tale scene at Hazelmere's side, but she was certainly feeling overly warm and the cool night air beckoned invitingly.

Hazelmere, correctly guessing her thoughts, made her decision for her by taking her arm. Together they strolled through the windows. Dorothea exclaimed at the sight of the formal gardens touched with moonlight. A few adventuresome couples had descended to the parterre below, where they appeared as pixie-like characters in the soft light. Without breaking the spell, Hazelmere strolled by her side to the far end of the terrace. He had a very good memory. There was an orangery built along the side of the house below the ballroom which could only be reached from the terrace. Knowing the Duchess of Richmond was a considerate hostess, he felt the orangery would be open. Coming to the end of the terrace and turning, he found that his confidence in the Duchess had not been misplaced.

'There's an orangery down these steps, which, if memory serves, gives on to the fountain court. Shall we investigate?'

The question was merely a formality. Dorothea was literally enthralled by the silvery beauty about her and, without thought, went down the steps by his side.

Inside the orangery, deserted save for themselves, they found the doors giving on to the fountain court thrown wide. Hearing the music of the fountains, Dorothea drew her hand from his arm and, looking very like a fairy queen, drifted to the open door to look out on the magical scene. The three fountains in the court were playing and the moonlight glistened and sparkled on each drop of water thrown up in the still night air to fall back with a silvery tinkle into the large marble bowls. She stood in the doorway, rapt in the beauty of the scene.

Silently Hazelmere shut the doors from the terrace and, coming up behind her, gently drew her back to lean against him. Feeling his hands about her waist, she allowed her head to rest against his shoulder. For some moments they were as still as the statues in the fountains. Then, prompted by her own particular devil, Dorothea turned her head to smile up at him. There was, after all, one certain way to precipitate matters.

His response was all she could have wished. Turning her slightly, Hazelmere swiftly bent his head to drop the gentlest of delicate kisses on her lips. As he raised his head her eyes opened wide. For one long moment they remained perfectly still, the hazel and green gazes fusing in the moonlight. Then, slowly, he turned her fully and deliberately drew her into his arms. She lifted her face and his lips found hers in a kiss that possessed her senses with gentle certainty. With infinite care he started her sensual education, his caresses deepening by imperceptible degrees so that her senses were never overwhelmed, but taught, step by steady step, to savour the exquisite delight he created. His control was absolute and

Dorothea, enfolded in his care, for the first time in her life, willingly let go of the reins.

She lost all track of time, gently led down paths where joy, as exquisite as dew on a buttercup, lay waiting to greet her. The sensual landscape conjured forth by his touch was a new frontier in which each discovery brought its own thrill. When, finally, he drew her back to reality she was dazed and breathless and exquisitely happy.

Then they were waltzing in the moonlit orangery to the music wafting through the open windows of the ballroom above. In no mood to protest, she gave herself up to the enjoyment of the moment. Hazelmere, looking down at her lovely face, serene and untroubled in the starlight, did likewise.

As the last chord sounded and they glided to a halt he firmly drew her arm through his and made for the door and the steps back to the terrace.

'Do we have to leave?' she asked, hanging back. 'It's so very lovely here.'

'Yes,' he replied uncompromisingly. If they stayed in this isolated spot a moment longer he knew very well what would happen. Which would all be very pleasant, except he had no idea what would happen next. After that little interlude he was no longer sure how far he could trust himself with her, and he had a shrewd suspicion that, innocent though she was, she was no more enamoured of the rules restricting their conduct than he was. It was bad enough that he had to exercise restraint for the both of them, as he was magnanimously doing at present, but if she started pulling in the opposite direction the temptation to capitulate might become too great. He groaned inwardly and closed his eyes to rid his mind of the intoxicating possibilities the thought conjured up. Opening them again, he tightened his grip on her arm and inexorably drew her back up the steps to the terrace. 'If we are missing at supper, your grandmama will have all her worst fears concerning me confirmed and will in all probability forbid me to speak to you!'

As she imagined the likelihood of his paying any attention to Lady Merion's strictures, a small, happy smile curved

Dorothea's lips, and she allowed him to lead her back into the ballroom.

Almost immediately they came face to face with Edward Buchanan. 'Miss Darent, you're flushed! Perhaps I might take you for a walk in the gardens? I'm sure Lord Hazelmere will excuse you.' The accusatory look he cast Hazelmere nearly did for Dorothea.

Hazelmere, who knew very well the cause of the delicate flush still apparent on her alabaster skin, smiled in a devilish way that brought his reputation forcibly to Edward Buchanan's mind, and said, 'On the contrary! Lord Hazelmere is about to escort Miss Darent to supper. If *you* will excuse *us*?'

Receiving a curt nod, Edward Buchanan found his quarry had somehow side-stepped him and escaped. The first uneasy glimmer that Miss Darent might fall prey to the wicked blandishments of tonnish society awoke in his unimaginative mind.

Out of earshot, Dorothea asked, 'Am I really flushed?' She felt delightful; not uncomfortable at all.

She could not interpret the slow grin that spread across the Marquis's face. 'Delightfully so,' was all the answer she got.

After much stopping to talk to acquaintances on the way, they finally gained the supper-room. Fanshawe and Cecily had saved them seats at a corner table well provided with an array of delicacies. As Hazelmere helped Dorothea to her chair Fanshawe, after one glance at her, caught his friend's eye, his look clearly stating that he had every idea of what they had been up to. Hazelmere grinned back.

Relieved to see him no longer in the hips, Fanshawe turned back to assure an excited and insistent Cecily that he would take her to see the fountain court.

When they rose from the table Fanshawe said to Hazelmere, 'Don't forget your promise to your mother! I've kept my side of it. I couldn't bear it if she was to quiz us all the way back to Cavendish Square.'

'Ye gods! I'd forgotten.' Hazelmere turned his most charming smile on Dorothea. 'Miss Darent, my mother is here somewhere in this mêlée and has made me promise to introduce you. Will you allow me to take you to her?'

She raised her fine brows, but consented to be led on a search for the Marchioness. As she moved through the crowd on Hazelmere's arm she could not resist saying, 'I'm tempted to ask why Lord Fanshawe is so anxious you keep your promise.'

Laughing down at her, he replied, 'I wouldn't if I were you. The answer would do nothing for your composure.' The caress in his eyes made her feel decidedly odd.

He finally located his mother, seated on a chaise in a corner of one of the salons, busily chatting to an acquaintance. On seeing them approach, this lady tactfully withdrew and Hazelmere made the promised introduction.

Lady Hazelmere had been prepared by her friends' letters to find Dorothea Darent a particularly pretty girl. The stunning goddess her son introduced was considerably more attractive than she had anticipated. She smiled delightedly at this vision in ivory satin.

Motioning Dorothea to sit beside her, the Dowager made very large eyes at her son, signifying how impressed she was by his taste. Hazelmere, correctly interpreting the glance, returned it with a smile clearly saying, 'Well, what did you expect?' Receiving in reply an unmistakable sign that she wished to be left alone with Miss Darent, he had little choice but to obey. Making his adieus to Dorothea, he bethought himself of another matter and departed to find Lady Merion.

Relieved of his distracting presence, Lady Hazelmere found that she was being regarded by an enormous pair of green eyes. With an ease born of long experience, she instituted a conversation on totally unexceptionable matters, carefully steering clear of any mention of her son. She quickly discovered that the child before her had poise and confidence, combined with a refreshing frankness. It was not difficult to understand her son's desire for the lovely Miss Darent. That he meant marriage she had no doubt, else he would never have consented to introduce her. As their conversation progressed she discovered that humour and a ready wit could be added to Miss Darent's charms and was well satisfied with his choice.

By the time Lord Alvanley came to claim Dorothea for the last dance of the evening Lady Hazelmere was wondering how much longer her son would wait. As Dorothea moved away on Alvanley's arm she wondered whether his conquest of the elegant young woman would be as smooth as he would certainly expect. In a flash of very unmaternal feeling she hoped that, for Dorothea's sake, it would not be *quite* that easy. Hazelmere was far too used to getting his own way—a set-down would make him much more human.

CHAPTER EIGHT

The next afternoon found the Marquis perusing various documents dealing with estate business which his mother had brought from Hazelmere. Over the years he had developed the habit of paying flying visits to his numerous estates while stationed in London for the Season, fitting these between his social engagements. This year, however, he had neglected business while pursuing Miss Darent. Never a lax landlord, he knew he could not put off visiting Hazelmere.

Glancing up at the clock on the mantel, he saw it lacked a quarter to three o'clock. The weather was fine, with a light breeze tossing the cherry blossoms from the trees in the Square. He rang for Mytton and gave orders for his curricle with the greys to be brought to the door immediately. He then went upstairs to throw a series of orders at Murgatroyd's head. Ten minutes later, immaculate as ever in top-boots and a coat of Bath superfine, he descended the steps of Hazelmere House. Climbing to the box-seat of his curricle, he nodded a dismissal to Jim Hitchin, adding, 'Be ready to leave for Hazelmere when I return.'

He tooled the curricle around to the other side of the square and pulled up outside Merion House. Tossing the reins to an urchin, he strode up the steps to the door. He was admitted by Mellow. 'Is her ladyship in, Mellow?'

'I regret to say, her ladyship is presently unavailable, my lord.'

Hazelmere frowned. 'In that case, perhaps you'll enquire whether Miss Darent can spare me a few minutes?'

'Certainly, my lord.'

Mellow showed him into the drawing-room and left to find

Miss Darent. Climbing the stairs, he wondered if he should
risk awakening his employer. After weighing the matter, he
rejected the idea. His lordship had his horses with him and
would not like to keep them standing. Finding Miss Darent
alone in the upstairs drawing-room, he conveyed his lordship's
message.

Dorothea, their visit to the Richmond House orchangery in
mind, was unsure of the propriety of seeing Hazelmere alone.
But Cecily had gone out driving with Lord Fanshawe, and
Lady Merion had still not emerged from her bedchamber. So
she descended to the drawing-room but cautiously left the door
open when she entered.

Hazelmere, on whom such little subtleties were not lost,
smiled warmly as he took her hand, kissed it and, as was fast
becoming his habit, did not release it.

'Miss Darent, will you come for a drive in the Park with
me?'

Ferdie had told her that Hazelmere, for the most chauvin-
istic of reasons, rarely took ladies driving in the Park. She was
therefore perfectly conscious of the honour being done her.
Deciding that she could not possibly forgo such an invitation,
she replied with alacrity, 'Why, yes, if you'll give me time to
find my pelisse.'

Releasing her hand, Hazelmere, long inured to feminine
ideas of time, felt constrained to add, 'Ten minutes, no more!'

Dorothea laughed over her shoulder as she disappeared from
the room. She surprised him by returning in less than ten
minutes and, as they left the house, revealed something of her
knowledge of him by exclaiming, 'Good heavens! You have
your greys!'

Retrieving the reins and suitably rewarding the attendant
urchin, Hazelmere climbed to the driving seat. As he leant
down to help her up to sit beside him he answered, 'As you
say, Miss Darent, my greys. And what do you know of my
greys?'

This shaft fell wide, however, as she could reply with perfect composure, 'Ferdie told me you rarely drive your greys
in the Park.'

Ferdie had told her rather more than this. Hazelmere's greys were considered to be the fastest and best matched pair in the country. His lordship, if Ferdie was to be believed, had been offered vast sums for them but, as he had bred and reared them on the Henry estates, he would not part with them for any price.

'Ah, Ferdie,' mused Hazelmere, suddenly seeing that Ferdie's line in inside intelligence could become a two-way street.

Conversation was necessarily suspended as he gave all his attention to negotiating the crowded streets, with the high-couraged and restless greys taking exception to numerous sights and sounds along the way. Dorothea could only admire his skill in successfully gaining the gates of the Park. Once inside, the curricle tooled along at a decent pace and Hazelmere turned his attention to her.

Much to his relief, she wore no hat, so that her face, surrounded by dark curls, was completely visible. As he watched she turned her head to smile up at him, brows lifting in mute question.

Carefully considering it in the dispassionate light of morning, Dorothea had reluctantly dismissed their interlude in the orangery as inconclusive. She had instigated it in the hope that his response would give her some clue to his feelings. But, while the result had been deliciously exciting, it had taught her little. That Hazelmere was well qualified to introduce her to forbidden delights had never been in doubt. While she wished with all her heart that he would say something, anything, to explain himself to her, she was depressingly certain that he would not choose the Park, with his greys in hand, as the place to do so. But presumably he had brought her here to tell her something.

'Miss Darent, I find I must leave London for a few days. Estate business demands my attendance at Hazelmere.'

'I see.' Dorothea was not overly put out by this revelation. If she had thought about it she would have assumed that he must need to visit his estates fairly regularly. Then she remembered her coming-out ball. The sky seemed to darken.

The face she turned to him was decidedly pensive as she wondered how to phrase her question.

Hazelmere, watching her thoughts pass across her face, solved her dilemma for her. 'I'll be returning on Tuesday evening, so I'll see you next on Wednesday night.'

As he watched the sunshine return to her face he felt he should need no further proof of her feelings for him. Her actions and responses in the orangery had been so very revealing. He was tempted to ask her then and there to marry him, but his real dislike of trying to converse with a lady while holding a highly dangerous pair of horses made him repress the impulse. There would be plenty of time later, in more appropriate surroundings. *God*! he thought, shaken. Imagine proposing in the middle of the Park!

They continued around the Park, stopping to exchange greetings with a number of acquaintances. Hazelmere, not wanting to keep his horses standing, kept these interludes to a minimum. As they completed their circuit he headed the greys for the gates. 'The weather is turning, Miss Darent, so I hope you'll not mind if I return you to Cavendish Square forthwith?'

'Not at all,' she replied, 'I know how honoured I've been to be driven behind your greys.'

Looking up, she found herself basking in that warm hazel gaze. 'Quite right, my child,' he murmured. 'And do remember to behave yourself while I'm away.'

Incensed by the proprietorial tone, she turned to utter some withering remark, but, quizzically regarded by those strangely glinting eyes, remembered just how often he had extricated her from difficult situations. She was saved from having to reply by their emergence into the traffic, his attention once more claimed by his horses. By the time they reached Cavendish Square she had convinced herself of the wisdom of ignoring his last remark.

Pulling up outside Merion House, Hazelmere jumped from the curricle and lifted her down. He escorted her up the steps and, as Mellow opened the door, raised her hand to his lips, saying with a smile, '*Au revoir*, Miss Darent. Until Wednesday.'

Sunday and Monday saw the Darent sisters attend a number of smaller functions in the lead-up to their own coming-out ball. While Cecily flirted outrageously with her young suitors, most as innocent as herself, Dorothea wisely refrained from giving any of the callow youths worshipping at her feet the slightest encouragement. However, no amount of icy hauteur seemed to deter Edward Buchanan. Unfortunately even Lady Merion was of the opinion that time was the only cure for that particular pest.

So, to her deep irritation, Dorothea found herself too often for comfort in Mr Buchanan's company. His conversational style drove her to distraction, while his continual and gradually more pressing attempts at gallantry awoke a quite different response. Her sanity was saved by the attentions of Lords Peterborough, Alvanley, Desborough and company, who, much to her delight, seemed almost as accomplished as Hazelmere in the subtle art of deflating pretensions.

Lady Merion sat staring bemusedly at the list in her hand. Was this really the best of all possible arrangements? She had been engaged in the arduous task of deciding the seating at her dinner table for Wednesday night since first thing on this dismal Tuesday morning. The house was a shambles, with caterers and florists coming in to set up their trestles and stands ready for the presentation of their wares the next night. The servants were everywhere—cleaning and polishing every bit of brass, silver and copper in the house, lovingly shining every lustre of every chandelier. Tomorrow night was the highlight of the Season as far as they were concerned and not one of Lady Merion's glittering guests was going to find the least little thing wrong.

Glancing at the ormolu clock on her mantel, she saw that it was nearly time for luncheon. In a last effort to detect any flaw in her design, she returned her attention to her list. Finally satisfied, she laid it aside and went downstairs to the morning-room, where all their meals this week had been served while the dining-room and drawing-room were redecorated. With the aid of that expert in all things fashionable, Mr Ferdie Acheson-Smythe, she had decided that her main rooms would look well in a clear pale blue, touched with white and silver, so much more striking than the common white and gold. This colour scheme was repeated throughout the main areas of the house and continued into the ballroom. The flowers for the ballroom were to be blue and white hyacinths, white wood anemones and trailing white jasmine.

The pale blue, white and silver theme would provide the perfect backdrop for her granddaughters' ball-dresses. The culmination of a prodigious effort, they were considered by Celestine among the best pieces her genius had ever created. Dorothea's dress had been both difficult and immensely satisfying. Celestine herself had scoured the warehouses to find precisely the right weight of silk in a green that perfectly matched Dorothea's eyes. The dress was shocking in its simplicity. Cut so low as to be ineligible for a younger débutante, the neckline was essentially parallel with the tiny puff sleeves, kept off the shoulder, leaving the shoulders quite bare. The bodice was shockingly snug. From the raised waistline the skirts smoothly flared over the hips, then fell heavily to the floor.

Cecily's dress, though far less stunning, was still a perfection of simplicity. Of a clear and pristine aquamarine silk, the creation, with rounded neckline and raised waist, trimmed with seed-pearls, set off her youthful figure to best advantage.

In spite of the lowering skies, the sisters had ridden in the Park as usual that morning and had been occupied since with their mail. Joining their grandmother at the luncheon table, they continued to chatter in their artless way, telling her whom they had seen and who had sent greetings. Gazing at their happy faces, she felt a pang of dismay. Soon, too soon, these young things would be gone and her house would return to its previous existence. She was not looking forward to such a quiet future at all.

* * *

Lady Merion had decreed that there would be no riding on the day of their ball. Both young ladies were to remain in bed until ten o'clock, when they could join her in the morning-room for breakfast and open the coming-out presents sent by their numerous wellwishers. They could walk around the park in the square if they wished, but after luncheon were to rest until it was time to dress. She had a horror of Cecily becoming feverish from excitement or, worse, of Dorothea succumbing to a migraine.

On hearing this plan for her day, Dorothea declared that she was more likely to become comatose from boredom. However, grateful to her grandmama for all her efforts on their part, she agreed to abide by her strictures.

By the time the sisters appeared at the breakfast table it was covered with bouquets and boxes and trifles of every imaginable type. Trimmer, Betsy and Witchett were called in to assist, and both girls, disclaiming any interest in food, settled down to sort through the welter of presents.

Entering upon this scene, Lady Merion stopped, thunderstruck. 'Good lord! I don't think I've seen anything to equal it!' She added two boxes to the piles, one in front of each of her granddaughters. 'There, my loves! I don't think any grandmama has had two granddaughters who've given her so much pleasure.'

Both girls impulsively rose and hugged and kissed her before opening her presents. To Cecily went a tiny pearl brooch made to adorn the neckline of her ballgown. Dorothea, opening the red leather case she found under the wrapping, gasped as her eyes fell on the single strand of perfect emeralds within. 'Oh! Grandmama! They're beautiful!'

After these gifts were tried on and duly admired Lady Merion urged them to continue opening their presents while she joined in the game of exclaiming and laughing over who had sent what.

While the presents today showed a greater degree of extravagance than the more common tributes, both girls had received their share of bouquets and poems and suchlike throughout the Season. However, while she frequently re-

ceived bouquets from Lord Alvanley and the other members
of Hazelmere's set, all of whom had, each in their own way,
worshipped at her feet, from the Marquis himself Dorothea
had not received so much as a primrose. She did not know
that Hazelmere, expert in such matters and knowing the opposition's ways too well, had omitted to send her such tributes
as a deliberate tactic. Consequently, when she came to a small
package amid the jumble and, unwrapping it, found a box from
Astley's she did not connect it with him.

It was not common to send débutantes jewellery. Intrigued,
she pushed aside the surrounding wrappings and cleared an
area so that she could examine this gift more closely. 'I wonder who sent this,' she murmured to herself.

Lady Merion heard her and came to her side. 'How very
odd! Open it, my dear, and let's see. There's sure to be a card
inside.'

However, on her opening the box no card was found. Inside
lay the most exquisitely delicate brooch, composed of emeralds and rubies in gold, in the shape of a blackberry. A slow
smile appeared on Dorothea's face. What audacity!

Lady Merion, seeing the smile, was at a loss. It was Cecily
who, looking up from her own concerns, saw the brooch in
her sister's fingers and immediately made the connection. 'Oh!
Is that from Lord Hazelmere?' Raising her brown eyes to Dorothea's blushing countenance, Cecily giggled.

Lady Merion grasped the straw. But what on earth did
blackberries have to do with Hazelmere? However, knowing
that gentleman, she guessed the gift was far from innocent.
She baldly stated, 'Dorothea, I forbid you to wear that tonight!'

'Oh, no! Don't do that, Grandmama! See, this tag from Mr
Astley says he has taken the liberty of designing the brooch
so it can be used as a pendant off the emerald string. How
very thoughtful.'

Examining the brooch and then the string of emeralds, Dorothea discovered the secret of joining them and regarded the
composite piece critically. It was perfectly balanced and
looked both expensive and utterly unique.

'Dorothea, I don't know what that brooch signifies, and I'm not sure I want to know,' declared Lady Merion in her most authoritarian tones. 'But, whatever Hazelmere means by it, you can't seriously intend to wear it tonight. Just think how conspicuous it will be! How on earth would you face him while wearing it?'

'Why, with my customary composure, I should hope,' returned her wilful granddaughter. 'I really couldn't refuse the challenge, Grandmama. You know I couldn't.'

Reflecting that she knew nothing of the sort, Lady Merion was visited by a strong suspicion that Hazelmere was leading Dorothea into deep waters. But, in the circumstances, there was little she could, in reality, do.

The only deviation from Lady Merion's rigid schedule was caused by Edward Buchanan. Without warning, he appeared on the doorstep and refused point-blank to accept Mellow's frigid denial of the ladies of the house. By dint of mentioning Herbert Darent, he prevailed on Mellow to admit him to the morning-room while that worthy conveyed a message to his mistress.

Lady Merion came downstairs, huffily indignant, and sailed into the morning-room. Five minutes later, looking slightly stunned, she emerged and went looking for her elder granddaughter.

Ten minutes later Dorothea, paler than usual, descended the stairs. She paused for a moment, eyeing the morning-room door with revulsion. Then, drawing a deep breath, she entered.

It was worse than she had imagined. Lady Merion had mentioned the bouquet of daisies—*daisies*!—already wilting. What she had not found words to describe was the incredible smug conceit of the man holding them.

'Ah! Miss Darent!' Abruptly words seemed to fail Mr Buchanan. Then, unfortunately, his tongue regained its major habit and he spoke. 'I suspect, my dear, that you know very well why I'm here.' His archness made Dorothea feel decidedly unwell. Luckily he was standing on the other side of a

small round table and she had every intention of keeping it
between them.

He seemed to find nothing remarkable in her silence and
continued with unabated cheerfulness. 'Yes, my dear! All right
and tight, I'm here to beg the honour of your hand! I doubt
you expected a declaration quite so soon, before your coming-
out even. Not many young ladies can claim to be settled so
successfully before being presented, what?'

She could stand it no longer. 'Mr Buchanan. I thank you
for your offer but I'm afraid I cannot consent to marry you.'

'Oh, no difficulty there, my dear. Edward Buchanan knows
how these things are done. Lord Herbert has already given his
consent. All we need now is for you to say the word and we
can announce it tonight at your ball.'

Hazelmere, rather more perceptive than Mr Buchanan, could
have told him that that was precisely the wrong thing to say
to a lady as independent as Dorothea Darent. Colours flying,
she made no effort to conceal the loathing she felt. 'Mr Buchanan. You appear to be labouring under a misapprehension.
Herbert Darent may be my guardian but he has no power to
coerce me into marriage. I will not accept your proposal. I
have no wish to be married to you. I trust I make myself plain?
And now, if you'll excuse me, we're very busy. Mellow will
show you out.'

She swept out of the door, head high, pausing to instruct
Mellow to see to their unwelcome visitor before continuing,
thankfully and triumphantly, upstairs.

Later that evening, just before her dinner guests were due
to arrive, Lady Merion stood in her hallway and watched her
granddaughters descending the stairs. Her bosom swelled with
pride and a well-earned sense of satisfaction. They were superb!

Cecily, leading, was a vision of childlike innocence, a twinkle in her big brown eyes belying any attempt at gravity. But
Dorothea! Breathtakingly lovely, she came elegantly down the
stairs, her innate poise allowing her to carry the stunning gown
to maximum effect. She was a sight that would stop any male

heart. Especially Hazelmere's! thought her ladyship with a
touch of vengeance as her eyes alighted on the blackberry
pendant. Dorothea had been right to wear it, she grudgingly
admitted, for the pendant set off the whole to perfection, lying
glinting green and red against her granddaughter's alabaster
skin.

Within minutes Mellow announced Ferdie, who had promised to come early to lend them his support. Entering the drawing-room, he stopped stock-still and simply stared.

'Oh, I say!' was all the elegant Mr Acheson-Smythe could
manage. At this evidence of appreciation all three ladies went
into whoops of laughter, and a far less formal atmosphere
greeted the remaining guests, who began to arrive promptly
thereafter.

The drawing-room was soon abuzz with conversation. Lady
Jersey and Princess Esterhazy complimented both girls with
obvious sincerity. As Dorothea moved away to talk to Miss
Bressington, Sally Jersey turned to Lady Merion. 'M'dear, I
just can't *wait* to see Hazelmere's face when he comes through
the door and sets eyes on that vision.'

'Sally, don't say things like that! I'm dreading that either
he or Dorothea or both will forget where they are and do
something quite scandalous tonight!'

'I hardly think, for once, anyone would blame him if he
did!'

At exactly that moment Mellow announced the Marquis of
Hazelmere and the Dowager Marchioness. While no one was
ill-bred enough to stare, Hazelmere was well aware that all
eyes, save one set of emerald green, were trained on him. He
resisted the temptation to look for Dorothea and instead, with
his usual urbane air, led his mother to pay their respects to
Lady Merion.

Lady Hazelmere, not under any such compulsion, sought
out Dorothea and in an undertone designed for him alone, said,
'My dear, you are lost! That girl is the most stunning sight I
have ever seen!'

Hazelmere, hazel eyes laughing, replied, 'Thank you,

Mama. I rather supposed that to be the case, seeing how closely all these tabbies are watching me.'

Lady Hazelmere chuckled and turned to compliment Lady Merion on her charges. Relinquishing his mother to the group of old friends around their hostess, Hazelmere skilfully drifted into the crowd.

The Hazelmere party was closely followed by the Eglemonts. Under cover of the bustle this created, with most attention being distracted by the sight of Lord Fanshawe greeting Cecily Darent, Hazelmere approached Dorothea where she stood talking to his younger sister, Lady Alison Gisborne. This vivacious blonde, having no doubt who her brother's inamorata was, had introduced herself to Dorothea. Seeing him, she smiled broadly and announced, 'Hello, Marc! Yes, I'm just going to see Mama, who I know is dying to say something to me!' She laughed up at him and departed.

'How well my younger sister understands me,' he murmured, raising Dorothea's hand to his lips as usual. He was thankful for the few minutes he had had to grow accustomed to the vision she presented.

Risking a glance up at him, Dorothea found his hazel eyes glinting, and as he smiled at her she felt that the rest of the room could disappear for all she cared. Smiling back, she said, 'I must thank you for your gift, Lord Hazelmere.'

'Ah, yes. I hoped it would act as a token of pleasant memories,' he replied, raising a long finger to touch the pendant and only just resisting the temptation to caress the skin on which it lay.

She had expected some outrageous remark. 'Yes, I always found Moreton Park woods particularly restful.' Her serenity was so complete that, if he hadn't known better, he could have thought she had forgotten her first meeting with him entirely.

Laughingly acknowledging the adept return, he took her breath away by murmuring provocatively, 'You have grown so very expert at fencing with me, my dear, that I fear I'll have to resort to…more direct methods.'

The emerald eyes flew to his, but just what she would have

said in response they never knew, for at that moment Marjorie Darent approached them.

While the rest of the company had the good manners not to interrupt the conversation between Miss Darent and Lord Hazelmere, Lady Darent felt no such restriction. Seeing Dorothea being monopolised by a man she considered one step removed from a rake, she saw her duty clearly. Recently arrived, she had not yet spoken to Dorothea and, being shortsighted, it was not until she was within a few feet that the full effect of Dorothea's gown struck her.

Favouring the Marquis with what she believed was a gracious smile, she spoke to Dorothea immediately. 'My dear! Don't you think a shawl would be more becoming over that gown?'

Hazelmere felt Dorothea stiffen and almost imperceptibly they drew closer together. 'I think not, Cousin,' replied Dorothea, holding her temper with a superhuman effort. 'I'm hardly cold. And besides,' she continued hurriedly, seeing that her cousin had missed the very large hint and was about to explain herself more fully, 'I would hardly embarrass Grandmama by adopting so provincial a style of dress.'

Lady Darent stiffened.

Only just preventing himself from applauding, Hazelmere intervened. 'Miss Darent, I believe my mother is trying to attract our attention. If Lady Darent will excuse us?' With a nod to that outraged lady, he firmly removed Dorothea from her orbit.

As they moved away he glanced down at the beauty by his side. 'Good girl! If you hadn't said that I'm afraid I had something much worse in mind. Remind me that, despite the other…skills I've yet to teach you, I don't need to teach you how to insult someone.'

A gurgle of laughter, quickly suppressed, greeted this sally, and Dorothea turned her sparkling eyes to his face. The Marquis's mother, towards whom they were headed, viewed this exchange with a peculiar smile. She had never thought to see her son so obviously in love.

The conversation continued to hum and the heat in the

drawing-room rose, until Mellow, resplendent in new long-tailed coat, announced dinner. Hazelmere, as the most senior of the peers present, would normally have led in Lady Merion, but Herbert Darent found that he was to perform this office, leaving the Marquis to attend Miss Darent. Cecily was squired by Lord Fanshawe, and the others obligingly took care of themselves.

The dinner was a resounding success and not a single incident occurred to mar Lady Merion's pleasure. Conversation flowed on all sides, even Marjorie finding in the half-deaf admiral by her side someone with whom she shared some common ground. As all had expected, Hazelmere and Dorothea seemed oblivious to all others, as were Cecily and Fanshawe opposite. Due to Lady Merion's strategic planning, no one was the least put out by this, except Lord and Lady Darent. Luckily those disapproving figures were too far removed to exert any dampening influence on the sparkling scene in the middle of the table.

With the removal of the last course, the ladies rose and departed for the drawing-room, leaving the gentlemen to their port. At a dinner preceding a ball the ritual separation was usually kept to a minimum. But Lady Merion was taking no chances. She had enlisted the aid of the Earl of Eglemont to ensure that Herbert did not prose on in his accustomed way and drive everyone else to distraction.

For this service Lord Eglemont was an inspired choice. He knew that none of the younger gentlemen present would have the least inclination to remain kicking his heels over the port. And who could blame them? In his view, a dinner and ball was the time for some fun, and even he would rather be back in the drawing-room, watching what devilment Marc and Tony, and even Lord Harcourt and Ferdie, could concoct, than listening to that pompous windbag Herbert Darent.

Herbert, therefore, found the discussion he instituted on the latest ideas of rotation farming taken out of his hands and wound up by Lord Eglemont, who then further usurped his role and led the gentlemen back to the drawing-room.

Lady Merion heaved a sigh of relief when she saw them

return. The room was pleasantly a-hum with conversation generated by the groups of young and old scattered through it. Lords Hazelmere and Fanshawe, re-entering the room to find the Misses Darent chatting avidly with groups of friends, wisely made no attempt to disengage them, but made themselves as inconspicuous as possible.

Hazelmere strolled over to his mother. 'Ah, Mama! I'd meant to ask earlier. Do you know if my esteemed elder sisters will be gracing the ball tonight?'

Lady Hazelmere's strait-laced elder daughters were every bit as great a burden to her as they were to her son. 'I fervently hope not, my dear!' She turned and, leaning across Sally Jersey, addressed Lady Merion. 'Hermione, you didn't invite Maria and Susan, did you?'

To both mother and son's dismay, Lady Merion nodded. 'Yes. And both accepted.'

Lady Hazelmere turned back to her son, pulling a face.

He bent to whisper in her ear. 'In that case, it would be wise if you dropped a word of warning in my loving sisters' ears, regarding the wisdom of giving myself and Miss Darent a suitably wide berth tonight.'

Lady Hazelmere looked at him in surprise. He smiled down at her in his usual maddening way before moving off into the room. She spent some minutes trying to solve the riddle, finally deciding that he must mean to do something that would incense her elder daughters. What it could be she had no idea but, as she turned to Sally Jersey sitting beside her, she found she was not alone in suspecting her son of being up to something.

'Anthea, what on earth is that boy of yours up to? He and Tony Fanshawe are behaving very coolly.'

'I've really no idea, Sally. You should know mothers are always the last to be told anything. But I must say,' she went on, 'I do think you're right. They're certainly planning something.'

As the time for the ball approached Lady Merion moved her dinner guests up to the ballroom. The florists and decorators had excelled themselves, but the exclamations and con-

gratulations of the ladies were soon drowned by the arrival of
the ball guests. The chatter and talk as acquaintances met
swept like a wave across the room as all the ton rolled up to
Lady Merion's ball.

Dorothea and Cecily were stationed at the head of the stairs
with their grandmother to receive the guests. For the next half-
hour they were completely absorbed in greeting and being presented to the ton at large. As the surge of arrivals started to
ease and then reduced to a trickle the ballroom was close to
overflowing, and all the glittering throng of the élite of London
society were present. The room looked magnificent, and Lady
Merion felt she had achieved the very pinnacle of success.
Catching Mellow's eye, she gave the signal to start the ball.
As he moved majestically down the room the guests parted to
clear an area for the first waltz.

Traditionally the first section of the first waltz was danced
only by the young lady in whose honour the ball was held.
Tonight Dorothea would go first down the room, followed by
Cecily, before the rest of the guests joined in. If strictest pro-
tocol was followed Dorothea would be partnered by Herbert
and Cecily by Lord Wigmore, Lady Merion's cousin. However, when approached by her ladyship, Lord Wigmore had
readily relinquished this task, chuckling when he heard who
was to take his place. Herbert was simply informed that, as
he did not waltz, a suitable replacement had been found. He
was put out but did not have the gumption to cause a fuss.
His grandmother wisely refrained from telling him who was
to lead his ward out.

She had also, under orders, not told her granddaughters who
their partners were for this all-important first dance. This had
placed no strain on her inventiveness, as neither girl had
thought to ask, both imagining that Herbert and Lord Wigmore
were inescapable fixtures. So, with inward trepidation, Lady
Merion, standing between the two girls at the top of the shallow steps leading down to her ballroom and, seeing the musicians preparing to strike the first chords, said, 'Off you go,
my loves! Your partners are arranged and will meet you at the

bottom of the steps. And my very best wishes for a most wonderful ball for you both!'

The sisters moved down the stairs, Dorothea slightly in advance, carrying herself with that self-confident air that drew all eyes. Inwardly she was dreading this dance. She knew Herbert could not waltz to save himself. The next few minutes could be hideously embarrassing. Then her already huge and glittering eyes widened even further as, stepping on to the ballroom floor, she saw the Marquis of Hazelmere coming towards her, magnificent and smiling as ever.

He bowed to her and she automatically curtsied gracefully. He raised her and she went into his arms with her usual total abandon, her face radiant and her eyes sparkling with laughter. As they turned with the dance she cast a quick glance across to find Cecily had been met by Fanshawe. She sighed with relief, and said in heartfelt accents, 'Oh! You have no idea how thankful I am that it's you!'

Hazelmere smiled as they slowly went down the room. 'Neither your grandmother nor I felt horrible Herbert was a suitable partner for you, nor that the not nearly so horrible but staid Lord Wigmore was quite right for Cecily.'

Alive to the silence around them, Dorothea, laughter in the big green eyes she did not dare take from his face, asked, 'Are we making a scandalous spectacle of ourselves?'

Hazelmere, still smiling, murmured, 'I rather suspect we are. But I doubt if it's for the reason you suspect.'

She looked her question.

For a moment the hazel eyes glinted. He elected to answer only half of the query. 'While my dancing the first waltz with you, and Tony with Cecily, is not precisely correct, it's nevertheless acceptable in the circumstances of your having no near male relatives other than Herbert, who everyone knows can't dance.'

'So they may disapprove but they can't condemn?'

'Exactly so.'

They had reached the end of the ballroom and Hazelmere expertly executed a difficult turn, sending them back through the other couples now on the floor.

'Incidentally,' he continued, 'this is also the one occasion when I can with impunity waltz twice with you. This dance is special and not listed on the programme and therefore doesn't count. So, my dear Miss Darent, may I have the double pleasure of the supper waltz and of escorting you to supper?'

Thinking that that would ensure a most enjoyable evening, she laughingly agreed. As the last notes drifted down the room they glided to a halt and he led her back to Lady Merion's side. Reluctantly relinquishing her, he kissed her hand and, with a peculiar smile that made her unruly heart somersault, disappeared into the gathering crowd of well-wishers.

Lady Hazelmere's reaction to that first waltz was much the same as that of many in the watching crowd. When Hazelmere took Dorothea into his arms the entire company held its breath, usually the prelude to an outburst of censorious whispering. However, all the censorious minds simultaneously realised that there was nothing particularly scandalous after all. A minute's reflection convinced the leading ladies that Lady Merion had pulled off a major coup. The gentlemen, almost to a man, found the incident highly entertaining.

What particularly tickled Lady Hazelmere's quirkish sense of humour was the outrage engendered in a large number of the more staid female breasts by the way her son and the lovely Dorothea danced. The ton had thought they were accustomed to the sight of Miss Darent in Lord Hazelmere's arms. But they had only seen them dancing in a crowd of other couples, not alone on a deserted ballroom floor. Tonight the first shock had come when Dorothea went so readily into his arms. But the way they moved together had really set the cat among the pigeons! So graceful, so completely attuned to each other that the intimacy which obviously existed between them was displayed for all to see. That performance had bordered on the indecent. Even more wonderful, thought the knowing Lady Hazelmere, was that not one word could be said of the matter. Not one single movement, not one flicker of an eyelash, had been in any way improper. The most censorious of the tabbies would not dare breathe a word for fear of being, quite justly, accused of having a mind of somewhat question-able taste. It was highly unlikely that her wicked son had not known how it would be. Equally certain that the lovely Dor-othea was quite innocent in the matter. Well, no, perhaps not innocent, amended her ladyship, but Dorothea could certainly not have known how revealing that dance would be. No gently nurtured female could possibly have gone through with it.

At least I now know why Marc wanted me to warn off Maria and Susan, she thought. And, thinking just how scan-dalised her elder daughters were bound to be, she laughed and went to carry out his commission.

For both Darent sisters their coming-out ball was the most enjoyable night of the Season. They were fêted and saluted at every turn. Dorothea danced with every one of Hazelmere's close friends, with whom she now enjoyed an easy acquain-tance. She also danced with Herbert, but in a quadrille, which he performed adequately if not gracefully. It was more than halfway through the evening before she found herself once more in the Marquis's arms, going down the floor in the sup-per waltz.

Guessing that she must have been making constant conver-sation, he did not press her to talk, merely murmuring, 'Tired, my lovely Dorothea?'

For a moment his use of her name did not register. Then she looked up and found all inclination to question his right to use it evaporating. Meeting his eyes, she felt that deliciously warm feeling spread over her. So she assented to the question with a smile, her long lashes dropping to veil her large green eyes from his gaze in a manner he recognised only too well.

Smiling, he wondered if he dared tell her how she looked when she did that, or what the action commonly conveyed, but decided that after such an explanation she would in all likelihood not speak to him for a week.

Suppertime was hilarious. As Dorothea and Cecily were the twin foci of attention, they could not sit together. Instead, Dor-othea and Hazelmere were surrounded by a reckless throng of his close friends. While he sat beside her, interpolating re-

marks only when the conversation threatened to get too deep
for her ears, they entertained her with numerous anecdotes,
many reflecting on Hazelmere himself. They knew he was perfectly capable of putting a stop to it any time he wished, so
when he made no move to dampen their spirits their hilarity
knew few bounds. In this way the half-hour devoted to supper
whizzed past until Dorothea was claimed by Lord Desborough
for the first of the last three dances of the evening.

At the end of the measure she was hailed by a small group
of her grandmother's acquaintances, older ladies whom she
had not yet had time to talk to. Laughingly dismissing Desborough, she went to spend a few minutes in their company.
Eventually excusing herself, Dorothea passed slowly through
the crowd, stopping to chat here and there, dispensing just the
right degree of notice at each halt. Turning from one such
encounter, she was addressed by Miss Buntton, a blonde ice-
maiden two years her junior. 'My dear Miss Darent,' said Miss
Buntton in her normal frigid accents. 'Your gown is really so
superb! Truly esoteric! But I fear my mama would never permit me to wear such a gown. She always says it does no good
to stand out in a crowd.'

Dorothea, long inured to Miss Buntton's waspish jealousies,
thought she really made it too easy. 'I'm sure, my dear Miss
Buntton, that you run no risk of displeasing your mama.' With
a smile of gentle malice, she was about to move on when
another, older woman, whose name she could not recall, standing on the other side of the blonde beauty, intervened.

'Miss Darent! I've been hoping to meet you. I'm Lady Susan Wilmot, Hazelmere's sister.'

Dorothea touched the hand graciously held out to her and
murmured something suitable. But Lady Susan was already
speaking. 'Yes, my dear. As I was just telling Miss Buntton,
I was so pleased to see Hazelmere doing his duty by you
tonight with that first waltz. He's so lax in certain responsi-
bilities, but, given that Lady Merion must have asked him, as
a favour, to replace Herbert, I was pleasantly surprised to see
him behave so acceptably. Perhaps it's a sign that he's contemplating settling down. Of course, the lady he marries must

have all the qualities—as she'll have to rule at Hazelmere. And naturally she can only come from the finest of family. Wealth, of course, is necessary; Hazelmere after all is one of the wealthiest himself.' Her ladyship smiled, gimlet-eyes, on Dorothea. 'I dare say I'm not giving away any secrets in saying that all the family have high hopes of our dear Miss Buntton here.'

'Oh?' Unable to escape the net of her ladyship's eloquence and feeling oddly depressed, Dorothea could not resist a glance at our Miss Buntton. Good lord! The girl was actually simpering!

At that moment a hand touched her arm. 'Dorothea! Here you are! Come and meet my brother-in-law. I've promised to introduce you.' Lady Alison Gisborne's eyes met her older sister's across the little group. Lady Susan coloured.

Missing the byplay, Dorothea, with relief, nodded to Lady Susan and Miss Buntton and gratefully departed to meet Andrew Gisborne.

As the closing strains of the last waltz drifted across the ballroom, and tired couples turned to find their parties, Dorothea found herself at the side of the ballroom on Lord Alvanley's arm. His lordship was scanning the room, obviously looking for someone. 'Ah, there he is!' Looking down at Dorothea, he explained, 'Marc asked me to return you to him after the dance.'

As they slowly made their way across the wide room, pausing to bid goodbye to departing guests, Dorothea saw Lady Alison pause by her brother, dragging on his arm to get his attention. For a moment Hazelmere listened as she spoke, clearly relating some message. Then she swiftly drew his head down to plant an affectionate kiss on his cheek and, with a cheerful wave, hurried to join her husband by the stairs.

By this time they had come up to the Marquis, who was conversing with an opulent beauty introduced earlier to Dorothea as Helen, Lady Walford. The four remained chatting for a few minutes as the company in the ballroom thinned. Then

Lord Alvanley suavely offered Lady Walford his arm and, after taking their leave of Dorothea, they left.

Hazelmere, seeing the appreciative grin on her face, said, 'Yes, Alvanley and I are very good friends.' Her smile deepened. After a pause he continued, 'My dear Dorothea, are you planning to ride in the Park tomorrow?'

This succeeded in capturing her attention from a group of guests nodding their goodbyes. 'Why, yes, I think so,' she replied.

'In that case, Ferdie and I, and probably Tony as well, will call for you at ten. Don't be late!' He kissed her hand and, recognising the portent of the flash in her green eyes, drew it through his arm; before she had time to tell him what she thought of his organisation of her morning, he strolled with her up the steps to her grandmother.

Lady Merion was exhausted. The evening had been an unqualified success, although in her opinion it would have proved less enervating if Dorothea and Hazelmere had been less accomplished dancers. However, she was not going to cavil at such a minor point and was in total charity with the world. Seeing them come up out of the deserted ballroom, she beamed. 'My dears! Such a success it's been!'

'And all due to you, Grandmama!' replied Dorothea, impulsively hugging the old lady.

'Now be off with you, child!' said her ladyship gruffly. 'Cecily has already retired. I'm sure Lord Hazelmere will excuse you.'

Hazelmere lifted her hand from his sleeve and, elegantly dropping a kiss on her wrist, said, 'Goodnight, Dorothea. I'll see you tomorrow morning.'

With another glance of green fire she was gone.

Lady Merion watched this exchange and, once her granddaughter was out of earshot, said, 'You do play close to the wind.'

'Only with your granddaughter,' came the outrageous reply. As she gasped he continued, 'Am I correct in thinking the horrible Herbert that gorgeous creature's guardian?'

Knowing she was being distracted from her main grievance, she was forced to reply, 'Yes, unfortunately.'

'No matter.' He shrugged, turning to take his leave.

But she had no intention of letting him escape so easily. Fixing him with a look that forcibly reminded him of his mother, she asked, 'When are you going to ask for her hand?'

'In my own good time,' he returned, unperturbed by this direct inquisition.

'So you intend to offer for her?'

At that he smiled. 'Do you doubt it?'

'After that first waltz, no one present could doubt it!' she retorted acerbically.

'Which is precisely as I intended.' With a smile of unruffled calm he bowed elegantly before descending the stairs.

Lady Merion watched his retreating back. For some reason she felt that, in spite of his cool handling of the affair, which she could not but applaud for the eminent good sense it showed, his success so far had been unnaturally easy. In her experience, headstrong young women like Dorothea were unlikely to appreciate his calm management of the affair. No, my lord, she thought, there's trouble ahead somewhere.

CHAPTER NINE

The riding party the next morning was a relaxed affair. From Cavendish Square came the Darent sisters, Hazelmere, Fanshawe, Ferdie and Mr Dermont. At the gates of the Park they were joined by Lord Harcourt and Miss Bressington. There were few others about at that hour, despite the clemency of the weather. Before long the three couples had parted, to amble down the glades and rides, totally absorbed with each other, while Ferdie and Mr Dermont were deep in discussion over the latest type of suiting.

As was often the case when she was alone in Hazelmere's company, Dorothea's composure was more apparent than real. She was having increasing difficulty maintaining the cool unconcern she felt was her only defence against those all-seeing hazel eyes. His presence physically disturbed her to the point where her mind no longer functioned with its customary clarity. Amid others, at balls and parties, where convention laid its restraining hand on his actions, she could retain sufficient command of her wits to deflect his subtle attacks. But when they were alone, with nothing to prevent him from leading her thoughts along avenues she knew to be as dangerous as they were exciting, she no longer felt confident of keeping him from guessing how deeply he affected her. In fact, she was no longer sure that she was hiding anything from him at all. She had no idea what he had made of her behaviour in the Duchess of Richmond's orangery. On the other hand, his imperious manners had abated not one whit. And he had yet to speak, even obliquely, of love.

As they rode side by side deep within the Park, far out of sight of the rest of their party, she was conscious of steadily increasing confusion. It was fraying her temper, particularly when the reprehensible creature beside her seemed not to know the meaning of uncertainty. His attitude was always one of complete assurance. She had a peculiar feeling of being inexorably caught up in something she did not comprehend, some trap baited with an irresistible lure, impossible to escape. And he was at the centre of it, drawing her ever closer.

Hazelmere took the opportunity to tell her he would again be away until some time in the next week. His brief trip to Hazelmere had revealed more examples of his neglect than his conscience would countenance. Having done all he could to impress upon the ton how definite his intentions towards her were, and what her response to his proposal was likely to be, he was determined to rectify the problems on his estates without delay. Other than the lady riding beside him, there was little to keep him in London; the débutante balls were not generally high on his list of enjoyable functions.

While she accepted the news of his projected absence prosaically enough, Dorothea was surprised by his final comments. 'In my absence, if you should need help in any way, you can trust Ferdie or Tony, or Alvanley, Peterborough or any of the others of our set, for that matter. We always help each other and they would unhesitatingly stand in my stead were there any need.'

She turned her wide-eyed gaze upon him, but was unable to see anything in his manner, other than a rueful twinkle in his eyes, to give her a clue as to what exactly he meant.

The twinkle was occasioned by the realisation that he had told her rather more than he had intended. He was slipping again. If she paused to consider she might wonder why his powerful friends should extend their protection to Miss Darent. That they would definitely do so to the future Marchioness of Hazelmere was a thought that might occur. He was sure she had no idea how publicly accepted their relationship had become and suspected that the realisation would be greeted, at least initially, with dismay, if not anger. It formed no part of his plans to force her hand thus early in the Season.

He then spent the best part of a pleasurable hour trying just

how far into the realms of the improper he could lead her. He
found it was rather further than his own rapidly diminishing
control made safe. So, with a skill born of extensive practice,
he adroitly disengaged, leaving her confused but with no idea
of where they had been headed.

They were the last to rejoin the group, and the look on
Hazelmere's face reminded Ferdie that he had a bone to pick
with his lordship, and Tony too, come to think of it! In otherwise perfect harmony, the group made its way out of the
Park and back to Cavendish Square, where Julia Bressington
was to spend the day.

A select masquerade ball was to be held the following
Thursday at the Bressingtons'. The Season's débutantes had
been clamouring for a masquerade. Such events, commonplace
some years previously, had fallen into disrepute because of the
licentiousness they provoked and the difficulty in policing acceptable standards of conduct. However, wilting under the
continued entreaties, a group of mothers had put their heads
together and devised a compromise. While the ball was to be
a masquerade, there were strict rules. Entry was by invitation
only and everyone had to wear plain black dominoes over
evening dress. Masks would be provided at the door, so the
hostesses would know each face before any were permitted to
enter.

Dorothea was disappointed when she realised that Hazelmere would not be back in time for the masquerade ball. She
considered not going herself but, as chaperons were not permitted in the ballroom and Lady Merion was therefore taking
a well-earned rest, Cecily did not like to go alone. To add to
this, Lady Merion made various obscure comments about not
wearing her heart on her sleeve or pining away just because
a certain nobleman was absent from town. Not being obtuse,
Dorothea took the point, and with good grace accompanied
Cecily to the ball.

Entering the hall of Bressington House, they handed in their
invitations and, approved by the hostesses, joined the queue
leading to a table where the Misses Bressington were distrib-

uting masks. The sight of Dorothea affected Julia Bressington strangely. She tittered and then, looking highly conspiratorial, surreptitiously handed over a note.

Dorothea, waiting in line, opened the missive. It contained only one sentence: 'Meet me on the terrace at midnight.' She felt sure there was only one person who would dare send her such a peremptory command. So Hazelmere was coming to the ball after all. Presumably he would be late and so would have less time to find her in the crush.

Her mask was tied tightly across her face by a giggling Julia, holding the hood of her domino in place and completely covering her hair. Despite this disguise, no sooner had she and Cecily stepped over the threshold than each was claimed by suspiciously tall, domino-clad figures.

Feeling a familiar arm about her waist and looking up into a pair of laughing hazel eyes, Dorothea instantly relaxed, laughing back.

'You're already here!'

'Already? How did you know I was coming at all?' he asked, thoroughly surprised.

'But you left me that note.' As she said the words a dreadful premonition seized her.

'What note? No. Wait.' He drew her into a window embrasure. 'Show me,' he commanded, holding out his hand.

Dorothea had put the note in the inside pocket of her domino. She drew it out and handed it to him.

Hazelmere read the single line of script, the lines about his mouth hardening. The idea of Dorothea attending the masquerade to fall victim to some gentleman as experienced as himself had been sufficient to drive him to conclude his business a day early. But what the hell was this note about?

Seeing Dorothea pale under her mask, he slipped his arm about her waist. Tucking the note into his pocket, he led her towards the centre of the room. 'Remind me, my love, to show you my signature some time. Then, if I ever send you a letter, you'll know it's from me.'

Deciding she was not going to be distracted by the ineligible epithet, which she knew had been included expressly for the purpose, she asked directly, 'But who is it from, if not you?'

Hazelmere considered telling her some fanciful tale, anything to make her forget the incident, but one glance at her determined face warned him that that particular ruse was unlikely to succeed. He eventually answered, 'I know no more than you, my dear.'

A waltz started up and Dorothea found herself circling the floor in his arms. By the time the dance concluded he had succeeded in convincing her to put aside her thoughts on the mysterious note and give her undivided attention to him. She learned that the principal attraction of a masquerade ball was that a lady could spend the entire evening in the arms of one gentleman without causing a furor. For his part, Hazelmere had no intention of letting her go. Luckily, as most of the couples in the ballroom were similarly invariant and Dorothea found nothing amiss with this arrangement, his possessiveness passed unnoticed.

After their second dance he drew her into a shadowed alcove. There, with Dorothea standing, unconsciously, within the comforting circle of his arm, they swapped their news.

'And Lord Peterborough has been *so* attentive,' sighed Dorothea, eyes dancing.

'Oh?' said Hazelmere, a frown in his eyes.

'Mmm,' she murmured in confirmation, adding innocently, 'He told me to tell you so.'

The laugh this elicited made her tingle. His hazel eyes were wreaking havoc with her composure. 'I must remember to thank Gerry next time I see him. In the meantime, sweet torment, come and dance.'

For the rest of the evening Hazelmere devoted himself to making her forget the existence of the note. He tried every trick he knew to bemuse and amuse her, hoping to divert her thoughts sufficiently to enable him to leave her, unsuspecting, with Fanshawe while he kept his midnight appointment. But while she certainly paid attention to all he said, blushing delightfully at his more provocative suggestions, she clearly possessed a distressingly calm and collected mind. He suspected that she guessed the reason for his behaviour and, short of kissing her in the middle of the ballroom, he could think of nothing that might succeed in distracting her. As midnight approached he gave up the attempt.

The rules for the ball called for a general unmasking at midnight. As the clock over the door approached five minutes to the hour Hazelmere, knowing that Dorothea, too, was keeping track of the time, drew her over to the windows leading on to the terrace.

'Are you sure you want to go through with this?' he asked.

'But of course!' She assumed that his evident wish to spare her the midnight meeting stemmed from the belief she would be overcome by some missish sentiment. She felt slightly aggrieved that he didn't know her better.

'Before I permit you to go out on that terrace I want you to promise you'll do precisely as I say.'

It was on the tip of her tongue to point out that it was her note and therefore her adventure, not his. And she certainly did not need his permission to go out on the terrace! But there was no time to argue, and the gleam of amusement in his eyes suggested that he had guessed her thoughts anyway. Mastering her annoyance, she agreed. 'Very well. I promise. What must I do?'

'Open the door and go out, but don't shut it behind you. I'll stay behind in the shadows. Walk on to the terrace but, whatever you do, don't go more than halfway to the balustrade. And only go a few yards either side of the door. Understand?'

She nodded. Satisfied, Hazelmere held the heavy curtain aside for her to slip past, and followed her into the darkened alcove between the curtain and the window. He opened this and Dorothea moved out on to the moonlit terrace.

Directly in front of her was a flight of stone steps leading down to a gravel path, with the lawns and shrubbery in deepest shadow beyond. Mindful of her instructions, she moved to her left, keeping close to the house. She had only gone a few paces when a voice came to her from somewhere near the steps.

'Miss Darent! This way!'

At exactly that moment someone inside the ballroom flung back the curtain over the next window along and opened it, but then, as the call for the unmasking was heard, closed it again.

The sound of running footsteps retreating along the gravel path came clearly to both Dorothea and Hazelmere, still in the shadows. Stepping up to her, he whispered, 'Stay here.' He went past her and lightly down the steps.

The last echoes of the footsteps were dying in the distance. The rhododendron bushes that bordered the terrace were dense and taller than Hazelmere himself. A most convenient setting for an abduction, he thought grimly. He was too wise to go searching in the darkened garden, leaving Dorothea unattended on the terrace, even though it seemed as though the mysterious leaver of notes had departed. Removing his mask and pushing back the hood of his domino, he returned to the terrace.

'There's no sign of anyone now,' he said. 'A pity, but no harm done.'

'But who could it be, to play such a silly joke?' she asked, tugging at the knots Julia Bressington had made in her mask strings.

'Here, let me.' He reached over her and undid the mask, removed it and pushed the hood back from her hair. Then, taking her face in both hands and tilting it up, he kissed her. After a moment his hands left her face to slip beneath her domino and gather her, unresisting, into his arms.

As the kiss deepened, Dorothea, again, lost all sense of time. He did no more than reinforce the lessons he had taught her in the orangery; there was no time for more. His experienced mouth claimed hers, gently persuading, while, under her domino, his hands drifted caressingly over her breasts, her waist and her hips. Then, reluctantly, he released her. Before she could recover he drew her hand through his arm and moved back to the door, saying in his usual manner, 'We'd best return to the ballroom before our absence becomes too difficult to explain.'

Back in the ballroom before she could gather her wits, Dorothea had no chance to say anything. They were quickly surrounded by friends, all laughing and talking at once. But during what was left of the ball she was conscious of the hazel eyes resting on her often, their expression doing nothing for her peace of mind.

Later, as they left the ballroom together, Hazelmere remembered the note. 'Incidentally, my love, should you get any further notes inciting you to do anything the least bit improper and which purport to come from me, you might remember I'm much more likely to make such suggestions in person.'

It was impossible to reply to that in any acceptable way. Dorothea wisely left it uncontested.

Leaving Bressington House a short time later, Lords Hazelmere and Fanshawe insisted on handing the Darent sisters into their carriage. Belatedly realising that she had allowed Hazelmere to monopolise her for the entire evening, Dorothea threw him a glance that she hoped conveyed her disapproval of his managing ways. She could hardly claim success, as he laughed and murmured in her ear that if she continued to cast such provocative looks at him he would be unable to resist the temptation to kiss her again. In the shadowy carriage drive he suited the action to the words, before helping a thoroughly flustered Dorothea into her grandmother's coach.

Hazelmere was more perturbed by the mysterious note and the incident on the terrace than he had let Dorothea guess. Walking back to Cavendish Square in company with Fanshawe, he considered the possible explanations.

Young heiresses had been abducted and held for ransom—that was one possible reason. However, most of the previous targets had been very wealthy. Dorothea, although commonly held to be well dowered, was not immensely rich. So, if it was an abduction attempt, the far more likely intention would be to have a touch at the Hazelmere coffers. It had never occurred to him that by making his interest in her so public he would make her a target for such attacks.

He considered the figure by his side. All was not well with his friend and, presuming from his silence on the matter that the cause was the younger Miss Darent, he did not like to add any extra burden to a brow already overwrought.

The romance between Fanshawe and Cecily was not proceeding as his lordship had hoped. He had discovered his love had a definite mind of her own and having once taken an idea into her head could hold to it buckle and thong in the face of all reason. She had objected to what she termed his proprietorial attitude at the masquerade, leaving him feeling decidedly rejected. While she had relented later, allowing him to escort her to their carriage, she had remained coldly aloof.

The two friends continued on their way, sunk in abstracted silence. They parted at the corner of Cavendish Square to retire to their respective chambers, troubled, for quite different reasons, over what the future held.

CHAPTER TEN

The Friday, Saturday and Sunday following the masquerade saw Hazelmere dancing attendance on Dorothea in a way that, had anyone still been watching, would have made them wonder at the power of love. Lady Merion was moved to make a number of rude comments to him when no one else was by, regarding the inadvisability of over-indulgence. Hazelmere listened politely and let the shafts fly by. He was thankful that his mother had returned to Hazelmere on Friday morning, archly refusing her dutiful son's offer of escort, saying she knew how many other things he had on his mind.

Keeping a watchful eye on Dorothea at the balls and parties in the evenings presented no great problem. He could with confidence leave her in the company of a great many friends, both his and her own. But from the time she returned from riding in the Park to the time she left Merion House for whichever of the evening's entertainments she was to attend, her day was a mystery to him.

On Friday he solved this by inviting her to drive with him in the Park in the afternoon. He almost committed the blunder of asking her to come out with him again on Saturday but, catching a glimpse of her face, realised that she was already becoming suspicious. She was quite capable of linking his sudden attentiveness with the incident at the masquerade. He returned to Hazelmere House and spent the rest of the afternoon trying to devise a means of keeping watch over her without being overly conspicuous.

The only other person he would have consulted was Fanshawe, but he was still having troubles of his own. He had to have better information on Dorothea's movements, but for

some while the means of acquiring such intelligence did not
present itself. It was only when a footman quietly entered to
light the fire that the penny dropped.

Summoning his butler, he asked, 'Mytton, is there any connection between my household and that of Merion House?'

Mytton, not sure what had occasioned this odd query, saw
no reason to equivocate. 'Young Charles, the footman, m'lord,
is walking out with Miss Darent's new maid.'

'Is he, indeed?' mused Hazelmere softly. He glanced up at
his terribly correct and equally shrewd henchman. 'Mytton,
you may tell Charles that I wish him to find out for me, if he
can, what Miss Darent's plans are for the morrow. He may
take whatever time he needs. But I must have the information
before tomorrow. Do you think he could accomplish such a
task?'

'Young Charles, if I may say so, m'lord, is a most capable
young man,' responded Mytton gravely.

'Very good,' replied Hazelmere, repressing a grin.

On returning home in the early hours of Saturday morning,
he found that Charles had been every bit as capable as Mytton
believed. Armed with Dorothea's plans for the next two days,
he was able to confine his appearances to her usual morning
rides in the Park, to a ball on Saturday night and to the party
she attended on Sunday evening. At the party, he found himself again under suspicion.

'Just what are you about now?' Dorothea enquired as they
glided around the room in the only waltz of the evening.

'I'd rather thought it was the waltz,' returned Hazelmere,
all innocence. 'I'm generally held to be reasonably good at it.'

Dorothea regarded him much as she would an errant child.
'And I suppose it has always been your habit to attend such
eminently boring parties as this?'

'Ah, but you forget, my love! My heart is at your feet.
Didn't you know?'

While the words were what she longed to hear, the tone left
Dorothea in no doubt of how she should treat them. She
laughed. 'Oh, no! You cannot distract me so easily. You'll

have to think up a far more plausible excuse for your presence here, of all places.'

'Is my being here so distasteful to you?' he asked, feigning seriousness.

Seeing the lurking twinkle at the back of the hazel eyes, she had no compunction in answering, 'Why, no! I believe I would welcome even Lord Peterborough in such company as this!'

He laughed. 'Very neat, my dear. But why, if this party is so boring, are you gracing it with your lovely presence?'

'I've no idea why Grandmama insisted on coming,' she admitted. 'Even she is not enjoying it, because Herbert and Marjorie are here. Thank heavens they leave for Darent Hall tomorrow. And Cecily! She's been going around as if the sky has fallen.' Fixing him with a direct look, she continued, 'Incidentally, if you have any interest in that matter, you could tell Lord Fanshawe to stop encouraging her to think herself up to all the rigs, because she's not. He has, and now she's annoyed because he won't let her do precisely as she wants. If he'll only tell her quite plainly he won't have it, she'll stop. She always responds to firm handling.'

'Unlike her elder sister?' murmured Hazelmere provocatively.

'Precisely!' answered Dorothea.

Hazelmere had the opportunity to deliver her message to Fanshawe the next day. Thanks to Charles's continuing efforts on his behalf, he learned that Dorothea and Cecily were to attend a select picnic at the home of Lady Oswey, escorted by that pink of the ton, Ferdie Acheson-Smythe. Feeling he could safely leave Dorothea's welfare in Ferdie's capable hands for the day, he collected Fanshawe and they departed to watch a prize-fight on Clapham Common. As the sisters were going to the theatre that evening in company with Lord and Lady Eglemont, Hazelmere felt no need to attend this function either. It was the early hours of the next morning when their lordships, thoroughly pleased with their day away from the rigours of the Season and somewhat the worse for wear, returned to Cavendish Square and their beds.

* * *

Ferdie and Dorothea departed Merion House on the Monday morning, expecting to pass a pleasant day at the Osweys' house by the Thames at Twickenham. Cecily was querulous and moody, labouring under the twin goads of feeling, on the one hand, that she had treated Lord Fanshawe unfairly and, on the other, of not wishing him to order her life for her.

Observing her elder sister, she wondered why Dorothea, much more independently minded than herself, acquiesced so readily to the Marquis's suggestions. Noting the absent-minded smile that hovered on her lips as she gazed unseeingly out of the carriage window, she concluded that her sister was obviously in love with Hazelmere. She, in contrast, had clearly mistaken her heart. For surely if she was in love with Fanshawe she would be perfectly happy to allow his judgement to prevail? But he had been horridly strict and old-fashioned about her impromptu acquaintance with some of the more dashing blades present at the masquerade. The sneaking suspicion that he had been right in telling her that acquaintance with those particular gentlemen would not be to her advantage did not improve her humour. In an altogether dismal mood, she alighted from the chaise at Oswey Hall.

However, the glorious sunshine, blue skies and gentle breeze—perfect conditions for a picnic by the stream in the bluebell wood—raised even Cecily's spirits. Soon she was one of a group of chattering damsels busily comparing stories of encounters with the more eligible bachelors of the ton. Rather too old for such girlish pastimes, Dorothea settled by one of the Oswey cousins, come up to town from her home in west Hampshire to spend the Season with her relatives. Reticent and shy, Miss Delamere was grateful to the beautiful Miss Darent, who seemed happy to talk with her of country pastimes. Dorothea, who had not thought of the Grange for weeks, was quite content to make conversation on the topics that in years past had been her primary concern.

No chaperons were present other than the indolent Lady Margaret Oswey. Settled on a pile of cushions in the clearing where the picnic was held, she had no wish to bestir herself. Consequently only those gentlemen who could be trusted to

keep the line even while out of her sight had been invited.
Ferdie was one of this select group. Lords Hazelmere, Fanshawe and friends were, of course, absent.

After the repast Ferdie escorted two of the younger misses
to see the fairy dell, so named because of the mixture of blue-
bells, crocuses and tulips which grew there. The dell was in
the woods they had passed on their way to the stream, and
was reached by a path which branched from the main one
some little way back towards the house. Having exclaimed to
their hearts' content over the colourful carpet lining the dell,
the two young things reluctantly allowed him to lead them
back towards the rest of the company. Emerging on to the
main track, one young lady on each of his arms, they were
approached by a footman in search of Miss Darent.

'She's with her ladyship by the stream, I think,' said Ferdie.
Perceiving the letter on the tray the footman was holding, he
asked, 'Is that for Miss Darent?'

Assured it was and had just been delivered by a groom,
Ferdie, in benign mood, said, 'Oh, I'll take it to her if you
like. Very good friend of Miss Darent.'

As the footman had seen Ferdie arrive with the Darent sisters, he saw no reason not to leave the missive in his hands.

Ferdie needed both arms to escort the young ladies back to
the stream, so he deposited the letter in the inner pocket of his
coat. On reaching the clearing, he relinquished his young
charges but found that Dorothea had gone for a ramble with
Miss Delamere. Ferdie spent the rest of the afternoon in a *tête-
à-tête* with Cecily. As she had reached the stage of needing
someone's shoulder to cry on, he did not have an easy time
of it. However, by the end of a lengthy discussion in which
featured all the real and imaginary shortcomings of an un-
named peer with whom he was well acquainted, he felt he had
made some headway in getting her to think of things from his
lordship's point of view, rather than only her own.

Although he had enjoyed his day, Ferdie heaved a sigh of
relief as the Merion carriage drew away from Oswey Hall late
in the afternoon. After his difficult time with Cecily he completely forgot the letter for Dorothea.

The next day this missive resurfaced. Dorothea and Cecily had sent a message that they would not be riding that morning. Ferdie assumed Cecily had had a difficult time the evening before. As Lord Eglemont was convinced she would shortly be his daughter-in-law, Ferdie's imagination did not have to work overtime to understand that their visit to the theatre might have proved an ordeal.

He was consequently breakfasting in languid style when his valet, Higgins, appeared at his elbow. 'I found this in your coat pocket, sir.'

As it was common for him to forget letters and notes and leave them in his clothing, Ferdie thought nothing of this and opened the unaddressed letter. Reading the lines within, he frowned. He turned the single sheet over and then back and read it once more. Propping it against the salt cellar, he stared at the letter as he finished his coffee. Then he refolded it and called his valet. 'Higgins, in which of my coats did you find this?'

'In the blue superfine you wore at Lady Oswey's picnic yesterday, sir.'

'Ah. Thought that might be it.'

Ferdie dressed rapidly and set out for Hazelmere House, fervently hoping that his cousin had not already departed for a morning about town. Luck favoured him. The Marquis was descending the steps of Hazelmere House in company with Fanshawe as he entered Cavendish Square. Out of breath, he waved at them. Staggering at seeing the impeccable Mr Acheson-Smythe in anything resembling a hurry, they halted and waited for him.

'Ferdie!' exclaimed Hazelmere. 'What the devil's got into you?'

'Never seen you move so fast in my life!' said Fanshawe.

'Need a word with you, Marc. Now!' Ferdie gasped.

Hazelmere saw that his cousin was looking unaccustomedly serious. 'Let's go back into the house.'

They re-entered Hazelmere House and headed for the library. Hazelmere sat behind the desk. Fanshawe perched on a corner of it and both looked expectantly at Ferdie, who had dropped into a chair facing them. Still struggling to catch his breath, he drew out the letter and threw it on the desk in front of his cousin. 'Read that.'

Hazelmere, suddenly equally serious, complied. Then he looked at Ferdie, his face impassive. 'Where did you get this?'

'Was supposed to be delivered to Dorothea at Lady Oswey's picnic. Met the footman on the way and offered to take it to her. Put it in my pocket and forgot it. Higgins found it this morning and, not knowing what it was, I opened it. Thought you'd like to see it.'

'So Dorothea never got it?'

Ferdie shook his head.

Fanshawe was totally in the dark. 'Will someone please tell me what is going on?' he pleaded.

Without comment Hazelmere handed him the letter. The message it contained read:

My dear Miss Darent,

I cannot imagine that the company at Lady Oswey's picnic is quite as scintillating as that to which you have become accustomed. So, why not meet me at the white wicket gate at the end of the path through the woods? I'll have my greys and we can go for a drive around the lanes with no one the wiser. Don't keep me waiting; you know I hate to keep my horses standing. I'll expect you at two.

Hazelmere.

Like Ferdie, Fanshawe had no difficulty recognising Hazelmere's writing and signature and knew the letter in his hand was a hoax. Eyeing his friend with an unusually grim look, he asked simply, 'Who?'

'I wish I knew,' replied Hazelmere. 'It's the second.'

'*What*?' The exclamation burst from Fanshawe and Ferdie in unison.

Laying the letter Ferdie had brought in front of him, Hazelmere opened a drawer and took out the note Dorothea had received at the Bressingtons' masquerade. Once they were side by side, it was clear that the same hand had written both. Fanshawe and Ferdie came around the desk to study them over his shoulders.

'When was the first one sent?' asked Fanshawe.

'The masquerade. That attempt would have succeeded to admiration except I returned to London a day earlier than expected. It was handed to Dorothea in the hall at Bressington House. She was surprised to find me already there. She'd believed the note. Hardly surprising, as it's exactly the sort of thing I might be expected to do.'

'You should have told me. We might have baited a trap!' exclaimed Fanshawe.

'We did spring the trap,' Hazelmere answered with a fleeting grin. 'Dorothea went out on to the terrace at midnight and I was in the shadows behind her. A voice, which neither of us recognised, called her towards the steps down on to the path. But then some others in the ballroom opened another door on to the terrace and whoever it was took fright. I wasn't about to give chase and leave Dorothea alone on the terrace.'

'And you saw nobody?' asked Ferdie. Hazelmere shook his head, going back to studying the second letter.

'Very likely she'd have gone to that gate if Ferdie'd remembered to give her the note,' said Fanshawe.

'No. She won't be caught by that ruse again,' said Hazelmere. 'But what puzzles me most is who the writer of these missives could be.'

'Got to be someone acquainted with you,' put in Ferdie.

'Yes,' agreed Hazelmere. 'That's what is particularly worrisome. I'd thought it was one of those abduction plots at first.'

'Shouldn't have thought the Darent girls were sufficiently rich to attract that sort of attention,' said Fanshawe.

'They aren't. I am,' replied the Marquis.

'Oh. Hadn't thought of that.'

All three men continued to study the letters, hoping that some clue to their writer's identity could be wrung from them. Fanshawe broke the silence to ask Ferdie, 'Why do you say whoever it is must know Marc?'

'Writing's not his, but the style is. Just the sort of thing he would say,' replied the knowledgeable Ferdie.

'Can't know you all that well. You never drive young ladies around, let alone behind your greys,' his lordship pointed out.

'With one notable exception,' corrected Hazelmere. 'To whit, Miss Darent.'

'Oh,' said Fanshawe, finally convinced.

'Precisely,' continued Hazelmere. 'It's someone who at least knows me well enough to write a letter in a style that could pass for mine. Someone who also knows I have driven Miss Darent behind the greys, who knows I'm very particular about keeping my horses standing and who knew I was out of town and not expected to attend the Bressington masquerade.'

'Therefore,' concluded Ferdie, 'one of us. Of the ton, I mean. At least as an accomplice.'

'That would appear the inescapable conclusion,' agreed Hazelmere. He continued to stare at the letters.

'What're we going to do?' asked Fanshawe.

'Can't call in Bow Street,' said Ferdie, decisively. 'Very heavy-footed. Create all sorts of rumpus. Lady Merion wouldn't like it; Dorothea wouldn't like it.'

'*I* wouldn't like it either,' put in Hazelmere.

'Quite so,' agreed Ferdie, glad to have this point settled.

'As far as I can see, the only thing we can do is keep a very careful watch over Dorothea,' said Hazelmere. 'She won't be taken in with any messages, but, as we don't know who's behind this, we'll have to ensure no one who could possibly be involved is given any chance to approach her alone.'

'Just us three?' Fanshawe enquired.

Hazelmere considered the question, the hazel gaze abstracted. 'For the moment,' he eventually replied. 'We can call in reinforcements if necessary.'

'What are they doing now?' asked Fanshawe.

'Resting,' replied Ferdie. Seeing their surprise, he explained. 'Went to the theatre last night with your parents, dear boy. Result—Cecily's exhausted.'

'Ah,' said Hazelmere with an understanding grin. Fanshawe frowned.

'Going riding with them this afternoon,' continued Ferdie, 'then the Diplomatic Ball at Carlton House this evening. That's easy—we'll all be there.'

'Well, Ferdie, m'lad,' said Fanshawe as he rose to leave, 'you'll just have to keep us informed of where Miss Darent means to be and then make sure at least one of us is there. Shouldn't be too hard. They can't be gallivanting all over town still, can they?'

Ferdie reflected that their lordships, normally engrossed in their own pursuits, had very little idea of just how crowded a young lady's calendar could be. He sincerely hoped they would not have to keep up their surveillance for long.

Moments later, as he descended the steps in their company, arriving on the pavement ahead of them, he gave voice to an idea that had been rolling around in his head for some time. 'Actually, as far as I can see, the easiest way to solve all these problems is for you two to hurry up and marry the chits! Then Marc could spend his entire day with Dorothea, if necessary, and Cecily wouldn't be moping around, and I could go back to living a quiet life again.'

Seeing that their receipt of this advice was not favourable, he hurriedly waved at them. 'No? I'm off! See you tonight at the ball.'

The Diplomatic Ball at Carlton House was so named because all the diplomatic corps and delegations stationed in London attended. Sponsored by the Prince Regent, attendance by all those invited was virtually obligatory. These included all the year's débutantes, the majority of the peers present in London and the élite of society. It amused the Prince to think that for one night in the Season they all danced attendance on him. While the cream of the ton considered this function supremely boring, the necessity of being present when the Prince arrived ensured that all summoned came early.

Knowing his Prince, Hazelmere realised that, while it was hardly likely that Dorothea would be kidnapped from the ball, both she and Cecily could face a threat from a different source. After discussing the possibilities, he and Fanshawe called at Merion House when they knew the sisters were riding with Ferdie. They found Lady Merion at home and, having outlined the perceived problem, it was agreed that both of them would accompany the Merion party to Carlton House, using the large Hazelmere town carriage.

Ferdie was taken aback at finding them in attendance when he called at Merion House that evening. A quick word from Hazelmere brought comprehension to his eyes. 'Good heavens! Never thought of that!'

'Never thought of what, Ferdie?' asked Dorothea. She had witnessed the exchange and, her curiosity aroused, had come to see if she could surprise from him some explanation for the appearance of their lordships.

Ferdie could never think quickly in such situations. He could find no glib words to answer her. Dorothea knew that if she waited long enough he was bound to say something helpful. She had reckoned without Hazelmere, who calmly stepped in with a blatant lie. 'Ferdie, I believe Lady Merion has been trying to catch your eye these minutes past.'

'What? Oh, yes! Got to see your grandmama.' With this explanatory aside to Dorothea, he crossed the room to her ladyship's side with the alacrity of a rabbit escaping a snare.

Dorothea looked at Hazelmere in disgust. 'Spoil-sport,' she said.

'It's hardly fair to try to trip Ferdie up. He's definitely not in your class. You can attempt to get the story out of me if you like.'

'As you obviously have no intention of telling me, it would be wasted effort, I fear,' she replied, adding, 'In such matters, I am, after all, definitely not in your class.'

'True,' returned Hazelmere, taking the wind out of her sails. The emerald glance he received in reply spoke volumes.

With Ferdie come, there was nothing more to delay their departure and soon they were settled in the carriage and on their way. The Hazelmere town coach was a luxurious affair and easily sat the six of them, despite the voluminous ball-

gowns peculiar to this affair. To some extent, the Diplomatic
Ball had temporarily replaced the more formal presentations
of previous years. Due to the problems besetting the royal
family, these had been suspended. But the tradition of all-
white, waisted, full-skirted ballgowns for the débutantes, worn
with white ostrich plumes in their hair, had transferred to the
Prince Regent's Diplomatic Ball.

The all-white ensemble made Cecily look ethereal. Dorothea, with her dark hair and green eyes contrasting with the
white, looked divine. As usual, Celestine had taken full advantage of Dorothea's age and figure and the bodice was cut
low, while the waistline had been subtly altered to emphasise
her tiny waist and the swell of her hips. On entering the Merion House drawing-room, Hazelmere, setting eyes on her,
knew he was justified in anticipating trouble at Carlton House.

It took no more than ten minutes to drive the short distance
to the Prince Regent's London residence, but, owing to the
crowds, it was nearly an hour before they reached the head of
the stairs and heard their names announced as they entered the
ballroom. As His Highness was convinced that he had a particular susceptibility to colds and chills, the rooms were already overheated. Dorothea was glad she had not brought a
shawl. Hazelmere, glancing down at her as she walked by his
side, uncharacteristically wished she had.

With Fanshawe escorting Cecily and Lady Merion on Ferdie's arm, they strolled down the ballroom, stopping to chat
to acquaintances and friends. They had agreed that the safest
place for the Misses Darent to make their curtsy to the Prince
Regent was where the élite of the ton usually congregated.
Lady Jersey and the other patronesses of Almack's would be
there, as would most of their lordships' close acquaintances.
In such august company, the chances of His Highness issuing
one of his unwelcome commands was considerably reduced.

They had reached this position and were busy greeting their
friends when a general stir running through the crowd announced the entrance of the Prince Regent. As the now portly
Prince, accompanied by two of his confidants, strolled down
the ballroom the assembled ranks of gentlemen bowed and the

ladies sank into the deepest of curtsies. This movement passed like a wave down the long room, arrested every now and again as His Highness paused to exchange a word with one of the favoured or, more frequently, to ogle a beautiful woman. Viewing this behaviour as her Prince approached, Dorothea thought it hardly appropriate for one of his years and position. In this, the majority of those around her agreed.

As the wave of curtsying ladies reached her, and the débutante to her left sank down, Dorothea did likewise, bowing her head as she had been taught. She was supposed to maintain this pose until His Highness had passed. While she waited, frozen into immobility, she realised that his feet, the only part of him within her range of vision, gaudily clad in bright red ballroom pumps with huge gold buckles, had stopped a short distance away. Risking an upward glance through her lashes, she discovered the Prince's protuberant pale blue eyes fixed on her. He smiled archly and came to take her hand and raise her to her feet.

As the others around her abandoned their obsequious stances she was aware of Hazelmere close behind her in the crush, a little way to her right, his hand now resting lightly at her waist. Mrs Drummond-Burrell moved slightly on her left. This movement, almost imperceptible though it was, distracted the Prince, who then became aware of those around her. She watched as the distinctly lecherous look faded, and then disappeared altogether, as His Highness's gaze met Hazelmere's over her right shoulder.

The Prince inwardly cursed. He had been informed that the most attractive débutante this year was Miss Darent, but that to suggest she might like to entertain him in private would be unwise, as she was considered by the ton to be virtually affianced to the Marquis of Hazelmere. While there were some among the peers he could ignore, Hazelmere was not one of them. But, seeing the luscious dark-haired beauty curtsying to him, he had entirely forgotten the warning until recalled to his surroundings by the censorious eyes of Mrs Drummond-Burrell and then Hazelmere's cool gaze. So, instead of what he had been going to say, he smiled in quite a different way, almost charmingly, and said, 'You are really very beautiful, my dear.' With a nod, he released her hand and, still smiling, moved on.

Dorothea sensed the almost palpable relief around her. As the Prince continued along the ballroom and the ranks of his subjects broke up she turned to Hazelmere and, not knowing how to phrase the question, raised her enquiring eyes to his.

'Yes, that was it,' he assented, smiling as he drew her hand through his arm. 'You did very well, my love.'

Ignoring provocation she knew to be deliberate, she asked, 'Why didn't you tell me he could be so…well, like that?'

'Because one can never tell if he will be.'

'Is that why I was with you and not with Grandmama?'

'His Highness is occasionally misguided enough to make… suggestions, which in your case would be totally inappropriate.'

'I see. And he would not do so while you were about but might well have done if I had been with Grandmama only?'

Hazelmere, who would have much preferred she had not realised that, merely nodded. He knew it would not be long before she deduced the reason that his presence had protected her from the Prince's importunities. After one glance at her pensive face he headed for the area of the huge ballroom given over to dancing.

At Carlton House the social rules that applied everywhere else did not hold sway. The principal ladies of the ton deplored the licence permitted under the Prince Regent's influence. Previously Hazelmere had found these lax standards very useful. Now he was concerned that Dorothea was not unknowingly led into difficulties through her innocence of just what was possible at Carlton House.

Reaching the dance-floor and hearing the musicians strike up, without a word he drew her into his arms and into the waltz. There were no dance cards at Carlton House and the waltz was the only dance permitted. She had not spoken again. Hazelmere, wishing that Carlton House had a deserted orangery, felt how stiff and distant she was as they glided down the floor. But as they progressed, in spite of herself, she relaxed into his familiar arms. He saw that they had attracted the attention of a number of gentlemen not normally present at any of the ton gatherings and determined to return her to Lady Merion immediately the dance ended. Looking down at her calm face, he realised with a jolt that he had no idea what she was thinking. She was normally so completely frank with him that it had not occurred to him that she could withdraw so entirely. Uncertain what to do for once in his life, he remained silent.

As the dance ended he raised her hand to his lips, bringing a familiar green spark to her enormous eyes. Smiling down at her, he drew her hand through his arm and led her to find Lady Merion. Relinquishing her to her grandmother with real regret, he was relieved to see Alvanley claim her for the next dance. To be overly attentive would only exacerbate her mood, so he resigned himself to not dancing with her again and drifted off in search of his friends.

Dorothea was in a state of utter confusion, which having to make a pretence of polite conversation did nothing to help. As the weeks of the Season had passed she had come to accept that she and Hazelmere would, in time, perhaps later in the Season, come to an understanding—a mutually agreed understanding. But now it appeared she was to have no say in the matter at all! Everyone already knew she would marry Hazelmere. Even the Prince Regent knew!

The sensation of being an entirely helpless puppet with Hazelmere pulling the strings fuelled her anger. While she had been falling desperately in love with him, worrying over whether or not he loved her, he had somehow convinced the world that she was his. How *dared* he take her so much for granted?

She fumed inwardly, her temper simmering, denied the natural outlet of confronting him in person. She spent three waltzes entirely consumed with plotting what she would say to him on the morrow. He would be made to realise that she was no milk-and-water miss to be manipulated to suit his convenience!

Dancing with one after another of his friends, all of whom,

she now realised, treated her as they would a friend's wife, did nothing to improve her temper. None of her partners guessed her true state; her composure was complete, her serenity convincing. It was, therefore, with an air of dangerous resklessness that she viewed the debonair Frenchman bowing before her and begging the pleasure of the next waltz. She had just been returned to her grandmama by Lord Desborough, who had moved away into the still considerable crowd.

With Lady Merion's consent she allowed the Comte de Vanée to lead her on to the floor. He had, so he informed her, only recently arrived from Paris. As he expertly guided her through the other dancers the Comte kept up a flow of general conversation, to which Dorothea paid little heed. Until she heard him mention Hazelmere's name.

Without hesitation she broke into his discourse. 'I'm so sorry, Comte, I'm afraid I didn't catch what you just said.'

'Ah, *mademoiselle*, I was only saying it is so like the Marquis to secure the most beautiful women as his mistresses— the lovely Lady Walford, for instance, whom you can see over there, talking with his lordship.'

Dorothea glanced where he indicated and glimpsed Hazelmere deep in conversation with Lady Walford, his dark head bent close to her fair one, listening intently. Even to her inexperienced eye, the pose argued a degree of familiarity. Feeling her heart literally descend to her slippers, she required every ounce of her well-practised poise to meet the Comte's eyes with her habitual calm. But that young man had felt her stiffen when she had seen Hazelmere and Lady Walford and was more than satisfied with his success. Too wise to belabour the point, he continued in his light-hearted recitation of ton affairs.

Unknown to the Comte, his words plunged Dorothea even deeper into misery than he could have hoped. If she was confused before, she was now utterly wretched. The sole vision in her tormented mind was of Hazelmere in intimate converse with Lady Walford. All the rest seemed to sink beneath a miasma of pain.

On the previous Sunday, before her departure for Darent

Hall, Marjorie Darent had sought a private interview with Dorothea, in order, as she saw it, to do her duty. 'As Herbert is your guardian and I am his wife,' she had carefully begun, 'I feel it is my duty to tell you it's common knowledge that Lord Hazelmere is trifling with your affections. I've been told he has acted in exactly this manner with many other susceptible young ladies. I regret to say, your resistance to his charm is most likely the attraction that draws him to your side. Neither Herbert nor I would wish to criticise your grandmama, but we are deeply pained to see you in the toils of such a man.'

Dorothea had listened with a patience born of her certainty that none of it was true. Marjorie had no idea how Hazelmere behaved towards her. And there was no chance that Lady Merion would blindly permit his attentions were these other than honourable.

Marjorie had gone on to enumerate his lordship's many failings—gambling, racing, addiction to boxing and other low forms of sport, finally coming to the point of her visit. 'It is my distressing duty to speak plainly to you, my dear. Lady Merion likely feels such subjects should not sully the ears of innocent maids, but, in the circumstances, it is right you should know. Forewarned, after all, is forearmed!'

Dorothea's lively imagination had run riot at this juncture. She was agog to learn what secret life Marjorie had invented for his lordship. The explanation, when it had come, was so mundane that she had almost giggled.

'My dear, the man is a rake! A very highly born rake, I'll agree. But a rake none the less! Why, the stories I've heard of his mistresses, many of them as well born as you or I, and all of them the most ravishing creatures. As you are yourself, my dear.'

The insinuation that Marjorie had managed to infuse into this last statement had nearly overset Dorothea. The idea of Hazelmere offering her a *carte blanche* was so ridiculous that she had had to take a deep breath to stop herself from laughing aloud and ruining her pose of polite attention. As it was, Marjorie had taken the indrawn breath to signify shock at his lordship's perfidy.

Her cousin had concluded by stating that neither Herbert nor she would countenance any further communication with the Marquis. Dorothea had managed to keep her temper by reminding herself it was her grandmother, not Marjorie, who had charge of her in London.

After Marjorie had left Dorothea had put her warnings entirely from her mind as the ludicrous imaginings she had been sure they were. But now that it seemed as if one, at least, of her cousin's facts was not wrong she was forced to question whether she really knew Hazelmere at all.

She had assumed there had been many women in his past—he could hardly have attained his undoubted experience of her sex without practice. But she had imagined these women were of the *demi-monde* and, furthermore, definitely in his past and not cluttering up his present life. Lady Walford, however, belonged to the ton, and she was obviously part of Hazelmere's present.

Dorothea heard not a single word of the rest of the Comte's conversation. Just before the dance ended she noticed Cecily dancing with Fanshawe. From her sparkling eyes, Dorothea concluded that they had made up their differences. Fanshawe, catching a glimpse of her through the throng, looked surprised, but they were immediately separated by the movement of the dance, so Dorothea failed to see what had excited his attention. At the end of the dance the Comte punctiliously delivered her to her grandmother and immediately took his leave of them, disappearing into the crowds. His departure was rapid because he, too, had seen Fanshawe's surprised look and, unlike Dorothea, knew the cause.

As the Comte could have predicted, it was not many minutes before Hazelmere materialised at her elbow. Immediately noticing her drawn face, he forebore to ask what the matter was, instead suggesting to Lady Merion that they could with impunity leave the ball, as the Prince had retired. Her ladyship, disliking the tone of the entertainment, readily agreed. As Fanshawe and Cecily reappeared at that moment, it only remained to find Ferdie before they could leave. This was easily accomplished, and the party departed Carlton House.

Seated opposite Dorothea in the carriage, Hazelmere desperately sought for a clue to what had so agitated her. Tony had told him that she had danced with one of the French diplomatic staff, a man of questionable standing. But it seemed unlikely that anything he could have said would have so overset her. He sensed that under her outward calm she was close to tears, but he had no idea why. Knowing he would get no chance to ask her directly, and so could not comfort her, only added to his frustration.

The carriage drew up outside Merion House and the ladies were escorted within. Ferdie left on foot and, sending the carriage on, Hazelmere and Fanshawe walked across the square. For more than half the distance Fanshawe kept up a rapturous monologue on the delights of love. He had made good use of Dorothea's advice, borrowing some of Hazelmere's arrogance to lend it weight, and it had been most successful.

Realising that Hazelmere was not responding and catching sight of his friend's serious face, Fanshawe exclaimed, 'Don't tell me you two have fallen out?'

Hazelmere grinned at the tone. 'To be perfectly truthful, I don't know whether we have or not.'

'Great heavens! You're worse than us!'

'Unfortunately true.'

'Well,' continued Fanshawe, 'why don't you just use Dorothea's advice on herself?'

'I have been reliably informed that firm handling will not work with the elder Miss Darent,' replied Hazelmere with the ghost of a smile.

'Which means very likely it will,' rejoined Fanshawe, still in exuberant vein.

'As a matter of fact, you speak more truly than you know,' returned Hazelmere as they parted on the steps of Hazelmere House.

Not as observant as Hazelmere, neither Lady Merion nor Cecily noticed the strained look in Dorothea's eyes. Her ladyship retired to bed with a headache, and Cecily was so bubbling over with her own happiness that for once her sister's pallor escaped her sharp eyes. To Dorothea's relief, she was able to retire to her bed without having to answer any difficult questions.

She lay staring at the window for what felt like hours. Her heart would not accept what her mind knew to be fact. While Hazelmere had been dancing attendance on her, making her lose her heart with his easy address and gentle caresses and those *wicked* hazel eyes, he had been simultaneously enjoying a far more illicit relationship with the beautiful Lady Walford. And what was more, she thought, wallowing in misery, that meant he was not in love with her at all.

It had taken her a long time to sort it out, but now, at last, she had it clear: Hazelmere had to marry, so he had decided she would do. Not the icily uncomfortable Miss Buntton, but a naïve country miss, not at home in the ton, someone who would be a sweet, conformable, entirely acceptable and totally manipulable wife, providing him with heirs and presiding over his household while he continued as he always had, enjoying the more exotic delights provided by the likes of Lady Walford. And, most likely, her apparent indifference was the lure that had drawn his eye. She was a challenge and a convenient conquest, all rolled into one.

For the first time since she had come to London she thought longingly of the Grange, where life had been so much simpler. No having to deal with imperious peers with beautiful mistresses who made one fall in love with them for entirely selfish reasons. It was close to dawn before she finally drifted into troubled sleep.

On entering his house, Hazelmere went into the library and, pouring himself a large brandy, settled down to stare into the dying fire.

When he had decided to wait until later in the Season before asking for Dorothea's hand he had not envisaged the current tangle of their affairs. He still had no clue what had gone wrong tonight and had no right to ask for an explanation. And, while previously she might have given him one, tonight she had realised how public he had made their relationship. She had not been pleased. God only knew what she would say if she learned that an announcement of their marriage was considered imminent! He grinned as he imagined her fury. Still, he could not regret his manipulation. After his behaviour in Moreton Park woods and at that blasted inn she would never have believed he was meek and malleable. If he had let her have her head in the matter of choosing her own husband she would undoubtedly have landed herself with some boring slowtop, too dimwitted to exercise any control over her. And she certainly needed someone to control her, to watch over her, to care for and cherish her—he shuddered to think what trouble she would have landed herself in had he not been there, time and again, to rescue her. Half the time she had not even recognised danger when she saw it. Such as in him.

That still surprised him. She certainly recognised the danger in Peterborough and Walsingham. But never, from that first moment in Moreton Park woods when he'd held her and kissed her as she'd never been kissed before, had she shown the slightest consciousness of danger in his company. Another one of her odd quirks, but one for which he was profoundly thankful.

He suspected that her dislike of his authoritarian ways stemmed from her habit of getting her own way in most things and of being able to manipulate people like Cecily, Lady Merion and Ferdie into doing much as she wished. Her refusal to attempt to wring from him the explanation for his presence at Merion House earlier in the evening suggested that she recognised the futility in cajoling or trying to manipulate him. Which was just as well. He had no intention of ever allowing her to do so. Still, he thought, a smile hovering at the corners of his mouth, he had no objection to her trying.

With a sigh he doggedly drew his mind back to his present problems. She had withdrawn from him and while, in normal circumstances, he would not have doubted his ability to bring her around, there were too many unexplained incidents occurring for him to feel easy. He glanced towards his desk, where the two mysterious notes lay in a drawer. There was someone else playing this hand and as yet he did not know who it was.

There was only one possible course of action. His steward on his Leicestershire estate was begging for his attendance. In travelling there, he would pass through Northamptonshire, not far from Darent Hall. Rapidly reviewing his engagements, he remembered a luncheon on the morrow. Very well, he would leave later in the day for Leicestershire and call in on horrible Herbert on the way back. Then, he supposed, he really should tell his mother, which meant an evening spent at Hazelmere. Seven days in all. He would be back in London by Tuesday next.

He did not like to leave her, but as he had no idea if any further attempt on her would be made, it would be wiser to solve the potential problem by marrying her as soon as possible. Abducting the Marchioness of Hazelmere would be a far more difficult task than abducting Miss Darent. In fact, he would make sure it was entirely impossible. He tossed off the last of the brandy and went to bed.

Comfortably settled between his silken sheets, he listened to Murgatroyd's footsteps die away down the hall. Their interlude in the Richmond House orangery had left no room for doubt of her feelings for him. And in her subsequent actions she had, albeit unwittingly, confirmed his hopes. She loved him. Beneath his frustration, that knowledge ran like a heady pulse, a constant source of joy and wonder. And from it had been born the patience to see the game through, to let her have her Season of independence before he claimed her. Aside from any other consideration, he had enjoyed her spirited resistance, her attempts, becoming less and less successful with time, to conceal her response to him. He sighed. For good or ill, her time had run out. Tuesday next would see the end of the game. And the start of so much more.

He stretched, conscious of the tenseness lying just beneath the surface. He should never have kissed her. Now every time he saw her he was shaken by an urgent desire to do it again. And every time he gave way to the impulse he was increasingly aware of an even more urgent desire to take her to bed.

The warmth of her hair, her smooth skin, the sweetness of her lips and, more than anything else, those tantalising green eyes had all become so strongly evocative that, for the first time in his considerable experience, his desire was no longer subject to his control. Aside from anything else, marrying her soon would end the torture. He slid himself into a more comfortable position and, thinking of emerald eyes, lost touch with reality.

CHAPTER ELEVEN

Next morning Lady Merion remained in bed, unwell after the stuffy atmosphere of Carlton House. Dorothea, unrefreshed by her troubled sleep, went to enquire after her health. Her ladyship immediately noticed the dark rings under her granddaughter's large eyes and insisted she remain in bed for the rest of the morning. Sure that if she rode in the Park this morning she would meet Hazelmere, and feeling that normal conversation with him was as yet beyond her, Dorothea agreed.

Cecily was undisturbed by the change in plans, as she had arranged to go driving with Fanshawe that afternoon. She wrote to Ferdie to cancel their morning engagement and, at Dorothea's suggestion, asked him to escort her sister for a ride that afternoon.

When the afternoon came Ferdie and Dorothea duly set off for the Park. Ferdie, not generally observant, noticed that Dorothea was not her normal self. Thinking to distract her, he rattled on about the Carlton House ball and the Prince Regent's set, and anything else that came into his head. Understanding his benign impulse, Dorothea tried to put on a happier face and to ignore the fact that he, too, seemed to consider her virtually betrothed to Hazelmere.

They had entered the Park and were ambling along the grass verge of the carriageway when, glancing ahead, she suddenly stopped. Breathlessly she cut into Ferdie's description of Lady Hanover's new wig. 'Ferdie, I want to gallop over to those trees. I think there are freesias growing there.'

Precipitately she set the bay mare cantering towards a stand of oak to their left. Ferdie, taken by surprise, turned his own horse to follow. As he did so his gaze alighted on an approaching carriage. It was Hazelmere's curricle, the Marquis driving his greys with Helen Walford beside him. The brief glimpse of his cousin's face before his horse moved off was quite sufficient to tell Ferdie that Hazelmere had seen Dorothea's sudden departure. The appalling fact that Dorothea had knowingly cut his cousin in the middle of the Park dawned on a horrified Ferdie.

'What on *earth* do you think you're doing?' he demanded as he came up with her by the trees. 'That was *Hazelmere*!'

'Yes, I know, Ferdie,' replied Dorothea, contrite as she realised that he was really distressed.

'Well, I'll be hanged if I know what you're up to,' he continued, 'but I can tell you that cutting people like Hazelmere in the middle of the Park is not the thing at all!'

'Yes, Ferdie. I'd like to go home now, please.'

'I should dashed well think so!' he exclaimed, knowing that Hazelmere would shortly be following them.

On the way back to Cavendish Square Ferdie tried to impress upon Dorothea the magnitude of her sin. Not knowing what had caused her to behave in such an extraordinary way, he felt that if he could induce her to behave with something like contrition when she shortly faced his cousin she might stand a better chance of surviving the ordeal. Ferdie knew, as few others did, that, while Hazelmere appeared to have the easiest of tempers, this was a fiction. The Marquis of Hazelmere had a very definite temper; he just did not lose it often.

Ferdie did not know that Dorothea was already acquainted with Hazelmere's temper. Seeing him driving his greys with the lovely Lady Walford by his side, she simply could not bear to stay and politely exchange pleasantries with them. Although she knew she had behaved badly and Hazelmere had every right to be angry, she, too, was decidedly aggrieved and was almost looking forward to an interview with his lordship. Luckily Ferdie had no idea of her thoughts—that anyone could look forward to an interview with Hazelmere in a rage was far too bizarre a concept for him to have understood.

Reaching Merion House, Ferdie escorted her indoors, past

the interested Mellow and into the drawing-room. There he got a glimmer of the underlying story. Dorothea, pacing about the room like a caged tigress, seemed to the distracted Ferdie to be more incensed than contrite.

'How *dare* he approach me while driving that woman?' she finally burst out.

Ferdie stared. 'What's wrong with driving Helen Walford?' he asked, fearing that her reason must be slipping.

'But surely you know? She's his mistress!'

'*What*?' Ferdie positively goggled. 'No! You've got that wrong! Very sure she's not Marc's mistress.'

Remembering his connection with Hazelmere, Dorothea paid no attention to him, convinced that he would take his cousin's side in any argument.

An imperious knock fell on the street door. Ferdie, glancing out of the window, saw Hazelmere's curricle standing outside.

Seeing Dorothea pointedly move away from the carriage-way, Hazelmere was thunderstruck. What the *devil* was she about, behaving like that to him? Too well attuned to his whereabouts to allow his entirely understandable rage to be evident, it was nevertheless some minutes before he could trust his voice to ask Helen Walford, 'My dear Helen, do you mind if I return you to your friends? I'm departing for Leicestershire shortly and I believe I've some unfinished business to attend to.'

Lady Walford was well acquainted with Hazelmere's temper, as she had often, in her childhood, been the cause of it. Looking into the hazel eyes, normally warm and amused, and finding them as cold and cloudy as agate, she merely smiled her agreement. She hoped Miss Darent had more backbone than the normal run of débutantes, for she was undoubtedly in for a most uncomfortable interview. The fact that Hazelmere was head over heels in love with her would not, as might be supposed, help her at all. Like all the Henrys, he possessed an unexpected puritanical streak which would lead him to demand of his wife-to-be a far higher standard of conduct than

he might tolerate in less favoured ladies. Consequently she
feared that his Dorothea was in for a particularly torrid time.

Having set Lady Walford down amid her friends, Hazelmere
drove immediately to Merion House. Arriving there, without
a word he threw the reins of his curricle to a bright-faced
urchin and strode up the steps to the door.

Admitted to the house by an intrigued Mellow, he merely
asked, in a deceptively gentle voice, 'Where is Miss Darent,
Mellow?'

'In the drawing-room, my lord.'

'Thank you. You need not announce me.'

He strolled across the hall and opened the drawing-room
door. Setting eyes on Ferdie, he smiled in a way that made
Ferdie decide to do whatever he wished. Holding the door
open, Hazelmere said, 'I believe you were leaving, Ferdie.'

There was no doubt about the command, but Ferdie, recognising the hardness in the hazel eyes, was having second
thoughts about the wisdom of leaving these two together. But
as he glanced at Dorothea his decision was unexpectedly taken
out of his hands. 'Goodbye, Ferdie,' she said.

So Ferdie went. He discarded the idea of telling his cousin
that Dorothea seemed to think Helen Walford was his mistress.
In his opinion, if anyone was going to talk to Hazelmere about
his mistresses it had better be Dorothea herself. Hearing the
drawing-room door shut with a click behind him, he decided
it might be wise to inform Lady Merion of the reason for, and
the likely outcome of, the interview being presently conducted
in her drawing-room.

Returning to the hall some five minutes later, having explained the situation as fully as he could to Lady Merion upstairs, he found the drawing-room door still shut. Viewing this
with misgiving, he departed for his lodgings.

After shutting the door behind Ferdie, Hazelmere moved
into the room. 'Very wise of you, my dear. There's no need
for Ferdie to get caught up in this.'

He paused to strip off his driving gloves and cast them on
a side-table. One glance at Dorothea, standing beside one of

the wing chairs by the fireplace, her hand clutching its back, informed him that she was every bit as angry as he was. He had no idea why, but the knowledge served to make him rein in his temper sufficiently to ask, in a relatively calm voice, 'Do you think you could possibly explain to me why you cut me in the Park?'

Despite the calmness, the undertones succeeded in igniting her smouldering temper. 'How *dare* you approach me while driving that woman?'

Looking into her furious green eyes, Hazelmere felt, like Ferdie before him, that he had lost the thread of the conversation. 'Helen?' he asked, mystified.

'Your mistress!' she replied scathingly.

'*My what*?' The words came like a whiplash, and Dorothea winced. Even angrier than before, Hazelmere moved to within a few feet of her, everything about him radiating barely leashed fury. Eyes narrowed, he asked, his voice deceptively soft, 'Who told you Helen Walford was my mistress?'

'I don't think that need concern you—'

'You mistake,' he broke in. 'It concerns me because Helen Walford has never been, is not and never will be my mistress. So who, my credulous Miss Darent, told you she was?'

Looking into the stormy hazel eyes, Dorothea knew she was hearing the truth. 'The Comte de Vanée,' she finally replied.

'A man of little importance,' he said dismissively. 'It may interest you to know that I have known Helen Walford since she was three. However,' he continued, moving forward so that he was standing directly beside her, forcing her to turn from the chair that up until then had been between them, 'that aside, you have still not explained why, regardless of what you might have thought, you presumed to censure me in such a public manner.'

Although his voice was low and even, Dorothea could not miss the suppressed anger. She knew she had been in the wrong, but his next words banished any notion of apologising.

'I've told you provincial manners will not do in London,' he continued. But there he stopped, for she rounded on him with such naked rage in her eyes that he was taken aback.

'How *dare* you speak to me of manners? Explain yours, if you can! I know you've been dancing attendance on me purely to see if you could make me fall in love with you, just because I didn't succumb to your legendary charm. Oh, Cousin Marjorie explained it all, so—'

That was as far as she got. Hazelmere paled as her words struck him. But as he caught the gist of her argument the already frayed rein he had kept on his passions snapped. In one swift, practised movement he swept her into his arms and his lips came down on hers in a kiss almost brutal in its intensity. Panicked, she struggled, but, as before, his fingers entwined in her hair, holding her head still, while the arm around her tightened, locking her in his embrace. And then, in the space of time between one heartbeat and the next, the tenor of the kiss changed to one of unbelievable sweetness. Her interest caught, her lips parted in response to his subtle command and she found herself floating in a sea of sensation. Dazed, she felt desire flooding through her, growing stronger with every second, rapidly building to a force she, in her inexperience, had no hope of restraining. She realised that she was responding in the most shameless way to his ardent kisses. She no longer cared. The only thought in her disjointed mind was the hope that he wouldn't stop.

His lips left hers to brush kisses on her upturned face, on her forehead, her eyelids, her chin and her delectable white throat. Recapturing her reddened lips, he gently explored the sweet softness within. She moaned, the sound an audible caress, her arms slipping around his neck, her fingers twisting in his dark hair as she held him to her. Inwardly smiling, he allowed the kiss to deepen, fanning the racing flames of her desire until they coalesced into a conflagration that threatened to consume them both. Then, reaching to the depths of a passionate nature that in every way matched his own, he demanded, and received, a surrender so complete and unequivocal that he knew beyond doubt she would be his, body and soul, whenever he so desired. Entirely satisfied, he drew her closer, moulding her body to his, allowing her to feel the extent of his desire for her.

Dorothea was nearly mindless. Some tiny part of her consciousness was detached enough to be shocked and horrified,
dismayed as his experienced hands roamed over her, his practised caresses sending ripples of desire from the top of her
head to her toes. The rest of her was in no mood to listen.
She supposed he would have to stop some time—but oh, she
would enjoy this while it lasted! Still, surely not even Hazelmere would seduce her in her grandmother's drawing-room?
Would he?

The tremor that ran through her jolted him to his senses.
He would have to leave her, and soon, if he was to leave her
at all. And, as they were in Merion House and not one of his
establishments, leave her he must. If he looked into her eyes
he would not be able to go. And at the moment he was in no
mood to talk to her. He needed time away from her to sort
out what had happened—right now he wasn't sure of anything
other than his physical need for her. And that required no
words to describe. He knew they had passed the point of easy
withdrawal; there was no gentle way to stop now. So, abruptly
bringing the kiss to an end, he released her and, disentangling
her hands from his hair, put her from him almost roughly,
before, turning brusquely, he walked straight to the door, picking up his gloves on the way, and, opening the door, left the
room.

In the hall he encountered Mellow. As his face had assumed
its normal mien and his hair was cut in a style that disguised
Dorothea's rumpling, Mellow assumed that there had been no
major fireworks. He hurried to open the door for his lordship.

Leaving the house, Hazelmere headed across the square to
his own mansion. While an observer unfamiliar with him
would have detected nothing amiss, he was experiencing a
degree of mental turmoil that effectively prevented him from
thinking clearly. Anger, frustration, hurt pride and a peculiar
sense of elation were only some of the emotions running riot
in his mind. He would have to leave, get out of London, before
his fevered brain would cool sufficiently to accurately assess
just where they now stood. Entering Hazelmere House and
seeing Mytton come forward from behind the green baize

door, he paused at the foot of the stairs. 'I've decided to leave for Leicestershire immediately. I expect to return on Tuesday next. Send Murgatroyd up to me and tell Jim to put the bays to and have the curricle at the front door in ten minutes.'

'Yes, m'lord,' replied Mytton, who, acquainted with the Marquis since that gentleman's childhood, returned immediately to the servants' hall to inform the household of his lordship's orders, adding that their master was in the devil's own temper. Without further discussion they all sped to their tasks, Murgatroyd almost running up the stairs.

Standing before the mirror to remove the diamond pin in his cravat, Hazelmere suddenly turned to his valet, hurriedly packing. 'Murgatroyd, see if you can catch Jim before he leaves the house. Tell him I've left the curricle outside Merion House. If he's already left for the mews you'd better send one of the footmen after him and come back to me.'

After one stunned moment Murgatroyd was out of the door and down the stairs as fast as dignity would allow. Hazelmere ruefully surveyed his own reflection. If his servants had not already realised the cause of his present mood, the fact that he had walked away and left his greys outside Merion House would doubtless clarify the issue.

Murgatroyd reached the servants' hall just as Jim, attired in the Hazelmere livery, was preparing to leave. Hearing his message, the entire population of the servants' hall simply stared. Then all those with any legitimate claim to be in the front of the house headed for the street door. Opening it and looking across the square to Merion House, Mytton, Jim, Murgatroyd and Charles gazed in silent awe at the curricle.

'My gawd! I'd never've believed it if I hadn't seen it for myself,' said Jim.

With much shaking of heads, they all resumed their activities, Jim crossing the square to retrieve the precious greys and Murgatroyd hurrying upstairs to inform his lordship that the carriage was being prepared.

In the end, Jim had to walk the bays for five minutes before his master appeared. On his way downstairs Hazelmere recalled the one player in the game who did not know where he

was going but should. He went into the library. His eye
alighted on a pile of correspondence, delivered that afternoon.
He flicked through the envelopes, leaving most unopened. His
attention was caught by a plain envelope of poor quality, addressed in a strong hand to 'Mr M. Henry'. Opening it, he
scanned the enclosed pages. When his eyes lifted he remained
standing, gazing at nothing, his long fingers beating a thoughtful tattoo on the desk-top. Then, with a frown, he crammed
the letter into his coat pocket and sat to compose a suitably
informative note to Ferdie. This was not easy. He still could
not concentrate properly, particularly when reviewing that interview at Merion House. Finally he wrote a simple set of
statements, informing Ferdie that he had to leave for Leicestershire on estate business and would be back in London on
Tuesday next, that Tony knew this, that he and Tony had
informed their close friends of the attempts on Dorothea over
lunch that day and they would assist in keeping an eye on her.
He ended with a simple request to Ferdie to look after Dorothea for him.

Signing this epistle, he bethought himself of one last item.
Raising his pen, he added a postscript. He would much prefer
if Ferdie could manage not to tell Dorothea of their fears for
her safety. Smiling ruefully, he fixed his seal to the letter and
rang for a footman. He did not have much confidence in Ferdie's ability to distract Dorothea once she became suspicious,
as she undoubtedly would long before he returned. Handing
the letter over with instructions that it be delivered to Mr Ache-
eson-Smythe's lodgings immediately, he strode out of his
house to the waiting curricle.

Released from that passionate embrace, Dorothea stood by
the chair, too stunned to move. Hearing the front door shut,
she put her fingers to her bruised lips. Her eyes slowly refocused. Then, drawing a shuddering breath, she went to the
door, opened it and, without even noticing Mellow, went up
the stairs to her chamber.

Lady Merion, hearing her footsteps, came out of the morning-room. Five minutes after Ferdie had left her she had come

downstairs. There was, she had felt, a limit to how long she could leave Dorothea alone with Hazelmere. All had been silent in the drawing-room. Taking a deep breath and waving Mellow away, she had opened the door. Seeing Dorothea locked in Hazelmere's arms, she had immediately closed it again. With a decidedly pensive expression, she had informed Mellow that she would sit in the morning-room and if anyone should call he was to show them in there. Now, glimpsing the retreating figure at the top of the stairs, she sighed. With a resigned air she rang for tea.

Despite her ignorance of the details of the recently conducted interview, she thought Dorothea would need at least half an hour to cry herself out. Far too wise to try to talk sense to a young lady in the first flush of tears, she calmly reviewed what she knew of the afternoon's events. None of it made a great deal of sense. She would have to extract sufficient details before she could begin to understand what it was about; she was too old to leap to conclusions.

Finishing her tea, she went purposefully upstairs.

Reaching her bedchamber, Dorothea shut the door, threw herself on her bed and gave way to her tears. For the first time in years she wept unrestrainedly, a mixture of relief, bewilderment and pent-up emotions pouring from her, disappointment and a barely recognised frustration lending their bitter flavour to her woe. For ten minutes the storm continued unabated. Finally, through exhaustion, the whirling kaleidoscope that was her mind slowed down and the racking sobs died. She was propped up against her pillows, dabbing ineffectually at her brimming eyes with a sodden handkerchief, when her grandmother knocked and entered.

Seeing her normally calm and collected granddaughter in the shadows of the bed, her large eyes enormous and swimming in unshed tears, Hermione walked over and plumped herself down on the end of the bed. Dorothea gulped and whispered, 'Oh, Grandmama, what am I to do?'

Recognising her cue, Lady Merion responded briskly. 'The first thing you'll do, my dear, is to wash your face and get yourself a fresh handkerchief. Go on, now. You'll feel a great deal better.' As Dorothea rose she continued, 'And after that I think we'll have a long talk. It's time you explained to me just what you and Hazelmere have been about.'

At that, Dorothea's green eyes returned to her grandmother's face, but she made no comment. While she washed and dried her face, and then ransacked her dressing-table for a clean handkerchief, the capacity for rational thought returned. Her grandmother undoubtedly deserved an explanation. But there were so many questions still unanswered. Pensive, she returned to her seat on the bed.

Lady Merion opened the conversation with a simple request to be told all about it.

Dorothea grimaced, then drew a deep breath and plunged in. 'Last night, at the ball, the Prince...well, it was obvious he believed...knew, that...there is...a...connection between myself and Lord Hazelmere. I realise, now, that most people know that some sort of...understanding exists between us.'

'After that first waltz at your come-out, I should think they would!' snorted Lady Merion.

'Waltz?' echoed Dorothea in confusion. 'What do you mean?'

Lady Merion sighed. 'I didn't think you knew.' She eyed her granddaughter shrewdly, then said, 'Over the past weeks your feelings for Marc Henry have been becoming daily more visible. Oh, I don't mean you wear your heart on your sleeve! Far from it. But no one, seeing the two of you together, could doubt your interest in him. And, given his attentiveness since the start of the Season, his intentions have been quite clear. Why, after your ball, he told me he would offer for you. In his own good time, he said. Just like him, of course.'

Dorothea listened to her grandmother's explanation, comprehension dawning. It occurred to her that she could do a great deal worse than to appeal to her experienced grandparent for further clarification. 'Actually,' she said, 'I wondered whether he was...well, merely looking for a suitable bride. He must marry. I gather his family have been badgering him for years to do so.' Resolutely she drew a deep breath and brought forth her most secret fear. 'When he met me in Moreton Park woods I think he got the idea from something I said that I had no expectations of marrying. And when I didn't behave like all the others I thought maybe he felt I would do.' She paused, gathering strength to continue. 'I wondered if he thought that, as I didn't have any great hopes of marriage, I'd be happy to enter into...I suppose the correct phrase is "a marriage of convenience", which would leave him free to continue with his mistresses as before.'

Lady Merion's face went blank. Then she threw back her head and laughed. When she could command her voice she said, 'Well! I'm glad Hazelmere's carefully orchestrated wooing has got the result it deserved.'

Bemused, Dorothea looked at her expectantly, but her grandmother waved aside the unspoken question. 'My dear Dorothea, I came into the drawing-room this afternoon while you and Hazelmere were...somewhat engaged. In my experience, a man contemplating a *mariage de convenance* does not set out to seduce his prospective bride before proposing.' A grin of unholy amusement still lit her ladyship's sharp face. 'After the way Hazelmere's been behaving over you, my dear, I should think you must be the last person in the ton to realise he's in love with you.'

'Oh.' Hope and a sneaking suspicion that it was all too good to be true warred in Dorothea's breast. Hope won, but the suspicion was not entirely vanquished.

Lady Merion broke in on her thoughts. 'Ferdie mentioned some misunderstanding over Helen Walford.'

'The Comte de Vanée told me she was Hazelmere's mistress. He denied it.'

Lady Merion almost groaned aloud. She closed her eyes. Finally opening them, she asked, her tone resigned, 'You asked him, I suppose?'

'Well, he wanted to know why I cut him in the Park,' said Dorothea, rapidly regaining her normal equilibrium. 'He said he'd known her since she was a child.'

'So he has. Helen Walford's father is a distant connection of Lady Hazelmere and, as a child, Helen often spent her sum-

mers at Hazelmere. In age she is some years younger than
Ferdie. She was something of a tomboy, and she often plagued
Marc and Tony, who treated her much as they treated Alison.
As I recall, they were always hauling her out of some scrape
or other, and with no very good grace, I can tell you!

'Helen unfortunately made a most unsuitable marriage. Arthur Walford was a rake and a gamester. He killed himself,
much to the relief of everyone. No one knows the full story,
but Hazelmere was involved. Helen once asked him how her
husband died. He told her she didn't need to know but should
content herself with the fact.'

'That certainly sounds very like him,' said Dorothea, sniff-
ing. Clearly Hazelmere's habit of managing things was a long-
standing and deeply ingrained characteristic.

'Anyway, Hazelmere has always treated Helen exactly as
he does Alison. I assume he was astonished that you thought
she was his mistress?'

Recalling his face at the time, Dorothea nodded. 'But why
did the Comte de Vanée tell me she was?'

'My dear, I'm afraid you'll have to get used to the malicious
tongues of certain people you meet. There are more than a few
who'd like to cause trouble for Hazelmere and will seek to
use you to do it.' Her ladyship paused, eyeing her granddaughter's elegant profile. 'Incidentally, I would not, if I were you,
ever bring up the subject of Hazelmere's mistresses. I grant
you, he has had a few. Well,' she amended, realising the in-
adequacy of this description, 'more than a few. A positive
parade, in fact, and all of them the most gorgeous of creatures!
But, my dear, Hazelmere's mistresses are very definitely *not*
your concern, and if he follows in his father's footsteps they'll
be confined to his past. It's highly unlikely, given how much
in love with you he is, that you'll find yourself having to turn
a blind eye to such liaisons in the future, unlike so many other
ladies.'

Dorothea inclined her head in acknowledgement of this excellent advice.

Lady Merion, watching her, saw tiredness creep over the
pale face. She leaned forward and patted Dorothea's hand re-

assuringly. 'My dear, you're worn out. I'll have a tray sent up, and you really should have an early night. We'll have to consider how best to go on but I think we should leave further discussion until tomorrow.'

Dorothea, feeling strangely wrung out and curiously elated at the same time, nodded her acquiescence and kissed her grandmother's cheek before Lady Merion, suddenly feeling her age, left the room.

When Trimmer brought her dinner tray to her, Dorothea, contrary to her expectations, was feeling quite hungry. Nibbling the delicate chicken, she pondered her state. None of what had happened should have been a shock. But the fact remained that things had changed. Somehow, hand in hand with the Marquis of Hazelmere, she had stepped from the safe shores of fashionable dalliance into a realm where forces stronger than any she had ever known seemed set to steal her very soul. Thinking of how she had felt in his arms that afternoon, she shivered. He would never let her forget how much she wanted him. He had certainly won that bet. Some part of her rational mind suggested, faintly, that she should be incensed over his subtle machinations which would so easily have overridden any objections from her. But the truth was... The truth was that she had no objections. None at all.

Absent-mindedly she picked up the bowl of Witchett's special tisane. Sipping it, she relaxed in her chair, the warmth of the fire welcome as night fell. Thinking back, she could not recall a single incident where he had seriously professed any devotion. That had been one of the factors that had drawn her to him. Beside all the others and their protestations of undying love, his calm authority had been a welcome relief. Instead, if she had been able to think clearly where he was concerned, she would have seen the true meaning behind that peculiar warmth which shone in his hazel eyes, the care he had continually shown her, even, as she had discovered the morning after, to the extent of hiring a bodyguard to watch the stairs during the night at that inn. It was not hard to believe her grandmother's view. But oh! What she would give to hear it, clear and unambiguous, from his lips.

She stared into the fire as if in the flames she would find his face. She had no firm idea of what was to follow and, as she yawned again, realised she was too tired to accurately assess the possibilities. They would have to wait until morning.

Trimmer entered and unobtrusively removed the tray. She helped Dorothea change, then silently withdrew.

Lying in the depths of the feather mattress, Dorothea heaved a deep sigh and snuggled down in the bed. Under the subtle influence of Witchett's tisane, she dropped into a deep and dreamless sleep.

Dorothea awoke early the next morning, refreshed but strangely lethargic. She stayed in her room, staring out of her window at the cherry trees in the Park, now in full leaf. At nine o'clock she emerged from her bedchamber and descended to the morning-room. Cecily, she was informed, was spending the morning with the Bensons in Mount Street and had cancelled their morning ride with Ferdie. Relieved of two worries, Dorothea gave silent thanks to be spared the traumas of satisfying her sister's curiosity. Having drunk a cup of coffee and nibbled a piece of toast, she decided it was still too early to go up to her grandmother. On impulse, she called for Trimmer and went for a walk in the square.

The sun was shining, and a light breeze blew wispy clouds across the sky. Revelling in the fresh air, she walked through to the other side of the park, paused to glance briefly at the silent mansion opposite, then briskly returned to Merion House. By now Lady Merion would have left her bed. Ascending the stairs, she was surprised to see Ferdie on his way down.

Having received his cousin's note, Ferdie had decided that if Dorothea was not to be told of the danger then it was high time someone informed her ladyship of the threats to her granddaughter. He had also been able to set Lady Merion's mind at rest regarding the inevitable gossip arising from the incident in the Park. At the party he had attended the previous night he had found this had incurred little attention, and what comment there was had described it as just a lovers' quarrel.

As luck would have it, Lady Jersey had witnessed the encounter. She had immediately afterwards attended a select tea party at Mrs Drummond-Burrell's and, of course, had bubbled over with the news of Miss Darent's odd behaviour and the Marquis's likely response.

While there had been more than a few disapproving comments, the tone had been set by Mrs Drummond-Burrell herself. A friend of Hazelmere's, she had been impressed by Dorothea and heartily approved the Marquis's choice. In response to a disparaging remark that Miss Darent had properly cooked her goose, as Hazelmere would never stand for such behaviour, that most steely of Almack's patronesses had coolly observed, 'Dear Sarah, I really don't think you fully appreciate Miss Darent. How often have any of us seen Hazelmere so much as thrown off balance?' The ensuing silence had assured her that she had captured the attention of the room. 'I cannot help thinking,' she had continued, 'that any young lady who can shake that gentleman's calm deserves our congratulations. If she can make the Marquis realise that he cannot control absolutely everything, I for one will applaud her.' Thus Dorothea's actions had come to be regarded as a successful attempt to defy his lordship, with the likely result being no more than a tiff.

Pausing to exchange greetings with Dorothea, Ferdie said, 'I'll call for you at three.'

'Oh, Ferdie, I don't know that I can.'

'Not a matter of can or can't, you must,' answered that knowledgeable gentleman. Realising that she did not understand, he suggested, 'Go see your grandmama. She'll explain.'

And with a nod and a wave he descended to the hall and, accepting his hat from Mellow, quit the house. Dorothea surrendered her pelisse to Trimmer and entered her ladyship's sanctum.

Lady Merion had already had much to think about that morning. The news that Dorothea had been the subject of two abduction attempts had shocked the old lady. But, considering the steps already taken to protect her, she could not think of anything more that could be done. She had rejected Ferdie's suggestion that Dorothea be warned, informing him that his cousin was already the cause of enough turmoil in Dorothea's life, without adding this to the account. Hazelmere's absence was not comforting. On the other hand, it would give Dorothea time to adjust to his idea of her future.

She had been pleasantly surprised and not a little relieved to hear of the lack of speculation over the scene in the Park. She particularly appreciated Ferdie's offer to ride with Dorothea in the Park that afternoon. 'Won't do for her to hide away, you know,' that young gentleman had sapiently remarked.

When Dorothea entered the room Lady Merion smiled and waved her to the comfortable chaise. 'You're looking a great deal better, my dear.'

'I feel a great deal better, Grandmama,' replied Dorothea, dutifully kissing her cheek and then gracefully sitting beside her.

Noting her calm and confident manner, Hermione nodded. 'I think it's time we had some plain speaking.' Having made this promising beginning, she paused to marshal her arguments. 'To begin with, I expect you'll admit Hazelmere has seriously engaged your affections?'

Smiling at the careful phrasing, Dorothea responded easily, 'I've been in love with Lord Hazelmere for some time.'

'As I said, he's already told me he intends offering for you. In his own good time,' continued her ladyship. 'But what I want to know is, how will you reply?'

A gurgle of laughter escaped Dorothea. 'Oh, Grandmama. Do you really think I'll have any choice?'

Lady Merion snorted. 'To be perfectly honest, my dear, I doubt it. Hazelmere is well aware of your feelings. And, from what I saw in the drawing-room yesterday, your *verbal* agreement is merely a formality.' She watched her calm and cool granddaughter blush rosily. 'Mind you,' she went on, 'it's a nuisance, having a husband who knows too much, but you can't have everything. Still, I don't think it's a bad bargain—

his father was just the same, and Anthea Henry was the happiest married woman in town.'

To Dorothea, it seemed safest to accept this assurance in silence.

Deciding that there was nothing more she could do to aid Hazelmere, Lady Merion continued briskly, 'Very well. Now we must decide how you should go on. You must not give the gossips any reason to suppose that anything other than the mildest of disagreements has occurred between you.'

Dorothea's brows rose in a thoroughly haughty manner.

'Quite!' nodded Lady Merion. 'But you'll be guided by me and Ferdie in this matter. Ferdie is so useful at times like these; he always knows how things will appear and what one must on no account do. You must continue to appear at all your engagements as usual, and you must appear entirely your normal self.' Looking at her granddaughter, she remarked acidly, 'That doesn't seem to be causing you any great difficulty at the moment.'

Turning huge green eyes upon her grandmother, Dorothea smiled in a serenely confident way, which, under the circumstances, Lady Merion found oddly disconcerting. 'Grandmama, I promise I'll behave at all times in a befitting manner. But you really cannot expect me to be the same as I was before the Diplomatic Ball.'

Lady Merion, not entirely sure of its portent, accepted the qualified assurance. 'One last thing. Ferdie told me Hazelmere has gone out of town until Tuesday, to one of his estates. Not,' she continued in response to the question in Dorothea's eyes, 'because of your quarrel. He'd already told his friends he meant to depart by yesterday evening.'

Digesting this news, Dorothea decided that, all in all, a few days to polish her newly discovered public persona without distraction would not go amiss. Besides, she was beginning to feel that there were a few tricks left to be played in the game between herself and the arrogant Marquis. When he next appeared, she intended to be well prepared.

CHAPTER TWELVE

Ferdie and Dorothea arrived at the Park and joined the groups of ladies and gentlemen milling about, exchanging greetings and the latest *on-dits*. More than a few eyes were directed Dorothea's way. Chatting in a relaxed and animated fashion with Lord Peterborough, riding beside her on his bay, she had herself well in hand. To all who were interested, she appeared entirely at ease.

Mrs Drummond-Burrell, sitting haughtily in her barouche, waved to them to attend her. As they drew up she complimented Dorothea on her looks and then embarked on a conversation with all three. At no time did she refer to the most noble Marquis of Hazelmere, nor the incident in the Park. Looking into the cool blue eyes, Dorothea smiled warmly, acknowledging the message.

Released from her side, they next fell victim to Lady Jersey. In stark contrast, she tried by every means possible to extract some comment from Dorothea on Hazelmere and what had happened after they had left the Park. Dorothea's practice in verbal fencing with his lordship left her well equipped to deal with opponents like Sally Jersey. She successfully turned aside all that lady's probing questions. As she accomplished this with an amused tolerance, very reminiscent of Hazelmere himself, Lady Jersey was more entertained than enraged by her refusal to be outwitted. Finally escaping her clutches, they rode on.

'Phew!' exclaimed Ferdie as soon as they were out of earshot. 'Never seen Silence so hell-bent on getting an answer!'

While they encountered a number of ladies similarly intent on learning the details of Dorothea's last meeting with the

Marquis, Lady Jersey's inquisition was by far the most comprehensive, and Dorothea easily handled these less inveterate busybodies.

On returning to Merion House, having parted from Lord Peterborough at the Park gates, Ferdie confessed to being thoroughly satisfied with Dorothea's performance. Overhearing this remark, addressed to her grandmother, Dorothea's eyes twinkled. 'Why, thank you, Ferdie,' she said meekly.

Not sure how to take this and finding her confidence slightly alarming, Ferdie assured them that he would call at eight to escort them to the evening's rout, and made his escape.

During the following days Dorothea found Hazelmere's friends keeping a protective watch over her and was amused by their endeavours to conceal this. Intrigued, she quizzed Ferdie for the reason and finally, in desperation, he retreated behind his absent cousin. 'Best ask Hazelmere if you want to know about it.' Correctly understanding this to mean that his lordship had left instructions that she was not to be told, she refrained from pushing Ferdie further. Finding that the words 'Hazelmere said so' acted as a talisman, Ferdie used the phrase increasingly. He fervently hoped his cousin would not be out of London longer than anticipated.

As she had all of Hazelmere's closest friends dancing attendance on her, Dorothea used the opportunity to lead them into describing their many interests and amusements. In so doing, they often gave her information on Hazelmere, and she slowly built up a more complete picture of his complex personality. For their part, his lordship's friends found the task of guarding her a pleasure. More than one found himself mesmerised by those large green eyes. Her natural assurance was much more apparent in Hazelmere's absence and, added to that, she now gave the impression of being fashionably distant, as if waiting for something or someone. However, not one of them found anything in her manner to suggest that she was other than completely content with Hazelmere's suit. So, roundly cursing his lordship's infernal luck, even the volatile Peterborough succumbed to her subtle invitation to be friends, and then the entire crew were her devoted slaves.

Fanshawe, viewing proceedings from the distance of his
pursuit of Cecily, now close to success, could think of only
one reason for Dorothea's serene manner. But, having heard
from Ferdie of their last meeting, and knowing from Cecily's
silence that Hazelmere had not proposed and forgotten to mention it, he was left wondering. From their friends' behaviour,
he guessed Dorothea had succeeded in the not inconsiderable
feat of adding them to her circle of doting admirers. Hazelmere
would get something of a shock when he found to what use
she had put his watchdogs. Luckily he was more likely to be
amused at their susceptibilities than annoyed at her success.
Life was going to be interesting when the Marquis returned to
town.

For Dorothea, the time passed in a dull whirl she would
readily have traded for the sight of his lordship's hazel eyes,
preferably smiling at her. She was not entirely looking forward
to her next private meeting with him, foreseeing a certain awkwardness in explaining why she had behaved as she had. But
she would rather have faced it sooner than later. Unfortunately
she could do nothing but wait and, with so many people endeavouring to please her, she felt it would be churlish to complain, even though her enthusiasm for fashionable pursuits had
waned.

The only truly dreadful moment occurred at the Melchetts'
ball on Saturday night. She might have guessed, had she
thought of him at all, that Edward Buchanan would, like a
distempered ghost, return to haunt her. He had heard of the
encounter in the Park and had listened with interest to the
speculation on the outcome. To his mind, Miss Darent's options were rapidly diminishing.

He accosted her as she stood by the side of the dance-floor
in company with Lord Desborough. Unfortunately the musicians had had a slight accident, and in the unexpected interval
the guests were strolling about, conversing in small groups.
Desborough had not previously met Edward Buchanan and so
accepted at face value his claim to acquaintance with Dorothea. Knowing she would be mortified by Mr Buchanan's gal-
lantries, Dorothea asked Desborough to fetch her a glass of

lemonade, hoping in the interval to dispose of her unwelcome suitor. Her plans backfired, and instead she found herself in a small ante-room with Edward Buchanan again pressing his suit.

'I have, after all, got your guardian's blessing. And now there are these rumours about your behaviour with Hazelmere. What I say, my dear, is that none of your fancy beaux will have you now.' He cocked an eyebrow at her and his ponderous voice gained in weight. 'Too top-lofty, that lot. You've queered your pitch there, right enough. You'd do well to lower your sights, my girl. Hazelmere and his set are out of your reach now. You should consider my proposal, indeed you should!'

Rigid with anger, Dorothea struggled to control her voice. 'Mr Buchanan! I will tell you for the last time: I do not wish, in any circumstances, to marry you! I trust that is plain enough. I will not change my mind. It was unwise in the extreme for Herbert to have encouraged your suit. I'm sorry, but I must return to the ballroom.'

She moved to sweep past him where he stood, his back to the door. As she did so Desborough, who had been looking all over for her, appeared there. Sheer relief showed on Dorothea's face. At the same moment Edward Buchanan grabbed her by the shoulders and attempted to kiss her. She struggled frantically, averting her face.

Almost instantly Buchanan was bodily plucked from her and thrown roughly against the wall. In considerable surprise he slid down to sit on the floor, his legs splayed out in front of him and an idiotic look on his face. Desborough, adjusting the set of his coat before offering his arm to Dorothea, turned at the last moment to say, 'Be thankful it was me and not Peterborough, Walsingham, or, God forbid, Hazelmere. Any of those three and you would be nursing rather more bruises and, very likely, a few broken bones as well. I suggest, Mr Buchanan, that you trouble Miss Darent no longer.' And, with that, he ushered a deeply grateful Dorothea back into the ballroom.

The upshot was that Hazelmere's friends never, ever, left

her unattended again, whether in the ballroom, the Park, or
any other gathering of the fashionable.

Hazelmere's entire attention was devoted to controlling the
frisky bays as he threaded through the crowded streets of the
capital. Once they had passed the village of Hampstead and
started over Finchley Common he dropped his hands and the
bays shot forward. With the horses driven well up to their bits,
the curricle rocketed past coaches travelling at conventional
speeds. Jim Hitchin, hanging on grimly behind, kept his lips
firmly shut and prayed that his master's customary skill did
not desert him. As the evening wore on and the shadows
started to spread, throwing inky patches across the road, concealing pot-holes and ruts, Jim expected their pace to ease.
But no change in speed was detectable as they left Barnet
behind and raced onwards up the Great North Road towards
the George at Harpenden, where they spent the night on such
trips as these.

Jim kept silent, more from fear of distracting the Marquis
than from reticence. But, when Hazelmere overtook the north-
bound accommodation coach just before St Albans on a tight
curve with less than inches to spare, Jim, in considerable
fright, swore roundly.

'What was that, Jim?' came Hazelmere's voice.

'Why, nothing, m'lord,' replied Jim. Unable to help himself,
he added, 'Just if you was to be wishful to break both our
necks I could think of few faster ways to do it.'

Silence. Then Jim heard his master laugh softly. 'I'm sorry,
Jim, I know I should not have done that.' And the curricle
slowed until they were bowling along at a safer pace.

Yes, and you're still up in the boughs, thought Jim. Just as
long as you keep this coach on the road, we'll survive.

It was late afternoon on Thursday when they reached Lauleigh, Hazelmere's Leicestershire estate between Melton
Mowbray and Oakham. His steward, a dour man named Walton, had not erred in demanding his attendance. There was an
enormous amount of work to be done and they made a start

on it that evening, going over the accounts and planning the activities of the next two days.

Walton, hearing from Jim of the likely change in his lordship's affairs, made sure that anything requiring his authorisation was dealt with. He was under no illusion that he would be able to summon his master north again that Season. Accustomed, like most of the Marquis's servitors, to keeping a weather eye out for his temper, in this case Walton guessed it was unlikely to be directed at him, and his flat tones droned in Hazelmere's ears incessantly over Friday and Saturday.

Hazelmere called a halt on Saturday afternoon and retired to his study, informing Jim that they would leave early the next morning. The events of the past two days, entirely divorced from those of the Season, had succeeded in restoring his calm. By forcing his mind to deal with such mundane affairs, he had managed to shut out the turmoil of emotions he had experienced on leaving Dorothea until now, when he felt infinitely more capable of dealing with them.

While it was warm in the south of the country, in Leicestershire the winds blew cool in the evening and the fire was alight. Pouring himself a drink, he dropped into the comfortable armchair before the hearth, stretching his long legs to the blaze. Cupping the glass in both hands, he gazed into the leaping flames.

Conjuring up the image of a pair of emerald eyes, he wondered what she was doing. Ah, yes. The Melchett ball. Away from the endless round of London during the Season, he was even more conscious of how much he wanted her by his side. That meeting in the drawing-room at Merion House had had about it an air of inevitability. He'd been so angry with her when he'd walked in the door—admittedly more from hurt pride than righteous indignation. And she'd been so surprisingly angry with him! Thankfully, she had promptly told him why. He grinned. All the dictates of how a young lady should behave had been overturned in the space of a few minutes. He could imagine no other female—apart from his mother, perhaps—who would dare let on that she even knew of his mistresses, much less question him on the subject.

As his relationship with Helen Walford was so well known among the ton, it had never occurred to him that a different version could be presented to Dorothea. Very clever of the Comte. He vaguely recalled some difficulty with Monsieur de Vanée over one of the barques of frailty who had at one time resided under his protection. What had been her name? Madeline? Miriam? Mentally he shrugged. The Comte's lies had undoubtedly been the cause of Dorothea's distress that night, coming on top of the incident with the Prince. Hardly surprising that she had baulked at meeting Helen and him in the Park.

But why, *why* had she flung that drivel about her being no more than a challenge at him? Even if Marjorie Darent had impressed it on her, surely she didn't believe it? He sipped the fine French brandy and felt it slide warmly down his throat. No—she hadn't believed Marjorie's tales. The Darents had left London on Monday, so any conversation between Dorothea and Marjorie must have occurred earlier. But Dorothea had behaved normally at that horrendous party on Sunday night. And at the Diplomatic Ball she'd been entirely unconcerned until the Prince's performance had opened her eyes too far. Even then, she had not been distraught, only, as he had expected, angry with him. It had only been later, after the Comte's interference, that she had been shattered and almost in tears. Well, his actions in her grandmother's drawing-room should have settled that. She couldn't possibly have missed the implication of that kiss.

It had not occurred to him until that day that by loving her he had put into her hands the power to hurt him. Since he was naturally strong and self-reliant, there were few close to him whose opinions mattered enough to affect him—his mother and Alison, Tony and Ferdie and, to a lesser extent, Helen. That was about it. And Dorothea mattered far more than all of them combined. But if such vulnerability was what one had to put up with, then put up with it he would. She had only lashed out at him because she was hurt by his imagined perfidy. He would simply ensure that such misunderstandings did not occur in the future.

So where did that leave them now? Much where they had been before, except that presumably she now knew he loved her. Assuming that events progressed as he intended, there was no reason that they could not be wed in a month or so. Then his frustrations and her uncertainties would be things of the past.

He brought his gaze back from the ceiling whence it had strayed and fixed it once more on the dancing flames. He was happily engaged in salacious imaginings in which Dorothea figured prominently when his housekeeper entered to inform him that dinner was served.

He reached Darent Hall, close to Corby and not far off his direct route, just before ten o'clock. He threw the reins to Jim, who had run to the horses' heads, with a command to keep them moving.

Admitted to the hall, he spoke to the butler. 'I am the Marquis of Hazelmere. I wonder if Lord Darent could spare me a few moments?'

Recognising the quality of this visitor, the butler showed him into the library and went to inform his master. Herbert was engaged in consuming a leisurely breakfast when Millchin announced that the most noble Marquis of Hazelmere required a few words with him. Herbert's mouth dropped open. After a moment he recovered himself enough to reply, 'Very well, Millchin, I'll come at once, of course. Where have you put him?'

Millchin told him and withdrew. Herbert continued to stare at the door. He had little doubt what Hazelmere wanted, but Marjorie had insisted that he was not in earnest and, even if he was, that he could not be considered suitable. In this instance, adherence to his wife's wishes was entirely impossible. Herbert was already uncomfortable before he entered his library to face Hazelmere, who somehow seemed more at home in the beautiful, heavily panelled room than its owner.

The interview was brief and to the point, conducted as it was by Hazelmere rather than Herbert. Having listened to the Marquis's request, Herbert felt forced to reveal that he had already given Edward Buchanan permission to address Dorothea.

At mention of Mr Buchanan, Hazelmere's look became uncomfortably intent. 'Do you mean to tell me you gave Buchanan permission to address your ward without checking his background?' The precise diction made Herbert even more nervous.

'I gather he owns an estate in Dorset,' he flustered. 'And, of course, he knows Sir Hugo Clere.'

'And learned from Sir Hugo that Miss Darent had inherited the Grange, no doubt. For your information, Edward Buchanan owns a tumbledown farmhouse in Dorset. He's penniless. The reason he's in London is that, after his most recent attempt to run away with a local heiress, Dorset is too hot for him. I'm surprised, my lord, that you take such little care over your duties as guardian.'

Herbert, brick-red with embarrassment, remained silent.

'I assume that, as you are acquainted with my family and my standing in society and as my wealth needs no detailing, you have no objection to giving *me* your permission to address Miss Darent?'

The scathing tones made Herbert wince. 'Naturally, should you wish to address Dorothea, of course you have my permission,' he said, squirming, then unwisely added, 'But what if she's already accepted Buchanan?'

'My dear sir, your ward is a great deal more discerning than you are.' Now that he had obtained Herbert's approval, the only other information Hazelmere required was the name of the family solicitors who would handle the marriage settlements.

Herbert was strangely diffident on this question. 'I believe Dorothea uses Whitney and Sons, in Chancery Lane.'

It took the Marquis a moment to assimilate this. Then he asked, eyes narrowed, 'So Miss Darent's solicitors are her own, not yours?'

'My aunt's crazy idea,' said Herbert defensively. 'She had the oddest notions. She decided it was best that both girls controlled their own fortunes.'

'So,' pursued Hazelmere, drawing on his gloves, 'when the Misses Darent marry, control of their fortunes remains in their hands?'

'Well, yes,' said Herbert, glancing directly at him. 'But that wouldn't worry you, surely? Her estate is nothing compared to yours.'

'Oh, quite,' agreed Hazelmere. 'I was merely wondering whether you gave that information to Buchanan. Did you?'

Herbert looked blank. 'No. He didn't ask.'

'I thought not,' said Hazelmere, a highly cynical smile curving his lips. Disclaiming any desire to dally with his relations-to-be, he re-entered the hall, to find that he was not destined to escape an encounter with Marjorie Darent. Her ladyship was looking even more severe than usual and directed a look of such magnitude at her husband that Hazelmere almost felt sorry for him.

'Lord Hazelmere—' she began.

But Hazelmere was determined that the conversational reins would remain in his hands. 'Lady Marjorie,' he countered. 'I'm sure you'll forgive my not staying. I've concluded the business I had with your husband and it's most urgent I return to Hazelmere at once. My mother, you realise.'

'Lady Hazelmere is ill?' asked Marjorie, struggling to keep abreast of this flow of information.

Hazelmere, unwilling to expose his mother to letters of condolence on her relapse, simply looked grave. 'I'm afraid I'm not at liberty to discuss the matter. I'm sure you understand.'

He bowed elegantly over her hand, nodded to Herbert and escaped.

He reached Hazelmere on Monday afternoon. His mother was resting, so, seeing the glint in his steward's eye, he gave his attention to the host of minor matters Liddiard had waiting for him. He delayed his appearance in the drawing-room until just before dinner. If they were free of servants his mother would lose no time in asking him why he was home, and he would rather face the inquisition after dinner than before.

As it transpired, he entered the drawing-room immediately

in front of Penton, his butler. Lady Hazelmere, recognising the
strategy, pulled a face at him as he bent to kiss her cheek. He
merely gave the smile he knew infuriated her, telling her as it
did that he was perfectly aware of what she wanted to say to
him but had no wish to hear it—at least, not yet. Her ladyship
reflected that her son was growing to resemble his father more
and more.

Over dinner he kept up a steady flow of inconsequential
anecdotes, detailing the fashionable happenings since she had
left London. Lady Hazelmere, knowing he would say nothing
to the point in front of the servants, listened with what interest
she could muster. Finally, after the covers were removed and
the servants withdrew, she drew a deep breath. 'And *now* are
you going to tell me why you're here?'

'Yes, Mama,' he replied meekly. 'Only I do think we might
be more comfortable in your parlour.'

Functioning in a similar way to Lady Merion's upstairs
drawing-room, her ladyship's parlour was a cheerful apartment
on the first floor of the large country house. The curtains were
already drawn, shutting out the twilight, and a small fire was
burning merrily in the grate. Lady Hazelmere sat in her favourite wing chair by the hearth, while her son, after pulling
it further from the flames, elegantly disposed his long limbs
in its partner opposite.

He then smiled at his impatient parent. Her ladyship, inured
by the years to such tactics, asked bluntly, 'Why have you
come to see me?'

'As you correctly suppose, to tell you I'm about to offer for
Dorothea Darent.'

'Very punctilious, I must say.'

'You know that I always am. In such matters as these, at
least.'

Aware that this was true, she ignored the comment. 'When
is the wedding to be?'

'As I haven't asked her, I cannot say. If I have my way, as
soon as possible.'

'I must say, I've wondered at your unusual patience.'

He shrugged. 'It seemed a good idea at the time. She'd only

just arrived in town, and if she'd refused it would have caused considerable awkwardness for a number of people.'

'Yes, I can appreciate that. But why the change of heart?'

He looked hard at her. 'Hasn't Lady Merion written to you this week?'

'Well, yes,' she admitted. 'But I'd much rather hear it from you.'

Hazelmere sighed and succinctly outlined the events preceding his departure from the capital. He also described the two attempts to abduct Dorothea, learning in the process that his mother already knew of these via a recently informed Lady Merion. When he finished, Lady Hazelmere looked at him, perplexed. 'But if she's in danger, why are you gallivanting all over the country?'

'Because the others are looking after her and it seemed more sensible to marry her as soon as possible and remove her from any danger at all,' he explained patiently. 'As I had to go to Lauleigh, I looked in on Herbert Darent on the way back.'

She eventually conceded. 'Yes, I suppose you're right, as usual. I assume Herbert was only too thrilled?'

'As a matter of fact, no,' he replied with a grin. 'I think that indescribable wife of his has convinced him I'm no better than a rake and shouldn't be allowed to marry into the family.'

Lady Hazelmere was speechless.

After a moment Hazelmere said, 'I take it you approve?'

His mother dragged her mind from contemplation of Lady Darent's manifold shortcomings. 'Of course! She's very suitable. In fact,' she said, warming to her theme, 'she's *eminently* suitable, as among her numerous qualities she can include the unique accomplishment of having attracted your interest!'

'Exactly so,' he returned, amused. 'And, as I've been at great pains to make our attachment abundantly clear to the ton, I really don't think the announcement will surprise.'

'When I think of that waltz at the Merion House ball!' Anthea Henry closed her eyes, continuing faintly, 'So very shocking of you, my dear!'

Hazelmere, not deceived, replied, 'Coming it much too strong, Mama!'

She opened eyes brimming with laughter. 'But it was! You had all the tabbies with their fur standing on end!'

Both mother and son allowed the conversation to lapse while they relived fond memories. Her ladyship finally stirred. 'When will you speak to her?'

'As soon as I can arrange to see her. Wednesday probably. If she's agreeable we'll come here for a few days. It would be useful, I imagine, for her to see the house.'

Lady Hazelmere sighed. Hermione's weekly letter had been perfectly candid. Clearly, despite minor misunderstandings, her arrogant son had, as usual, triumphed, and all would proceed as he decreed. Even the headstrong Dorothea had apparently been tamed. If things continued in this fashion Marc would soon grow to be utterly impossible. She had had such hopes of Dorothea. Still, at least she would now have a daughter-in-law. Even if nothing else, they could swap stories of her impossible son. And, knowing her son, she could look forward, with as much confidence as possible in such matters, to a grandchild within the year. The thought cheered her. So, resigned, all she said was, 'Yes, that would be wise. We'll have to arrange to refurbish the apartments next to yours.'

CHAPTER THIRTEEN

Hazelmere returned to London, driving a new pair of black horses, leaving the bays in the country to recuperate. The curricle flashed into the mews behind Hazelmere House late in the afternoon. Discussing the performance of the new pair with Jim, he strolled out of the stables as Ferdie rode into the mews, leading two horses.

Thoroughly worn out with his role as chief confidant and protector, Ferdie was delighted to see his cousin. Dismounting and handing over the reins to Jim, he reflected that the source of the horses the Darent sisters rode was one of the better kept secrets in this whole affair. He could imagine what Dorothea would say when she learned that her bay mare had all along belonged to Hazelmere. He hoped they would be married by then and she could discuss the subject with Hazelmere rather than him. He turned to his cousin. 'Relieved to see you back!'

'Oh?' The black brows rose interrogatively.

'Not that anything's happened,' he hastily assured him. 'But Dorothea knows something's going on and it's getting more and more difficult to know what to say.'

'Poor Ferdie! It sounds as if it's all been too much for you.'

'Well, it has!' returned Ferdie, incensed. 'Here she's gone and turned all your friends into her most devoted slaves—oh, yes! Didn't expect that, did you?' He had the satisfaction of seeing the hazel eyes widen. Nodding decisively, he continued, 'Rather think it's been her holding the reins in your absence, not us!'

Hazelmere, eyes dancing, sighed. 'I see I was mistaken in thinking it safe to leave you all in charge of Miss Darent. I might have guessed it would turn out the other way. Why on

earth you have allowed her to assume the whip hand, I know
not. Obviously I'll have to intervene and save you all.'

'All very well for you. It's you she loves, not us! Never
seen a lady so capable of making us all jump to her tune.
Better take her in hand straight away!'

Hazelmere laughed at this blatant encouragement. 'Believe
me, Ferdie, I intend to—with all possible speed. But not tonight, I think. It's Alvanley's dinner for me. I can't remember
if there's anything else on.'

'No, nothing of note. I'm to escort Dorothea and Cecily to
a quiet little party at Lady Rothwell's. Just the younger crew,
so I'm looking forward to an uneventful evening. Mind,
though! Tomorrow she's all yours!'

'Oh, quite definitely!' As they strolled back into Cavendish
Square Hazelmere added, 'In fact, you can assist in your own
relief by informing Dorothea that I'll call on her tomorrow
morning.'

Regarding his cousin with misgiving, Ferdie answered,
'Well, I'll tell her. But she'll probably insist on going riding
or think up some important engagement on the spot.'

'In that case,' Hazelmere said, his voice silky smooth, his
lips curving in anticipation, 'you had better add, in your most
persuasive tones, that she would do very much better to meet
me next in private rather than public.'

Ferdie, doubting that he could deliver that statement with
quite the force Hazelmere could, nodded reluctantly. 'Yes, all
right, I suppose that'll do it.'

'You can take it from me that it will,' responded Hazelmere
gravely. Laughing at Ferdie's outraged countenance, he
clapped his cousin on the shoulder and went into his own
house, leaving Ferdie to wander on to his lodgings.

Some two hours later Fanshawe was attempting to tie his
neckcloth in the latest fashion when the knocker on his door
was plied with unusual insistence. With an oath he discarded
his latest attempt and testily recommended his man, standing
mute with an armload of fresh specimens, to see who on earth
it was.

A minute later, just as he was once again engrossed, the door opened.

'Hartness, who on earth have you sent these to? They're too floppy to do anything with!'

Came an amused voice in reply, 'A poor cobbler always blames his lathe.'

He twisted around, ruining any chance he had of correctly tying his next attempt. 'Oh, you're back, are you?'

'As you see,' replied Hazelmere. 'I'd said I would be, after all.'

'Never know where you'll be or not. Where'd you get to—just Leicestershire?'

'Lauleigh, Darent Hall and Hazelmere,' responded the Marquis.

Fanshawe took a moment to work this out. 'Thought that might be it,' he said sagaciously. 'Have you seen Dorothea yet?'

'No. I thought that after my flying around the country I deserve Alvanley's dinner. And Ferdie tells me they're to attend a boring party tonight, so all should be safe until tomorrow.'

'Tomorrow. Good! Where'd you say Darent Hall was?'

'Ah, lies the wind in that quarter?'

'You're not the only one who can suddenly decide for reasons unknown to get leg-shackled to a managing female!' responded his lordship tartly.

Laughing, Hazelmere said, 'It's in Northamptonshire, not far from Corby. Easy to find if you ask. Here! For the lord's sake, let me tie that or Jeremy will be wondering what's become of us! Stand still!'

He rapidly tied his friend's cravat, his long fingers creasing the stiff material into the required folds. 'Right, done. Now let's get going!'

Fanshawe, admiring the finished product, mused, 'Not bad.'

Finding his coat thrown at his head, he laughed and, putting it on, joined Hazelmere on the stairs.

Jeremy Alvanley had been in the habit of giving a dinner for his closest friends every year for six years. It had become

an event in their calendar, a gentlemen-only gourmet affair
with the best of the latest vintages to wash the delicacies down.
All their set made every effort to attend, and the occasion
usually proved highly entertaining. This year's dinner was no
exception. The conversation flowed as freely as the wine.
Much of this consisted of regaling Hazelmere with the problems they had faced in looking after Miss Darent. All of them
knew of the scene in the Park, but none of them could begin
to imagine what had happened afterwards. However, they were
well acquainted with Hazelmere and had therefore been surprised at Dorothea's subsequent performance. Finding him in
his normal benign mood, none of them was quite sure what
to think. But, as he was obviously genuinely entertained by
the stories of their difficulties, they took every opportunity to
impress on him how arduous their labours had been.

Though they did not know it, their stories confirmed for
Hazelmere what Ferdie and later Fanshawe had told him:
clearly Dorothea had taken charge, realising that, to some extent, they were acting under his direction. That she had succeeded in captivating them was apparent. He was amused to
hear that the only sure way they found to escape her subtle
questioning had been to invoke his name. That this had succeeded told him that she had known precisely what she was
about in her handling of this group of gentlemen whom he
would have described as among the most hardened to feminine
wiles.

During the evening Desborough paused by his chair to en-
lighten him regarding Edward Buchanan. The black brows
drew together. Then he shrugged. 'I might have expected him
to make some such attempt. Thankfully, you were there.' With
a quick smile Desborough moved on.

After dinner it was their custom to adjourn to White's for
the rest of the evening, or, more correctly, until the small hours
of the next morning. By eleven o'clock they were deeply engrossed in play.

Ferdie, Dorothea and Cecily arrived at Lady Rothwell's
punctually at eight, to find carriages waiting to convey them

to a surprise party at Vauxhall. Neither Dorothea nor Ferdie was enthusiastic; Cecily was ecstatic. As it was virtually impossible to withdraw politely, Dorothea and the even more reluctant Ferdie were forced to accept the change with suitable grace.

At the pleasure gardens Lady Rothwell had hired a booth facing the dancing area, gaily lit with festoons of coloured lanterns. The younger folk joined in the dancing, while Dorothea and Ferdie stayed in the booth, watching the passing scene. Lady Rothwell sat keeping a shrewd and motherly eye on all her young charges.

Dorothea had heard that Hazelmere was expected to have returned that day. Speculation on their next meeting was consuming more and more of her time. Glancing at her pensive face, Ferdie recalled his cousin's message. He could hardly deliver it in Lady Rothwell's hearing. 'Would you like to view the Fairy Fountain, Miss Darent?'

Dorothea had no wish to view the Fairy Fountain but thought it odd that Ferdie should imagine she would. Then she caught the faintest inclination of his head, and, intrigued, agreed. Lady Rothwell made no demur to their projected stroll and Dorothea left the booth on Ferdie's arm. Once out of sight and sound of her ladyship, she lost no time. 'What is it you wish to tell me, Ferdie?'

Thinking she had a bad habit of making it difficult to lead up to things by degrees, Ferdie answered baldly, 'Met Hazelmere this afternoon. Gave me a message for you.'

'Oh?' she replied, bridling.

Not liking the tone of that syllable and fast coming to the conclusion he should have told his high-handed cousin to deliver his own messages, Ferdie was forced to continue. 'Said to tell you he would call on you tomorrow morning.'

'I see. What a pity I shall miss him! I do believe I have to visit some friends tomorrow morning.'

'Told him so.' Ferdie nodded sagely. Under Dorothea's bemused gaze, he hurriedly explained, 'Told him you would very likely be engaged.'

'And?'

Liking his role less and less, Ferdie took a deep breath and continued manfully, 'He said to say you would do better to meet him in private rather than in public.'

The undisguised threat left Dorothea speechless. Seeing her kindling eyes, Ferdie decided it was time to return to safer and more populated surroundings than the secluded walk they had entered. 'Take you back to her ladyship,' he volunteered.

Seething, Dorothea allowed him to take her arm and they retraced their steps. She was incensed. More than that, she was *furious*! How *dared* he send such a command to her? However, as she strolled back to the booth by Ferdie's side common sense reasserted itself. If her last meeting with Hazelmere was any guide, she would be wise to avoid provoking him further. The thought of refusing his suggested interview only to meet him next in the middle of a ballroom was enough to convince her to accede to his request.

Shortly after Dorothea and Ferdie had left, Lady Rothwell was joined by Cecily, thoroughly enjoying herself, accompanied by Lord Rothwell. Noticing Cecily's high colour, her ladyship sent her son for some ices from the pavilion. Cecily sat down beside her and was in the middle of a delighted description of the sights when they were interrupted by a knock on the door.

At her ladyship's command, an individual in attire proclaiming the respectable gentleman's gentleman entered the booth.

'Lady Rothwell?'

'Yes?'

'I have an urgent message for Miss Cecily Darent.' The man proffered a sealed letter.

At a nod from Lady Rothwell, Cecily took it, broke the seal and spread open the single sheet. Reading it, she paled. Reaching the end, she sat down weakly in the chair, allowing her ladyship to remove the letter from suddenly nerveless fingers.

'Good heavens!' exclaimed Lady Rothwell, quickly perusing the missive. 'My dear, I'm so sorry!'

'I must go to him,' said Cecily. 'Where's my cloak?'

'Don't you think you should wait for Dorothea and Ferdie?'

'Oh, no! They might be half an hour or more! Surely there can be no impropriety? I must not delay. Oh, please, Lady Rothwell, please say I may go?'

Her ladyship was not proof against Cecily's huge pansy eyes. But it was with definite misgiving that she watched her disappear down the walk to the carriage gate in the company of Lord Fanshawe's man.

Ten minutes later Ferdie and Dorothea regained the booth. Lady Rothwell had sent her son away and was trying to rid herself of a strong suspicion that she had erred in allowing Cecily to leave. She looked up with relief.

'Oh, Ferdie! I'm so glad to see you. And you too, my dear. Cecily received a most disturbing message and has gone off with Lord Fanshawe's man.'

Neither Ferdie nor Dorothea understood much of this, but, seeing the letter her ladyship was holding out, Ferdie took it.

To Miss Cecily Darent,
I am writing on behalf of Lord Fanshawe, who is currently in my surgery, having sustained serious wounds in a recent accident. His lordship is in a bad way and is asking for you. I am sending this note by the hand of his servant and I hope if he finds you you will allow this individual, who his lordship assures me is trustworthy, to escort you to his lordship's side. I need hardly add that time is of the essence.

Yours, et cetera,
James Harten, Surgeon.

'Oh, dear!' said Dorothea.
'Gammon!' said Ferdie.
'I beg your pardon?' asked Dorothea.
'This letter,' he explained. 'It's a hoax.'
'But how do you know?' wailed Lady Rothwell.
'Because I know it's Alvanley's dinner tonight and then they always go on to White's. Every year, always the same. So wherever Tony is, Marc's with him. Bound to be. And

Marc would never allow this. You may not know, but I do. Devilishly starchy on some things, Hazelmere.'

Dorothea, knowing this to be the truth, gave voice to her thoughts. 'But if it is a hoax, to what purpose?'

Ferdie realised they had all made a mistake in forgetting there were two Darent sisters. Dorothea and Lady Rothwell were obviously expecting him to answer. 'Sorry to have to say this, but I'm afraid she's been abducted.'

'I knew there was something wrong,' wailed her ladyship. 'Oh, dear! Whatever shall I tell Hermione?'

'Ferdie, what should we do?' asked Dorothea, wasting no time in histrionics.

Ferdie, whose brain could, under stress, perform quite creditably, paused for a moment. 'Who else knew of this letter?'

'No one,' answered Lady Rothwell. 'William was out getting ices at the time and I didn't like to show it to him.'

'Good. Dorothea and I will leave and return to Merion House. If any demand or message is sent, that's where it'll be. Lady Rothwell, you'll have to tell everyone Dorothea was feeling unwell and that Cecily and I took her home.'

Her ladyship, reviewing this plan, approved. 'Yes, very well. And Dorothea, tell Hermione I'll keep silent about this. I feel responsible for letting Cecily go and I dread to think what your grandmother will think of me, my dear.'

Nodding, Dorothea murmured thanks and reassurances before she and Ferdie left for the carriages.

In spite of the coachman's best efforts, the journey to Cavendish Square took twenty tense minutes. Admitted to Merion House by a surprised Mellow, they found, as suspected, a recently delivered letter addressed to Dorothea. Lady Merion was attending a card party at Miss Berry's and would not be home for hours.

Ushering Dorothea into the drawing-room and shutting the door on Mellow, Ferdie nodded to the letter. 'Best open it. Have to know what they want.'

Dorothea broke the cheap seal and read the contents of the single sheet, Ferdie looking over her shoulder.

My dear Miss Darent,

I have your sister in safe keeping and if you wish to see her again you will do exactly as I say. You should immediately set out in your carriage and travel to the Castle Inn at Tadworth, south of Banstead. Do not bring anyone with you or nothing will come of your visit and your sister's reputation will assuredly be lost. If you do not arrive before dawn I will be forced to conclude that you have informed the authorities and I will then have to flee the country, taking your sister with me. I am sure I can rely on your good sense. I remain,

Your most obedient servant,
Edward Buchanan, Esq.

'Good God! The bounder!' said Ferdie, disgust etching his fair face. 'You can't possibly go to that place.' After a pause he added, 'But someone's going to have to.'

Dorothea's mind was racing. In a way, it was partly her fault that Cecily had been abducted. If only she had been more careful of her younger sister and not so absorbed with her own affairs. It was Cecily for whom they had come to London to find a husband. Maybe she could have been firmer with Edward Buchanan, though it was difficult to see how. Weighing up the possible courses of action available to her, she answered Ferdie at random. 'Yes, but who? And how?'

Ferdie had little doubt as to the who and how. 'Best thing we can do is get hold of Hazelmere. Tony'll be with him and they'll know what to do. Sort of thing Marc's good at.'

Dorothea's absent gaze abruptly fixed on Ferdie's face. She had no difficulty understanding his comments. But inwardly she groaned. The memory of how affairs stood between herself and the Marquis, never far from mind, reeled into focus. After the way they had parted the last thing she needed was this. To meet him next with a calm request to extricate her sister, essentially her responsibility, from the clutches of one of her own importunate suitors was a prospect she could not face. 'No, Ferdie,' she said with calm decision. 'There's no need for Hazelmere or Fanshawe or anyone else to be involved.'

Ferdie simply looked blank. Then stubborn. There ensued a totally unprofitable ten minutes of wrangling. Finally Dorothea suggested a compromise. 'If you fetch Grandmama, then she can decide what to do.'

Relieved, Ferdie headed for Miss Berry's.

It was over an hour later that Mellow opened the door to his mistress. On reaching the Misses Berry's trim little house, Ferdie had sent in a message that Dorothea was ill and consequently Lady Merion's presence was required at Merion House. Instead of resulting in Lady Merion's coming out, he had been summoned in. Lady Merion had been engaged in a thrilling rubber and had desired to know how desperately ill her granddaughter, last seen in rude health, had become. Under the amused gaze of what had seemed like half the ton, Ferdie had been forced to assure her ladyship that Dorothea's state was not critical. With a smile her ladyship had settled down to finish her game.

But now, as she surrendered her fur wrap, Lady Merion looked anything but complacent. A worried frown had settled over the sharp blue eyes as she led the way into the drawing-room. Ferdie followed and shut the door.

'Where's Dorothea?' asked Lady Merion.

Ferdie's face was blank as he scanned the room, almost as if he expected to find Dorothea hiding in a corner. The pale blue eyes stopped when they reached the white square tucked into a corner of the mirror on the mantelpiece.

Lady Merion, following his gaze, walked over and twitched the envelope free. It was addressed to her. She smoothed out the sheet. Then, one hand groping wildly, she sank into a chair. Under her powder she paled, but her voice when she spoke was firm. 'Drat the girl! She's gone off to get Cecily herself.'

'*What*?'

'Precisely!' Lady Merion read the note again. 'A lot of gibberish about being responsible for the mess.' She snorted. 'Says she can handle Buchanan.'

A pause developed, Ferdie, for once, too incensed to break

it. Eventually Lady Merion spoke again. 'I'm not so sure she can handle that man. I think we should summon Hazelmere anyway. Dorothea seems set against it, but in the circumstances he should be told. It's time she realised that, as she's virtually affianced to him, she simply can't go careering off about the countryside like this, let alone keep it hidden from him.' The sharp blue eyes turned on Ferdie. 'So how do we get hold of him?'

Ferdie came to life. 'Tonight it's easy. You write a note and we'll send it to him at White's. One night of the year you can be sure he's there.'

Lady Merion nodded briskly and, going to the small escritoire, dashed off a note to Hazelmere.

Ferdie, engaged in some hard thinking, looked up as she sealed it. 'Don't address it. I'll do that.'

Lady Merion raised her brows but relinquished her seat without comment. Picking up the pen, Ferdie frowned, then inscribed the front of the note with his cousin's full title.

Summoning Mellow, Ferdie put the note into his hands and instructed him to ensure its immediate delivery to White's. No answer was expected. Together with Lady Merion, he settled down to wait.

As Ferdie had predicted, both Lords Hazelmere and Fanshawe were at their accustomed positions in the gaming-room. Hazelmere was holding the bank, and the rest of the table was comprised of their friends, all making every effort to break the bank. They had been playing for a little over an hour and had just got pleasantly settled in.

Hazelmere, dealing the next hand, was surprised to find an attendant at his elbow with a letter on a salver. Completing the deal, he picked up the letter and, glancing at the direction, used the silver-bladed knife to break the seal. He laid the missive on the table and returned his attention to his cards.

He had immediately recognised Ferdie's handwriting, but could not understand why his cousin should suddenly start to send letters to him under his full title. In fact, he could not understand why Ferdie would send him a letter at this time of

night at all. Despite giving only half his mind to the game, he
succeeded in concluding the first round and, while the other
players were considering their next bids, he opened the letter.

The reason for Ferdie's departure from normal behaviour
was instantly apparent. Rapidly scanning the lines, he managed to control his expression so that those watching could
tell nothing from it. The letter ran,

> My dear Hazelmere,
> Cecily has been abducted by Edward Buchanan. In a note
> he has demanded Dorothea's attendance at some inn. Af-
> ter sending Ferdie to get me, Dorothea left for the inn.
> Ferdie suggests you may be able to help. We are at Mer-
> ion House.
>
> Yours, et cetera,
> Hermione Merion.

Refolding the letter, Hazelmere stared pensively at the
cards. Then, placing the letter in his coat pocket, he turned
once more to the game. He rapidly brought this to a conclusion, refusing the opportunity to draw Markham further into
the bidding. Pushing back his chair, he signalled to an attendant to remove the pile of rouleaus from in front of him. 'I'm
very much afraid, my friends, that you'll have to continue
without me,' he said smoothly.

'Trouble?' asked Peterborough.

'I trust not. Nevertheless, I'll have to return to Cavendish
Square. Will you take the bank, Gerry?'

While Hazelmere and Peterborough concluded their trans-
action for transfer of the bank, Fanshawe frowned at the table.
He had also recognised Ferdie's writing. Finally catching Hazelmere's eye, he raised his brows questioningly. Receiving
an almost imperceptible nod in return, he also withdrew from
the game. Minutes later the two friends descended the steps
of White's. Once clear of the entrance, Fanshawe asked, 'What
is it? Not your mother?'

Hazelmere shook his head. 'Wrong side of Cavendish

Square.' Without further comment he handed the letter over. They stopped under a street-lamp for Fanshawe to read it.

'Good lord! Cecily!'

'I'm afraid we protected Dorothea too well and so he changed his plans a trifle.' Seeing Fanshawe still staring at the letter, Hazelmere removed this firmly from his grasp, saying, 'I suspect we should hurry.'

They covered the distance to Cavendish Square in less than ten minutes. Admitted to Merion House by the thoroughly intrigued Mellow, Hazelmere did not wait to be announced but led the way into the drawing-room.

Lady Merion started up out of her chair. 'Thank God you're here!' Despite her wish to appear calm, the unexpected worry was a taxing burden. She was no longer young.

Hazelmere smiled reassuringly and, after bowing over her hand, settled her once more. Hearing the increasing commotion from the other side of the room as Fanshawe tried to piece together what had happened, he intervened. 'I think we should start at the beginning.'

His voice cut through the altercation with ease. Fanshawe and Ferdie looked at him, then his lordship abandoned his belligerent stance and Ferdie his defensive one. They seated themselves, Ferdie opposite Lady Merion and Fanshawe on a chair pulled over from the side of the room.

Hazelmere nodded his approval and perched on the arm of the chaise. 'You start, Ferdie.'

'Took Dorothea and Cecily to Lady Rothwell's, as I'd said. We all thought it was to be a quiet little party. Turned out to be a visit to Vauxhall.'

'Couldn't you have stopped it?' interposed Fanshawe.

Ferdie looked at Hazelmere and replied, 'Knew you wouldn't like it, but nothing to be done. Dorothea and Cecily wouldn't have understood. Couldn't simply refuse and come away.'

Hazelmere nodded. 'Yes, I see. What then?'

'At first all seemed fine. Nothing untoward. Young people only and no flash characters. Took Dorothea for a stroll.' Nodding to Hazelmere, he explained, 'Your message. When we

got back to the booth Lady Rothwell told us Cecily had gone.
A servant had come with a letter for her.' Fishing in his coat
pockets for the letter, Ferdie continued, 'Fellow told Lady
Rothwell he was your man, Tony. Here it is.'

He handed the crumpled note to Fanshawe. As he read it
his lordship's face grew unusually grim. Handing it on to Hazelmere, he looked at Ferdie. 'And she went with him?'

'Lady Rothwell tried to stop her, but you know what Cecily
is. After that we came straight back here.'

'One moment! Did anyone other than Lady Rothwell know
what happened?' asked Hazelmere.

'No, luckily,' replied Fanshawe. 'And she's promised to
keep mum. Going to say Dorothea was unwell and Cecily and
I escorted her home.'

'She's a good friend,' put in Lady Merion. 'She won't say
anything unhelpful.'

'And then?' prompted Hazelmere.

'We found the letter from Buchanan waiting when we got
here.'

'Where's this letter?' asked Fanshawe.

Lady Merion and Ferdie tried to remember where they had
put it. Then her ladyship realised it was on the escritoire. Hazelmere retrieved it and remained standing while he read the
single sheet, Fanshawe looking over his shoulder.

'Is the writing the same as the others?' asked Fanshawe.

Hazelmere nodded. 'Yes, all the same. So it was Edward
Buchanan all the time.' He folded the letter and returned to
the chaise. 'What happened next?'

'I suggested we send for you. Seemed the best idea. Dorothea didn't agree. Insisted there was no need. Couldn't see
it, myself. Then she suggested I fetch Lady Merion. Meek and
mild as anything! Thought that was a good idea, so I did.
Didn't know she'd go haring off as soon as my back was
turned! Didn't let on at all!' Ferdie's anger returned in full
force.

Hazelmere smiled.

Lady Merion frowned. 'Well? Aren't you going after her?'

The black brows rose, a touch arrogantly. 'Of course. While

I dare say Dorothea may manage Buchanan well enough, like you, I would feel a great deal happier if I knew exactly what was going on. However,' he paused, hazel eyes fixed on an aspidistra in the corner, 'it occurs to me that flying off in a rush might land us in a worse tangle.'

'How so?' asked Fanshawe, seating himself again.

'At the moment Cecily is presumably at the Castle Inn at Tadworth, in the company of Edward Buchanan and associates. Dorothea must have left before midnight and it'll take her close to three hours to make the journey. It's now after twelve-thirty. We can probably make the distance in two hours, so we should reach the inn not far behind her.' He paused for breath. 'However, if we go flying down there we end with both Darent sisters mysteriously disappearing from London, and on the same night you and I, Tony, also mysteriously disappear. And what do we do when we catch up with them? Bring them back to London? But we wouldn't reach here until morning. The gossips would have a field-day.'

As the truth of his words sank in, Lady Merion grimaced.

Ferdie's pale face went blank. 'Oh.'

'So what are we going to do?' asked Fanshawe.

Hazelmere grinned. 'The problem is not insurmountable.' Glancing at Lady Merion's worried face, he added with a smile, 'It's a pity your inventive elder granddaughter isn't here to help, but I think I can contrive a suitable tale. Ring for Mellow, Ferdie.'

Hazelmere asked for his groom to be summoned from Hazelmere House. While they waited he was silent, an odd smile touching the corners of his mouth. At one point he roused himself to ask whether Dorothea had gone alone.

Lady Merion answered. 'Her note said she was taking their maid, Betsy, and of course Lang, her coachman, will be driving.'

Hazelmere nodded as if satisfied and relapsed into silence.

Jim entered the room, cap in hand. Hazelmere studied him for a moment and then, smiling, began in a soft voice that Jim knew well. 'Jim, I have a number of orders which it's vital you carry out to the letter and with all possible speed. The first thing you'll do is fig out the greys.'

'*What*?' This exclamation broke from both Ferdie and Fanshawe simultaneously.

'No! Really, Marc! Can't have thought! The greys on bad roads at night!' blustered Ferdie.

Jim, watching his master, merely blinked. Fanshawe opened his mouth to protest, then caught his friend's eye and subsided.

'There's no point in having the fastest pair in the realm if one cannot use them when needed,' remarked Hazelmere. Turning back to Jim, he continued, 'After you've seen the greys put to, get a stable-boy to walk them in the square. Saddle the fastest horse in the stables—Lightning, I think. And then ride first to Eglemont.' Turning to Fanshawe, he asked, 'Your parents are at home, aren't they?'

'Yes,' replied his lordship, mystified.

'Good. You, Jim, will demand to see Lord Eglemont, or, failing him, her ladyship. You'll tell them Lord Fanshawe will arrive before morning with Cecily Darent. He'll explain when he arrives. You're then to ride to Hazelmere and speak to the Dowager. You'll tell her that I'll arrive before morning with Miss Darent. Again, I'll explain when I arrive.' Suddenly grinning, he added, 'It's probably just as well you won't know the whole story, so you can deny knowledge with a clear conscience.'

Jim, knowing the Marquis's mother well, grinned back. Hazelmere nodded a dismissal.

Fanshawe had worked out some of the plan in his friend's head and was grinning. Hazelmere refused to meet his eye, and instead turned back to Lady Merion and Ferdie. 'I'll only go through this once. We don't have time for repeat performances. Listen well and, if you see any points I've missed, say so. We have to ensure the story is watertight.'

Satisfied he had their attention, he started, 'Some time much earlier in the Season I unwisely described to Dorothea the beauties of seeing Hazelmere Water at sunrise. Dorothea told Cecily, and between them they made my life and yours, Tony, unbearable until we agreed to organise an excursion to see this wonder. With the aid of our respective parents, a plan was hatched. It's best to see this spectacle on a clear morning, and because none of us wished to spend a week or more in the country waiting for such an opportunity it was agreed that on the first clear moonlit night we would drive down in the carriage, view the Water at dawn, visit Hazelmere and Eglemont and return to town later.' With a nod at Lady Merion he added, 'The party was to include your ladyship. Tonight is a clear moonlit night with the promise of a fine morning to follow. Perfect for our projected expedition. Did you say something, Tony?'

Fanshawe had put his head on his arms with an audible groan. Looking up, he said, 'All very well to save their reputations, but what about ours?'

Hazelmere grinned. 'I don't expect this story to fool our friends. It's the rest of the ton I'm concerned about.' He paused. 'Console yourself with imagining how grateful Cecily is bound to be when you tell her of your sacrifice to preserve her reputation.'

Lady Merion snorted. She wondered if Hazelmere expected Dorothea to be grateful. Then he was speaking again.

'To continue. It was arranged that Lady Merion and the Misses Darent would decide on the most appropriate night and then contact the two of us. At the Rothwells' party the girls realised tonight was the most suitable in weeks. So they excused themselves from the party on the pretext that Dorothea was ill and returned to Merion House. They sent a message to us at White's. Ferdie helped with that. And all the gaming-room saw me get the letter, and then we both left to return to Cavendish Square. So far, all's well. Then, after we arrived and agreed tonight was suitable, Ferdie went to fetch Lady Merion. What excuse did you give for summoning her ladyship, Ferdie?'

'That Dorothea was ill.'

'So that fits too. However, when you arrived home, Lady Merion, it was you who felt truly unwell. Sufficiently unwell, at least, to baulk at a night drive down to Hazelmere. But rather than postpone the outing, and seeing that as of this afternoon Dorothea and I are betrothed...'

Hazelmere broke off, seeing the sensation this announcement had caused. 'No,' he continued in a weary tone, 'I haven't asked her yet, but I do have horrible Herbert's blessing and she's not going to get the chance to refuse, so we will be by the time we return to London.'

He paused but, when no one made any comment, continued, 'Where was I? Oh, yes! In these circumstances, you suggested the maid Betsy could go in your stead. We left immediately. Dorothea and I went down in the curricle with Jim and Tony, and Cecily followed in the carriage with Betsy. We had decided that, as the Season is somewhat flat at the moment, we would all spend a few days in the country. So that is exactly what has happened and is going to happen.'

A pause ensued while they considered the tale. Lady Merion's mind was reeling as she considered the possible outcomes when Hazelmere calmly informed Dorothea that she was to marry him. She wished she could be there to see it. But it would do Marc Henry the world of good to meet some opposition for a change. She had little doubt he would succeed in overcoming it. So, an expectant smile curving her lips, she remained silent.

Then Hazelmere spoke again. 'Now for the loose ends. You and I, Tony, are shortly to leave for Tadworth to remove the young ladies from Buchanan's hands and from there we'll proceed to Hazelmere and Eglemont. Lady Merion, you remain here and ensure we have no more rumours. Ferdie, you are the final player and you've probably got the most vital role.'

At these words Ferdie looked highly suspicious. Long acquaintance with his cousin made him wary of such pronouncements. 'What am I to do?'

'First, I want you to place a notice of my betrothal to Dorothea in tomorrow's *Gazette*. There should be time. Then you must very subtly ensure the story of our romantic escapade is broadcast throughout the ton.'

'No!' groaned Fanshawe, pain writ large on his countenance. 'We'll never be able to show our faces at White's again!'

Hazelmere's smile broadened. 'Even so. If everyone is exclaiming over our idiotic behaviour they're unlikely to go looking for other explanations of tonight's doings.' Turning back to Ferdie, he asked, 'Have I missed anything vital?'

Ferdie was running the whole tale over in his mind. He brought his gaze back to his cousin's face, his eyes alight. 'It's good. No gaps. I think I'll drop in on Ginger Gordon tomorrow. Haven't seen him in ages.'

This was greeted by another moan from Fanshawe. Sir 'Ginger' Gordon was an inveterate gossip, Sir Barnaby Ruscombe's chief rival. Even a few words in his ear could be counted on to go a very long way.

'Good! That's settled.' Hazelmere glanced at the clock and rose. 'Come on, Tony. We'd better go.' Taking Lady Merion's hand, he smiled confidently down at her. 'Don't fret. We'll bring them off without harm.'

Turning to Ferdie, Hazelmere noted the smile of pleasant anticipation on his face. 'Don't get too carried away, Ferdie. I do wish to live in London, you know.'

Startled out of his reverie, Ferdie hastened to reassure his cousin that everything would be most subtly handled. As Fanshawe had finished taking his leave, Hazelmere merely threw him a sceptical glance as he moved to the door.

The friends strode rapidly across Cavendish Square. As they reached Hazelmere House Fanshawe said, 'I'll go and get changed. Pick me up when you're ready?'

Hazelmere nodded and entered his house. Moments later his servants were flying to do his bidding, and inside ten minutes, attired more suitably for driving about the country at night, he mounted his curricle behind the restive greys and swept out of the square. Taking Fanshawe up at his lodgings, they made good time through the deserted city streets. Once clear of the suburbs, Hazelmere allowed the horses their heads and the curricle bounded forward.

Edward Buchanan's master plan began to hiccup from the start. The first phase was the abduction of Cecily Darent from

Vauxhall Gardens. Having assumed that she was no different
from the usual débutante, he was unprepared for the spirited
resistance she put up when he grabbed her on one of the shadowy paths. Assisted by his valet, he had secured her hands
and gagged her, but she had managed to kick him on the shin
before they had bundled her into the carriage. Thus warned,
he had kept her bound and gagged until he had been able to
release her into the parlour, the only one in the Castle Inn,
and lock the stout oak door on her.

The Castle Inn was a small hostelry. Not far from the major
roads, it was sufficiently removed to make interruption by unexpected guests unlikely. The front door gave directly on to
the taproom. Edward Buchanan stayed by the fire in the low-
ceilinged room, sipping a mug of ale and smugly considering
the future. It had finally dawned on him that the desirable Miss
Darent, she of the Grange, Hampshire, as nice a little property
as any he had seen, had ripened like a plum and was about to
fall into the hand of the Marquis of Hazelmere. And his lordship didn't even need the money. It was grossly unfair. So he
had set about rectifying the error of fate. But Miss Darent
seemed possessed of an uncanny ability to side-step his snares.
His attempts at the masquerade and the picnic had both come
to naught. This time, however, he prided himself he had her
measure. To save her young sister, she would, he was certain,
deliver herself, and her tidy little fortune, into his hands. Her
fight with Hazelmere and his lordship's absence from town
had relieved his horizon of its only cloud. He smiled into the
flames. Then, bored with his own company, he rose and
stretched. Miss Cecily had been alone for nearly an hour. It
should, therefore, be safe to venture in and discuss the beauties
of the future with his prospective sister-in-law.

Opening the door of the parlour, he sauntered in. A vase of
flowers flew at his head. He ducked just in time and the vase
crashed against the door.

'*Get out!*' said Cecily in tones reminiscent of Lady Merion.
'How *dare* you come in here?'

He had expected to find her weeping in distress and fear,

totally submissive and entirely incapable of accurately throwing objects about the room. Instead she stood at the other end of the heavy deal table that squatted squarely in the middle of the chamber. On its surface, close to her hand, were ranged all the potential missiles the room had held. Eyeing these, he assumed an authoritative manner.

Waving his hand at her ammunition, he said in a confident tone, 'My dear child! There's no cause for such actions, I assure you!'

'Gammon!' she said, picking up a small salt cellar. 'I think you're mad.'

A frown marred Edward Buchanan's contentment. 'You shouldn't say such things of your future brother-in-law, m'dear.'

It took Cecily all of a minute to work it out. 'But Dorothea won't marry you.'

'I assure you she will,' returned Edward Buchanan with calm certainty. He pulled a chair up to the table and sat, a wary eye on the salt cellar. 'And why not? Hazelmere won't have her now, not after she cut him in the Park. And none of her other beaux seems all that keen to come up to scratch. And after she comes down here to spend the night with me— well, just think of the scandal if she doesn't marry me after all.'

'Good lord! You really must be mad! I don't know what happened between Dorothea and Hazelmere in the Park, but I do know he's only gone out of town to his estates. He's expected back any day now. If he finds you've been trying to…to pressure Dorothea into marrying you, well…' Words failed Cecily as she tried to imagine what Hazelmere really would do in such a situation.

But Edward Buchanan was not impressed. 'By the time his lordship finds out, it'll be too late. Your sister will be promised to me and Hazelmere will never stand for the scandal.'

'What scandal? If he killed you it would be simple to hush it up. Tony told me there's little Hazelmere couldn't do if he wished it.'

A niggling doubt awoke in Edward Buchanan's stolid brain.

Memories of the tales of Hazelmere's prowess at Gentleman Jackson's boxing salon reverberated in his head. And Desborough's warning flitted through his consciousness. He shook such unhelpful thoughts aside. 'Nonsense!'

But Edward Buchanan was to find, as Tony Fanshawe already had, that Cecily's mind was of a peculiarly tenacious disposition. She continued to dwell longingly on the possible outcome once Hazelmere learned of his plans. No amount of persuasion could shake her faith that he would find out, and that sooner rather than later. As her description of the likely punishments in store for him passed from the general to the specific Edward Buchanan found himself totally unable to divert her attention. She was trying to recall what drawing and quartering entailed when she was interrupted by a knock on the door.

With enormous relief he rose. 'That, I believe, will be your sister, m'dear.'

Dorothea had spent the journey to Tadworth more in consideration of the possibilities of her next morning's encounter with Hazelmere than in worry over her imminent encounter with Edward Buchanan. She had no real fear of the bucolic Mr Buchanan and did not pause to question her ability to deal with him. She planned to march into the Castle Inn and, quite simply, walk out again with Cecily. If Edward Buchanan was so Gothic as to believe he could bend her to his will by such melodramatic tactics he would shortly learn his error. Her only worry was that her grandmother would bow to Ferdie's exhortations and inform Hazelmere. Hopefully, Lady Merion would hold firm. That way she could get Cecily and herself safely back to London and meet his lordship in the morning, having lost no further ground, bar the lack of a few hours' sleep.

Lang found the inn without difficulty. Entering, Dorothea saw at a glance that this was a respectable house. Reassured, she left Betsy and Lang seated in the taproom and knocked on the parlour door. When it opened she swept through, head held high, without so much as a glance at the man holding the door. She advanced towards her sister, stretching out her hands in greeting. 'There you are, my love.'

The sisters exchanged kisses and Dorothea pulled off her gloves. 'Did you have a pleasant trip down?' she enquired.

Moving back to his chair after shutting the door, Edward Buchanan began to feel that all was not proceeding as it should.

Cecily took her cue from Dorothea. Ignoring their captor, they happily conversed in the most mundane manner, as if nothing at all untoward had occurred. Dorothea moved to the fire to warm her chilled hands.

Suddenly Edward Buchanan could stand it no longer. 'Miss Darent!'

Dorothea turned to look at him, disdain in every line. 'Mr Buchanan. I had hoped, sir, that you would by now have come to your senses and that I would not be forced into conversation with you.'

The repressive tones stung. But Edward Buchanan had not come thus far to be easily turned aside. 'My dear Miss Darent, I realise the events of the evening have come as a shock to you. But you must consider, m'dear. You're here. I'm here. You need to be married. I'm only too willing to oblige. If you think about it, I'm sure you'll see that Edward Buchanan's not such a bad bargain.'

Eyes blazing, Dorothea replied scornfully, 'You, sir, are unquestionably the most distasteful character it has been my misfortune to meet. I dare say you think you've been clever. Personally I doubt it! I cannot for the life of me understand your obsession with marrying me. However, other than as a source of irritation, it concerns me not in the least. By your presence you reveal yourself as anything but the gentleman you purport to be, and neither my sister nor I have the slightest wish to converse with you further!'

Edward Buchanan purpled alarmingly as the comprehensive condemnation poured over him. Rising abruptly, he knocked over his chair. 'Ah, but I think you'll change your mind, m'dear. You wouldn't want it broadcast that I was alone with your lovely young sister for some hours tonight.'

Both Dorothea and Cecily whirled to face him, contempt written clearly on their faces. But before either could speak Edward Buchanan went on, 'Oh, yes. I think you'll change your mind. You've scuttled your chances with Hazelmere. Wouldn't do for your sister to let Fanshawe off the hook, too.'

Cecily was fairly hopping with rage. 'Thea, don't you listen to him! Oooh, just *wait* till Tony and Hazelmere hear of this!'

Dorothea laid a restraining hand on Cecily's arm as that spirited damsel was about to launch forth into further vituperative outpourings. Drawing herself to her full height, she spoke clearly, a distinctly martial light in her green eyes. 'Mr Buchanan. There will be no scandal. My sister and I will shortly be leaving this charming inn and returning to town in our carriage, accompanied by our maid.'

Edward Buchanan jeered, 'And what's to stop me passing on the tale of what happened here tonight?'

Dorothea's eyes opened wide. 'Why, Hazelmere, of course.' She would have given anything not to have needed recourse to his lordship, but, as far as she could see, he was the best deterrent she had. Cecily's happiness was at stake now and she would do anything necessary to preserve her younger sister.

Her calm reference to the Marquis temporarily rattled Edward Buchanan. Then he recovered. 'Nice try, m'dear. But it won't do. Aside from the fact that all the ton knows you quarrelled with his arrogant lordship, I happen to know he's out of town. By the time he returns, the damage will be done.'

The gaze Dorothea bent on the hapless Mr Buchanan would have frozen greater men. 'My dear sir, if your information on the Marquis's movements is so reliable I presume you also know that he returned to London today. As for our relationship, I have no intention of edifying you with an explanation. Suffice to say that Lord Hazelmere has requested an interview with me tomorrow morning.' She paused to let her words sink in. Then she turned to Cecily. 'Come, my love. We should start back. I wouldn't like to be late for my meeting with Hazelmere.'

But Edward Buchanan was not yet defeated. 'Easy to say,

m'dear. But even if he is in town, who's to say he'll hear about it? No, I'm afraid I really can't let you leave.'

His stubborn belligerence ignited Dorothea's temper. 'Oh, you silly man! I hope Hazelmere *doesn't* hear about it. The only reason I came down here is so that there's no reason for him to be involved. And if only you'd see sense you'd be assisting us to leave with all speed!'

'Hah! So he doesn't know!'

'He didn't know when I left, but I wouldn't wager a groat that he doesn't know by now.'

'There's still time to get married,' mused Mr Buchanan. 'I've a special licence and there's a clergyman of sorts in the village.'

Cecily's mouth dropped open. 'You're quite mad,' she informed Mr Buchanan.

'Mr Buchanan!' said Dorothea in tones of long suffering. 'Please listen to me! I will not marry you. Not now, not tonight, not ever.'

'Yes, you will!'

Dorothea opened her mouth to deny this charge but it remained open, her words evaporating, as a calm voice drawled from the doorway, 'I'm shattered to disappoint you, Buchanan, but in this instance Miss Darent is quite correct.'

All eyes turned to see the Marquis of Hazelmere, standing in the doorway, shoulders negligently propped against the frame.

CHAPTER FOURTEEN

Dorothea would have given everything she possessed to know how long Hazelmere had been standing there. Across the room her eyes locked with his. Then, smiling faintly, he straightened and crossed to stand before her, taking her hand and kissing it, as was his habit. Dorothea struggled to master her surprise as the usual light-headedness swept over her. Under the warm hazel gaze she blushed. Hazelmere retained his clasp on her hand as he turned to view Edward Buchanan.

Fanshawe had been standing immediately behind Hazelmere and had entered the room in his wake, pointedly shutting the door after him. Cecily, with a suppressed squeal, had run to his side.

The arrival of their lordships left Edward Buchanan, at least temporarily, with nothing to say and nowhere to go. He was barely able to believe the evidence of his eyes, and all trace of intelligence had left his face, leaving it more bovine in appearance than ever. With the rug effectively pulled from under him, he stared in mute trepidation at Hazelmere, who stood, calmly regarding him, a considering light in the strange hazel eyes.

'Before we continue this singularly senseless conversation I should point out to you, Buchanan, that, on her marriage, Miss Darent's estate remains in her hands.'

Cool and precise, Hazelmere's words affected Edward Buchanan as if a bucket of iced water had been dashed in his face. For a matter of seconds sheer astonishment held him silent. Then, 'Why, that's...that's... I've been grossly deceived!' he blustered. 'Lord Darent has misled me! And Sir Hugo!'

Cecily, Fanshawe and Dorothea received these interesting revelations in fascinated silence. Hazelmere said, 'Precisely. That being so, I think you'll need a holiday to recover from your…exertions, shall we say? A long holiday, I should think. On your estates in Dorset, perhaps? I have no wish to see your face again, in London or anywhere else. If I do, or if it comes to my ears you are again indulging in the practice of abduction or in any way inconveniencing anyone, I'll send your letters to the authorities with a full description of what took place. As all the notes are in your handwriting, and one is very conveniently signed, I'm sure they'll take a great interest in you.'

The steely words effectively reduced Edward Buchanan's grand plan to very small pieces. With his great chance fast disappearing downstream, he glanced wildly, first at Fanshawe and Cecily, and then at Hazelmere, Dorothea at his side, her hand still firmly held in his. 'But the scandal…' His voice trailed away as he encountered Hazelmere's eyes.

'I'm afraid, Buchanan, you seem to be labouring under a misapprehension.' The tones were icy enough to chill the blood in Edward Buchanan's veins. He suddenly recalled some of the other stories about Hazelmere. 'The Misses Darent are on their way to visit Fanshawe's and my families on our estates, escorted by their maid and coachman. Fanshawe and I were delayed in leaving town and so arranged to meet them here.' There was a slight pause during which the hazel eyes calmly surveyed Mr Buchanan. 'Are you suggesting there is anything in that which is at all…improper?'

Edward Buchanan paled. Thoroughly unnerved, he hastened to reassure the Marquis, the words fairly tripping from his tongue. 'No, no! Of course not! Never meant to imply any such thing.' One finger had gone to his neckcloth as if it was suddenly too tight. Retreat, disorderly or otherwise, seemed imperative. 'It's getting late. I must be away. Your servant, Misses Darent, my lords.' With the sketchiest of bows he made for the door, slowing as he realised that Fanshawe still stood with his back to it. At a nod from Hazelmere, Fanshawe opened the door, allowing an agitated Edward Buchanan to escape.

Instantly the sounds of a hurried departure reached their ears. Then the main door of the inn slammed shut and all was quiet.

Inside the parlour the frozen tableau dissolved. Cecily openly threw herself into Fanshawe's arms. Dorothea saw it and wished she could be similarly uninhibited. As things were, she felt barely capable of preserving her composure.

'Oh, God! What a nincompoop!' said Fanshawe. 'Why'd you let him escape so easily?'

'He's not worth the effort,' replied Hazelmere absent-mindedly, his eyes searching Dorothea's face. 'Besides, as he said, he'd been misled.'

Dorothea, trying to look unconscious of his meaning and failing dismally, tried to steer the conversation into lighter fields. 'Misled! I've been trying for weeks to get rid of him. If *only* I'd known!' It suddenly dawned on her to wonder how Hazelmere had known. She felt strangely giddy.

Hazelmere saw her abstracted gaze. Noticing the assorted objects on the table, he seized on the distraction. 'Have you been using the abominable Mr Buchanan for target practice?'

Dorothea, following his gaze, was diverted. 'No. That was Cecily. But she only threw a vase of flowers at him.'

Looking to where she pointed, he saw the shards of the shattered vase. 'Does she often throw things?' he asked faintly.

'Only when she's angry.'

While he considered her answer Hazelmere picked up Dorothea's cloak and draped it over her shoulders. 'More to the point, does she hit anything?'

'Oh, usually,' Dorothea replied, strangely engrossed with the ties of the cloak. 'She's been doing it since she was a child, so her aim is really quite good.'

Glancing at Fanshawe, absorbed with Cecily, Hazelmere could not repress a grin of unholy amusement. 'Do remind me, my love, to mention that to Tony some time. I should warn him of what he's about to take on.'

Dorothea smiled nervously. Hazelmere reached around her to retrieve her gloves and handed them to her. Correctly interpreting his nod, she put them on. She looked up, to find his hazel eyes warmly smiling.

'I think we should leave this inn forthwith. Aside from getting you and Cecily safely away, it's by far too crowded for my liking.'

She smiled back, ignoring the little thrill of anticipation the words and tone drew forth, perfectly content to do whatever he wished, just as long as he continued to smile at her in that deliciously peculiar way. As usual, he had assumed command. But she could hardly argue with the efficient way he had got rid of Edward Buchanan. In the circumstances, she felt she could safely leave discussion of his managing ways until they had returned to London. There was still that interview to be endured, after which they would doubtless discuss what possibilities the future held. She reminded herself she still had no unequivocal proof of the nature of his feelings for her.

Hazelmere escorted Dorothea into the taproom, closely followed by Fanshawe with Cecily. Seeing her chicks being ushered safely out, Betsy heaved a sigh of relief and came forward with Lang to hear their instructions.

Hazelmere consulted his watch. It was already close to four. In the curricle he could reach Hazelmere in just over an hour. The carriage would take closer to two. Dawn would be before six. He turned to Fanshawe with a grin. 'I'll leave you with the coach and Betsy, of course.'

Dorothea, who had moved with Cecily to reassure the clucking Betsy, looked up. Hazelmere smiled blandly back at her.

'Yes, I thought you would,' replied Fanshawe, disgusted at the thought of two hours' frustrating travel with his love and her maid. 'We'll make directly for Eglemont. Cecily can see Hazelmere Water some other time. Preferably not at dawn, what's more! To think I'm going to be saddled with this and I won't even reap the rewards!' He tried to scowl at his friend but could not resist the rueful laughter in the hazel eyes.

'Never mind,' replied Hazelmere, aware that Dorothea had missed little of their exchange. 'I rather think I've got more to explain than you.' He moved to Dorothea's side and outlined the dispositions for the next phase of their journey. He accomplished this without explanation, and was about to lead Dorothea outside when she regained the use of her tongue.

'But there's no need for this at all! Couldn't we simply go back to London?' A long drive alone with Hazelmere had not figured in her plans.

Hazelmere stopped and sighed. 'No.'

Dorothea waited for him to explain, but when instead he took her arm she stood her ground. 'I realise it would not be wise for all of us to return together, but there's no reason Cecily and I cannot go back in the carriage with Betsy, and you two can go down to your estates, then return to London later.'

Hazelmere caught the grin on Fanshawe's face. It could hardly be missed; it was enormous. Noting the stubborn set of Dorothea's chin and the flash of determination in her green eyes, he silenced her in the only effective way he knew. Under the bemused gazes of the innkeeper, Betsy, Lang, an intrigued and approving Cecily and a still grinning Fanshawe, he pulled her against him and kissed her. He did not stop until he judged her incapable of finding further words to argue with.

When Dorothea's wits finally returned she was on the box-seat of Hazelmere's curricle, the Marquis by her side, smartly heading his greys out of the inn yard, setting them on the road leading south. She glanced up at his profile, clearly visible in the bright moonlight. Her determination to force a clear declaration from him grew. Aside from anything else, if what had just occurred was any indication of how he planned to settle disagreements between them in future, unless there was some balance in their relationship, she would never win any arguments at all. Her mind made up, she reviewed her options.

The road between Tadworth and Dorking was narrow but otherwise in good condition. Which, reflected Hazelmere, was just as well. The hedges on either side cast shadows over the road, and despite the silvery moonlight he could not see far ahead. And his love would not remain silent for long. One glance as they left the inn had convinced him that she was merely gathering her forces. He glanced at her now and found her looking speculatively at him. Her brows rose in mute question.

He smiled back and returned his attention to his horses. He had no intention of initiating a conversation. Let her make the first move.

This was not long in coming. 'Are you ever going to tell me just what has been going on?'

Thinking 'No' by far the safest answer, he regretfully settled for, 'It's a long story.'

'How long before we reach Hazelmere?'

'About an hour.'

'Plenty of time to explain, then. *Even* with your greys in hand.'

'But we have to reach Hazelmere Water before dawn.'

'Why?'

Glancing down at her lovely, confused countenance, he smiled reassuringly. 'Because that's the supposed reason for this midnight jaunt, and so at least one of you, having been so insistent on seeing it, had better do so. Just in case someone like Sally Jersey, who has also seen it, asks for a description.'

Raising her eyes to his face, Dorothea asked in weary resignation, 'Just what *is* this tale you've woven? You had much better tell me from the beginning if I'm supposed to convince the likes of Lady Jersey of the truth of it.'

Content to keep the conversation on relatively safe ground, Hazelmere obliged. He started by telling her what happened after she had left Merion House. 'You'll have to remember to make your peace with Ferdie.'

'Was he terribly bothered?'

'Incensed.' He sketched the outline of the story, omitting to tell her that they were supposedly betrothed. He spent some minutes impressing on her the magnitude of Fanshawe's and his sacrifices in saving Cecily's and her reputations. Hearing her chuckle over Ferdie's mission to spread the tale far and wide, he hoped he had diverted her mind from what he had not explained.

Recovering from her giggles, Dorothea mentally reviewed what she had heard, her eyes fixed on the offside horse. This midnight drive was possibly the best chance she would ever have of extracting information from Hazelmere. In normal circumstances, his physical presence was so distracting that it was a constant battle of mind against body to formulate sensible questions, let alone combat his evasive answers. But, since he was now perched on the box-seat beside her, his hands occupied with the reins and his attention divided between his horses and herself, the odds were more even. She would certainly have to encourage him to take her driving more often in future. Silent, they passed through Dorking and into the country lanes leading to Hazelmere. Bringing her gaze back to his face, she said in the most non-committal of tones, 'What were the other notes Mr Buchanan had sent?'

He recalled a comment of Ferdie's that she had a habit of asking questions so it was impossible to sidle out of them. Resigned to the inevitable, he answered, 'He made two previous attempts to abduct you. That was something I didn't foresee when I decided to convince the ton of my interest in you.'

The moonlight had completely faded and sunrise was not far off. They had crossed the Hazelmere boundary, and the look-out over the ornamental lake known as Hazelmere Water was not far ahead.

After a considerable pause while she tried to analyse his actions in all this Dorothea said, 'I take it the first was the Bressington masquerade?'

'Yes. There's nothing you don't know about that, except I knew it wasn't a joke. That was why I was suddenly so ridiculously attentive, even attending that boring party that Sunday. I don't know what I would have done if I hadn't been able to learn your engagements. Did you know one of my footmen is walking out with your maid?'

Dorothea regarded him with a fascinated expression. He grinned and continued, 'The second attempt was at the picnic you attended with Ferdie. He forgot to give you a note delivered while you were there. It was unaddressed, so he opened it when his man found it the next day. It was supposedly signed by me, but Ferdie knows my signature and so he brought it to me. Tony was with me at the time, so after that both of them knew.'

'When did the rest of your friends find out?'

Impossible to deny it. 'On Wednesday, at a luncheon. I had to leave town, and Tony and Ferdie couldn't hope to keep you in sight all the time.'

'Did it never occur to you to tell me?' she asked.

'Yes. But I couldn't see what good it would do.' Seeing her frown, he sighed. 'Who could know if and when the next attempt might be made?'

The silence on his left was complete. After a minute he risked a glance and found she was regarding him quizzically. 'You're quite abominably high-handed, you know.'

He smiled sweetly and replied, 'Yes, I know. But only with the best of intentions.'

The curricle topped a gentle rise and just beyond the crest Hazelmere turned the horses on to the grass verge, cropped to form a look-out. 'And that,' he announced, 'is Hazelmere Water.'

With the sun breaking over the distant horizon, the scene spread beneath her feet was breathtakingly beautiful. He jumped down from the curricle and tied the reins firmly to a bush. He lifted her down and together they descended a flight of shallow steps cut into the escarpment. These led to a small plateau beneath the crest where a stone bench stood by an old oak. An uninterrupted view of the valley below unfurled at their feet. Hazelmere Water was a large ornamental lake edged by clumps of willows. There was an island in the middle with more willows, and a summer-house, painted white, showing through the lacy foliage. Swans cruised slowly on the gentle currents of the stream that fed the lake from one end and exited at the other.

As the sun climbed higher the colours of the scene changed constantly from the first cool sepia tones through the warm pink tints of early sunrise and the golden glow of increasing light, until finally, as the sun cleared the hills behind the lake and shone forth unhindered, the bright greens of the grass and willows and the deep blue of the lake showed clear and intense.

Seated on the bench, Dorothea watched in speechless delight. Hazelmere, beside her, had viewed the sight on many occasions. He still found pleasure in it, but today had eyes only for the woman beside him. Returning to London with the firm intention of settling their past and future in one fell swoop, he had found that, instead of waiting patient and secure for him to declare himself, his independent love had gone haring off in the middle of the night to do battle with Edward Buchanan. It really should not have surprised him. While he had little doubt she would have handled the matter after a fashion, her disposition to manage matters her own way had given him an irresistible opportunity to bring their frustrating courtship to its inevitable climax. But now, despite her apparent calm, she was defensive. To be trying to keep him at a distance after all that had passed between them seemed rather odd, even for his independent love. He watched her; delight in the scene before her glowed on her expressive face. Inwardly he sighed. He was going to have to find out what it was that was worrying her. The reins of this affair of theirs had continually tangled; he couldn't remember when he'd had so much difficulty with a woman. And now he had a sneaking suspicion that, while he had thought he had got the reins untangled and running free, they had somehow got snagged again.

With the sun riding the sky, Dorothea turned towards him, her eyes glowing. 'That was the most beautiful sight I've ever seen! I'm afraid Lord Fanshawe will have to bring Cecily here at dawn after all.'

Hazelmere had lost interest in Fanshawe and Cecily. 'Just as long as it's you who tells him so. Having consigned him to two hours in that carriage with Cecily and your Betsy, I fear I'm not at present riding high in his esteem.'

Dorothea, suddenly breathless, looked down and found that he had hold of her hand. She felt him move to draw her to him. Knowing that if he kissed her she would lose any chance of retaining sufficient control to force any admission, positive or negative, from him, she resisted. He immediately stopped. For a moment silence, still and deep, engulfed them. Dorothea, her eyes downcast, did not see the long lips curl into a wry smile. Hazelmere could think of only one way to precipitate matters, so he took it. 'Dorothea?' His voice was entirely devoid of its usual mocking tone. 'My dear, will you do me the honour of becoming my wife?'

Despite the fact that she had expected the question, for one long moment she thought the world had stopped turning. Then, her eyes still locked on his hand, gently clasping hers, she struggled to find words to extricate herself from the predicament the question had landed her in. How typical of him! If she simply said yes, she would never learn the truth.

'My lord, I am sensible…very sensible of the honour you do me. However, I… I am not convinced there is…any real…reason or…or basis for marriage between us.' In the circumstances, Dorothea felt quite pleased with the outcome. Nicely vague.

Although not surprised, Hazelmere still felt as if he had been winded. How on earth had she come to that wonderful conclusion? Clearly he was going to have to explain a few things to his beloved. Assuming it was his motives she question, he went direct to that issue. 'Why do you imagine I want to marry you?'

Hearing the sincerity in his voice, she felt forced to reply truthfully. Now was no time for missish sentiment. 'You have to marry. I gather you want a conformable wife, to give you heirs and manage your households.' She paused, then added, 'Someone who would not interfere with your present lifestyle.'

For once, he missed the oblique allusion. 'There's nothing in my present lifestyle that marriage to you would disrupt.' For some reason, far from reassuring her, the statement seemed to have the opposite effect.

Dorothea gulped. For one instant she almost convinced herself that she didn't want to know. Then she shook her head. 'In that case, I really don't think we…would suit.'

Hazelmere was entirely at sea. He had no idea what she was talking about, but he heard the catch in her voice. Foreseeing

an unprofitable and probably distressing time ahead if they
continued in this roundabout fashion, he decided to gamble all
on one throw. Cutting tangled reins was the fastest way, after
all. Provided you could hold the horses afterwards. Possessing
himself of both her hands, he drew her around to face him.
'If you're adamant that is true, then of course I'll not press
you. But, if you wish to convince me what you say is so,
you'll have to look at me, my love, and tell me you don't love
me.'

Her heart had sunk like lead at his first sentence. The second
threw her into total disarray. *How could she do that?* In the
long silence that ensued she could feel his eyes on her, still
warm. If she looked up she would lose.

'Dorothea?'

Mute, all she could do was shake her head.

'Why? My dear, you'll have to give me some explanation.'
His voice, unbearably gentle and stripped of its usual lightness,
brought her close to tears. She tried to look up and failed.
Wrenching her hands free, she stood and took a few agitated
steps, stopping beside the trunk of the oak. Her scheming was
turning this into a nightmare. Heavens! What on earth had she
started?

Hazelmere watched her. Clearly she was struggling with
some imagined demon, but he could hardly deal with it unless
she told him what it was. Calmly he stood and strolled to stand
behind her. Taking her by the shoulders, he firmly turned her
to face him. One hand at her waist held her lightly while the
other gently tilted her face up. She stubbornly kept her lovely
and far too revealing eyes lowered. 'Dorothea, why won't you
marry me?'

Impossible not to answer. In the end, in a voice so small
that she could hardly recognise it as her own, she said, 'Because you don't love me.'

For nearly a minute Hazelmere, dazed, remained perfectly
still. Then enlightenment dawned, and with it came relief. Dorothea, equally immobile, suddenly felt his hands shake. Startled, she looked up and saw, to her disbelieving fury, that he
was laughing! Really laughing! Outraged, she flung away. Or

tried to, but he had seen her intention in those beautiful eyes
and held on to her, pulling her roughly into his arms and
holding her, hard, against him. Rage seared through her, leav·
ing her strangely wan. Then his voice, muffled as he spoke
against her hair and still shaking with suppressed laughter,
reached her. 'Oh, sweetheart! What a gem you are! Here I
went to the most extraordinary lengths to convince the entire
ton, or at least all those who mattered, that I was *irrevocably*
in love with you and the only person who didn't notice was
you!'

Already stiff and unyielding, she went rigid. She looked up.
'You *don't* love me!'

The dark brows rose. The hazel eyes, still laughing, gently
quizzed her. 'Don't I?'

She tore her eyes from that mesmeric glance. If she was
ever to learn the answers she had to pose the questions. 'What
about that bet?' she asked, trying to sound scornful and not
succeeding in the least.

He propped his shoulders against the oak, still holding her
against him. 'Young men with too much money and not
enough sense. There are always bets on such things. It's nothing new. There are bets on Fanshawe and Cecily, and Julia
Bressington and Harcourt, and a few other couples, too.'

Her eyes had returned to his during this explanation. 'Really?'

He nodded, smiling. She dropped her eyes to his shoulder
while she considered that. Hazelmere studied her face. When
she remained silent he continued, 'Furthermore, my love, I feel
constrained to point out that, had I been seeking a suitable and
complaisant wife, I would hardly choose a lady whom I have
had to twice rescue from scandalous situations in public inns.'

'But it wasn't my fault in either case!' protested Dorothea
indignantly. She had glanced up into the teasing hazel eyes
but quickly broke the connection. In a small voice she added,
'I thought perhaps you felt being married to me would be
more…comfortable than being married to Miss Buntton.'

'Miss Buntton?' said Hazelmere incredulously. He shuddered. 'My dear, being married to a hedgehog would be more

comfortable than being married to Miss Buntton.' Dorothea smothered a giggle. 'Whoever put that idea…oh, Susan, I suppose?'

Dorothea nodded. Then another thought occurred. 'You're not marrying me because of the…possible scandal over tonight?'

'After I've gone to such lengths to ensure there'll be no scandal? Of course not.' As she persisted in keeping her eyes down, he added a clincher. 'Besides, if that were so, how is it that I've already got Herbert's permission to address you?'

That brought her head up. 'You *have* asked his permission!'

'My dear Dorothea, you really should strive to rid yourself of these ramshackle notions you cherish of me. I wouldn't ask you to marry me if I didn't have Herbert's permission to pay my addresses to you.'

The pious tone pricked her temper. 'What about your mistresses?' she asked.

The hazel eyes caught hers. 'What about them?'

She was at a loss. 'How should I know?' she said in exasperation.

'Precisely!' The dry tone left her in no doubt of what he meant. Their eyes held, then he sighed. 'If you must know, I dismissed my last mistress when I returned to London last September, after meeting you. I've had enough mistresses for a lifetime. I want a wife.'

Her gaze had drifted to his cravat and her hands, trapped between them, were apparently occupied in smoothing its folds. Hazelmere sighed. 'My dear, delightful, idiotic Dorothea, *do* look at me. I am trying, apparently unsuccessfully, to convince you that I love you. The least you can do is pay attention!'

Dorothea had exhausted her questions. Obediently she looked up. When her eyes once more locked with his Hazelmere nodded approvingly. 'Good! For your information, my love, I've been in love with you from, I think, the moment I first saw you picking blackberries in Moreton Park woods. What's more, my reputation notwithstanding, I am not in the habit of seducing village maids *or* débutantes.'

The green eyes widened. Slightly breathless, she said, 'I thought that was part of the bet.'

Goaded, Hazelmere replied, 'The only reason I've been seducing you, albeit in stages, is because I can't seem to keep my hands off you!' At her surprise, he continued, 'Oh, yes! If you think I have power over you, you have just as much power over me.'

The thoroughly feminine smile that spread across her lovely features prompted him to tighten his arms around her. 'Now that I've got your full attention, my love, what *can* I do to convince you I love you?'

Assuming his question to be purely rhetorical, Dorothea lifted her face for his kiss. His lips gently brushed hers in a series of teasingly gentle kisses that satisfied her not at all. She wriggled her hands free and drew his head more firmly to her. She felt rather than heard his satisfied chuckle, then his lips settled over hers in a long engagement that, despite his intentions, drifted deeper with each passing minute. At some point he pushed her cloak back, allowing him access to her body, still clad in the thin silk evening gown of the night before. Too soon they reached the same point they had in Lady Merion's drawing-room. Hazelmere, still in control despite his raging desire, mentally cursed. He should not have let it go this far. There was no way he would even consider taking her here. Her first time she should remember with joy, not distaste. But he had already left her in this state once before. He couldn't do that again.

He raised his head to look at her. Her eyes were huge and glittering, deepest emerald under heavy lids. She moved, unconsciously seductive, pressing her body against him. With a ragged sigh he turned them around so her back was against the trunk of the oak. He bent his head and his lips burned a trail to the hollow of her throat. Expertly his long fingers undid the column of tiny buttons closing her bodice and loosened the laces beneath. As his hand gently cupped her naked breast she moaned softly. His lips found hers again, letting their passions ride. There were other ways she could be satisfied. And he knew them all.

Much later, when she was wrapped once more in her cloak and resting comfortably in his arms, he felt her draw a deep breath and sigh happily. He chuckled and dropped a kiss on the top of her head. 'Does that mean you've agreed to marry me?'

Dorothea smiled dreamily. Without looking up, she asked, 'Do I have any choice?'

'Not really. If you don't consent now I'll take you to Hazelmere, lock you in my apartments and keep you there until I get you with child. Then you won't have any choice at all.'

At that she looked up, laughing. 'Would you?'

The hazel eyes glinted. 'Without hesitation.'

She smiled, a slow, infinitely smug smile. She felt the arms around her tighten. 'In that case, I'd better agree.'

He nodded. 'Very wise.' His eyes searched her face for a moment, as if trying to gauge her state of mind. Then he sighed. 'I suspect I should take advantage of your contented state to tell you that the notice of our betrothal will appear in today's *Gazette*.'

For a moment the implication did not register. Then she asked, 'How on earth…?'

'I asked Ferdie to put it in. It's wiser to keep the tabbies happy wherever possible.' His arm around her, he started to move towards the steps.

Feigning anger, Dorothea stopped dead. 'So *that's* why you're so insistent I marry you!'

The arm around her tightened again, drawing her to him once more. 'Don't start that again. I'm marrying you, you disbelieving woman, because I love you!' He kissed her soundly, then pulled her on to the steps. 'Besides which,' he continued conversationally, 'if I don't have you soon, I'm going to go out of my mind.'

Amused, he watched his love blush delightfully.

'The house is over the next rise. Knowing my mother, the entire household has probably been waiting for hours.'

Dorothea was eager to catch her first glimpse of Hazelmere, and as the curricle topped the rise she looked down on the huge sandstone mansion, honey-coloured in the sun, sprawling across the opposite side of the valley. Descending the gentle slope and crossing the bridge over the stream from the lake, the curricle swept through the gates in the low stone wall separating the formal gardens from the rest of the park. Hazelmere held the greys to a trot as they followed the winding drive through acres and acres of perfectly tended gardens and lawns, past shrubberies and fountains, until the curricle reached the broad sweep of the gravel court before the main entrance.

Jim Hitchin came running to take the reins, grinning with relief at seeing the horses in one piece. He had never doubted his master would return all right and tight with the lady beside him, so had wasted no thoughts on them.

Hazelmere jumped down and lifted Dorothea down. At the first sound of wheels on the gravel, Lady Hazelmere, who had been waiting in the morning-room since five o'clock, had come to the door to welcome them. She was agog to learn just why her usually correct son had seen fit to drive through the night, apparently alone with Miss Darent in an open curricle. One look at his face warned her not to ask.

Correctly surmising that they had been up all night, she immediately whisked Dorothea upstairs to the large chamber she had had prepared. It was only then that Dorothea removed her cloak, and as she moved towards the window the light fell full on her. Lady Hazelmere rapidly revised her assessment of her son's behaviour and, turning, shooed out her maid, who had come in to help. Instead she helped the sleepy girl to bed, lending her one of her own nightgowns and forbearing to ask any questions, even as to the whereabouts of her missing clothing. The tell-tale signs of her son's lovemaking, showing clearly on the perfect skin, would fade by the time she awoke. No need to further embarrass the child, or to expose her to the censorious mind of her sharp-eyed maid. Her own maid, Hazelmere had informed her, along with his valet, would arrive from London later.

Leaving Dorothea already halfway asleep, Lady Hazelmere went downstairs in search of her son. Hazelmere, aware of his mother's curiosity, knew that if she once caught him she would not let him go until she had all the story. He had therefore refused point-blank to pay any attention whatever to Liddiard and had repaired with all possible speed to his apartments before she could materialise and waylay him.

Baulked of all prey, her ladyship spent the rest of the morning in comfortable speculation on what her son and the lovely Dorothea had been up to.

Hazelmere woke to the rattle of curtains. Sunlight streamed into the large apartment. He closed his eyes again. He had left orders to be woken at one. He supposed it was one.

Then memory returned and the events of the early morning swam into focus. The severe lips curved in a smile of pure happiness. A discreet cough interrupted his recollections. He reluctantly opened his eyes and located Murgatroyd, standing by the bed, disapproval in every line.

'I wondered, my lord, what you wished me to do with these?' From finger and thumb hung suspended a garment, which, after a few moments of total bewilderment, Hazelmere recognised. 'I found them in the pocket of your driving cloak, m'lord.' Never, in all the years he had been valeting, had Murgatroyd had to deal with such an occurrence. He was badly discomposed.

Raising his eyes to the face of his henchman, now devoid of all expression, Hazelmere sternly repressed the urge to laugh. As soon as he could command his voice he said, somewhat breathlessly, 'I suppose you had better return them to their owner.'

Something very like shock infused the countenance of his imperturbable valet. 'My lord?' Incredulity hung in the air.

'Miss Darent,' supplied Hazelmere, sorely tried.

Murgatroyd assimilated this information, his face wooden. 'Of course, my lord.' He bowed and had almost reached the door before Hazelmere spoke again.

'Incidentally, Murgatroyd, Miss Darent and I are to be married in a few weeks, so I'm afraid you'll have to get used to such happenings.'

'Indeed, my lord?' Murgatroyd's breast seethed with a whole range of emotions. He had never before valeted to a married gentleman, preferring the regularities of bachelor households. It was the reason he had left his last position. But he had been very comfortable in Hazelmere's employ. And Miss Darent, soon to be her ladyship, was a very lovely woman. And the Marquis was...well, Hazelmere. The rigid features relaxed into something approaching a smile. 'I'm sure I wish you both very happy, my lord.'

Hazelmere smiled his acknowledgement and dropped back on to his pillows as Murgatroyd left in search of Trimmer.

The next five days passed in a rush of activity. Hazelmere had decreed they were to be married at St George's in Hanover Square in just over two weeks. There was a wealth of detail to be discussed and decisions made. A constant stream of couriers passed between London and Hazelmere, carrying orders and information. On that first afternoon Tony Fanshawe and Cecily dropped by on their way back to London. On hearing the news, Cecily was ecstatic; Betsy promptly burst into tears.

From Lady Merion came the news that the whole town was a-buzz with the tale of their trip to Hazelmere Water and, far from there being any undesirable comment, everyone was describing it as the romance of the Season. As Dorothea refolded her grandmother's letter Hazelmere smiled wickedly across the breakfast table. 'Just as well they'll never know what really happened at Hazelmere Water.'

Dorothea gasped, then, outraged by the knowing look on his face, threw a roll at him. Ducking, he protested, 'I thought only Cecily threw things!'

They decided to return to London on Monday. Hazelmere spent Sunday afternoon with Liddiard. He would only be able to spare a single day in the run-up to their wedding for dealing with any further business. Liddiard was to be in ultimate charge of all his estates until they returned from their wedding trip to Italy.

Dorothea, time hanging heavy on her hands, went to sit in the sunken rose garden. It had been five days since they had arrived; five days since that morning above Hazelmere Water. And in those five days Marc had been politely attentive but curiously distant. They had exchanged nothing but the most chastely light kisses—no passionate embraces, no delicious caresses. It was ridiculous! What on earth was the matter now?

A swish of silk skirts heralded Lady Hazelmere's approach. The two women had become firm friends. With a smile her ladyship settled herself on the stone bench beside her soon to be daughter-in-law, and, as was her habit, took the bull by the horns. 'What's the matter?'

Used by now to her ways, Dorothea grimaced. 'It's nothing, really.'

Lady Hazelmere's shrewd eyes studied the younger woman. Then she made an educated guess. 'Hasn't Marc slept with you yet?'

Dorothea blushed rosily.

Her ladyship laughed musically, then reassured her. 'Don't get upset, child. I couldn't help notice you were missing a rather vital article of clothing when you arrived. I presume you didn't set out from London like that?'

In spite of herself, Dorothea grinned. 'No.'

'Well,' said her ladyship, examining the tips of her slippers as they peeped from under the hem of her stylishly elegant gown, 'Marc seems to be taking after his father in more ways than one. It's something of a shock to think you're marrying a rake and find instead that, at least before the wedding, you'd get the same treatment from the Archbishop's son.'

Dorothea giggled.

'Well, maybe not quite the same,' amended Lady Hazelmere. 'But all the Henry men are like that—scandalous on the one hand and puritanical on the other. It's decidedly confusing. Mind you, I doubt there have been many virgin brides in the family, either.'

Dorothea sat up straighter. 'Oh?'

'A word of advice, my dear: if you don't wish to be forced to wait the full two weeks until your wedding, you'd better do something about it. You're leaving for London tomorrow and once there, if I know Marc, you'll have no chance to force the issue. If, on the other hand, you break his resistance now, you should have no trouble in London.'

'But he seems so very distant, I wondered if perhaps he—'

'*Distant*? What on earth happened at Hazelmere Water?' exclaimed her ladyship. 'That sort of thing, let me tell you, just doesn't happen if a man is "distant". Marc's keeping as far away from you as possible because he doesn't trust himself—he knows he's too close to the edge with you, that's all. If you want him to make love to you before your wedding you'll just have to give him a push.'

Dorothea, eyes round, regarded her soon to be mother-in-law. The novel idea of forcing such an issue with her stubborn and domineering betrothed had an attraction all its own. 'How?'

Tucking her arm into Dorothea's, Lady Hazelmere smiled joyously. 'Let's go and look at your wardrobe, shall we?'

That evening Hazelmere arrived in the drawing-room, just ahead of Penton, as usual, to escort his betrothed and his mother into dinner. As he crossed the threshold his eyes went to Dorothea. He blinked and checked, then smoothly recovered himself.

Throughout the meal he struggled to keep his eyes away from the vision in ivory silk seated on his right. But for once his mother seemed curiously silent, leaving Dorothea and himself to carry the conversation. In the end he forced himself to keep his eyes on her face. That was bad enough, but not nearly so disturbing as the rest of her. Where in hell had she got that gown? Presumably Celestine—simplicity was her hallmark. An ivory sheath with a bodice so abbreviated that it barely passed muster, with an overdress of silk gauze so fine that it was completely transparent. The entire creation was held together by a row of tiny pearl buttons down the front. He had never been so thankful to see the end of a meal as he was that night.

He watched Dorothea and his mother retire upstairs to the parlour. With a sigh of relief he went into the library. Half an hour later, settled in one of the huge wing chairs before the fire, a large brandy by his side, he was deep in the latest newssheet when he heard the door shut. Looking up, he stood as Dorothea came towards him, calm and serene as ever, a book in her hands. 'Your mother has retired early so that she'll be able to farewell us in the morning. I thought I'd come and sit with you for a while. You don't mind, do you?'

He smiled in response to her smile and settled her in the wing chair opposite his. She opened her book and seemed to be quite content to sit quietly reading. He returned to his newssheet.

For a while only the ticking of the huge grandfather clock in the corner and the occasional crackle from the fire disturbed the peace. Glancing up, he saw she had laid aside her book and was calmly watching the leaping flames. The light from the fire flickered in a rosy glow over her still figure, striking coppery glints from her dark hair. He forced his attention back to the newssheet.

After reading the same paragraph four times, and still having no idea what it said, he gave up. He laid the paper aside. In one smooth movement he rose and, crossing to her, took her hands; raising her, he drew her into his arms. He looked down into her emerald eyes, then bent his head until his lips found hers. The room was still; only the flames rose and fell, illuminating the figures locked together before the hearth. When the kiss finally ended they were both breathing raggedly. The hazel and green eyes locked for a time in silent communion, then Hazelmere bent to lightly brush her lips with his. 'I love you.'

Hardly daring to speak in case the magic surrounding them shattered into a million shards, Dorothea barely breathed the words, 'And I love you.'

The severely sculpted lips lifted in a decidedly wicked smile. 'Let's go to bed.'

Many hours later Dorothea, blissfully sated, snuggled herself against the long length of her husband-to-be. They had come up to his room; her room next door was not yet refurbished. Her clothes, and his, were scattered in a trail from the door to the hearth. They had first made love, exquisitely, on the huge daybed before the fire. Later they had moved to the even larger four-poster, where they now lay. With a soft, contented sigh she settled herself to sleep, one arm across his chest, his arm around her, holding her close.

Suddenly, in the darkness, Hazelmere chuckled. Then he shook with silent laughter. 'Oh, God! What on earth will Murgatroyd say this time?'

Dorothea murmured sleepily and dropped a kiss on his collarbone. She had no idea who Murgatroyd was and was not particularly interested. She was too busy savouring the novel sensation of having won an argument with her arrogant Marquis. Even if she did not win another for a considerable time, she doubted it would bother her. She was bound to be far too contented to care.

Fair Juno

CHAPTER ONE

Martin Cambden Willesden, fifth Earl of Merton, strode purposefully along the first-floor corridor of the Hermitage, his principal country residence. The scowl marring his striking features would have warned any who knew him that he was in a foul mood. A common saying among the men of the 7th Hussars had been that if any emotion showed on Major Willesden's face the portents were bad. And, thought ex-Major Willesden savagely, I've every right to feel furious.

Recalled from pleasant exile in the Bahamas, forced to leave behind the most satisfying mistress he had ever mounted, he had landed in gloomy London to face an uphill battle to extricate the family fortunes from the appalling state they had, apparently unaided, tumbled into. Matthews, the elder, of Matthews and Sons, his and his family's man of business, had warned him that the Hermitage was in need of attention and would not, in its present state, meet with his approval. He had thought that was all part of the old man's attempt to persuade him to return to England without delay. He should have recalled Matthews' habit of understatement. Martin's lips thinned. The grim look in his grey eyes deepened. The Hermitage was in even worse case than the investments he had spent the last three weeks reorganising.

As he paced the length of the corridor, the crisp clack of boot-heels penetrated his reverie. In a state bordering on shock, Martin stopped and stared down. There were no runners! Just bare wooden boards and, to his critical eye, they were not even well-polished.

Slowly, his grey gaze lifted to take in the sombre tones of

decaying wallpaper framed by faded and musty hangings. A pervasive chill inhabited the gloom.

His frown now black, the Earl of Merton swore—and added yet another item to the catalogue of matters requiring immediate attention. If he was ever to visit the Hermitage again, let alone reside for more than a day, the place would have to be done up. Downstairs was bad enough—but this! Description failed him.

Setting aside his aggravation, Martin resumed his determined progress towards the Dowager Countess's rooms. Since his arrival eight hours ago, he had postponed the inevitable meeting with his mother on the grounds of dealing with the problems crippling his major estate. The excuse had not been exaggeration. But the critical decisions had been made; the reins were now firmly in his grasp.

Despite such success, his hopes for the coming interview were less than certain. Curiosity brushed shoulders with a lingering wariness he had not thought he still possessed.

His mother, Lady Catherine Willesden, the Dowager Countess of Merton, had terrorised her household for as long as Martin could recall. The only ones apparently immune from her domination had been his father and himself. His father she had excused. He had not been so favoured.

He halted outside the plain wooden door that gave access to the Dowager's apartments. Despite all that lay between them, she was his mother. A mother he had not seen for thirteen years and whom he remembered as a cold, calculating woman with no room in her heart for him. How much of the blame for the decay of his ancestral acres could be laid at her door? The question puzzled him, for he knew her pride. In fact, he had a good few questions, including how she would deal with him now; the answers lay beyond the door facing him.

Recognising the instinctive squaring of his shoulders as his habit when about to enter his colonel's domain, Martin's lips twitched. Without more ado, he raised a fist to the plain panels and knocked. Hearing a clear instruction to enter, he opened the door and complied.

He paused just beyond the threshold, his hand on the door-knob and, with a practised air of languid ease, scanned the room. What he saw answered some of his questions.

The tall, upright figure in the chair before the windows was much as he remembered, more gaunt with hair three shades greyer, perhaps, but still retaining that calm air of determination he so vividly recalled. It was the sight of the gnarled and twisted hands resting, useless, in her lap and the peculiar rigidity of her pose that alerted him to the truth. They had told him she kept to her room, a victim of rheumatism. He had interpreted that as a fashionable response to a relatively minor ailment. Now, reality stared him in the face. His mother was an invalid, bound to her chair.

Pity stabbed him, sharp and fresh. He remembered her as an active woman, riding and dancing with the best of them. Then his eyes locked with hers, chilly grey, haughty as ever—and more defensive than he had ever seen them. Instantly, he knew that pity was the very last thing his mother would accept from him.

Despite the real shock, his face remained impassive. Unhurriedly, he closed the door and strolled into the room, taking a moment to acknowledge the round-eyed stare of the only other occupant of the large chamber—his eldest brother's relict, Melissa.

Catherine Willesden sat in her high-backed chair and watched her third son approach, her features as impassive as his. Her lips thinned as she took in his long, powerful frame, and the subtle elegance that cloaked it. The light fell on his features as he drew nearer. Her sharp eyes were quick to detect the hardness behind the elegance, a ruthless determination, a hedonism ill-concealed by the veneer of polite manners. It was a characteristic she was honest enough to recognise.

Then he was before her. To her horror, he reached for her hand. She would have stopped him if she'd been able but the words stuck in her throat, trapped by her pride. Warm, strong fingers closed over her gnarled fingers. Her surprise was swamped beneath a sudden rush of emotions as Martin's dark head bent and she felt his lips brush her wrinkled skin. Gently, he replaced her hand in her lap and dutifully kissed her cheek.

'Mama.'

The single word, uttered in a gravelly voice deeper than she recalled, jolted Lady Catherine to reality. She blinked rapidly. Her heart was beating faster. Ridiculous! She fixed her son with a frown, struggling to infuse an arctic bleakness into her grey eyes. The slight smile which played about his mouth suggested that he was well aware he had thrown her off balance. But she was determined to keep this black sheep firmly beneath her thumb. She could, and would, ensure he brought no further scandal upon the family.

'I believe, sir, that I sent instructions that you were to attend me here immediately you reached England?'

Entirely unperturbed by his mother's icy glare, Martin strolled to the empty fireplace, one black brow rising in polite surprise. 'Didn't my secretary write to you?'

Indignation flared in Lady Catherine's pale eyes. 'If you are referring to a note from a Mr Wetherall informing me that the Earl of Merton was occupied with taking up the reins of his inheritance and would call on me at his earliest convenience, I received it, sirrah! What I want to know is what the meaning of it is. And why, once you finally arrived, it took you an entire day to remember the way to my rooms!'

Observing the unmistakable signs of ire investing his mother's austere features, Martin resisted the temptation to remind her of his title. He had not expected to enjoy this discussion, but, somehow, his mother no longer seemed as remote nor as truly hostile as he recalled. Perhaps it was her infirmity that made her appear more human? 'Suffice it to say that the Merton affairs were in a somewhat deeper tangle than I had understood.' Placing one booted foot on the brass fender, Martin braced an arm against the heavily carved mantel and, with unimpaired calm, regarded his mother. 'However, now that I have managed to spare you some time away from the damnable business of setting this estate to rights, perhaps you could tell me what it is you wish to see me about?'

By the conscious exercise of considerable will-power, Lady

Catherine kept surprise from her face. It wasn't his words that shook her, but his voice. Gone entirely were the light, charming tones of youth. In their place, there was depth containing a great deal of hardness, harshness, with the undertones of command barely concealed beneath the fashionable drawl.

Inwardly, she shook herself. The idea of being cowed by this scapegrace son was ludicrous. He had always been impudent—but never stupid. Such languid insolence would be a thing of the past, once she made his position clear. Wrapping herself in haughty dignity, Lady Catherine embarked on her son's education. 'I have much to say concerning how you should go on.'

Exuding an attitude of polite attention, Martin settled his shoulders against the mantelpiece, elegantly crossing his long legs before him, and fixed his mother with a steady regard.

Frowning, Lady Catherine nodded towards a chair. 'Sit down.'

Martin's lips twisted in a slow smile. 'I'm quite comfortable. What are these facts you needs must inform me of?'

Lady Catherine decided not to glare. His very ease was disconcerting. Much better not to let on how disturbing she found it. She forced herself to meet his unwavering gaze. 'Firstly, I consider it imperative that you marry as soon as possible. To this end, I've arranged a match with a Miss Faith Wendover.'

One of Martin's mobile brows rose.

Seeing it, the Dowager hurried on. 'Given that the title now resides with the third of my four sons, you can hardly be surprised if, in my estimation, securing the succession is a major concern.'

Her eldest son George had married to please his family but Melissa, dull, plain Melissa, had failed lamentably in satisfying expectations. Her second son Edward had died some years previously, part of the force which had successfully repelled The Monster's invasion. George had succumbed to the fever a year ago. Until then, it had never dawned on the Dowager that her impossible third son could inherit. If she had thought of it at all, she would have expected him to die, somewhere,

on one of his outlandish adventures, leaving Damian, her favourite, as the next Earl.

But Martin was now the Earl; it was up to her to ensure
that he toed the line.

Determined to brook no opposition, Lady Catherine fixed
her son with a commanding eye. 'Miss Wendover is an heiress
and passably pretty. She'll make an unexceptionable Countess
of Merton. Her family is well-respected and she'll bring considerable land as her dower. Now you are here and the settlements can be signed, the marriage can take place in three
months' time.'

Prepared to defend her arrangements against a storm of protest, Lady Catherine tilted her chin at an imperious angle and
regarded the lean figure propped by the fireplace with keen
anticipation. Once again, she was struck by the changes, enveloped by a unnerving sense of dealing with a stranger who
was yet no stranger. He was looking down, his expression
guarded. Unexpectedly curious, Lady Catherine studied her
son. Her last memories of Martin were of a twenty-two-year-
old, already steeped in every form of fashionable vice—drinking, gambling and, of course, women. It was his propensity
for dabbling with the opposite sex that had brought his tem-
pestuous career to a sudden halt. Serena Monckton. The beauty
had claimed Martin had seduced her. He had denied it but no
one, least of all his family, had believed him. But he had
steadfastly resisted all attempts to coerce him into marrying
the chit. In a fury, her husband had bought off the girl's family
and banished his third son to a distant relative in the colonies.
John had regretted that action bitterly, regretted it to his dying
day, quite literally; Martin had always been his favourite and
he had died without seeing him again.

Intent on finding evidence that the son of her memories had
not in truth changed, Lady Catherine acknowledged the broad
shoulders and long, lean limbs with an inward snort. He still
possessed the figure of Adonis, hard and well-muscled through
addiction to outdoor pursuits. His long-boned hands were
clean and manicured; the gold signet his father had given him
on his twenty-first birthday glowed on his right hand. The hair

that curled about his clear brow was as black as a raven's wing. All that she remembered. What she could not recall was the strength engraved in the chiselled features, the aura of confidence which went further than mere arrogance, the graceful movements that created an impression of harnessed power. Those she could not remember at all.

Unease growing, she waited for some show of resistance. None came.

'Have you nothing to say?'

Startled from his reverie, induced by memories of the last time his mother had insisted he marry, Martin lifted his gaze to the Dowager's face. His brows rose. 'On the contrary. But I would like to hear all your plans first. Surely that's not the sum of them?'

'By no means.' Lady Catherine threw him a glance that would have wilted lesser men and wished he would sit down. Towering over her, he seemed far too powerful to intimidate. But she was determined to do her duty. 'My second point concerns the family estates and businesses. You say you've been acquainting yourself with them. I wish you to leave all such matters in the hands of those retainers George hired. They're doubtless better managers than you could ever be. After all, you can have no experience of running estates of such size.'

A muscle at the corner of Martin's mouth quivered. He stilled it.

Lady Catherine, absorbed in ordering her arguments, missed the warning. 'Lastly, once you and Miss Wendover are married, you will reside here throughout the year.' She paused to eye Martin speculatively. 'You may not yet realise, but it is my money that keeps the Merton estates afloat. Remember, I wasn't a nobody before I married your father. I've allowed what passed back to me through settlements on your father's death to be drawn upon for living expenses as the estates are unable to pay well enough.'

Martin remained silent.

Confident of victory despite his impassivity, Lady Catherine advanced her trump card. 'Unless you agree to my conditions,

I'll withdraw my funds from the estate, which will leave you destitute.' On the word, her eyes flickered over the long frame still negligently propped against the mantelpiece. The subtle hand of a master showed in the cut of his dark blue coat; the pristine state of his small clothes was beyond reproach. Gleaming Hessians completed the picture. Martin, his mother reflected, had never been cheap.

The object of her scrutiny was examining the toe of one boot.

Undeterred, the Dowager added a clincher. 'Should you choose to flout my wishes, I'll see you damned and will settle my fortune on Damian.'

As she made this final, all-encompassing threat, Lady Catherine smiled and settled back in her chair. Martin had always disliked Damian, jealous of the fact that the younger boy was her favourite. Knowing the battle won, she glanced up at her son.

She was unprepared for the slow smile which spread across his dark face, softening the harsh lines, imparting a devilish handsomeness to the aristocratic features. Irrelevantly, she reflected that it was hardly surprising that this son, of the four, had never had the slightest trouble winning the ladies to his side.

'If that's all you have to say, ma'am, I have a few comments of my own.'

Lady Catherine blinked, then inclined her head regally, prepared to be gracious in victory.

Nonchalantly, Martin straightened and strolled towards the windows. 'Firstly, as regards my marriage, I will marry whom I please, when I please. And, incidentally, if I please.'

The stunned silence behind him spoke volumes. Martin's gaze skimmed the tops of the trees in the Home Wood. His mother's suggestions were outrageous, but entirely expected. However, while her machinations were unwelcome, he understood and respected the devotion to family duty that prompted her to them. Even more to the point, they confirmed his supposition that she had had no hand in the decline of the Merton fortunes. As she was tied to her room, her household under the sway of an unscrupulous factor he had derived great satisfaction from verbally flaying before evicting him in the time-honoured way, he doubted his mother had any idea of the state of the rest of the house. Her chambers were in reasonable condition, better than any others in the rambling mansion. The factor had succeeded in intimidating the rest of the staff and, very likely, had gulled Melissa and possibly even George into believing that the decay was unavoidable. And if the section of gardens he could now see was the only fragment of the grounds still deserving of the title, how could his mother know the rest was wilderness? Martin paused by the window, his fingers drumming lightly on the wide ledge. 'Apropos of Damian, I should point out that he will hardly thank you for rushing me to the altar. He is, after all, my heir until such time as I father a legitimate son. Considering his current pecuniary embarrassments, he's unlikely to appreciate your motives in assisting me to accomplish that deed, and in such haste.'

Lady Catherine stiffened. Martin spared a glance for his sister-in-law, huddled back in her chair, listening intently to the exchange between mother and son while ostensibly absorbed with her embroidery. One brow rising cynically, Martin turned to his mother's fury.

'How *dare* you!' For a moment, rage held the Dowager speechless. Then the dam broke. 'You will marry *as I say*! To think of any other course is out of the question! The arrangements have been made.'

'Naturally,' Martin replied, his voice cool and precise, 'I regret any inconvenience your actions may cause others. However,' he continued, on a sterner note, 'I am at a loss to understand what gave you the impression that you were empowered to speak for me in this matter. I find it hard to believe that Miss Wendover's parents were so ill-advised as to imagine you did. If they have, in truth, done so, their discomfiture is the result of their own folly. I suggest you inform them without delay that no alliance will occur between Miss Wendover and myself.'

Stunned, Lady Catherine blinked. 'You're mad! I would be

mortified to do so!' She sat bolt upright, her hands twisting in her lap, her expression one of dawning dismay.

Martin quelled an unexpected urge to comfort her. She would have to learn that the youth who left this house thirteen years before was no more. 'I hesitate to point out that any embarrassment you might feel has been accrued through your own machinations. It would be well if you could bring yourself to understand that I will not be manipulated, ma'am.'

Unable to meet his stern gaze, Lady Catherine glanced down at her crabbed fingers, conscious for the first time in years of an urge to fuss with her skirts. Suddenly, Martin looked very like—sounded very like—his father.

When his mother remained silent, Martin continued calmly, his tone dry. 'As for your second point, I can inform you that, having become thoroughly acquainted with my inheritance, I've rescinded all the appointments made by George. Matthews and Sons and Bromleys, our brokers, together with our bankers, Blanchards, remain. They date from my father's time. But my people are now in charge of this estate and the smaller estates in Dorset, Leicestershire and Northamptonshire. The men George hired were bleeding the estate dry. It's beyond my comprehension, ma'am, why even you did not question the story that estates of the size of the Merton holdings were, within two years of my father's death, mysteriously no longer able to support the family.'

Martin paused, tamping down the anger simmering beneath his calm. Just thinking of the state of his patrimony was enough to summon his demons. Surmising from his mother's stunned expression that she needed a few minutes to adjust to his revelations, he let his gaze wander the room.

Lady Catherine's mind was indeed reeling. A niggling memory of the odd look old Matthews had given her when, angry at Martin's inheriting, she had given vent to her frustrations in a long catalogue of his shortcomings, returned with a thump. She had been taken aback by the man's quietly tendered opinion that Mr Martin was just what the Merton estates needed. Martin, expensive profligate that he was, was hardly the sort she had expected Matthews to support. Later, she had learned that Martin had engaged the same firm his family had long used to represent him in his business dealings. It had come as something of a shock to realise that Martin had the sort of dealings with which a firm such as Matthews and Sons would assist. Matthews' comment had bothered her. Now she knew what he had meant. Damn him—why had he not explained more fully? Why had she not asked?

After gazing at Melissa's bent head, pale blonde flecked with grey, and recalling his conclusion of years before that nothing much actually went on inside it, Martin turned back to his mother. As he guessed rather more of her thoughts than she would have wished, his lips twisted wryly. 'You're quite right in saying that I've little experience in running estates of this size—my own are considerably more extensive.'

Confirming as they did that her third son had changed in more ways than met the eye, his words seriously undermined Lady Catherine's composure. They more than undermined her plans.

At her thunderstruck look, Martin's grin converted to a not ungentle smile. 'Did you think your prodigal son was returning from a life of deprivation to hang on your sleeve?'

The glance she threw him was answer enough. Martin leant back against the window-ledge, long legs stretched before him. 'I'm desolated to disappoint you, ma'am, but I'm in no need of your funds. On my return to London, I'll instruct Matthews to call on you here, to assist in redrafting your will. I pray you hold to your threat to disown me. Damian will never forgive you if you don't. Besides,' he added, grey eyes gleaming with irrepressible candour, 'he needs the support that the news that he's your beneficiary will bring. If nothing else, it should relieve me of the necessity of repeatedly rescuing him from the River Tick. As far as I'm concerned, he may go to the devil in whatever way he chooses. If he uses your money to do it, I'll be even better pleased. However, regardless of what you may choose to do, no further monies from your settlements will be used for the Merton estates, in any way whatever.'

Martin examined his mother's face, sensitive to the encroachments of age on past beauty. After her initial shock, she had drawn herself up, her eyes grey stone, her lips compressed as if to hold back her incredulity. Despite her ailment, there was a deal of strength and determination still discernible in the gaunt frame. To his surprise, he no longer felt the need to strike back at her, to impress her with his successes, to demonstrate how worthy of her love he was. That, too, had died with the years.

'And now to your last stipulation.' He pushed away from the window-ledge, glancing down to resettle his sleeves. 'I will, of course, be residing for part of the year in London. Beyond that, I anticipate travelling to my various estates as well as visiting those of my friends, as one might expect. I also anticipate inviting guests to stay here. As I recall, during my father's day, the Hermitage was renowned for its hospitality.' He looked at his mother; she was staring past him, plainly struggling to bring this new image of him into focus.

'Of course, such visits will have to wait until the place is refurbished.'

'*What*?' The unladylike exclamation burst from Lady Catherine's lips. Startled, her gaze flew to Martin's face, her question in her eyes.

'You needn't concern yourself about that.' Martin frowned. There was no need for her to know how bad it really was; she would be mortified. 'I'm sending a firm of decorators down once they've finished with Merton House.' He paused but his mother's gaze was again far-away. When she made no further comment, Martin straightened. 'I'm returning to London within the hour. So, if there's nothing further you wish to discuss, I'll bid you goodbye.'

'Am I to assume these decorators will, on *your* instruction, redo these rooms as well?' The sarcasm in Lady Catherine's voice would have cut glass.

Martin smothered his smile. Rapidly, he reviewed his options. 'If you wish, I'll tell them to consult with you—over the rooms that are peculiarly yours, of course.'

He could not, in all conscience, saddle her with the task of overseeing such a major reconstruction, and, if truth be known, he intended to use this opportunity to stamp his own personality on this, the seat of his forebears.

His mother's glare relieved him of any worry that she would react to his independence by going into a decline. Reassured, Martin raised an expectant brow.

With every evidence of reluctance, Lady Catherine nodded a curt dismissal.

With a graceful bow to her, and a nod for Melissa, Martin left the room.

Lady Catherine watched him go, then sought counsel in silence. Long after the door had clicked shut, she remained, her gaze fixed, unseeing, on the unlighted fire. Eventually shaking free of her recollections, she could not help wondering if, in her most secret of hearts, despite the attendant difficulties, she was not just a little bit relieved to have a man, a real man, in charge again.

Downstairs, Martin briskly descended the steep steps of the portico to where his curricle awaited, his prize match bays stamping impatiently. A heavy hacking cough greeted him, coming from beyond the off-side horse. Frowning, Martin ignored the reins looped over the brake and, patting the velvety noses of his favourite pair, rounded them to find his groom-cum-valet and ex-batman Joshua Carruthers propped against the carriage, eyes streaming above a large handkerchief.

'What the devil's the matter?' Even as Martin asked the question, he realised the answer.

'Nuthing more'n a cold,' Joshua mumbled thickly, waving one gnarled hand dismissively. He gulped and stuffed the handkerchief in his breeches pocket, revealing a shiny red nose to his master's sharp eyes. 'Best get on our way, then.'

Martin did not move. 'You're not going anywhere.'

'But I distin'ly 'eard you say nuthin' on earth woul' induce you to spen' the night in this ramshackle 'ole.'

'As always, your memory is accurate, your hearing less so. I'm going on.'

'No' without me, you're not.'

Exasperated, hands on hips, Martin watched as the old soldier half staggered to the back of the curricle. When he had to brace himself against the curricle side as another bout of coughing shook him, Martin swore. Spotting two stable boys gazing in awe, whether at the equipage or its owner Martin was not at all sure, he beckoned them up. 'Hold 'em.'

Once assured they had the restless horses secured, Martin grasped Joshua by the elbow and steered him remorselessly towards the house. 'Consider yourself ordered back to barracks. Dammit, man—we wouldn't get around the first bend before you fell off.'

In vain, Joshua tried to hang back. 'But—'

'I know the place is in a state,' Martin countered, sweeping his reluctant henchman back up the steps. 'But now I've got rid of that wretched factor, the rest of the staff will doubtless remember how things should be done. At least,' he added, stopping in the gloomy front hall, 'I hope they will.'

He had given orders that the household should conduct itself as it had previously, in his father's day. Enough of the staff remained for him to expect a reasonable outcome. All locals, many from generations of Merton servitors, they had been overwhelmed by the outsider George had installed over them. Freed from the tyrannical factor, they seemed eager to return the Hermitage to its proper state.

Joshua sniffed. 'What about the horses?'

Martin's lips twitched but he suppressed the urge to smile, assuming instead a repressively haughty attitude. His brows rose to chilling heights. 'You aren't about to suggest I don't know how to take care of my cattle, are you?'

Muttering, Joshua threw him a darkling glance.

'Get off to bed, you old curmudgeon. When you're well enough to ride, you may take a horse from the stables and come on to London. It'll have to be that hack of George's; it's the only animal remaining with sufficient resemblance to the equine species to meet your high standards.'

Not at all mollified, Joshua humphed. But he knew better than to argue. Contenting himself with a last warning— 'There's rain on the way, so's you'd best take heed'—he stumped down the hall towards the faded baize-covered door at its rear.

Smiling, Martin returned to his curricle. Dismissing the wide-eyed lads, he climbed to the box seat and clicked the reins. The carriage swept down the weed-choked drive. Martin did not glance back.

As he passed through the gateposts marking the main entry, through the heavy iron gates, half off their hinges, Martin heaved a heartfelt sigh. For thirteen years, his home had glowed in his memory, a place of charm and grace, an Elysian paradise he had longed to regain. Fate had granted him his wish but, as fickle as ever, had denied him his dream. The charm and grace had vanished, victim to the neglect of the years since his father had had it in his care.

He would restore it—bring back the gracious beauty, the calming sense of peace. On that he was determined. Martin's jaw set, his eyes glinted, grey steel in the afternoon sun. In truth, he was glad to leave behind the travesty of his dream. He would remain in London until the work was done. When next he saw his home, it would once again be the place he had carried in his heart through all the years of his roaming. His particular paradise.

The road to Taunton loomed ahead. Checking his team for the turn, Martin cast a quick glance to the west. Joshua had been right—there was rain on the way. Pursing his lips, Martin considered his options. If he stopped at Taunton, London the next day would be a tough order. He would make for Ilchester—he and Joshua had passed the previous night at the Fox in tolerable comfort. Decision made, Martin dropped his hands, letting the horses stretch their legs. From memory, there was a short cut, just south of Taunton, which would see him in Ilchester before the coming storm.

Two hours later, the curricle swayed perilously as the wheels hit yet another rut. Martin swore roundly. He reined in his team to peer ahead into the gathering gloom. The short cut, dimly remembered as a fair road, had not lived up to expectations. A low mutter came from the west. Martin scanned the horizons, barely visible beneath the low-lying cloud. He doubted he could even make the London road before the storm struck.

He was gently urging the horses over the rutted stretch, dredging his memory in an effort to recall any nearby shelter, when a scream rent the air. The horses plunged. Rapidly bringing them under control, Martin leapt from his perch and ran to their heads. He caught hold of their bits just in time to prevent them rearing as a second scream sliced through the night. No doubt about it, a woman's scream, coming from the woods just ahead. Swiftly, Martin tied the team securely to a nearby gate and, grabbing the pair of loaded pistols from beneath the seat, made for the trees. Once in their shadow, he took care to move silently, thanking the years of his misspent youth, when he had often gone poaching on his father's preserves with young Johnny Hobbs from the village.

Some distance into the wood, he froze. Before him lay a small clearing, a track leading into it from the opposite direction. Sounds of a struggle came from an ill-assorted trio, waltzing in the shadows in the centre.

'Keep still, you little…!'

'*Ow*! Gawd! She bit my finger, the doxy!'

As one man pulled away, the group resolved into two burly men dressed in unkempt frieze and a lady, unquestionably a lady, in a silk gown which shimmered in the twilight. The larger of the men succeeded in grabbing the woman from behind, trapping her arms by her sides. Despite her efforts to kick him, he managed to hold her.

'Listen, missus. The master said to hold you 'ere and not to harm a single hair of your head. Now how's we to do that if'n you don't stop still?'

The exasperation in the man's voice brought a sympathetic smile to Martin's face. The clearing was too large to allow him to creep up on them. Quietly, he worked his way around so that the man holding the woman would have his back to him.

'You fools!' The woman and her captor teetered perilously. 'Don't you know the price for kidnapping? If you let me go, I'll pay you double what your master will!'

Martin's brows rose. The woman's voice was unexpectedly mature. Clearly, she had not lost her head.

'Maybe so, lady,' growled the man nursing his finger. 'But the master's gentry and they're mean when crossed. No—I don't rightly see as how we can oblige.'

Holding both pistols fully cocked, Martin stepped from the trees. 'Dear me. Haven't you been taught to always oblige a lady?'

The man holding the woman let her go and swung to face Martin. In the same moment, Martin saw the second man draw a knife. He had a clear shot and took it, the ball passing into the man's elbow. The man dropped the knife and howled. His comrade turned to the source of the sound and so missed the pretty sight of ex-Major Martin Willesden, soldier of fortune and experienced man at arms, being laid low by a right to the jaw, delivered by a very small fist. Martin, his attention on the man he had shot, did not see the blow coming. His head jerked back from the contact and struck a low branch. Stunned, he crumpled slowly to the ground.

Helen Walford stared at the long form stretched somnolent at her feet. God in heaven! It wasn't Hedley Swayne after all! The discharged pistol, still smoking, was clutched in the man's left hand. His right hand held a second pistol, cocked and ready. She darted forward and grabbed it. Catching her skirts in one hand, she leapt over the sprawled form and swung to train the pistol on her captor, hampered in his efforts to reach her by the body between. 'Keep your distance!' she warned. 'I know how to use this.'

Noting the steadiness of the pistol pointed at his chest, the man who had held her decided to accept her word. He glanced back at his accomplice, now on his knees, moaning in pain. He threw Helen a malevolent glance. 'Blast!'

He eyed her menacingly, then turned and stumped over to his mate. Helping him up, he growled, 'Let's get out of this. The master's bound to be along shortly. To my mind, he can sort this lot out hisself.'

His words carried to Helen. Her eyes widened in shock. 'You mean this man isn't your master?' She spared a glance for the still form at her feet. Heavens! What had she done?

The men looked at the crumpled figure. 'That swell? Never set eyes on him afore, missus.'

'Whoever he be, he's goin' to be none too pleased with you when he wakes up,' added the second man with relish.

Helen swallowed and gestured with the gun. Grumbling, the two rogues made their way to the edge of the clearing where stood a disreputable gig pulled by a single broken-down nag. They clambered aboard and, whistling up the horse, departed down the rough track.

Left alone in the gloom with her unconscious rescuer, Helen stood and stared at the recumbent form. 'Oh, lord!'

Thus far, her day had been a resounding disaster. Kidnapped in the small hours, bundled up in a distinctly odoriferous blanket, bustled from one carriage to another until the sounds of London had been left far behind, she had spent the day being battered and jostled, tied and gagged, trussed and trapped in a worn-out chaise. Her head was still pounding. And now she had been rescued, only to lay her rescuer low.

With a groan, Helen pressed a hand to her temple.

Fate was having a field day.

CHAPTER TWO

The back of his head hurt. Martin's first thought on regaining consciousness convinced him he was still alive. But, when his lids fluttered open, he realised his error. He had to be dead. There was an angel hanging over him, her golden hair lit by an unearthly radiance. A sudden twinge forced his eyes shut.

He could not be dead. His head hurt too much, even though it was cradled in the softest lap imaginable. A delicate hand brushed his brow. He trapped it in one of his. No spectre, his angel, but flesh and blood.

'What happened?' He winced, pain stabbing behind his eyes.

Helen, bending over him, winced in sympathy. 'I'm dreadfully afraid that I hit you. On the jaw. You stumbled back and hit a branch.'

When a spasm of pain—or was it irritation?—passed over her rescuer's strong features, Helen's guilt increased. As soon as the rattle of the gig had receded, she had fallen on her knees beside her victim. Quelling all maidenly hesitation—she was hardly a maiden, after all—she had bent her mind to ministering to the injuries she had caused. His shoulders were abominably heavy, but, eventually, she had managed to lift his head on to her lap, gently stroking back the raven locks that had fallen across his brow.

Martin held on to her hand, reluctant to let his anchor to reality slip. It was a small hand, the bones delicate between his fingers. Gradually, the pounding in his head subsided, leaving a dull ache. He put up his free hand to feel the bruise on his chin. Just in time, he remembered not to try and feel the bump on his head. It was, after all, resting on her lap and she sounded like a lady.

'Do you always attack your rescuers?' Martin struggled to sit up.

Helen helped him, then sat back on her heels to look at him, open concern in her eyes. 'I really must apologise. I thought you were Hedley Swayne.'

Gingerly, Martin examined the lump rising on the back of his skull. Her voice, if nothing else, confirmed his angel's station. The soft, rounded tones slid into his consciousness like warmed honey. He frowned. 'Who's Hedley Swayne? The master who arranged your abduction?'

Helen nodded. 'So I believe.' She should have guessed this man wasn't Hedley—his voice was far too deep, far too gravelly. Feeling at a distinct disadvantage due to the unfortunate circumstance of their meeting, she studied her hands, clasped in her lap, and wondered what her rescuer was thinking. She had had ample opportunity to admire his length as he had lain stretched out beside her. A most impressive length. The single comprehensive glance she had had, before his head had hit the branch, had left a highly favourable impression. Despite her predicament, Helen's lips twitched. She could not recall being quite so impressed in years. Reality intruded. She had hit him and knocked him out. *He*, doubtless, was not impressed at all.

Surreptitiously observing his damsel in distress as she knelt beside him in the shadowy twilight, Martin could understand his earlier conviction that she was an angel. Thick golden curls rioted around her head, spilling in chaotic confusion on to her shoulders. Very nicely turned shoulders, too. A silk evening gown which he thought would be apricot under normal light clung to her shapely curves. He could not guess how tall she was but all the rest of her was constructed on generous lines. He glanced at her face. In the poor light, her features were indistinct. An unexpectedly strong desire to see more, in better light, possessed him. 'I take it this same Hedley Swayne is expected here at any moment?'

'That's what the two men said.' Helen spoke dismissively.

In truth, she could summon little interest in her abductor; her rescuer was far more fascinating.

Slowly, Martin got to his feet, grateful for his angel's steadying hand. His faculties were a trifle unsettled, his senses distracted by her nearness. 'Why did they leave?' She was quite tall; her curls would tickle his nose if she were closer, her forehead level with his lips. Just the right height for a tall man. Her legs, glorious legs, were deliciously long. He resisted the urge to examine them more closely.

'I held the second pistol on them.' Sensing his distraction and worried that she might have caused him serious injury, Helen frowned, trying to study his expression through the gloom. Reminded of his pistols, she bent to retrieve them, her silk skirts clinging to her shapely derrière.

Martin looked away, shaking his head to dislodge the fantasies crowding in. Damn it! The situation was potentially dangerous! Definitely not the time for idle dalliance. He cleared his throat. 'In my present condition, I feel it might be wise to leave before Mr Swayne arrives. Unless you think it preferable to stay and face him?'

Helen shook her head. 'Heavens, no! He'll have a coach and men with him. He never travels without outriders.' Her contempt for her abductor rang in her tone. A sudden thought struck her. 'Where are we?'

'South of Taunton.'

'Taunton?' Helen stood, the pistols hanging from her hands, and frowned. 'Hedley mentioned estates somewhere in Cornwall. I suppose he was going to take me there.'

Martin nodded; the explanation was likely, given their present location. He glanced around to reorientate himself, then reached for his pistols. 'If he's likely to come with friends, I suggest we depart forthwith. My curricle's in a lane beyond the wood. I was passing when I heard your screams.'

'Thank heaven you did.' Belatedly, Helen shook out her skirts. 'I held very little hope we would be near any main road.'

She glanced up at her rescuer, to find he was studying her, the shadows concealing his expression.

Martin smiled, a little wryly. His angel was not out of the woods yet. 'I hesitate to disabuse you of such a comforting thought, but we're some way from any main road. I was taking a short cut through the lanes in the hope of reaching the London road before the storm.'

'You're going to London?'

'Eventually,' Martin conceded. The branches above obscured too much of the sky to let him judge the approach of the rainclouds. 'But first we'll have to find shelter for the night.'

With a last glance about, Martin offered her his arm.

Quelling a rush of uncharacteristic nervousness, Helen placed her hand on his sleeve. She had no choice but to trust him, yet her trust in gentlemen was not presently high.

'Was it from London you were taken?'

'Yes,' Helen felt no constraint in revealing that much but the question reminded her to be wary until she knew more of her rescuer, fascinating though he might be.

Absorbed in negotiating the numerous hurdles in the congested path through the trees without further damaging her gown, Helen felt the calm certainty with which she normally faced her world return. Her rescuer's strong arm assisted her over the blockages. The subtle deference in his attitude effectively dispelled her fears, settling a cloak of protectiveness about her. Relieved to find his behaviour as gentlemanly as his elegance, she relaxed.

Martin waited until they were some distance from the clearing before appeasing his burgeoning curiosity. The question burning his tongue was who she was. But that, doubtless, would be best left for later. He contented himself with, 'Who is Hedley Swayne?'

'A fop,' came the uncompromising reply.

'You mistook *me* for a *fop*?' Despite the potential seriousness of their plight, Martin's latent tendencies were too strong to repress. When she turned her head his way, eyes wide, her lips parted in confusion, his eyes wickedly quizzed her.

Helen caught her breath. For an instant, her eyes locked with her rescuer's. Three heartbeats passed before, with a desperate effort, she wrenched her gaze free and snatched back her wandering wits. 'I didn't see you, remember.'

At the sound of her soft and slightly husky disclaimer, Martin chuckled. 'Ah, yes!'

A fallen tree blocked their path. He released her to step over it, then turned and held out his hands. From beneath her lashes, Helen glanced up at his face. A strong, intriguing face, rather more tanned and harsh-featured than one was wont to see. She wondered what colour his eyes were. With a calm she was not entirely sure she possessed, she put her hands into his. His strong fingers closed over hers; a peculiar constriction tightened about her chest. Helen glanced down, ostensibly to negotiate the fallen tree, in reality to hide her sudden frown at the ridiculous skitterishness that had attacked her. Surely she was too old for such girlish reactions?

Resuming his place by her side, Martin glanced down at her bent head, perfectly sure, now, that the tremor he had felt in her fingers had not been a figment of his over-active imagination. Highly experienced in the subtleties of this particular form of play, he sought for some topic to get her mind off him. 'I trust you've suffered no harm from your ordeal with those ruffians?'

Determined not to let her ridiculous nervousness show, Helen shook her head. 'No—none at all. But they were under orders to take care of me.'

'So I heard. Nevertheless, I dare say you've had your wits quite addled by fright.'

Despite an unnerving awareness of the presence by her side, Helen laughed. 'Oh, no! I assure you I'm not such a poor creature as all that.' She risked a glance upwards and saw her rescuer's dark brows rise. The look he bent on her was patently disbelieving. Her smile grew. 'Very well,' she conceded, 'I'll admit to a qualm or two, but when they were plainly being as gentle as they knew how I could hardly quake for fear of my life.'

'I've rescued an Amazon.'

The bland statement floated above her curls. Helen chuckled and shook her head, but refused to be further drawn.

As the trees thinned, she resolutely turned her mind to her present predicament. With the uncertainty of her abduction receding, she was conscious of an oddly light-hearted response to this new set of circumstances. Twilight was drawing in; she was walking through woods, very much alone, with an unknown gentleman. While she was quite convinced of his quality, she was not nearly so sure it was safe to approve of his style, much less his propensities. Nevertheless, trepidation was not what she felt. Unbidden, a smile curved her lips. Not since childhood had such a whimsical, adventurous mood claimed her; the same buoyant exuberance had whirled her through her most outrageous childhood exploits. Why on earth it should surface now, in response, she was sure, to the stranger by her side, she had no idea. But the thrill of exhilaration tripping along her nerves was too marked to ignore. In truth, she had no wish to ignore it—life had been too serious, too mundane, for too long. A little adventure would lighten the dim prospect of her lonely future.

They emerged from the trees. In the narrow lane, a fashionable curricle was outlined against the gathering gloom, a pair of high-stepping bays restlessly shifting between the shafts. Impulsively, Helen gasped, 'What beauties!'

The lines of both equipage and horses spoke volumes. Clearly, her rescuer was a man of means. Smiling, he released her beside the carriage, going to the horses' heads to run a soothing hand over their noses.

Helen eyed the curricle, wondering if, in her slim evening gown, it was possible to gain the box seat perched high above the axle with reasonable decorum. She was about to attempt the difficult climb when a pair of strong hands fastened about her waist and she was lifted, effortlessly, upwards.

'Oh!' Her eyes widened; she bit back a most unladylike squeal. Deposited gently on the seat, she blushed rosy red. 'Er... thank you.' The smile on her rescuer's face was decidedly wicked. Abruptly, Helen busied herself with settling her skirts, while, under her lashes, she watched him untie the reins.

It wasn't just the fact that she knew she was no lightweight, nor that no man before had ever lifted her like that, making her feel ridiculously delicate. It wasn't even the impression of remarkable strength that lingered with the memory of his hands gripping her waist. No. It was her quite shocking response to that perfectly mundane little intimacy that was tying her nerves in knots. Never in her life had she felt so odd, so thoroughly witless. What on earth was the matter with her?

Her rescuer swung up beside her. He moved with the ease of a born athlete, compounding the impression of leashed power created by the combination of understated elegance and sheer size. A deliciously fascinating impression, Helen was only too willing to admit. Then he glanced at her.

'Comfortable?'

She nodded, the simple question dispelling any lingering fears. In her estimation, no blackguard would ask if his victim was comfortable. Her rescuer might make her nervous; he did not frighten her.

A drop of rain fell on Martin's hand as he clicked the reins. The sensation drew his mind from contemplation of the woman beside him and focused it on more practical matters. Night was closing in and, with it, the weather.

He levelled a measuring glance at his companion. When he had lifted her to the box seat, getting a good glimpse of a pair of shapely ankles in the process, he had confirmed the fact that her dress was indeed silk, fine and delicate. Furthermore, his experienced assessment told him her fashionable standing extended to wearing no more than a fine silk chemise beneath. In the wood, the warmth of the afternoon had been trapped beneath the trees but now they were in the open and the temperature was dropping. The neckline of her gown was cut remarkably low, a fact which met with his unqualified approval; the tiny puffed sleeves, badly crushed, were set off her shoulders. Even in the poor light, her skin glowed translucently pale. She was not yet shivering, but it could only be a question of time. 'If you'll forgive my impertinence, why are you gallivanting about without even a cloak?'

Helen frowned, considering. How much was it safe to reveal? Then, unconsciously lifting her chin, she took the plunge. 'I was at Chatham House, at a ball given for Lady

Chatham's birthday. A footman brought a note asking me to meet…a friend on the portico.'

In retrospect, she should have been more careful. 'There were…circumstances that made that seem quite reasonable at the time,' she explained. 'But there was no one about—at least, that's what I thought. I waited for a moment or two, then, just as I was about to go back inside, someone—one of those two ruffians, I think—threw a coat over my head.'

Helen shivered slightly, whether from the cold or the memory of her sudden fright she was not sure. 'They bundled me into a waiting carriage—it was still early and there were no other coaches in the drive.' She drew a deep breath. 'So that's why no cloak.'

'I see.' Martin trapped the reins under his boot and reached behind the seat to drag his greatcoat from where it was neatly stowed. He shook it out and flung it about his companion's distracting shoulders, then calmly picked up the reins. 'What makes you think it was this Hedley Swayne behind your abduction?'

Helen frowned. In reality, now that she considered the matter more closely, there was no firm evidence to connect Hedley with the kidnap attempt.

Observing her pensive face, Martin's brows rose. 'No real reason—just a feeling?'

At the superior tone rippling beneath the raspy surface of his deep voice, Helen drew herself up. 'If you knew how Hedley's been behaving recently, you wouldn't doubt it.'

Martin grinned at her prickly rejoinder and infused a degree of sympathy into his, 'How has he been behaving?'

'He's forever at me to marry him—heaven only knows why.'

Pressing his lips together to suppress the spontaneous retort that had leapt to his tongue, Martin waited until his voice was steady before asking, 'Not the obvious?'

Absorbed in cogitations on the vagaries of Hedley Swayne, Helen shook her head. 'Definitely not the obvious.' Suddenly recalling to whom she was speaking, she blushed. Praying that the poor light would conceal the fact, she hurried on. 'Hedley's not the marrying kind, if you know what I mean.'

Martin's lips twitched but he made no comment.

Helen considered the iniquitous Mr Swayne, a slight frown puckering her delicate brows. 'Unfortunately, I've no idea why he wants to marry me. No idea at all.'

They proceeded in silence, Martin intent on the bad road, Helen lost in thought. The land about was open pastures, separated by occasional hedgerows, with not even a farmhouse to be seen. A stray thought took hold in Martin's mind. 'Did you say you were at a ball when they grabbed you? Have you been missing since last night?'

Helen nodded. 'But I went in my own carriage—not many of my friends have returned to town yet.'

'So your coachman would have raised the alarm?'

Slowly, Helen shook her head. 'Not immediately. I might have gone home in some acquaintance's carriage and my message to John got lost in the fuss. That's happened before. My people wouldn't have been certain I was truly missing until this morning.' Her brows knit, she considered the possibilities. 'I wonder what they'll do?'

For his own reasons, Martin also wondered. The possibility of being mistaken for a kidnapper, and the consequent explanations, was not the sort of imbroglio he wished to be landed in just at present—not when he had barely set foot in England and had yet to establish his bona fides. 'You'll certainly cause a stir when you reappear.'

'Mm.' Helen's mind had drifted from the shadowy possibilities of happenings in London, drawn to more immediate concerns by the presence beside her. Her rescuer had yet to ask her name, nor had he volunteered his. But her adventurous mood had her firmly in its grip; their state of being mutually incognito seemed perfectly appropriate. She felt comfortably secure; appellations, she was sure, were unnecessary.

Absorbed in the increasingly difficult task of managing his team over the severely rutted track, Martin racked his brains for some acceptable avenue to learn his companion's name. Their situation was an odd one—not having been formally introduced, he did not expect her to volunteer the information. He balked at simply asking, not wanting her to feel impelled to reveal it out of gratitude for her rescue. Yet, without it, could he be sure of finding her in London? He ought, of course, to introduce himself, but, until he was more certain of her, was reluctant to do so.

Another drop of rain and a low mutter from the west jerked his mind back to practicalities. Skittish, the horses tossed their heads. He settled them, carefully edging them about a sharp corner. The dark shape of a barn loomed on the left, set back in a field and screened on the west by a stand of chestnuts. The mutter turned into a growl; lightning split the sky.

With a grimace, Martin checked the horses for the turn into the rough cart track leading to the barn. He glanced at his companion, still lost in thought. 'I'm afraid, my dear, that before you you see our abode for the night. We're miles from the nearest shelter and the horses won't stand a thunderstorm.'

Startled from her reverie, Helen peered ahead. Seeing the dark structure before her, she considered the proposition of spending the night in a barn with her rescuer and found it strangely attractive. 'Don't mind me,' she replied airily. 'If I'm to have an adventure then it might as well be complete with a night in a disused barn. Is it disused, do you think?'

'In this area? Unlikely. Hopefully there'll be a loft full of fresh straw.'

There was. Martin unharnessed the horses and rubbed them down, then made them as secure as possible in the rude stalls. By now very grateful for the warmth of his thick greatcoat, Helen clutched it about her. She wandered around the outside of the barn and discovered a well, clearly in use, by one side. Before the rain set in, she hurried to draw water, filling all the pails she could find. After supplying the horses, she splashed water over her face, washing away the dust of the day. Refreshed, she belatedly remembered she had no towel. Eyes closed, she all but jumped when a deep chuckle came from behind her, reverberating through her bones, sending peculiar shivers flickering over her skin. Strong fingers caught her hand; a linen square was pushed into it. Hurriedly, Helen mopped her face and turned.

He stood a yard or so behind her, a subtle smile twisting his firm lips. He had found a lantern and hung it from the loft steps. The soft light fell on his black hair, glossing the curls where they formed over his ears and by the side of his neck. Hooded grey eyes—she was sure they were grey—lazily regarded her. Helen's diaphragm seized; her eyes widened. He was handsome. Disgustingly handsome. Even more handsome than Hazelmere. She felt her throat constrict. Damn it! No man had the right to be so handsome. With an effort, she masked her reactions and swept him an elegant curtsy. 'Thank you most kindly, sir—for your handkerchief and for rescuing me.'

The subtle smile deepened, infusing the harshly handsome face with a wholly sensual promise. 'My pleasure, fair Juno.'

This time, his voice sent tingling quivers down her spine. Fair Juno? Shaken, Helen held out the handkerchief, hoping the action would cover her momentary fluster.

Taking back the linen square, Martin let his eyes roam, then abruptly hauled back on the reins. Dammit—he was supposed to be a gentleman and she was very clearly a lady. But if she kept looking at him like that he was apt to forget such niceties.

Smoothly, he turned to a rough bin against one wall. 'There's corn here. If we grind some up, we'll be able to have pancakes for supper.'

Helen eyed the blue-suited back a touch nervously, then turned her gaze, even more dubiously, on the corn bin. Were pancakes made of corn? 'I'm afraid...' she began, forced to admit to ignorance.

Her rescuer threw her a dazzling smile. 'Don't worry. I know how. Come and help.'

Thus adjured, Helen willingly went forward to render what assistance she could. They hunted about and found two suitable rocks, a large flat one for the grinding base and a smaller, round one to crush the corn. After a demonstration of the accepted technique, Helen settled to the task of producing the cornmeal, while her mentor started a small fire, just outside the barn door, where the lee of the barn gave protection from the steady rain.

Every now and then, a crack of lightning presaged a heavy roll of thunder. The horses shifted restively, but they settled. Inside the barn, all was snug and dry.

'That should be sufficient.'

Seated on a pile of straw, Helen looked up to find her mentor towering beside her, a pail of water in one hand.

'Now we add water to make a paste.'

Struggling to keep his eyes on his task, Martin knelt opposite his assistant and, dipping his fingers in the water, sprinkled the pile of meal. Helen caught the idea. Soon, a satisfyingly large mound of soft dough had been formed. Helen carried the dough to the fire in her hands, while Martin brought up the heavy rock.

She had seen him wash an old piece of iron and scrub it down with straw. He had placed it across the fire. She watched as he brought up the water pail and let a drop fall to the heated surface. Critically, he watched it sizzle into steam.

Martin smiled. 'Just right. The trick is not to let it get too hot.'

Confidently, he set two pieces of dough on to the metal surface and quickly flattened them with his palm.

Helen pulled an old crate closer to the fire. 'How do you know all this?'

A slow grin twisted Martin's lips. 'Among my many and varied past lives, I was a soldier.'

'In the Peninsula?'

Martin nodded. While they cooked and ate their pancakes, he entertained her with a colourful if censored account of his campaigning days. These had necessarily culminated with Waterloo. 'After that, I returned to…my business affairs.'

He rose and stretched. The night was deepest black about them. It was as if they were the only souls for miles. His lips twisted in a wry grin. Stranded in a barn with fair Juno—what an opportunity for one of his propensities. Unfortunately, fair Juno was unquestionably gently bred and was under his protection. His grin turned to a grimace, then was wiped from his face before she could see it. He held out a hand to help her to her feet.

'Time for bed.' Resolutely, he quelled his fantasies, insistently knocking on the door of his consciousness. He inclined his head towards the ladder. 'There are piles of fresh straw up there. We should be snug enough for the night.'

Helen went with him readily, any fears she had possessed entirely allayed by the past hours. She felt perfectly safe with him, perfectly confident of his behaving as he ought. They were friends of sorts, engaged in an adventure.

Her transparent confidence was not lost on Martin. He found her trust oddly touching, not something he was usually gifted with, not something he had any wish to damage. Reaching the foot of the ladder, he unhooked the lantern. 'I'll go up first.' He smiled. 'Can you climb the ladder alone?'

The idea of being carried up the ladder, thrown over his shoulder like a sack of potatoes, was not to be borne. Helen considered the ascent, then shrugged out of his greatcoat. 'If you'll take that up, I think I can manage.'

Briskly, Martin went up, taking the coat and the lantern with him. Then he held the lantern out to light her way. Helen twisted her skirts to one side and, guarding against any misstep, carefully negotiated the climb.

Above her, Martin swallowed his curses. He had thought coming up first was the right thing to do, relieving her of the potential embarrassment of accidentally exposing her calves and ankles to his view. But the view he now had—of a remarkable expanse of creamy breasts, barely concealed by the low neckline of her gown—was equally scandalous. And equally tempting. And he was going to have to spend a whole night with her within reach?

He gritted his teeth and forced his features to behave.

After drawing her to safety, he crossed to the hay door and propped it ajar, admitting the cool night air and fitful streaks of moonlight, shafting through breaks in the storm clouds. He extinguished the lantern and placed it safely on a beam. Earlier in the evening, he had brought up the carriage blanket from the curricle. Spreading his greatcoat in the straw, he picked up the blanket and handed it to her. 'You can sleep there. Wrap yourself up well or you'll be cold.'

The air in the loft was warmer than below but the night boded ill for anyone dressed only in two layers of silk. Gratefully, Helen took the blanket and shook it out, then realised there was only one. 'But what about you? Won't you be cold, too?'

In the safety of the dark, Martin grimaced. He was hoping the night air would cool his imagination, already feverish. Only too aware of the direction of his thoughts, and their likely effect on his tone, he forced his voice to a lighter pitch. 'Sleeping in a dry loft full of straw is nothing to the rigours of campaigning.' So saying, he threw himself down, full-length in the straw, a good three yards from his coat.

In the dim light, Helen saw him grin at her. She smiled, then wrapped the blanket around her before snuggling down into his still warm coat. 'Goodnight.'

'Goodnight.'

For ten full minutes, silence reigned. Martin, far from sleep, watched the clouds cross the moon. Then the thunder returned in full measure. The horses whinnied but settled again. He heard his companion shift restlessly. 'What's the matter? Afraid of mice?'

'*Mice*?' On the rising note, Helen sat bolt upright.

Silently, Martin cursed his loose tongue. 'Don't worry about them.'

'*Don't*…! You must be joking!'

Helen shivered, an action Martin saw clearly as a shaft of moonlight glanced through the hay door and fell full on her. God, she was an armful!

Hugging the greatcoat about her, Helen struggled to subdue her burgeoning panic. She sat still, breathing deeply, until another crack of thunder rent the night. 'If you must know, I'm frightened of storms.' The admission, forced through her chattering teeth, came out at least an octave too high. 'And I'm cold.'

Martin heard the querulous note in her voice. She truly was frightened. Hell! The storm had yet to unleash its full fury—

if he did nothing to calm her she might well end up hysterical. Revising his estimate on which was the safer—spending an innocent night with fair Juno or campaigning in Spain—he sighed deeply and stood up, wondering if what he was about to do qualified as masochism. It was certainly going to make sleep difficult, if not impossible. He crossed to where she sat, huddled rigid beneath the blanket. Sitting beside her, on his coat, he put his arm about her and gave her a quick hug. Then, ignoring her confused reluctance, he drew her down to lie beside him, her head resting on his shoulder, her curls tickling his chin. 'Now go to sleep,' he said sternly. 'The mice won't get you and you're safe from the storm and you should be warm enough.'

Rigid with panic, Helen held herself stiffly within his encircling arms. Heaven help her, she did not know which frightened her most—the storm, or the tempest of emotions shattering her confidence. Nothing in her extensive experience had prepared her for spending a night in a stranger's arms but, with the storm raging outside, she could not have forced herself from her safe haven if the stars had fallen. And she was safe. Safe from the elements outside. Gradually, it dawned that she was also safe from any nearer threat.

Reassurance slowly penetrated the mists of panicky confusion assailing her reason. Her locked muscles eased; the tension left her limbs. The man in whose arms she lay was still and silent. His breathing was deep and even, his heart a steady thud muffled beneath her cheek. She had nothing to fear.

Helen relaxed.

When she melted against him, Martin stifled a curse, willing his muscles to perfect stillness.

'Goodnight.' Helen sighed sleepily.

'Goodnight,' Martin replied, his accents clipped.

But Helen was still some way from sleep. The storm lashed the countryside. Inside the barn, all was quiet. Martin, very conscious of the warm and infinitely tempting body beside him, felt her flinch at the thunderclaps. In the aftermath of a particularly violent report, she murmured, 'I've just realised I don't even know your name.'

Helen excused her lie on the grounds of social nicety; she had been wondering for hours how to approach the subject. Their unexpected intimacy gave her an opening she felt justified in taking. It was part of the adventure for him not to know her name, but she definitely wanted to know his.

'Martin Willesden, at your service.' Despite his agony, Martin grinned into the darkness. He was only too willing to serve her in any number of ways.

'Willesden,' Helen repeated, yawning. Then, her eyes flew wide. 'Oh heavens! Not *the* Martin Willesden? The new Earl of Merton?' Helen twisted to look up into his face.

Martin was entertained by her tone. "'Fraid so,' he answered. He glanced down, but her expression was hidden by the dark. 'I presume my reputation has gone before me?'

'Your reputation?' Helen drew breath. 'You, dear sir, have been the sole topic of conversation among the tabbies for the last fortnight. They're all dying for you to show your face! Is the black sheep, now raised to the title, going to join polite society or give us all the go-by?'

Martin chuckled.

Helen felt the sound reverberate through his chest. The temptation to stretch her hands over the expanse of hard muscle was all but overwhelming. Resolutely, she quelled it, settling her head once more into his shoulder.

'I've no taste for the melodramatic.' Martin shifted his hold, adjusting to her position. 'Since landing I've been too busy setting things to rights to make my presence known. I'm returning from inspecting my principal seat. I'll be joining in all the normal pastimes once I get back to London.'

'"All the normal pastimes"?' Helen echoed. 'Yes, I can just imagine.'

'Can you?' Unable to resist, Martin squinted down at her but could not see her face. He could remember it, though— green-flecked amber eyes under perfectly arched brown brows, a straight little nose and wide, full lips, very kissable. 'What do you know of the pastimes of rakes?'

Helen resisted the temptation to reply that she had been married to one. 'Too much,' she countered, reflecting that that, also, was true. Then the oddity of the conversation struck her. She giggled sleepily. 'I feel I should point out to you that this is a most *improper* conversation.' Her tone was light, as light-hearted as she felt. She was perfectly aware that their present situation was scandalous in the extreme, yet it seemed oddly right, and she was quite content.

Martin's views on their situation were considerably more pungent. Sheer madness designed to make his head hurt more than it already did. First she had hit him on the jaw, and caused him to crack his skull. Now this. What more grievous torture could she visit on him?

With a soft sigh, Helen snuggled against him.

Martin's jaw clenched with the effort to remain passive. A chuckle he could only describe as siren-like escaped her. 'I've just thought. I escaped from the clutches of a fop only to spend the night in the arms of one of the most notorious rakehells London ever produced. Presumably there is a moral in this somewhere.' She giggled again and, to Martin's profound astonishment, as innocently and completely as a child, fell asleep.

Martin lay still, staring at the rough beams overhead. Her admission to a knowledge of rakes and their activities struck him as distinctly odd. Also distinctly distracting. Before his imagination, only too willing to slip its leash, could bring him undone, he put the peculiar statement aside for inspection at a later date—a safer date. Given fair Juno's apparent quality, taking her declaration at face value and acting accordingly might not be wise.

With an effort, he concentrated on falling asleep. First, he tried to pretend there was no woman in his arms. That proved impossible. Then he tried thinking of Erica, the mullato mistress he had left behind. That did not work either. Somehow Erica's dark ringlets and coffee-coloured skin kept transforming to golden curls and luscious white curves. Instead of Erica's small, dark-tipped breasts, he saw fuller white breasts with dusky pink aureoles. His experienced imagination had no difficulty in filling in what the apricot silk gown hid—a subtle form of mental torture. Finally, after making a vow to learn fair Juno's name and track her down once she was restored to her family and no longer under his protection, Martin forced himself to think of nothing at all.

After an hour, he drifted into an unsettled doze.

CHAPTER THREE

Early morning sunlight tickled Martin's consciousness awake. Luckily, he opened his eyes before he moved, not something he always did. What he saw stopped him from reacting on impulse to the warm softness in his arms. Biting back his curses, he extricated himself from the clasp of silken limbs and, without disturbing fair Juno, got down from the loft as fast as he was able.

He greeted the horses, then went outside. The sky was clear, the air fresh and clean. The storm had drenched the countryside but the sun now shone bright. A good day for travelling. After stretching his legs, he was about to go inside and wake his companion in adventure when he bethought himself of the state of the roads.

A few paces down the cart track saw his plans revised. Used to travelling on gravel or the hard-surfaced highways, he had forgotten they were on byways not much more than cattle tracks. The track from the barn turned to a quagmire before it reached the road. The road itself was little better. Closer inspection suggested a few hours would suffice to render it passable, at least as far as he could see.

Resigned to the wait, he returned to the barn.

He climbed to the loft and found fair Juno still asleep. The morning sunlight spilled through the hay door, gilding the curls that escaped in random profusion from the simple knot on the top of her head. Her lips were slightly parted in sleep, her breathing shallow. A delicate blush tinted her perfect complexion. An ivory and gold goddess, or so she seemed to him. He stared long and hard at the vision, drinking in the symmetry of her features, the arch of her brows and the warm

glow of full lips. Most of the rest of her was concealed by the
folds of the carriage blanket, much to his relief. Only one arm,
nicely rounded in a distinctively feminine mould, showed bare,
ivory-sheathed, nestling on the straw where he had laid it
down.

Who was she? Quietly, Martin descended the ladder. Let
her sleep—after the storm, she probably needed the rest.

Once more on firm ground, he rubbed his hands over his
face. In truth, he could do with a few hours of extra sleep, but
he was not fool enough to try relaxing in the straw by fair
Juno's side.

The morning was far advanced before Helen awoke. For a
full minute, she lay, confused and disorientated, before recollections of the previous evening returned her to full understanding.

She was alone in the loft. Abruptly, she sat up. Then she
heard his voice, dimmed by distance. After a moment, she
realised he was outside, talking to the horses. Hurriedly, she
scrambled out of the carriage blanket. She shook it and folded
it neatly before laying it, along with his coat, on the edge of
the loft by the ladder. Then, with a last glance to make sure
he was still outside, she gingerly descended the ladder, her
skirts hiked to her knees.

Relieved to have reached the ground undetected, she let her
skirts down, brushing ineffectually at the creases. She pulled
a wisp of straw from her hair, grimacing at the thought of how
she must look. There was a pail of fresh water beside the
ladder, the linen handkerchief she had used the day before
draped over the side. Quickly, she splashed her face and rinsed
her hands. She was patting her face dry when she heard his
step behind her.

'Ah! Fair Juno awakes. I was just about to roust you out.'

Helen turned. In daylight, her rescuer was even more distressingly handsome than in lamplight. The broad shoulders
seemed broader than ever; his height was no dream. Small
wonder he had made her feel weak and small. The aquiline
features held a touch of harshness, but the impression might

be due to his tan. Helen blinked and found his grey eyes laughingly quizzing her. She prayed her blush was not detectable. 'I'm so sorry. You should have woken me earlier.'

'No matter.' Martin reached for the harness he had left on the wall of the stall. He had wondered what colour her eyes would prove to be in daylight. Pools of amber and limpid green highlighted with gold, they were the most striking features of a remarkably striking package. He thanked his stars he had not seen her in daylight before being forced to spend a night by her side. Her blush suggested she felt much the same. Martin knew for a certainty that relaxing with rakes was much easier in the dark but he did not want her to retreat behind a correct façade. He smiled and was relieved when she smiled back. 'The roads are only just dry enough to attempt the curricle.'

Helen followed him outside, pausing to breathe deeply of the fresh morning air. She saw him struggling to harness the restive horses and went forward to help, approaching steadily so as not to spook the highly strung beasts. Catching hold of the bit of the nearside horse, she crooned sweet nothings and stroked the velvet nose.

Martin nodded his approval, pleasantly surprised by her practical assistance. Together, they efficiently hitched the pair to the curricle.

Holding the reins, he went to her side, intending to lift her to the box seat.

'Er—I left the blanket and your coat in the loft.' The words tumbled out. Helen prayed that he would not notice her fluster. Panic had risen to claim her at the mere thought of him touching her again. After the past ten minutes' surreptitious observation, she could not understand how she had had the nerve to survive the night.

One black brow rose; the grey eyes rested thoughtfully on her face. Then he handed her the reins. 'I'll get them. Don't try to move 'em.'

He was back in two minutes, but by then she had steeled herself for the ordeal. He stowed the blanket and coat behind the seat, then reached for the reins. Helen relinquished them.

An instant later, his hands fastened about her waist. A moment of weightlessness followed, before she was deposited, gently, on the seat.

As she fussed about, settling her skirts, Helen reflected that new experiences were always unsettling. Just what it was she felt every time he touched her she could not have said—but she had no doubt it was scandalous. And delicious. And very likely addictive, as well. Doubtless, it was one of those tricks rakes had at their fingertips, to make susceptible women their slaves. Not that her late and wholly unlamented husband had had the facility. Then again, she amended, giving the devil his due, Arthur had never had much time for her, the gawky sixteen-year old he had wed for her fortune and supplanted within weeks with a more experienced courtesan. However, none of the countless admirers she had had since her return to social acceptability had ever affected her as Martin Willesden did.

The curricle jerked into motion. Her eyes fell to his hands, long, strong fingers managing the reins. His ability probably owed more to his undeniable experience—the experience that glowed in the smouldering depths of those grey eyes. Whatever it was, wherever its origin, he was dangerous—a fact she should strive to remember.

The sun found her face; Helen tilted her head up and breathed in the fresh scent of rain-washed greenery. Her mental homily was undoubtedly apt, but, try as she might, she could not take the threat seriously. This was an adventure, her first in years. She was reluctant to allow strictures, however appropriate, to mar the joy. The situation was, after all, beyond outrageous; decorum and social niceties had necessarily been set aside. Why shouldn't she enjoy the freedom of the moment?

'We should reach Ilchester for a late breakfast.'

Helen wished he had not mentioned food. Determined to keep her mind from dwelling on her empty stomach, she cast about for some suitably innocuous topic. 'You said you'd been visiting your home. Is it near here?'

'The other side of Taunton.'

'You've been away for some time, haven't you? Was it much changed?'

Martin grimaced. 'Thirteen years of mismanagement have unfortunately taken their toll.' The silence following this pronouncement suggested that his anger at the fact had shown in his tone. He sought to soften the effect. 'My mother lives there, but she's been an invalid for some years. My sister-in-law acts as her companion but unfortunately she's a nonentity—hardly the sort to raise a dust when the runners disappeared.'

'Disappeared?' Shocked incredulity showed in fair Juno's eyes, echoed in her tone.

Reluctantly, Martin grinned. 'I'm afraid the place, beyond my mother's rooms, is barely habitable. That's why I was so set on heading back to London without delay.' Reflecting that had this not been the case he would not have had the honour of rescuing fair Juno, Martin began to look on the Hermitage's shortcomings with a slightly less jaundiced eye. Considering the matter dispassionately, something he had yet to do, he shrugged. 'It's not seriously damaged—the fabric's sound enough. I've a team of decorators at work on my town house. When they've finished there, I'll send them to the Hermitage.'

Intrigued by the distant look in his eyes, Helen gently prompted, 'Tell me what it's like.'

Martin grinned. His eyes on his horses, and on the ruts in the road, he obliged with a thumbnail sketch of the Hermitage, not as he had found it, but as he remembered it. 'In my father's day, it was a gracious place,' he concluded. 'Whenever I think of it, I remember it as being full of guests. Hopefully, now I've returned, I'll be able to restore it to its previous state.'

Helen listened intently, struck by the fervour rippling in the undercurrents of his deep voice. 'It's your favourite estate?' she asked, trying to find the reason.

Martin considered the question, trying to find words to convey his feelings. 'I suppose it's the place I call home. The place I most associate with my father. And happier memories.'

The tone of his last sentence prevented further enquiry. Helen mulled over what little she knew of the new Earl of

Merton and realised it was little indeed. He had clearly been out of the country, but why and where she had no idea. She had heard talk of a scandal, unspecified, in his past, but, given the anticipation of the hostesses of the *ton*, it was clearly of insufficient import to exclude him from their ballrooms and dinners.

While he conversed, one part of Martin's mind puzzled over the conundrum of his companion. Fair Juno was not that young, nor yet that old. Mid-twenties was his experienced guess. What did not seem right was the absence of a ring on her left hand. She was undeniably beautiful, attractive in a wholly sensual way, and the sort of lady who was invited to Chatham House. The possibility that she was a lady of a different hue occurred only to be dismissed. Fair Juno was well-bred enough to recognise his potential and be flustered by it— hardly the hallmark of a barque of frailty. All in all, fair Juno was an enigma.

'And now,' he said, bringing their companionable silence to an end, 'we should put our minds to deciding how best to return you to your home.' He glanced at the fair face beside him. 'Say the word, and I'll drive you to your door.' Entirely unintentionally, his voice had dropped several tones. Which, he thought, catching Juno's wide-eyed look, merely indicated how much she affected him.

'I don't really think that would be altogether wise,' Helen returned, suppressing her scandalous inclinations. He was teasing her, she was sure.

'Perhaps not. I had hoped London starchiness had abated somewhat, but clearly the passing of the years has yet to turn that particular stone to dust.' Martin smiled down into her large eyes, infusing his expression with as much innocence as he was capable. 'How, then?'

Helen narrowed her eyes and stared hard at him. 'I had expected, my lord, that one of your reputation would have no difficulty in overcoming such a minor obstacle. If you put your mind to it, I'm sure you'll think of something.'

It was a decidedly impertinent speech and provoked a decidedly audacious reply. The gleam in the grey eyes gave her warning.

'I'm afraid, my dear, that if you consult my reputation more closely you'll realise I've never been one for placating the proprieties.'

Realising her tactical error, Helen retreated to innocence. How silly to try to deflate a rake with outrageousness. 'Don't you really know? I confess, I'd thought you would.'

For an instant, the grey eyes held hers, suspicion in their depths. Then their quality subtly altered. She was conscious of a stilling of time, of her surroundings dimming into blankness. His grey eyes, and him, filled her senses. Then his lips twisted in a gently mocking smile and he looked away.

'As you say, fair Juno, my experience is extensive.' Martin slanted another glance her way, and saw a slight frown pucker her brow. 'I suspect it might be best if we try for one of the minor inns, just before Hounslow. I'll hire a chaise and escort for you there.' When the frown did not immediately lift, he smiled. 'You may give the coachman instructions once you reach the outskirts of London.'

'Yes,' said Helen, struggling to preserve her calm in the face of the discovery that grey eyes of his particular shade seemed to possess a strange power over her. For a moment, she had been mesmerised, deprived of all will, totally at his mercy. And it had felt quite delicious. 'I suppose that will do.'

Her tone of reluctant acceptance brought a smirk to Martin's lips, quickly suppressed. What a very responsive yet oddly innocent goddess she was. His interest in her, already marked, was growing by the minute. Just as well that they had agreed to part that evening. 'We should reach Hounslow before dark,' he said, eager to settle that point.

They journeyed on in silence. Martin pondered how to broach the subject of her name; Helen pondered him. He was, without doubt, the most attractive man she had ever met. It was not just his physical attributes, though there was no fault to be found with those. Neither could his manners, polished and assured though they were, account for the effect. It was, she decided, something far more fundamental, like the raspy growl of his deep voice and the fire banked like coals in the smoky grey eyes.

'Do you spend much of your year in the country, fair maid?'

The question jolted Helen back to reality. 'I often visit at—' She broke off, then continued smoothly, 'At friends' houses.'

'Ah.'

The quality of the glance that rested fleetingly upon her face confirmed her suspicion. He was trying to learn more of her.

'So you spend most of your year in London?'

'Other than my visits.'

Conversation rapidly degenerated to a game of quiz and answer, he trying to glean snippets of information, she trying to avoid revealing any identifying fact while politely answering all his queries.

'Do you attend the opera?'

'During the season.'

'In friends' boxes?'

Helen threw him a haughty look. 'I have my own box.'

'Then no doubt I'll see you there.' Martin smiled, pleased to have scored a hit.

Realising her slip, Helen had no choice but to be gracious. She inclined her head. 'Countess Lieven often joins me. I'm sure she'll be only too pleased to meet you.'

'Oh.' Stymied by the mention of the most censorious of the patronesses of Almack's, Martin looked suitably chagrined. Then his brow cleared. 'A capital notion. I can sue for permission to waltz in Almack's. With you.'

At the thought, Helen had to laugh. The vision of Martin Willesden stalking the hallowed boards, an eagle among the lambs, setting all the mother ewes in a flap, was intensely appealing.

It was Martin's turn to look haughty. 'Do you think I won't?'

Abruptly, Helen found herself drowning in smouldering grey, warmed and shaken to the core. Dragging her eyes from his, she looked ahead. 'I…hadn't imagined you would be attracted to the mild entertainments of the Marriage Mart.'

'I'm not. Only the promise of all manner of earthly pleasures could get me over its threshold.'

Helen was not game to try to cap that. She rapidly became absorbed in the scenery.

A slow smile curved Martin's lips before he gave his attention to his horses. He could not recall ever enjoying thirty minutes of conversation with a female half as much. In fact, he could not recall any other woman he had ever favoured with half an hour of verbal discourse. Fair Juno was a novelty, her mind quick and adroit. Innocent though the information he had gained was, it confirmed his suspicion that she had attained a position in the *ton* normally reserved for older matrons. Or widows.

At the thought, he let his eyes roam in leisurely appraisal over the curvaceous form beside him. She felt his gaze and glanced up, a slightly nervous smile hovering on her rosy lips.

Helen saw the predatory gleam in the grey eyes and accurately read their message. Dragging her dignity about her, the only protection she possessed, she arched one brow in spirited defence, perfectly ready to continue their banter. But the reprobate by her side merely smiled in a thoroughly seductive way and gave his attention to his horses. Helen transferred her gaze to the scenery, her lips irrepressibly curving in appreciation. Conversing with a rake while free of the normal strictures, protected from any physical consequences by the fact he had both hands full of high-tempered horseflesh, was every bit as scandalously exciting as she had ever, as a green girl, imagined it would be. It was all deliciously dangerous but, in this case, completely safe. She had realised as much some miles back. It was a game that, in this particular instance, she could play with impunity. She was in his care and, instinctively, she knew he would honour that charge. While she remained under his protection, she was safe from him.

Heaven help her later.

But, of course, there would be no later. Helen stifled a sigh as reality intruded, impossible to deny. The future, for them both, was fixed. When he reached London, he would be the focus of the matchmaking mamas—with good reason. He was

titled, wealthy and hideously handsome to boot. Their darling
daughters would make cakes of themselves trying to catch his
grey eyes. And, inevitably, he would choose one of them as
his wife. Some well-dowered, biddable miss with an immaculate reputation. A widow, with no pretensions to property,
with a murky marriage to a social outcast behind her and nothing more than her connections to recommend her, was a poor
bargain.

Inwardly, Helen shook herself. Reality began in London.
There was no need to cloud her day of adventure with such
dismal forebodings. She tried to force the image of Martin
Willesden paying court to a sweet young thing from her mind.
In truth, the tableau was somewhat hazy. It was hard to believe
that a man of his tastes, as demonstrated by their dalliance of
the past half-hour, would settle to marriage with a sweet young
thing. Doubtless, he would be the sort who kept a mistress or
two on the side. Well, who was she to complain? Her husband
had done the same, with her blessing. Not that her blessing
would have been forthcoming had Martin Willesden been her
husband.

With a determined effort, Helen redirected her thoughts. He
wanted to know her name. She could tell him, but her ano-
nymity was a comforting sop to her conscience. Besides
which, when he reached London and learned who she was, he
would realise such a connection was unsuitable, for no one
would ever believe it innocent. If she refused to tell him her
name, he would not feel obliged to acknowledge her when he
met her again. Then, too, many men felt widows were fair
game and she would hate him to consider her a potential candidate for his extramarital vacancy. All in all, she decided, he
did not need to know her name.

Martin wondered what thoughts held his goddess so silent.
But the peace of the morning was soothing about them and
he made no move to interrupt her reverie. Despite not knowing
her name, he felt confident of finding her in the capital. London might be the teeming hub of the nation, but its hallowed
halls were trod by few. A gold and ivory goddess would be
easy to trace.

The road widened then dipped. A ford lay ahead. Engrossed in contemplation of the predictable delights of waltzing with fair Juno, Martin automatically checked his pair, then sent them into the shallow water at a smart trot.

The horses' hooves clopped on the gravelly surface of the opposite bank; they slowed, then leaned into the traces and strained. The carriage wheels stuck fast, rocking the occupants of the box seat to full awareness of their predicament.

Helen clutched the side of the seat, then turned a wide-eyed look on her rescuer as a muttered expletive was belatedly smothered.

Martin shut his eyes in frustration. He had forgotten that minor fords were often not paved. The heavy rain had washed silt into the ford; his wheels felt as if they were six inches deep.

With a heavy sigh, he opened his eyes. 'We're stuck.'

Helen glanced around at the swiftly moving stream. 'So we are,' she agreed helpfully.

Martin cast her a warning look. She met it with unlikely innocence. Grimacing, he lifted his gaze to scan their surroundings. About them, the silence of woods and fields lay unbroken by human discord. No smoke rose above the trees to give hint of a nearby cottage. Memory suggested they were still some miles from the London road.

With a groan, Martin shortened the reins. 'I'll have to get down and find some stones. Can you hold them, do you think?'

A mischievous grin lit Helen's face. 'I was under the impression that no out-and-outer would ever entrust his cattle to a mere woman.'

Martin grimaced. '*Touché*. I wouldn't—except that I wouldn't give a farthing for their behaviour if I simply tied the reins to the rail. The devils would sense the absence of a master and they'd be off as soon as the stones were in place.' He glanced down into the large green eyes. 'All they need is a light touch on the reins for reassurance—and you seem to know your way about horses.'

Helen reached for the reins. 'I do. But if you spook them

by throwing stones, I'll drive off and leave you to your fate.
So be warned!'

Martin laughed at her melodramatic tone and relinquished
the reins. He stood carefully and removed his coat, placing it
over the seat before jumping down from the carriage. The
water covered his ankles. With an inward sigh for his gleaming
Hessians, he splashed to the bank and cast about for stones to
place beneath and before the wheels.

Helen watched, the reins held gently in both hands. Every
now and then, she felt a tug as the horses lived up to their
owner's expectations and tested their freedom. They were
clearly unhappy to be standing stock-still, half in and half out
of the stream, rather than stretching their legs along the high-
way. As the minutes ticked by, Helen became infected with
their impatience. Martin had to go further and further afield to
find stones to lay in the mud before the wheels. She had no
idea of the time, but thought it close to noon. How far were
they from London?

Then her reckless self emerged and shouldered aside her
worries. This was adventure and in adventure important things
took care of themselves. Things would turn out all right; she
need not concern herself—fate was in charge.

Determinedly light-hearted, she started to hum, then, as
Martin had disappeared upstream, lifted her voice in the refrain
from an old country air.

Martin heard the lilting melody as he returned with yet more
rocks. He paused for a moment, out of sight, and let her gentle
contralto wash over him, waves of song lapping his consciousness. The sound was close to a caress. With a chuckle, Martin
moved forward. A siren's song, no less.

She checked when she saw him, but when he raised one
brow in question she raised one back and, tilting her chin,
resumed her song.

With a broad smile, Martin settled the stones he carried to
best effect and headed back for more. In truth, he found fair
Juno's fortitude somewhat remarkable, he who would have
sworn he knew all there was to know of women. But this
woman had not whined at the delay, nor raised peevish quib-

bles about the consequences. Consequences neither he nor she could do anything to avoid. Had she realised yet?

An interesting question. Yet, he reflected, fair Juno was no one's fool.

Three more trips and there were enough rocks to attempt to break free of the cloying mud. Hands on hips, Martin stood by the side of the carriage and looked up at his assistant. 'I'll have to push the carriage from behind. Do you think you can hold them, once they gain the bank?'

A look of supercilious condescension was bestowed upon him. 'Of course,' Helen said, then deserted the high ground to ask, 'Do you think they'll bolt?'

With a half-smile, Martin shook his head. 'Not if you keep the reins short.' He moved to the back of the curricle, praying that that was so. 'When I say so, give 'em the office.'

On her mettle, Helen obediently waited for his call before clicking the reins. The horses heaved, the curricle slowly edged forward. Then the wheels gained firm purchase and the carriage abruptly left the water. The horses pulled hard. Suppressing her sudden fear, stirred to life by the strength of the great beasts sensed through the reins, she determinedly hauled back, struggling to hold them. She applied the brake to lock the wheels, and the carriage skidded slightly.

Then Martin was beside her, taking the reins from her suddenly weak fingers.

'Good girl!'

The approval in his voice warmed her; the glow in his eyes raised her temperature even more. To her annoyance, Helen felt herself blushing. An odd sensation of weakness, not quite faintness but surely an allied affliction, bloomed within. She shifted along the seat, making room for him, supremely conscious of the large body when it settled once more by her side.

To her relief, Martin seemed content to resume their journey without further delay, leaving her to the task of shackling her wayward thoughts. Never before had they been so astray. And, if she was any judge at all of the matter, Martin Willesden was the type of man who could sense a wayward feminine thought at ten paces. Her present safety might be ensured, but she did not need to lay snares for her future.

Having learned his lesson somewhat belatedly, Martin devoted as much of his attention as he could summon to driving. The London road was gained without further mishap. Soon, they were bowling along at a spanking pace. Even so, it was past two o'clock when, accepting the inevitable, Martin checked and turned into the yard of the Frog and Duck at Wincanton.

He turned to smile into Juno's questioning eyes. 'Lunch. I'm famished, even if, being a fashionable woman, you are not.'

Helen's eyes widened slightly. 'I'm not that fashionable.'

Martin laughed and jumped down. He reached up to lift fair Juno to the ground, noting her slight hesitation before, without fuss, she drew nearer and let him grasp her waist.

Flustered again but determined not to show it, Helen accepted Martin's proffered arm. He led her up the steps to the inn door, then stood aside to allow her to enter. As she did so, the head groom, having laid eyes on the horses his ostlers had taken in charge, came hurrying to ask Martin's orders.

Alone, Helen crossed the threshold, thankful for the cool dimness within. She was feeling unduly warm. The door gave directly on to the taproom, a large chamber, low-ceilinged and cosy with a huge fireplace at one end. Alerted by the noise outside, the landlord was coming forward from his domain on the other side of the room. Seeing her, he stopped. And stared. Helen became aware that all the other occupants of the tap, six in all and all male, were likewise transfixed. Then, to her discomfort, a leering grin suffused the landlord's face. Faint echoes appeared on his patrons' faces, too.

Simultaneously realising what a sight she must present, and the likely conclusion the landlord had drawn, Helen drew herself up, ready to defend her status.

There was no need. Martin came through the door and stopped by her side. One comprehensive glance was all it took for him to grasp the conclusion the inhabitants of the Frog and

Duck had jumped to. He scowled at the landlord. 'A private parlour, host, where my wife can be at ease.'

The growled command wiped the leer from the landlord's face so fast, he had no expression ready to cover the ensuing blankness.

Helen was not sure whether to laugh or gasp. *Wife*? In the end, she covered her left hand with her right and, tipping up her chin, looked down her nose at the landlord, a feat assisted by the fact that she was taller than he. The man shrank as obsequiousness took hold.

'Yes, m'lord! Certainly, m'lord. If madam would step this way?'

Bowing every two paces, he led them to a neat little parlour. While Martin gave orders for a substantial meal, Helen sank, with a little sigh of thankfulness, into a well-padded armchair by the hearth, carefully avoiding the mirror above the mantelpiece. She had little real idea how bad her state was, but could not imagine knowing would help.

Martin heard her sigh. He glanced at her, then said to the landlord, 'We had an accident with our chaise. Our servants are following behind, with our luggage. Perhaps,' he continued, raising his voice and turning to address a weary Juno, 'you'd like to refresh yourself above stairs, my dear?'

Helen blinked, then readily agreed. Led to a small chamber and supplied with warm water, she washed the dust of the road from her face and hands, then steeled herself to examine the damage her adventures had wrought in her appearance. It was not as bad as she had feared. Her eyes were sparkling clear and the wind had whipped colour into her cheeks. Clearly, driving about the countryside with Martin Willesden agreed with her constitution. In the end, she undid her hair and reformed the mass of curls into a simpler knot. Her dress, the apricot silk marred by a host of creases, was beyond her ability to change. Other than shaking and straightening her skirts, there was little else she could do.

Returning to the parlour, she found their repast laid out upon the table. Martin rose with a smile and held a chair for her.

'Wine?'

At her nod, he filled her glass. Then, without more ado, they applied themselves to the task of demolishing the food before them.

Finally satisfied, Martin sat back in his chair and put aside contemplation of their problems the better to savour his wine while quietly studying fair Juno, absorbed in peeling a plum. His eyes slid over her generous curves—generous, ample— such words came readily to mind. Along with luscious, ripe and other, less acceptable terms. Martin hid a smile behind his goblet. All in all, he had no fault to find in the arrangement of fair Juno's dispositions.

'We won't reach London tonight, will we?'

The question drew Martin's gaze to her lips, full and richly curved and presently stained with plum juice. A driving urge to taste them seared through him. Abruptly, he refocused his mind on their problem. He raised his eyes to Juno's, troubled green and concerned. He smiled reassuringly. 'No.'

Helen felt justified in ignoring the smile. 'No', he said, and smiled. Did he have any idea of the panic she was holding at bay by dint of sheer determination?

Apparently, he did, for he continued, more seriously, 'Getting stuck in that ford has delayed us too much. However, I draw the line at driving my horses through the night, not that that would avail us, for I can't see arriving in London at dawn to be much improvement over our current state.'

Helen frowned, forced to acknowledge the truth of that remark. He would not be able to hire a chaise for her if they passed by Hounslow in the middle of the night.

'And, before you suggest it, I refuse to be a party to any scheme to hire a chaise for you to travel alone through the night.'

Helen's frown deepened. She opened her mouth to argue.

'*Even* with outriders.'

Helen shut her mouth and glared. But his tone and the set of his jaw warned her that no argument would shift him. And, in truth, she had no wish to spend the night jolting over the roads, a prey to fears of highwaymen and worse. 'What, then?' she asked in her most reasonable tone.

She was rewarded with a brilliant smile which quite took her breath away. Luckily, he did not expect her to speak.

'I had wondered,' Martin began diffidently, unsure how his plan would be received, 'if we could find an inn where neither of us is known, to put up in for the night.'

Helen considered the suggestion. She could see no alternative. Raising her napkin to wipe her lips, she raised her eyes to his. 'How will we explain our disreputable state—and our lack of servants and luggage?'

The instant she asked the question, she knew the answer. Deliciously wicked, but, she reasoned, it was all part of her adventure and thus could be viewed with a lenient eye.

Pleased by her tacit acceptance of the only viable plan he had, Martin relaxed. 'We can tell the same story I edified our host with—that we've had an accident and our retainers are following behind with the luggage.'

Still a little nervous of the idea, Helen nodded. Did he intend to claim they were wed?

'Which reminds me,' said Martin, sliding the gold signet from his right hand. 'You had better wear this for the duration.' He held the heavy ring out and dropped it into her palm.

Helen studied the ring, still warm from his hand. Obviously, they were to appear married. She slipped it on to the third finger of her left hand. To her surprise, its weight, in that remembered place, did not evoke the expected horror. Instead, it was strangely reassuring, a source of strength, a pledge of protection.

'Very well,' she said. She drew a deep breath and purposefully added, 'But we'll have to have separate rooms.' Determined to be clear on that point, she raised her eyes to his darkly handsome face and beheld a haughty expression.

'Naturally,' returned Martin repressively. It would undoubtedly be safer that way. Aside from anything else, he would need to get some sleep. He studied Juno's fair countenance and the need to know her real name grew. Given that they were to masquerade cloaked in wedded bliss, he felt that their increasing intimacy justified a request for enlightenment. 'I rather think, my dear, that, given our new relationship, it might be appropriate if I knew your name.'

Engrossed in fantasies revolving around their new relationship, Helen gave a start. 'Oh.' She thought once more of the matter, inwardly acknowledging her reluctance and her reasons for it. Eyeing the handsome face, the strangely compelling eyes fixed on hers, she admitted to an urge to tell him, to confide in a man so transparently at ease in her world. But hard on the heels of that feeling came a premonition of how he would look when he heard her name. He would know of her husband; they would likely have met. What would he feel—pity? Revulsion, albeit carefully cloaked? Doing anything to damage the closeness she sensed between them was repugnant.

Letting her gaze fall, she picked up her napkin, creasing the folds between her fingers. 'I…really…' Her words trailed away. How to explain what she felt?

Martin smiled a little crookedly. He would have liked her to confide in him but the point was not worth disturbing her over. 'You really feel you shouldn't?'

Helen threw him a grateful look. 'It's just that the adventure seems more…complete—and,' she added, determined at least to have some of the truth, 'my behaviour more excusable if I continue incognito.'

Smiling more broadly, Martin inclined his head in acceptance. 'Very well. But what should I call you?'

With a gentle smile that, unbeknown to her, held an element of sweet shyness quite at odds with her years, Helen said, 'You choose. I'm sure you can invent something appropriate.'

Her smile very nearly overset Martin's much tried control. He had thought it strengthened by the years, but fair Juno was temptation beyond any he had ever faced. Invent something? His mind was seething with invention, did she but know it. But, as knowledge of his thoughts would hardly be conducive to allowing her to continue with reasonable calm in his company, he could only be thankful that they did not show in his face.

They did show in his eyes. Even with the table between them, Helen saw the smoke rise and cloud the grey. Stormy heat caressed her. Mesmerised, she sat and waited, breathless and trying to hide it. Heaven forbid that he ever realise how much he affected her!

'Juno,' Martin said, just managing to keep his voice within acceptable range. 'Fair Juno.' His smile was entirely beyond his control, laced with wicked thoughts and scandalous suggestion.

Helen lifted one brow, trying to pour cold water on the flames she could feel flickering around them. 'I hardly think, my lord, that such an allusion is appropriate.'

His smile only gained in intensity. 'On the contrary, my dear. I feel it entirely appropriate.'

Helen tried to frown. Juno—queen of the goddesses. How could she argue with that?

'And now, having settled our immediate future, I suggest we get on our way.' Martin rose and stretched, letting languid grace cloak his haste. If he did not get out of here soon, and back to the relative safety of the curricle's box seat, he would not answer for the consequences. Exposure to fair Juno was sapping all will to resist his rakish inclinations. And he had dinner with her, alone, to look forward to. He had need to recoup what strength he could.

He went around the table and helped her to her feet. Tucking her small hand into the crook of his arm, he led her to the door. 'Come, my lady. Your carriage awaits.'

CHAPTER FOUR

They had chosen the Bells at Cholderton as their overnight stop. The small town nestled just south of the London road, the major traffic passing by without pause. The Bells was an old house, less frequented in these days of rapid travel but still in sufficiently good state to hold promise of a comfortable night.

Shown into a private parlour, Helen glanced about at the faded elegance. She nodded in approval, her haughty demeanour supporting their fiction. Martin had told their story, his natural arrogance wiping out any possibility of disbelief. Lord and Lady Willesden required rooms for the night. The landlord found nothing amiss with the request; he was, in fact, only too pleased to see them.

'My good wife will have your supper ready directly, m'lord. There's duck and partridge, with lamb's-foot jelly and a wine syllabub to follow.'

Languidly superior, Martin nodded. 'That should do admirably.'

When the door closed behind the little man, Martin glanced her way, laughter lurking in his grey eyes. 'Just so,' he said, his smile warming her every bit as much as the fire in the grate.

Feeling her nervousness increase as he drew nearer, Helen turned to hold out her chilled fingers to the blaze. When the sun had slipped beneath the horizon, he had insisted she don his greatcoat. Her fingers went to the heavy garment to ease it from her shoulders. Instantly, he was beside her. His fingers brushed hers.

'Here, let me.'

She had to, for she could not have moved if the ceiling had fallen. His gentle touch, so simple but almost a caress, and the velvety quality cloaking his rumbling growl, drowned her senses in dizzying distraction. The effect he had on her was intensifying with time. How on earth was she to survive the evening?

As soon as he stepped away from her to drop the coat over a chair, Helen sank into the armchair by the fire. She drew a deep breath, forcing herself to meet his intent gaze when he turned once more to face her.

Martin studied the vision before him, reading her unease with accomplished certainty. If circumstances had been different, she would have every reason to feel threatened. As things stood, she was safe. Or at least, he amended, safe enough. He knew she could sense his attraction and was hourly more entertained by her efforts to hide her consciousness of him. Entertained and intrigued. Clearly, fair Juno, if widow she was, was not one of those who dispensed her favours with gay abandon.

As he watched, a small frown creased Juno's brow.

'Why aren't you travelling with a groom or tiger?'

Elegantly disposing his long limbs in the chair opposite hers, Martin smiled, perfectly ready to converse on such innocent topics. 'My groom fell victim to a severe head cold. I left him at the Hermitage.' Considering that fact, privately Martin owned to some relief that Joshua had not been perched behind, cramping his style.

'Does the Hermitage have many farms attached?'

'Six. They're all leased to long-term tenants.'

Succeeding questions, which Martin was shrewd enough to know were far from artless, led them to a discussion of farming and the care of estates. He could appreciate Juno's desire to avoid questions on town pursuits; such topics were likely to give him more clues to her identity. Yet her opinions on the organisation of farm labour and the problems faced by tenant farmers were equally revealing. Her knowledge of the subject could not have been acquired other than through firsthand experience. All of which added to his mental picture of

fair Juno. She had spent a goodly portion of her life on a large
and well-run estate.

A brisk knock on the door heralded the landlord. 'Your
dinner, m'lord.' Carrying a heavily laden tray, he entered,
closely followed by a buxom woman with tablecloth and cut-
lery. Together, they efficiently laid the table, then bowed and
withdrew.

Rising, Martin held out his hand. 'Shall we?'

Placing her hand in his, Helen ruthlessly stifled the thrill
that shot through her at his touch, assuming her most regal
manner as she allowed him to lead her to the table and seat
her at one end. The slight smile which played about his lips
suggested he was not deceived by her worldly air.

Thankfully, the food gave her a safe topic for discussion.

'I have to admit to ignorance of the latest fads. Thirteen
years is a long time away from the boards of the fashionable.'

Encouraged by this admission, Helen ignored the laughing
understanding lighting his grey eyes and launched into a catalogue of the latest culinary delights.

When the landlord re-entered to draw the covers, Helen
grasped the opportunity to retreat to the chair by the fire. She
heard the door shut behind their host and wondered, a little
frantically, how she was to manage for the next two hours.

'Brandy?'

Turning to see Martin at the sideboard, decanter in hand,
she shook her head. Did he but know it, he did not need any
assistance to befuddle her wits.

Helping himself to a large dose, undoubtedly required if he
was to sleep with Juno, alone, next door, Martin came to stand
by the fire, one booted foot on the fender, his shoulders
propped against the mantelpiece.

'Your man is not going to be impressed with your boots.'

Martin followed her glance and grimaced. 'I'll have to entrust them to the boots here. Joshua will, in all probability,
never forgive me.'

Helen smiled at his nonsense. Despite the tingling of her
nerves, due entirely to her company, she felt relaxed and at
peace, not a state she had had much experience of over her

life. Content, she thought, searching for the right word. Engaged in a most scandalous escapade and I feel content. How odd.

Catching Martin's gaze as it rested lightly upon her, she smiled. He smiled back, a slow, pensive smile, and she felt the heat rise inside her. Her eyes locked with his, smoky grey and intent, and she felt her will start to slip from its moorings.

Sounds of an arrival disrupted their silent communion. Martin turned to stare at the door. The noise beyond rose until it resolved into the clamour of many voices. An invasion had found the Bells.

Helen frowned. 'What could it be?'

Equally at sea, Martin shook his head. 'Too late for a scheduled stop, I would have thought.' Inwardly, he hoped that whatever company had sought shelter at the inn did not include any who might recognise either Juno or himself. If it ever became known, there was no possibility that their escapade would be viewed as innocent.

The noise outside subsided to a steady hum. Almost immediately, the landlord arrived to satisfy their curiosity.

'Excuse me, m'lord, but it seems a night for accidents. The night coach for Plymouth's lost a wheel just up the road. The smith says as it can't be fixed 'til the morrow, so's we're having to put up all the passengers here. If it be all the same to you and her ladyship,' he said, ducking his head in Helen's direction, 'I've put you in the main chamber. It's got a huge bed, m'lord—you won't be disappointed. But there's more people than we have beds as 'tis, so I didn't think as how you'd mind.'

The man looked hopefully at Martin. Martin looked back, wondering how Juno was taking the news. From his point of view, the disaster was a damned nuisance. But if he insisted on separate rooms, they would probably end up sharing with some less suitable bedfellows—the sort who travelled on the night coach. And, all in all, with the extra men in the house, he would much rather Juno was safe by his side, even if he got no sleep as a result. 'Very well,' he replied in his most languid voice. He heard the hiss of Juno's indrawn breath and suppressed a smile. 'In the circumstances, your best chamber will have to do.'

Obviously relieved, the landlord bobbed his head and departed.

Martin turned to meet Juno's reproving gaze. One black brow rose. 'In truth, my dear, you'll be far safer with me than alone this night.'

There was no answer to that. Helen dragged her gaze from his face and fastened it on the flames leaping and dancing about the large log in the grate. The prospect of sleeping in the same bed as Martin Willesden left her feeling numb. It was shock, she supposed. She had slept in his arms in the loft last night, but a loft was not the same as a bed. Her adventure was taking a decidedly dangerous turn. No—it was impossible. She would have to think of some alternative.

But she had still to discover another way from the impasse when, at Martin's suggestion, they went upstairs to their room, the largest chamber as promised. A welcoming fire burned in the grate, a bed which was every bit as huge as her fevered imagination had anticipated stood against one wall. The room was comfortably furnished, the age of the hangings disguised by the soft candlelight. Martin held the door for her, then followed her in.

The click of the latch jolted Helen to action. She swung to face him, clasping her hands firmly before her. 'My lord, this is impossible.'

He smiled and moved past her to the window. 'Martin,' he said, throwing a mild glance over his shoulder. 'You'd better stop "my lording" me if we're supposed to be married.'

Martin checked the window, opening it a crack to let in some air, then rearranged the heavy drapes. He strolled back to the middle of the room, pausing to shrug out of his coat. He draped it over the back of a chair, then smiled at Juno, still standing, uncertain and nervous, near the door. 'It's not impossible,' he said, beckoning her forward. 'Come here by the fire and let me unlace your gown.' He ignored the alarm flaring in her eyes. 'Then you can wrap yourself in the sheet and be as modestly garbed as a nun.'

Helen considered his words, her nerves in knots, her mind incapable of finding any way out. When his hand beckoned again, with increasing imperiousness, she walked hesitantly forward, her eyes reflecting her troubled state.

With a reassuring smile, Martin took her hand and drew her to face the fire. Behind her, he found the lacings of her silk gown. His practised fingers made short work of the closures. He resisted the temptation to part the sides of the garment and run a fingertip down her spine, clad only, as he had suspected, in a fine silk chemise. 'Stay there a moment. I'll fetch the sheet.'

Helen stared at the flames, her cheeks rosy red. So far, his behaviour had been as reassuringly unthreatening as his words. It was her own inclinations that were undermining her confidence. She was perfectly well aware of how close she stood to having an illicit affair with one of the most notorious rakes in England. All she needed to do was to give him a sign that she would welcome his advances and she would learn what it was that made rakes so sought after as lovers. Martin Willesden was temptation incarnate. But her common sense stood firmly in her way, prosaically pointing out that the last thing she needed was a fling, an affair of the moment, based on nothing more than a passing attraction. That had never been her style.

The sheet descended over her shoulders.

'I'll look the other way. I promise not to peek.'

Helen did not dare look to see just where he was or if he complied. Hurriedly, she slipped the silk dress down, letting it puddle about her ankles while she wrapped the sheet around and about her, tucking the ends in to secure it. She stepped out of her dress and bent to pick it up.

The sheet rustled as she moved and Martin turned around, just in time to see her pick up her dress. He admired the view before she straightened, shooting him an uncertain look. The firelight gilded her curls, sheening softly on the exposed ivory shoulders and arms. The ache in his loins, a niggling pain for the past twenty-four hours, intensified. Determined to ignore it, he grinned at her. 'If you get into bed, I'll tuck you in.'

Discovering the teasing glint inhabiting his grey eyes, Helen glared, but obediently moved to the bed. 'Where are you going to sleep?' There was no armchair in the room.

Martin's grin grew. 'As the landlord said, it's a large bed.' He unbuttoned his waistcoat then started on the laces of his shirt.

Helen stopped and stared. 'What are you doing?'

His control under strain, Martin grimaced. 'Getting ready for bed. I'll be damned if I sleep another night in these clothes.' At the look on fair Juno's face, a picture of scandalised horror, he growled, 'For God's sake, woman! Get into bed and turn the other way. You know you're perfectly safe.'

Which was more than he knew, but the longer she stood there, wide green eyes on him, the more danger she courted. When she blinked, then climbed rapidly on to the bed, curling up on one side and pulling the covers about her ears, Martin let out a sigh of relief.

Nerves skittering uncontrollably, Helen lay and stared at the wall. The candles were snuffed, but the flames from the fire shed enough light to see by. She heard his Hessians hit the floor, then the door opened as he stood them in the corridor for the boots to attend to. He closed the door and she heard the muffled sounds of him undressing. She wished she could stop listening, but her nerves, at full stretch, would not let her. Then the bed at her back sagged. With a small squeak, she clutched the side of the mattress to stop herself from rolling into him.

In spite of his pain, Martin chuckled. He had not anticipated that difficulty. 'Don't worry. You have my word as a gentleman that I won't take advantage.'

That's not what I'm worried about! Helen kept the thought to herself. She was scandalised, tantalised, terrified by the possibilities. It had been a long time since she had been in bed with a man, and that never innocently. Last night in the straw did not count—that had been quite different—that had not been a bed. This was definitely a bed. To her horror, her thoughts kept sliding to how easy it would be to relax, to let herself drift back in the bed, until she met the hard, heavy body indenting the mattress behind her.

In the dark, Martin mentally gritted his teeth. His loins were as girded as they could get. But the warm perfume of her hair tickled his senses; his body was alive to her nearness. If last night had been difficult, tonight would be torture. As the fire-light faded, leaving them in comforting darkness, he realised she was stiff and rigid beside him, definitely not asleep.

'You needn't worry I'll move in the night. I sleep very soundly.' Once I sleep, he added silently. 'I suspect it's some-thing to do with having been in the army. One slept when one could, usually in far from comfortable surroundings.'

'How long were you in the Peninsula?'

Her question, muffled by the bedclothes, reminded Martin of an ascerbic comment made by some high-ranking hostess, to the effect that there was nothing so boring as hearing of men's military exploits. He seized the idea. Within ten minutes, the woman's astuteness was confirmed. He paused in the middle of a detailed description of his second major battle. No sound beyond the crackle of the fire disturbed the stillness of the chamber. Then his straining ears caught the soft huff of Juno's breathing, shallow and even. She was asleep.

He smiled into the darkness, oddly elated, as if he had suc-ceeded in winning another battle. Knowing she was asleep allowed him to relax. As he slipped into slumber, he sternly reminded himself to make sure he woke properly—before he moved.

The reminder was needed. He awoke to find that, as he had expected, he had passed the night without stirring. He was no nearer to where Juno had laid her head than before. Unfortu-nately, Juno herself had moved. A lot closer. She had some-how insinuated herself into his arms, her head comfortably settled on his chest. One naked arm lay about his waist.

And her sheet had ridden up in the night. He could feel her silken limbs entwined with his.

Martin clenched every muscle he possessed and willed his body to compliance. Carefully, excruciatingly slowly, he dis-

entangled their limbs, trying not to glance at her legs, too
worried about waking her to draw the sheet down. He was
naked; if she woke now, she was going to get a shock.

It was a relief to leave the warmth of the bed. Quickly, he
dressed and escaped downstairs.

He found the landlord in the taproom, serving some of the
male passengers from the coach. There were others still asleep
on some of the benches. After greeting the man and asking
after the weather, Martin casually asked, 'Have our servants
by any chance appeared?'

The landlord shook his head. 'No, m'lord. No one's been
by this morning.'

Frowning direfully, Martin swore. 'In that case, I'll hire one
of your carriages. My wife can go on to town while I backtrack to find out what's become of our people.'

The landlord was all sympathetic help. He assured Martin
of the quality of his carriage and that the coachman and groom
could be trusted to see her ladyship safe into London.

'Very well,' said Martin, tossing a small purse to the man.
'Have the carriage ready. I'll want her ladyship on her way
immediately after we breakfast.' Martin glanced about the taproom and remembered the sensation Juno had caused the previous day. 'Perhaps you could send a tray upstairs?'

'Certainly, m'lord. I'll send my missus up directly.'

Martin returned upstairs, pausing to gather his strength before tapping lightly on the door and entering. To his relief,
Juno, fair as ever, was out of bed and fully dressed.

Helen was seated before the small dressing-table, setting her
hair once more into a neat knot. She turned when Martin entered, returning his smile as calmly as she could. She had
woken to find him gone, but had found herself in the middle
of the bed, her protective sheet twisted high on her thighs. The
coverlet had been over the top, but she could not begin to
think of where he had been when he had awoken. 'Good morning.'

Her pulse accelerating, she turned back to the mirror.

'A fair morning it is.' Martin came to stand beside the dressing-table, propping his shoulders against the wall.

To Helen's sensitised senses, he exuded an overwhelming aura of potent masculinity. Struggling to keep her wits focused, she listened as he told her of his arrangements.

'With luck, you'll be home shortly after midday.'

Despite the fact that home was where she wished to be, Helen was acutely aware of a dull, shrinking feeling as he pronounced the end to their adventure. Suddenly, the morning seemed less bright.

Their breakfast arrived and was laid out on the small table by the window. Bidden to attend, Helen tried to shake off her attack of the dismals and respond to his banter as she should. He had been a knight in shining armour, in truth, and she owed him a great deal. So she put a brave face on her irrational despondency and replied brightly to his comments.

She would have been mortified to know the ease with which Martin read her thoughts. Clearly, Juno had never mastered the art of prevarication. Her expression was open, her eyes a direct reflection of her mood. He accurately sensed her feelings, and her desire to keep them hidden. Wisely, he made no reference to his knowledge, but was inordinately pleased that she should feel saddened at having her time in his company brought to an end. It would make it so much easier to draw her to him when next they met.

Breakfast over, he escorted her downstairs. The day was fine; Juno did not need his coat. He paused, holding her beside him on the steps of the inn. The carriage which was to convey her to London stood ready before them, as neat and clean as the landlord had said. The coachman and groom were burly fellows, both with the open honesty of countrymen. Juno would be safe in their care. He looked down into her clear green eyes. A wry smile twisted his lips. 'I've told them they should take you to London but that you'll make up your mind where you wish to go when you get there. I've paid them fully, so you don't need to worry about that.'

Helen felt breathless. 'I don't know how to thank you, my lord,' she began, her voice soft and low so that none would hear them. 'You've been of inestimable help.'

Martin's smile broadened. 'The pleasure was entirely mine,

fair Juno.' He lifted her hand from his sleeve and placed a
kiss on her trembling fingertips.

'Your ring,' Helen whispered.

Smoothly, reluctantly, Martin drew the heavy signet from
her finger and replaced it on his. He raised his eyes to gaze
deeply into hers. 'Until next we meet.'

Helen smiled tremulously, aware of a desire to lean into his
warmth, to clutch at his hand.

Quite where the idea sprang from Martin could not later
have said. But it suddenly occurred to him that he was mas-
querading as her husband. And being her husband gave him
certain rights. Furthermore, being a rake, he would be mad not
to take advantage of those rights. His lips lifted in a wholly
devilish smile.

Helen saw the smile. Her eyes widened. But she got no
chance to do anything at all. One strong arm slipped about
her, pulling her firmly against him, while the fingers of his
other hand tipped her face up. His lips closed over hers, confidently, possessively. And time stood still.

For an instant, she held firm against that too knowledgeable
kiss, but the subtle invitation to greater intimacy was too compelling to resist. Her lips parted; he took immediate advantage,
tasting her, teasing her, languidly, expertly exploring her,
sending her mind whirling into fathomless sensation. She was
dimly aware of the tightening of his arms about her. She
melted against him, seeking to press herself against his muscled length. It was utterly delicious, this invitation to delight.
The heady taste of him filled her senses; she was oblivious to
all else but him.

Reluctantly, Martin brought the kiss to an end, wishing he
could take their interaction further but knowing that was, for
the moment, impossible. But at least he had left her with something to remember him by, until he found her in London and
continued her seduction.

Looking down into her dazed eyes, he smiled and, too wise
to attempt conversation, led her to the carriage. The groom,
studiously straight-faced, jumped down and opened the door.
Martin helped his goddess into the coach and saw her settled

comfortably. He raised her hand to his lips. 'Farewell, fair Juno. 'Till next we meet.'

Helen blinked. The message in his eyes was clear. Then the door was shut. A minute later the carriage lurched into motion. She resisted the urge to scramble to the window, to stare back at him until he was out of sight. There was no need. ''Till next we meet,' he had said. She had no doubt he meant it.

Still shaken, Helen drew a ragged breath. If only dreams could come true.

In the inn yard, Martin stood and watched the carriage until it disappeared along the road to London. His impulse was to order his curricle and follow as fast as he was able. But she could not escape. He would find her in London, of that he was sure.

She was one goddess he had every intention of worshipping.

CHAPTER FIVE

Three weeks later, Helen was in her chamber, studying the contents of her wardrobe to determine what could, and could not, be used for the upcoming Little Season, when her maid, Janet, put her head around the door.

'You've a visitor, m'lady.'

Before Helen could extricate herself from the silks and satins and ask who, Janet had gone.

'Bother!' Helen sat on her heels and wondered who it was. The familiar excitement that had simmered just below her surface ever since she had returned to town blossomed. But it could not be him, she reasoned, not at eleven in the morning. With a sigh, she stood and shook out her primrose morning gown, before seating herself before her dressing-table to straighten her curls.

Her reappearance in the capital had caused a minor sensation among her friends but, luckily, thanks to the discretion of her servants, her disappearance had not been broadcast throughout the *ton*. Hence, while she had had to sustain a somewhat strained interview with Ferdie Acheson-Smythe, who had read her a lecture on the ills likely to befall women of her class who kept scandalous secrets, and a much more rigorous cross-examination from Tony Fanshawe, the entire episode had passed off without major catastrophe. Throughout her explanations, she had managed to keep the names of her abductor—for she had no evidence that it had really been Hedley Swayne—and her rescuer—who was far too scandalous to be acknowledged—to herself. In this, she had been lucky. Circumstances, in the form of the birth of his son and heir, had kept her self-appointed guardian, Marc Henry, Marquis of Hazelmere, at home in Surrey. If she had had to face his sharp hazel eyes, she was sure she would have been forced to the truth—the whole truth. Thankfully, fate had spared her.

Descending the stairs, she was conscious of anticipation still pulsing her veins despite the sure knowledge that she would not meet a pair of stormy grey eyes in her small drawing-room. Those eyes, and their warmth, had haunted her; the memory of his lips on hers lay, a jewel enshrined in her memories. But if he looked for her, he would learn her name. And then he would know. Her silly dreams could never come true.

Startling eyes did indeed meet her when she entered her drawing-room, but they were emerald-green and belonged to Dorothea, Marchioness of Hazelmere.

'Helen!' Dorothea jumped to her feet, elegantly gowned as always, her face alight with a happiness so radiant that Helen's breath caught in her throat.

'Thea—what on earth are you doing here? I thought you'd be fixed at Hazelmere for months.' Helen returned the younger woman's warm embrace. They had become firm friends since Dorothea's marriage to Hazelmere, just over a year ago. Helen's connection with Hazelmere dated from her childhood; she was distantly connected with the Henrys and had spent many of her summers with Hazelmere's younger sister in Surrey.

Helen held Dorothea at arm's length, conscious of a pang of dismal jealousy that she would never experience the joy that shone from Dorothea's face. 'How's my godson?' she asked, smiling determinedly.

'Darcy's fine.' Dorothea smiled back, linking her arm in Helen's. Together, they strolled through the open French windows and into the small courtyard.

An ironwork seat with a padded cushion stood facing the bank of flowerbeds, the sun-warmed house wall at its back. As they sank on to the cushions, Dorothea explained, 'I've installed him on the second floor of Hazelmere House. Mytton doesn't know how to react. As for Murgatroyd—he's torn between pride and handing in his notice.'

Helen grinned. Hazelmere's butler and his valet were well-known to her. 'But how did you convince Marc you were well enough to come to town? I was sure he would keep you in semi-permanent seclusion until Darcy was in leading strings, at the very least.'

'Quite simple, really,' explained Dorothea airily. 'I merely pointed out that if I was well enough to share his bed I was certainly well enough to endure the rigours of the Season.'

Helen's laughter pealed forth. 'Oh, gracious!' she gasped, once she was able. 'What I would have given to have been able to see his face.'

'Yes,' agreed Dorothea, emerald eyes twinkling. 'It really was quite something.' She turned to study Helen. 'But enough of my managing husband. What's this I hear of a disappearance?'

With practised ease, Helen told her tale. Dorothea did not press her for the details she omitted, merely remarking at the end of the story, 'Hazelmere hasn't heard and I don't see any reason to tell him.' With a quick smile, she continued, 'What I came here to do was invite you to dinner on Thursday. Just the family, those who are in town. It's too early yet for anything formal and we'll have enough of that once the Season begins. You will come, won't you?'

'Of course,' said Helen. Then she grimaced. 'Mind you, by then Hazelmere will have heard about my escapade. You may tell him from me that there's no reason for him to concern himself over it and I won't take kindly to being interrogated over the dinner-table.'

Dorothea laughed and squeezed her hand. 'I'll make sure he behaves.'

Reflecting that she had perfect confidence in her friend's ability on that score, Helen smiled at the thought of the mighty Hazelmere being managed, on however small a scale, by his elegant wife.

Dorothea rose. 'I have to hurry for I've yet to catch Cecily.' Helen escorted her guest to the door.

'Come early, if you can,' Dorothea urged. 'Darcy's always so good with you.' With an affectionate hug and a cheery wave, Dorothea went down the steps to the street and was handed into the waiting coach by her footman.

Helen watched her depart, then, smiling, went back upstairs to see which of her gowns would do for Thursday.

Martin strolled down St James's oblivious of the noise and bustle that surrounded him. He had yet to learn fair Juno's name, an aberration he had every intention of rectifying with all possible speed. Returning to town in her wake, he had expected to be able to make enquiries the next day. Fate, however, had stepped in and engineered a crisis on his Leicestershire estate. His presence had been necessary; the ensuing wrangle had forced him to post down to London in search of documents, then back to the country to see his orders executed. When the dust had finally settled, three weeks had flown.

He had woken this morning determined to make up for lost time. White's seemed the obvious place to start. He had never let his membership lapse, despite the years spent far afield. Consequently, when challenged, he felt perfectly confident in directing the porter to the membership lists. All proved in order. From the man's change in manner, Martin assumed his ascension to the title was common knowledge. He was bowed into the rooms with all due deference.

He strolled through the interconnecting chambers, pausing to scan the scattered groups for signs of familiar faces. As it transpired, it was they who recognised him.

'Martin?'

The question had him turning to meet hazel eyes on a level with his own. Delighted, Martin grinned. 'Marc!'

They shook hands warmly. After they had exchanged their news, and Martin had duly exclaimed over his friend's recent marriage, Hazelmere gestured to the rooms ahead.

'Tony's here somewhere. He's married too. To Dorothea's sister, as it happens.'

Martin turned laughing eyes on him. 'That must have caused comment. How did Tony take the ribbing about always following your lead?'

'Strangely, this time, I don't think he cared.'

They found Anthony, Lord Fanshawe, and various other members of what had once been Martin's set, ensconced in one of the back rooms. Martin's entrance caused a mild sensation. He was bombarded with questions, which he answered with good grace, picking up the threads of long-ago friendships, and, to his surprise, gradually relaxing into what had once been his milieu. With so many present, he put aside his questions on fair Juno. To Hazelmere or Fanshawe, his oldest friends, he might admit to an interest in an unknown widow. But to raise speculation in so many minds was not his present aim.

Leaving the club some hours later, still in company with Hazelmere and Fanshawe, he wryly reflected that at least he had made a start at re-establishing himself socially.

They were about to part, when Hazelmere stayed him. 'I've just remembered. Come to dinner tomorrow—we're having an informal affair, just family. Tony's coming, so you can meet both our wives.' He smiled proudly. 'And my heir.'

'God, yes!' said Fanshawe. 'Come and add to the mood. It'll be chaos anyway.'

Martin could not help his laugh. 'Very well. I have to confess I'm dying to meet your paragons.'

'Six, then. We still dine early at present.'

With a nod and a wave, they parted. Striding along the pavement in the direction of his newly refurbished home in Grosvenor Square, Martin mused that the new Lady Hazelmere might well be one who could assist him in discovering fair Juno's identity.

Letting himself into his front hall, he surrendered his cane and gloves to his butler, Hillthorpe, who had instantly materialised from beyond the green baize door. Strolling the corridor to his library, Martin was struck again by the silence of the large house. In his memories, there had always been people around—children, friends of his brothers, friends of his parents. All gone now. Only his mother, tied to her room in Somerset, and his younger brother Damian remained. And God knew where Damian was, nor yet how long he was likely to remain. Martin's expression hardened, then he shrugged aside all thought of his younger brother. Damian could take care of himself.

Sinking into a newly upholstered chair, a glass of the finest French brandy in his hand, Martin considered his house. It was empty—indubitably empty. He needed to fill it—with life, with laughter. That was what was still missing. He had rectified the damp and the decay and had cast forth the unscrupulous. The structure was now sound. It was time to turn his mind, and energies, to rebuilding a family—his family.

Hazelmere's transparent pride in his wife and son had impressed him. He knew Marc, and a few hours had sufficed to assure him that the bonds of similarity that had drawn them to each other in earlier years still persisted.

Perhaps that was why fate had thrown fair Juno at his head?

Martin's lips twisted in a self-deprecatory smile. Why could he not just admit that he was besotted with the woman? There was no need to invoke fate or any such infernal agency. Juno was very real and, to him, wholly desirable. And, for the first time in his life, he was not contemplating a temporary relationship, limited by his interest. He was quite sure his interest in Juno would never die.

With a grin, Martin raised his glass in a silent toast. To his goddess. He tossed off the brandy, then, laying down the glass, left the room.

Thursday evening was mild and clear. Martin walked the few blocks to Cavendish Square. He was admitted to Hazelmere House by the butler, Mytton, whom he recognised and who, to his amazement, recognised him.

'Welcome back, my lord.'

'Er—thank you, Mytton.'

Hazelmere strolled into the hall. 'Thought it was you.'

Martin shook hands but his eyes were drawn to the woman who had followed his host into the hall. Fair-skinned and slender, a wealth of auburn hair crowned a classically featured face. Martin glanced at Hazelmere, his brows lifting in question.

The smile on the Marquis's face was answer enough. 'Permit me to introduce you to my wife. Dorothea, Marchioness of Hazelmere—Martin Willesden, Earl of Merton.'

Martin bowed over the slim hand that was bestowed on him; Dorothea curtsied, then, rising, looked up at him frankly, green eyes twinkling. 'Welcome, my lord. We've heard so much about you. You see me positively preening, such is the cachet of being the first hostess to entertain you.'

The low voice invited him to laugh with her at society's vagaries. Martin smiled. 'The pleasure is entirely mine, my lady.' She was, he thought, entirely enchanting, just right for Hazelmere. His gaze shifted to his friend's face. Hazelmere was watching his wife, the proprietorial gleam in his hazel eyes pronounced.

'But do come in and meet the others.' Dorothea took his arm and led him towards the drawing-room.

Hazelmere fell in on his other side. 'You have to exclaim over the heir, too,' he murmured, hazel eyes dancing with laughter.

They paused on the threshold of the large drawing-room. A babble of gay voices, unaffected by polite restraint, filled the air. Martin scanned those present, noting Fanshawe, with a pretty blonde chit at his side, talking to an older woman whom he recognised as Marc's mother, the Dowager Marchioness. Martin remembered her with affection; she was one of the few who had not condemned him over the Monckton affair. By her side was an even older woman in a purple turban. She looked vaguely familiar but he could not place her.

His gaze travelled on to a group before the fireplace— And froze. A woman stood before the hearth, a baby balanced on one hip, cradled in one curvaceous arm. The light from the wall sconce glittered over her golden curls. Her ample charms were exquisitely sheathed in topaz silk; pearls sheened about her throat. She was taller than the dandy she had been talking to, a slim, slight figure with pale blond hair. But his entrance had brought an abrupt halt to their discourse. Eyes of pale green, wide with shock, were fixed on him.

With a slow, infinitely wicked smile, Martin made straight for fair Juno.

As he crossed the large room, he was aware of Dorothea by his side, chattering animatedly. Her comments led him to understand that she thought he was interested in seeing her son. Martin's smile deepened; his eyes locked with fair Juno's. The sight of her, with a baby on her hip, affected him more strongly than he wished to admit. No desire, in a life strewn with desire, had ever been so strong. He wanted to see her standing before his fireplace, with his son in her arms. It was that simple.

Helen couldn't breathe. The sight of Martin in the doorway had quite literally scattered her wits. In the middle of a sentence, in reply to a question of Ferdie's, her voice had simply suspended, stopped, her mind totally focused on the rake across the room. And now he was coming to her side! With an effort, she drew breath, and panic rushed in. Her gaze lifted to his and was trapped in clouds of grey. The quality of his smile registered. It was devilish. Repressing a shiver of pure anticipation, Helen dragged her mind free of his spell. Heavens! She was going to have to do better than this—where had her years of experience flown to?

Then Dorothea was there, reaching for her son. 'Let me introduce Lord Darcy Henry.'

Helen handed Darcy over, desperately struggling to find her mental feet. Dorothea held Darcy for Martin to admire. The Earl of Merton barely glanced at Hazelmere's heir.

'He's nearly two months old.' Dorothea looked up to find that her husband's old friend was not even looking at her son. She stared at Martin, then realised he was staring at Helen. Dorothea followed his gaze and beheld her usually impervious friend mesmerised, bedazzled, wholly hypnotised by Lord Merton's grey gaze.

Fascinated, Dorothea was glancing from Martin to Helen and back again when her husband appeared by her side. Ex-rake that he was, Hazelmere took in the scene in one, comprehensive glance.

'Martin, Lord Merton, allow me to introduce Helen, Lady Walford, Darcy's godmother.' Hazelmere turned to his wife. 'Perhaps, my dear, you'd better take Darcy back to the nursery.' With an innocent air, the hazel gaze returned to Helen. 'And perhaps, Helen, you could introduce the others—or at least those Martin can't recall?'

With a benedictory smile, Hazelmere moved off, firmly removing his by now intrigued wife.

Finding his field clear, Martin allowed a rakish smile to surface. He moved to Helen's side, one black brow rising quizzically. 'Revealed by the hand of fate, fair Juno.'

The softly spoken words caressed Helen's ear, sending a delicious shiver down her spine. 'Helen,' she whispered back urgently, searching for some semblance of equilibrium. She dared not look at him until she had found it.

'You'll always be fair Juno to me,' came the outrageous reply. 'What man of flesh and blood could let that image go? Just think of the memories.'

Helen decided she had better not—her composure was rattled enough already.

Calmly, Martin appropriated her hand and dropped a light kiss on her fingers, smiling at the tremor of awareness the action provoked.

Wide-eyed, Helen glanced up at him, only to glance away rapidly. The glow in his eyes suggested he was going to be outrageous; his smile was a declaration of devilish intent.

Indignation came to her rescue. 'I take it you're acquainted with Hazelmere?'

Martin's eyes danced. 'We're old friends—very old friends.'

Of that Helen had not a doubt. For years, Marc had sternly protected her from the advances of the rakes of the *ton*; now, in his own drawing-room, he had all but handed her into Martin Willesden's arms. Typical! Helen repressed a most unladylike snort.

With his usual good manners, Ferdie had drifted away when Martin had approached so purposefully. With a warning glance for the reprobate beside her, Helen raised her voice. 'Ferdie— have you and Lord Merton met?'

It transpired that they had not. Helen performed the introductions, adding for Martin's benefit, 'Ferdie is Hazelmere's cousin.'

Martin frowned slightly. 'The one who rode his father's stallion?'

To Helen's amusement, Ferdie blushed. 'Didn't think anyone would remember that.'

'I've a particularly good memory,' Martin averred, his eyes seeking Helen's. Trapping her gaze, he added, his voice low, 'Particularly vivid.'

It was Helen's turn to blush. Studiously avoiding Ferdie's interested eye, she placed a hand on Martin's sleeve, risking the contact in the pursuit of greater safety. 'Have you met Dorothea's grandmother, my lord?' With a nod for Ferdie, she purposefully steered Martin in the direction of the dowagers, hoping that in their presence he would get little opportunity to exercise his facility for unnerving innuendo.

To her relief, as they circulated among Hazelmere's guests, Martin behaved in a manner which when she later had time to consider it, only confirmed her assessment of his experience and expertise. He chatted easily with whoever she introduced him to, the ready charm she had always associated with the most dangerous species of rake very apparent. However, at no time did he give any indication of wishing to leave her side. In fact, his attitude declared that, had it been permissible, he would unhesitatingly have monopolised her time.

He made his preference so clear that both the Dowager, Marc's mother, and Lady Merion, Dorothea's grandmother, took great delight in twitting them both over it.

'I gather you've been in the colonies for some years, my lord. I dare say it takes time to remember our ways?'

The pointed look Lady Merion bent on Martin should, by rights, have flustered even him. Yet, to her horror, Helen heard his deep voice reply, 'Having but recently laid claim to an exceptionable memory, I can hardly now advance forgetfulness as my excuse, ma'am.'

For the life of her, Helen could not resist glancing his way. The grey eyes were glowing and fixed on her face.

'Perhaps, my lord, you should seek guidance in achieving

your re-entry to society?' The Dowager Marchioness's eyes were even more innocent than her son's. 'Perhaps Lady Walford would be willing to assist?'

Helen blushed furiously.

'A capital notion, ma'am.' With a smile for the delighted dowagers that relieved Helen of any need to speak, Martin drew her from their questionable safety.

Her composure severely compromised, Helen tried to act calmly, tried to convince herself that, in the present circumstances, it was she who should be in control, not he, but in that she failed miserably. As the evening progressed, and they went into dinner, she was not even surprised to find that Martin had somehow arranged things so that it seemed natural for him to lead her in and sit on her right.

Under cover of an uproarious discussion on the latest of the Prince Regent's peccadilloes, Martin leaned closer and asked, 'Will you consent to a drive with me in the Park, fair Juno?'

Helen sent him a glittering glance, intended to convey her disapproval of his continued use of that name. He received it with an unrepentant smile.

'Good. I'll call for you at eleven tomorrow.'

Before she could do more than gasp at his effrontery, he was offering her a dish of crab. Helen drew a determined breath. 'My lord...' she began.

'My lady?' he promptly replied, grey eyes intent.

Frantically searching for some means of bringing him to a sense of his shortcomings in respect of accepted procedures, Helen looked deep into his eyes, saw them calmly predatory, and knew she stood no chance of turning him from his purpose. His gaze held hers and the fire shrouded by the grey glowed bright. One brow rose. Abruptly, Helen looked down at her plate.

Smoothly, Martin turned back to the company, a confident smile curving his lips.

Nerves aflutter, Helen decided she would do well to regroup before she took on an opponent of Martin Willesden's calibre.

When they adjourned to the drawing-room, the men eschewing their port in favour of joining the ladies, a different light was cast on Martin's propensities. It was Cecily, Lady Fanshawe, who opened Helen's eyes to what had, until that moment, escaped her notice, preoccupied as she had been with Lord Merton's potential for outrageousness. The youthful Cecily, just seventeen, had bubbled about the company in her usual fashion, but had missed being introduced to Martin earlier. Helen performed the introduction and was slightly startled by Cecily's reaction. The big pansy brown eyes opened wide; Lady Fanshawe simply stared.

'*Ohh*,' she finally breathed, her round eyes taking in as much of Martin as she could.

Tony Fanshawe came up in time to witness his wife's response. With a deep sigh, he took her arm.

'Go away, Martin,' he said, and, with a long-suffering look, drew Cecily around. About to lead her off, he paused and glanced back, wicked lights gleaming in his blue eyes. 'On second thoughts, why not take Helen away, too?'

Helen glared. They were *insufferable*, the lot of them! A gaggle of unrepentant rakes.

Martin's chuckle brought her around to face him. 'What a very good idea.' The nuance he managed to infuse into the words sent her eyes flying wide. Somehow, his fingers had trapped her hand. Held by the glow in his grey eyes, smoky now with an emotion she was coming to recognise, Helen could only stare as he raised her hand to his lips. The gesture was so simple, yet heavy with meaning. The lingering touch of his lips, a warm caress on her fingertips, sent a succession of shivers through her.

In desperation, Helen blinked—and saw him through Cecily's eyes. She was used to men being the same height as she, but Martin was a good half-head taller. His dark hair curled lightly; there was the faintest trace of silver at his temples. The grey eyes, so mesmeric, were watching her from under arched and hooded lids. The lines at their corners suggested that laughter came easily to their owner. His cheeks were lean and tanned, his lips fine-drawn and firm. One glance at his jaw gave warning of his temper.

With a little sigh, Helen acknowledged the face and moved

on to the figure. She was a large woman, junoesque in truth, but he made her feel small. His shoulders were wide, his chest broad, leaving an impression of lean muscle cloaking a large and powerful frame. She knew he moved gracefully, as an athlete would; the idea of waltzing with him was more than just attractive.

As she realised, with a jolt, just how long she had stood staring, her eyes flew to his. Heightened consciousness, of him, of her susceptibility, of how much he could see, threatened to overwhelm her. Her breath caught in her throat. She looked away, nervous, confused and more at sea than she had ever been. 'Can you see Ferdie anywhere?'

Martin heard the panic in her tone. Smiling, he dutifully scanned the room. Her response was encouraging but now was not the time to press her further. With consummate ease, he took charge. 'He's by the fireplace.' Tucking her hand into the crook of his arm, he strolled back into the fray of conversation.

Grateful for his understanding, for she knew it was that, Helen took the opportunity he gave her to reassemble her faculties and get her feet back on the ground. As they circulated about the big room, she recalled a comment of Dorothea's that being in Marc's care often felt like being caught in a web, with him, the spider, in the centre. That was exactly how she now felt, except that it was Martin at the centre of her web. It was a protective web; the bonds did not hurt. But they were there, inescapable, unbreakable.

Her relief was very real when Hazelmere approached them, saying to Martin, 'Tony and I are for White's. Gisborne—' he waved in the direction of his brother-in-law '—is coming, too. Are you for the tables?'

Martin smiled. 'Lead the way.'

Hazelmere laughed. 'I didn't think you'd have changed.' With a nod for Helen, he left them.

Martin had taken possession of her hand. Helen glanced up and discovered that the expression in his eyes went far beyond the acceptable, a warm and distinctly intimate caress. He raised her fingers to his lips.

'Until tomorrow, fair Juno.'

It was all she could do to nod her farewell.

Much later, in the privacy of her chamber, Helen stared at her reflection in the mirror, and wondered when such madness would end.

CHAPTER SIX

Not soon, was Helen's conclusion when, the next day, Martin called as promised to take her for a drive in the Park. Bowling along beneath the trees, their leaves just beginning to turn, perched in her familiar spot beside him on the box seat, she discovered that he intended to give her no chance to ponder the wisdom of the outing. Instead, he seemed intent on following the Dowager Marchioness of Hazelmere's advice and enlisting her aid.

'Who is that quiz in the shocking purple toque?'

Helen followed his glance. 'That's Lady Havelock. She's a bit of a dragon.'

'And looks it. Does she still hold sway with the Melbourne House set?'

'Not so much these days, now that Lady Melbourne lives so retired.' Helen raised her hand in acknowledgement of a bow from a painted fop.

'And who's he?'

At the possessive growl, Helen's lips twitched. 'Shiffy? Sir Lumley Sheffington.'

'Oh.' Martin glanced again at the white-painted face above an outrageous apricot silk bow. 'I remember now. I'd forgotten about him—entirely understandable.'

Helen giggled. Shiffy was one of the more memorable figures among the *ton*.

Martin kept up a steady stream of questions—on the other occupants of the Park, on the happenings in town and whether certain personages were as he remembered them. Engrossed with her answers, Helen did not notice the passage of time.

Their hour together vanished more swiftly, and with greater ease, than she had expected.

Descending the steps of Helen's small house in Half Moon Street, having seen his goddess safely inside, Martin startled Joshua, standing at the bays' heads, with an exceedingly broad grin. Gaining the box seat and retrieving the reins, Martin waved Joshua to his perch. 'The day bodes fair, my projects proceed apace—what more could a man ask for?'

Scrambling up behind, Joshua rolled his eyes heavenwards. 'No mystery what's come over you,' he muttered, *sotto voce*, making a mental note to learn more of Lady Walford. In blissful ignorance of his henchman's deductions, Martin gave his horses the office, well-pleased with his beginning.

As the week progressed, he had even more reason for satisfaction. His re-entry to the *ton* was accomplished more easily than he had hoped. A visit to the theatre, escorting fair Juno to view the latest of Mrs Siddons' dramatic flights, had brought him to the notice of the major hostesses. The pile of white cards stacked upon his mantelpiece grew day by day. Eschewing all subtlety, he determined which of the parties his delight intended to grace by dint of the simple expedient of asking. Thus forearmed, he felt assured of enjoying those assemblies he deigned to attend.

Climbing the stairs to Lady Burlington's ballroom for the first of the larger gatherings on his list, Martin spared a moment to contemplate how the *ton* would receive him. Invitations were one thing, but how would they treat the black sheep in the flesh? If he was to marry Helen, the *ton's* approbation was a hurdle he would have to clear.

He need not have worried.

'Lord Merton!' Lady Burlington positively pounced on him. 'I'm so thrilled you could find time to attend my little party.'

Replying all but automatically to his hostess's gushing comments, Martin reflected that, from what he could see, her 'little party' numbered over one hundred.

'Pleased you could come.'

The gruff accents of Lord Burlington were a welcome re-

lease. After shaking hands, Martin moved into the room, only
to find himself surrounded. By women.

Blonde hair in ringlets, black hair in curls, every shade and
hue pressed in on every side. A medley of perfumes washed
over him, light fractured in their gems. 'Lord Merton!' was
on each pair of lips. The hostesses of the *ton*, many the very
women who had, thirteen years before, closed their doors in
his face, all but fell over themselves in their eagerness to impress him with their credentials. Manfully quelling an unnerving impulse to laugh in their powdered faces, Martin drew on
his experience, cloaking his antipathy with just the right degree of patronising superiority, and accepted their admiration
as became one who knew how their games were played.

'I do hope you'll find time to call.'

Martin allowed a black brow to rise at the tone of that particular invitation, coming from a blonde whose eyes vied with
her diamonds in hardness. He could hardly be unaware of the
heated glances some of the younger matrons were flinging his
way. Cynically, he wondered if, had he returned as plain Martin Willesden, unadorned with an earldom and colossal wealth,
he would have been welcomed quite so enthusiastically.

Due to the importunities of the more clinging mesdames, it
was late before Martin saw Helen. Instantly, he knew she was
aware of him, but, unsure of whether he would notice her, she
was making every effort not to notice him. With a devilish
smile, he nodded a brief but determined farewell to his court
and escaped across the ballroom to his goddess's side.

Helen knew he was approaching long before he reached her.
It was not simply that the majority of female eyes in the vi-
cinity had suddenly found a common target, nor that Mrs
Hitchin, with whom she was conversing, had stopped, slack-
jawed, in the middle of a sentence, her eyes fixed on a point
beyond Helen's left shoulder. Her flickering nerves would
have told her he was near and getting nearer even had she
been blindfold.

Quelling her traitorous senses, ignoring her increasing pulse,
Helen turned and, smoothly, surrendered her hand into his.

'My lord.' His fingers closed about hers in a warm, possessive clasp. Determined not to fluster, Helen curtsied.

Martin raised her, then, slowly, deliberately, holding her gaze with is, he carried her fingers to his lips.

For an instant, Helen could have sworn that the entire host held its breath. Kissing ladies' hands was a gallantry no longer common; pray heaven that they put it down to his years away. She, of course, knew better. The glow in his eyes warmed her, the smouldering grey igniting a familiar warmth within.

To her relief, years of ballroom etiquette came to her rescue. 'My lord, pray allow me to present Mrs Hitchin.'

Martin had no interest in Mrs Hitchin. He bestowed a civil nod upon the lady, and a comforting smile. But he did not let go of Juno's hand. Instead, he tucked it into his arm. 'My dear Lady Walford, there's a waltz about to start. I do hope Mrs Hitchin will excuse us?'

Helen blinked. How *dared* he simply walk up and appropriate her? Then full understanding of what he was suggesting broke upon her. A waltz? Held in his arms—and she could imagine just how. Heaven help her—how was she to manage? Just the thought made her feel weak.

In panic, she looked about for assistance. Mrs Hitchin was no use; the woman was positively basking in the glow of Martin's smile. But before she could find a lifeline to cling to, Martin was moving towards the area of the room given over to the dancers.

'I promise not to bite.'

His words, gentle in her ear, stiffened her resolve. She was being silly—missish, she who did not know the meaning of the word. He would not do anything truly outrageous in the middle of a ballroom, would he?

And then he was drawing her into his arms, holding her every bit as close as she had feared. They joined the whirling couples on the floor. A host of emotions she had never experienced before being exposed to Martin Willesden threatened to overcome her. Helen struggled to quell them. She could not—must not—let him get away with this...this commandeering of her senses.

'My lord,' she said firmly, raising her eyes to his.

'My lady,' he replied, his tone investing the term with meaning far beyond the mundane, his eyes confirming his intent.

Helen felt her eyes grow round. Great heavens! He was seducing her. In the middle of Lady Burlington's ballroom, with half the *ton* looking on. Rapidly revising her estimates of his potential, she allowed her lids to veil her eyes and sought for a lighter note. 'Does polite society thus far meet with your approval?'

Martin smiled. 'I hardly know. I've had so little in recent years to compare it with.' He felt her relax, and took the opportunity provided by negotiating the tight turn at the bottom of the room to draw her more firmly against him. 'But, as far as the company goes, I've some reservations.'

'Oh?' Thankful that he was prepared to converse reasonably, Helen decided to overlook the almost imperceptible tightening of his arm about her. 'Why is that?'

'Well,' said Martin, frowning as if considering his words, 'it's the female element I have most trouble with.'

Suspicion bloomed in Helen's mind. What did a rake consider reasonable conversation? She felt compelled to give him the benefit of her doubt and asked, 'What is it that particularly troubles you?'

The concerned look he threw her almost had her believing his, 'It's their predatory tendencies that worry me.' When she looked sceptical, he added defensively, 'It's most unnerving to a fully licenced rake to find himself the pursued rather than the pursuer. Just imagine it, if you can.'

'Strange,' said Helen, green eyes glinting. 'I could almost believe I know just how you feel.'

At that he smiled, a dazzling smile that overloaded her senses and sent them spinning. By the time she had collected them, the music had ceased. 'Perhaps I should return to—' In confusion, Helen bit her lip. Heavens, she was no débutante to be returning to a chaperon's side! What was she thinking of—what was it the man by her side made her think of?

Martin chuckled, following her thoughts easily. 'Fear not,

fair Juno. Your reputation is safe with me.' He paused then added in a pensive tone, 'As for the rest of you, though…' The shocked glance she sent him had him chuckling again.

When, a few minutes later, he relinquished her to Lord Alvanley, still flustered but recovered enough to throw him a speaking glance, he reflected that he had spoken no more than the truth throughout their exchanges. Which was odd enough. But he did, in fact, find the cloying interest of the unmarried females repelling and suspected his feeling sprang, as he had told her, from his liking to be the driving force behind his relationships. Her far more natural response to him was gratifying; her attempts to hide it, believing, correctly, that it gave him far more influence over her than she would like, made her irresistibly attractive to a man of his ilk. Given his long-term plans for her, he had no intention that her reputation should suffer at his or anyone else's hands. And he felt positively righteous that he had gone so far as to give her clear warning of his intent.

Halo glowing, he strolled about the room, waiting for the time to claim her for supper.

Dancing with friends and acquaintances who demanded no more from her than polite conversation gave Helen time to consider Martin Willesden's words. Not for the life of her could she fathom what he meant. If it had not been for the fact that he knew she was a connection of Hazelmere's, she might have suspected he intended to set her up as his mistress. But she knew enough of the peculiar code of the rake to know that Hazelmere's protection would not be challenged by a friend. But, if not that, then his words could only mean he was on the lookout for a wife and believed she would suit.

Inwardly, Helen sighed, and wished it were so. But he was wrong—and the sooner he learned his error the better. He was going to break her heart if he did not desist from his determined pursuit. None knew better than she that, while her birth was perfectly acceptable and her connections beyond reproach, being the relict of a social outcast would not be considered a suitable background for the new Countess of Merton. That position should rightly be reserved for one of the *incompar-*

ables, or, at the very least, a richly dowered débutante. She had never been one of the former, though she had, for a bare month before her marriage, been one of the latter.

The cotillion came to an end. Lord Peterborough, whom she had known forever, bowed elegantly over her hand. 'Thank you, Gerry,' she said, smiling. 'You're always such an eligible *parti*.'

His lordship laughed and offered her his arm. Supper was being served downstairs. Helen raised her hand to place it on his sleeve but, to her surprise, warm fingers closed about hers.

'Ah, Gerry. I have to tell you Lady Birchfield is looking for you.'

Lord Peterborough glared. 'Dammit, Martin! Lady Birchfield can look all she likes. The woman's old enough to be m'mother.'

'Really? I'd no idea you were so young.' Martin's eyes gleamed. 'It's just as well I've arrived to escort Lady Walford to supper. It wouldn't do for her to be thought a cradle-snatcher.'

Having deprived both Lord Peterborough and fair Juno of the power of speech, Martin smoothly drew Helen's hand through his arm and, with a genial nod to his friend, steered her in the direction of the supper-room.

By the time Helen found her tongue, she was seated at a small table in an alcove of the supper-room, a plate of delicacies before her. Fixing the reprobate opposite with a steely glare, her bosom swelled. 'Lord Merton...' she began.

'Martin, remember?' Martin grinned at her. 'You didn't really believe I'd let you go into supper with anyone else, did you?'

Staring into teasing grey eyes, Helen felt totally befuddled. Should she answer yes or no? If she said yes, he would only take the opportunity to tell her she should have known better—which was true. And saying no was out of the question. In the end, she glared. 'You're impossible.'

Martin smiled. 'Have a lobster patty.'

Helen gave up. It was simply too easy for him to pull the rug from beneath her feet in private. She had yet, she reflected,

to learn how to keep him at a proper distance. If she did not
master the art soon, it would be entirely too late. Already, she
had noticed a few curious looks cast their way. Still, as far as
the *ton* knew, he could merely be looking her over, seeking
congenial company until the Little Season got into full swing
and he set about the serious task of finding a suitable wife.

Pleased by her capitulation, Martin devoted his considerable
talents to distracting her, in which endeavour he was so successful that, by the time he returned her to the ballroom, she
was thoroughly flustered. In the circumstances, he forbore to
claim another dance, contenting himself with placing a most
improper kiss in her palm before leaving her to less threatening cavaliers.

The Burlington ball marked the beginning of Martin's campaign. He was assiduous in attending whatever ball or party
Helen Walford graced, paying her such marked attention as
could not be misconstrued. He took great delight in teasing
her, knowing that she, of all who watched him, was the furth-
erest from divining his purpose. Many had marked his predilection for her company; he did not, in truth, give a damn. He
fully intended to go a great deal further than mere predilection.

Everything he learned of her confirmed his certainty that
she was the one woman he wanted before his fireplace. She
was accepted and respected, unquestionably good *ton*. Her maturity was transparent, but, while she clearly understood the
rules of the game, she had never, to anyone's knowledge,
played. Not the closest scrutiny uncovered any degree of partiality for the numerous gentlemen who claimed her as friend.
She was much admired, by the women as well as the men—
no mean feat in these days of cut-throat beauty.

It was a week into the Little Season when his pursuit of her
took him to the dim portals of Almack's. The Marriage Mart
had never been one of his favourite venues. As a youth, he
had labelled it the Temple of Doom—forswear happiness, all
ye who enter here. With a grimace, he gathered his resolution
and trod up the steps. Helen was within and he had determined
to conquer not only her, but this last bastion of the *ton*.

The porter admitted him to the hall, but, not being a regular, there he had to wait for one or other of the patronesses to grant him permission to enter the rooms. As luck would have it, it was Sally Jersey who swept out in response to the porter's summons, her large eyes wide and incredulous.

'Good God! It *is* you!'

Martin grinned wryly and bowed. 'Me, myself and I, alone.' He smiled winningly. 'Will you allow me to enter, dear Sally?'

Lady Jersey was no more immune to rakish charm than the next woman. But she knew Martin Willesden, and knew of the scandal in his past. She was also one of those who had never believed it. She eyed the tower of potent masculinity before her and frowned. 'Will you promise not to cause any undue flutter?'

Martin put back his head and laughed. 'Sally, oh, Sally. What an impossible stipulation.'

When he eyed her wickedly, Lady Jersey was forced to acknowledge the truth of his words. 'Oh—very well! I never believed that Monckton chit anyway,' she muttered.

Martin captured her hand and bowed low. 'My thanks, Sally.'

'Oh, go on with you!' said Lady Jersey. 'You make me feel old.'

'Never *old*, Sally.' With one last wicked grin, Martin headed for the ballroom.

He had hoped to slip unnoticed to the side of the room, from which vantage point, being so tall, he would have been able to locate Helen. Instead, to his horror, he was mobbed but feet from the door. While he had been speaking to Sally, word of his arrival had gone the rounds. To his incredulous gaze, it appeared that every fond mama with an insipid daughter in tow had gathered near the entrance for the express purpose of accosting him.

'My dear Lord Merton—I'm Lady Dalgleish—a very old friend of your mama's. Pray allow me to present...'

'Such an exciting career as you've had, my lord. You must take the time to tell my dear Annabelle all about it—she just *adores* tales of foreign places.'

Never in his life had Martin faced such a trial. It quickly transpired that, as virtually none could claim acquaintance due to his prolonged sojourn overseas, they had all decided to ignore such niceties and introduce themselves. The reason for his thirteen-year absence was entirely overlooked.

'You must come to my soirée next week. Just a *very* select few. You'll be able to converse with Julia so much more easily without such a horde about.'

Even Martin blinked at that. They were shameless, the lot of them. The temptation to tell them all to go to hell was strong, but Sally would never forgive him. And he wanted to see Helen, who was undoubtedly one of the many enjoying the unexpected entertainment.

In the end, Martin simply stood stock still and let them come at him, steadfastly refusing to ask any young lady to dance, nor to accept any invitation to look over a chit's finer points during a stroll around the rooms. He knew that none of the hostesses would be so bold as to suggest he dance with any of the young things, regardless of their parents' wishes. It was the first time he had ever had reason to be thankful for his past.

Finally, the attack faltered. In between deflecting the none too subtle invitations, he had managed to locate Helen in a small knot of ladies at the far end of the room. Sensing a hiatus, he made a bid for freedom before his besiegers had a chance to regroup.

Gracefully, Martin bowed to the stalwart matron planted plumb in front of him, her two freckle-faced daughters flanking her. 'Your pardon, ma'am. I fear I must leave you. So pleasant to have met your daughters.' With a vague smile, he beat a hasty retreat.

Helen had certainly noticed the crowd by the door and recognised the dark head at its centre. It was no more than she had expected—his due, nothing more. With an inward sigh, she made an effort to immerse herself in her friends' discussion. Lord Merton would have his hands full with the debs from now on.

'My dear—my *very* dear Lady Walford.' Martin did not try

to keep the relief from his voice. 'What a pleasure it is to see you—at last.'

Helen jumped and turned, knowing who she would see before she did. No one else had a voice that could frazzle her senses. 'My lord.' She curtsied. As usual, he raised her and appropriated her hand, as if she had made him a present of it. She had come to accept that particular trick as inevitable, knowing no way of stopping him. But she had yet to come to grips with the warmth in his eyes as they rested on her, and the promise that glowed in their depths.

Breathlessly, she introduced the three ladies in her circle. To her surprise, Martin did not try to remove her but stayed by her side, chatting politely, charming her friends utterly.

When Helen's friends moved away, to talk to other acquaintances among the growing crowd, Martin dropped the reserve he employed in such social situations. He glanced down into Helen's green eyes, his own entirely devoid of guile. 'You'll have to be my mentor in this particular theatre of war. Where else can we go to be safe?'

Helen looked her astonishment. 'Safe?'

Martin smiled a little ruefully. 'I'm claiming your protection.' When she still looked bemused, he added, 'In return for my earlier efforts on your behalf.'

A slight blush staining her cheeks, Helen let her eyes slide over his impressive length. 'However could *I* protect *you*? You're bamming me.'

'No such thing—rake's honour.' Hand over his heart, Martin grinned. 'The matchmaking mamas are out to leg-shackle me, I do assure you. They're hunting in packs, what's more. If I'm to retain any degree of freedom, I'll need all the help I can get.'

Helen smothered a giggle. 'You can't just not take any notice. You'll have to choose a wife some time.'

The grey eyes holding hers suddenly became intent. But his voice was still even when he asked, 'You don't seriously suppose I'd marry any of the delicate debs?'

'But…it's what's expected of men of your position.' Helen coloured, then abruptly glanced away. Not only was this a most improper conversation, but she had nearly blurted out that hers had been such a conventional marriage. That, she was the first to admit, was hardly a recommendation.

To her unease, the grey eyes were still trained on her face. She could feel them, compelling her to return his regard. Unable to withstand the subtle pressure, she glanced up. Her eyes locked with his.

Martin smiled gently, and raised her hand to his lips, his eyes holding hers steadily. 'I'll never marry one of the debs, my dear. My tastes run to women of more…voluptuous charms.'

If Helen had had any doubts over what he intended her to understand by that, the look in his eyes would have dispelled them. For good measure, when she blushed, his eyes dropped to caress the ripe swell of her breasts, more revealed than concealed by the current craze for low necklines. Helen felt her cheeks flame.

'Martin!'

His eyes returned to her face, gentle laughter in the grey depths. 'Mmm?'

What could she say? She should talk to him of reality, of all the reasons she was ineligible. Now was the time. Determined to halt his mad schemes before they went any further, before her heart was totally torn in two, Helen raised her eyes to his. 'My lord, you cannot marry me. My husband was Arthur Walford—you must have known him. He committed suicide, but only after being hounded from the *ton*. He gambled away everything he owned, including my settlements. With such a background, I'm no suitable wife for you.'

All Martin's levity had flown. The expression in his eyes, intent yet infinitely gentle, did not waver; his thumb moved caressingly over the back of her hand. 'My dear, I know all this. Did you think I would care?'

The room was whirling. Helen could not breathe. 'But…'

Martin's smile grew. Confidently, he drew her to stroll beside him. If they remained stationary for much longer, someone would stop to talk. 'My dear Helen, I've never been one to act in accordance with society's dictates. I've been a rake and a gamester for as long as anyone here can recall. I assure you, none will think it the least odd that I, of all men, should choose to marry a more mature woman rather than saddle myself with some mindless flibbertigibbet.'

A nervous giggle assured him that she had accepted the truth of that. 'Now enough of your quibbles. If this is merely a ploy to deny me your protection, I take leave to tell you 'tis a shabby trick.'

'As if you need my protection.' Helen followed his lead in moving from the topic of marriage, trying to regain their usual, lightly bantering tone. Her mind was in a whirl. What he had suggested was beyond her wildest dreams; she would need time to consider the possibilities. Her brain was too overloaded to make much sense of it now, particularly not with him by her side. 'I'm quite sure you could rout all the matchmaking mamas without difficulty.'

'Unquestionably,' agreed the rake by her side. 'But, having done so, I'd be cast out from these hallowed halls, bidden never to return, and thus would be unable to see you on Wednesday nights. Not a prospect I relish. So, in the interests of your Wednesday nights, madam, will you consent to act as my protector?'

Helen could only laugh. 'Very well. But only within strict limits.'

Martin frowned. 'What limits?'

'You must not misbehave with me.' She glanced up, trying for stern implacability. 'No dancing more than two waltzes, and never two together. In fact,' she added, recalling his ability to think up new and ever more disturbing ways of dealing with her, 'no going beyond the line in any way whatever.'

'Unfair! How do you imagine I'll control my rakish tendencies? Have pity, fair Juno. I can't reform in an instant.'

But Helen stood firm. 'That's my best offer, my lord.' When his brows rose, she added, her own brows rising, 'You'd hardly ask me to place my own position here in jeopardy?'

Martin sighed in mock-defeat. 'You drive a hard bargain, sweetheart. I capitulate. In the interests of my own skin, I accept your conditions.'

It was a full minute before Helen registered the ineligible epithet and by then it was too late to gasp.

To her considerable relief, Martin did behave impeccably for the rest of the evening. She had no illusions as to how outrageous he could be if he put his mind to it. His 'rakish tendencies', as he called them, were remarkably strong. But not even the highest stickler could have faulted his performance—beyond the fact that he remained anchored to her side.

After the excitement of Almack's, Helen had expected to endure a sleepless night. Instead, drugged with unaccustomed happiness, she had slept the sleep of the innocent. Unheralded but sure of his welcome, Martin had called to take her driving at eleven. What with entertaining a small procession of afternoon visitors, all agog to hear anything she might have to say about the Earl of Merton, and then dressing for dinner at Hatcham House, Helen found herself once more in Martin Willesden's arms, waltzing down a ballroom, without having had more than a moment to spend in consideration of his words of the previous night.

'Tell me, fairest Juno, is it normal for such affairs as this to be so refreshingly free of the *jeunes filles*?'

Martin's voice in her ear summoned her wits from besotted contemplation of how very strong he was and how helpless he made her feel. Helen blinked. 'Well,' she temporised, glancing about at the crowd and noticing he was right, 'I suppose it's because the Hatchams are rather out of the deb set— their own children are all married. And Lord Pomeroy is giving a ball for his daughter tonight, too, so many of the younger folk will be there, I expect.'

Martin frowned slightly. 'I don't suppose I can convince you to eschew the larger balls—at least for this year?'

Helen returned his mock-frown with one of her own. 'After avoiding the *ton* and the matchmaking mamas for the past thirteen years, the least you can do is allow them a try at you.'

'But just think how pointless such an undertaking on their parts will be.' His expression became earnest. 'Shouldn't I, in

the interests of the social good, and the matchmaking mamas'
constitutions, simply give them all the go-by?'

The music ceased and they whirled to a halt. Taking his
arm all but automatically, Helen fell to strolling by his side.
'By no means!' She could not yet see where his conversation
was taking them. 'It's your duty to be seen at the major functions.'

Martin grimaced. 'You're absolutely sure?'

Warily, Helen nodded.

'Ah, well.' He sighed. 'In that case, just as long as you're
there to protect me, I suppose I'll have to attend.'

'My lord, I cannot be forever at your side.' She could see
where he was headed now.

'Why not?'

The grey eyes, impossibly candid, held hers.

'Because…' Helen struggled to assemble her reasons—her
rational, sensible reasons. But, under the power of his grey
gaze, they went winging from her head. They had halted by
the side of the ballroom and she had turned, the better to look
into his face. The eyes holding hers seemed to look deeper,
reach deeper, to touch some chord within her and make it sing.
Then, as she watched, he was distracted. His eyes left hers,
focusing on some vision a few feet behind her.

'Speaking of protection…' Martin drew her hand through
his arm, securing her by his side.

'Martin—*darling*! How positively *thrilling* to see you
again—after all these years!'

Helen stifled a wince at the arch tones. Small wonder that
Martin wished to avoid the mesdames if that was the treatment
they accorded him. She felt the muscles of his arm tense beneath her fingers. Helen shifted slightly, to stand more definitely by his side, where she sensed he wanted her, and found
herself staring at blonde curls much paler than her own, arranged about a face rather older than her own. But not old
enough to be a matchmaking mama. The woman cast the barest of icy smiles in her direction before turning big, pale blue
eyes on the new Earl of Merton.

The new Earl remained stubbornly silent.

The lady continued unabashed. '*Such* a surprise, my dear. You should have called.' A look of unlikely ingenuousness suffused the pale face. 'Oh! Of *course*. You wouldn't know! I'm Lady Rochester now.'

For Helen, the penny dropped with the name. She stifled the urge to look up at Martin, to see what he was making of her ladyship's performance. Lady Rochester was a widow of some years standing, one of those who, while credited with birth sufficient to enter the *ton* and title sufficient to open most doors, was nevertheless on the outer circle of polite society. No scandal had ever touched her name, but consistent rumour still tarnished it.

Martin's silence was beginning to strain her ladyship's smile. But her voice was determinedly conspiratorial when she said, 'My dear Martin, I've so much to tell you. Perhaps, such old friends as we are, we should repair to some place rather more private to review our histories? If Lady Walford will excuse us?'

The last was said with a dismissive smile. Her ladyship reached for Martin's other arm. Helen stiffened, and would have drawn her hand from Martin's sleeve except that his hand, covering hers, tightened, strong fingers gripping hers.

'I think not.'

Helen blinked, very glad that Martin did not use that particular tone to her. Shafts of ice and arctic winds would have been warmer. Intrigued by this by-play, for it was transparently obvious that there was more to the exchange than she yet knew, she watched Lady Rochester's face pale to blank-white.

'But—'

'As it happens,' Martin continued, repressive coldness in every syllable, 'Lady Walford and I were about to take a stroll on the terrace. If you'll excuse us, Lady Rochester?'

With a distant nod, Martin steered Helen past the importunate Lady Rochester, leaving her ladyship to stare, dumbfounded, at their backs.

Within minutes, they were strolling on the long terrace in relative isolation. Helen felt the tension ease from Martin's long frame. Who was Lady Rochester that she should draw such a violent, albeit suppressed reaction from Martin? Out of the blue, the answer flew into Helen's head.

'Oh! Is she the one who—?' Abruptly, she cut off her words; embarrassment rose to smother her.

Beside her, she felt rather than heard Martin's sigh.

'She's the one who engineered the little drama that saw me exiled from England.'

Engineered? What drama? Helen wished she had the nerve to ask.

Martin stared out over the darkly shadowed gardens, seeing the shadows from his past. He did not want them to cloud his future. There was no one within earshot. 'When I was twenty-two, Serena Monckton, now Lady Rochester, was a débutante. She quite literally threw herself at my head.' He glanced down at Helen's face, and saw the little frown of concentration that dragged at her brows. He smiled. 'As I told you, I have a constitutional dislike of being pursued. In this case, however, I underestimated the opposition. Serena engineered a compromising situation—and then cried rape.'

Helen's brows flew but she said nothing.

'Unfortunately, that little contretemps came on top of the discovery by my father of a rash of gambling debts—nothing overly outrageous, only what was to be expected from a youth such as I was. But my father was determined to keep me in line. Serena's little ploy was the last straw. He issued an ultimatum.'

Despite his clipped tones, and the effort he was making to tell his story without emotion, Helen heard the pain, dulled by the years but still there, an undercurrent that had sprung to life immediately he had mentioned his father.

'Either I married the chit or he'd send me to the colonies. I chose the colonies.' Martin raised his brows, considering his life in brief. 'All in all, that was the luckiest decision of my life.' His lips curled. 'Perhaps I should thank Serena. Without her efforts, I doubt I would be worth quite as much as I am today.'

Helen threw him a soft smile. Hesitantly, and only because

she was desperate to know, she asked, 'Did your father learn the truth later?'

There was a distinct pause before the answer came. 'No. I never saw him again. He died two years after the event, while I was still in Jamaica.'

Helen did not need to ask herself if she had heard the truth. Every particle of her being knew that she had. No matter how accomplished an actor, no man, she felt sure, could manufacture the emptiness, the intense loss, that vibrated in the deep, gravelly voice. She had heard vague murmurings of the scandal in his past. She was pleased that he had told her of it— now she could disregard it.

They paced the length of the terrace to where a series of shallow steps led down to a fountain surrounded by an area of parterre. A number of couples were strolling in the fresh night air, seeking relief from the closeness of the ballroom.

Glancing at the serious face beside him, Martin smiled. She was so easy to read. He felt curiously honoured that she should concern herself with his long-ago hurts. But it was time she smiled again. 'Can I tempt you from the terrace, fair Juno? I promise not to abduct you.'

Helen looked up and smiled as the implication of his words registered. A disavowal of any negative response to being abducted by him had almost reached her lips before, horrified, she stilled the words. Fancy admitting to a desire to be kidnapped—by a rake, no less! Her wits were becoming thoroughly untrustworthy when he was by her side. She covered her confusion by drawing away and sweeping him a curtsy. 'Why, thank you, my lord. A brisk turn about the fountain will doubtless clear my head.'

Martin's brows rose. 'Does it need clearing? What's it full of?'

You, was her thought. But his eyes were quizzing her. Determined not to be jockeyed into making any revealing disclosures, Helen put her nose in the air and her hand on his arm. 'The fountain, my lord.'

His soft laugh set every nerve tingling.

'As you command, fair Juno.'

CHAPTER SEVEN

The Little Season progressed and, with it, Martin's campaign. By the time the first flurry of balls had faded into memory, and the trees in the Park had begun to shed their leaves, he felt it was time to re-evaluate his position. Helen Walford was his—that was quite clear to him. Hopefully, it would, by now, also be quite clear to the *ton* at large. Watching his fair Juno from the side of Lady Winchester's ballroom, his shoulders propped against the panelled wall, he spared a moment in fond amazement that she, alone, was still uncertain on the matter, unsure that the future he had planned for her would ever come true.

He had taken great delight in conveying, by every subtle means at his disposal, just how exciting her future would be. She was fascinated. Her insecurity stemmed, he surmised, from her unhappy marriage—a fact he had no difficulty believing. Arthur Walford must have been all of fifteen years her senior.

'I wonder…is it possible to tempt you to the card-room?'

At the familiar languid tones, Martin smiled and shifted his gaze sideways to the Marquis of Hazelmere's face. 'Unlikely.'

Hazelmere sighed. 'I thought not. I'll have to hunt up Tony.' He clapped Martin on the shoulder and was turning away when he paused to add, 'Just remember—the sooner you resolve this matter, the sooner you can join us. It doesn't do to forget your friends.' With a smile of the most complete understanding, Hazelmere moved on.

Turning back to the ballroom in time to see Helen throw a laughing smile at her partner—Alvanley and therefore perfectly safe—Martin smiled wryly. He had only just arrived, yet the urge to monopolise Lady Walford's company was growing stronger by the minute. He would resist the tug yet awhile; there was a limit to all things—even the leniency of the *ton* towards one who they were now convinced had been wrongfully slighted. Martin's smile grew. In truth, the past no longer haunted him. His only concern was for the future. But the approbation of the *ton* would be important to the future Countess of Merton, so he was pleased to have secured that elusive cachet.

As to the future itself, he had no doubts. In fact, if he was forced to the truth, he would have to admit that he had made up his mind to wed Helen Walford the instant he had seen her standing before the Hazelmeres' fireplace. The only consideration that had kept him from a declaration was a desire not to startle her—or the *ton*. The *ton* was now taken care of. She was still slightly nervous over what she knew would shortly be her fate, but, if anything, that touch of the wide-eyed innocent only made him more eager to make her his.

The music came to an end and the guests milled across the floor. Conversation rose to cloak the scene lit by the heavy chandeliers. The curls in the ladies' artfully arranged coiffures sheened; jewels winked about their throats. Their gowns swirled, the colours of spring flowers about the trunks of the darker-garbed males.

Juno had her own little court. Over the heads of the throng, Martin watched as she smiled and traded quips. Her gown of palest amber became her fair charms to admiration. With an inward glow, he noted the way her eyes lifted every now and then to scan the company. She had yet to see him. Then, as he watched, waiting for the right moment to make his presence known, a fop in a coat of a peculiar shade of green insinuated himself at Helen's side.

Martin came away from the wall. He started across the floor, automatically smiling and nodding at those he knew, his attention focused on the man beside Helen. He had noticed him, and his interest in Lady Walford, before. Discreet enquiry had elicited the information that he was one Hedley Swayne, Esquire, of a small but prosperous estate in Cornwall. Despite

the lack of firm evidence, it was entirely possible that Hedley
Swayne had indeed been behind Helen's kidnapping. The *ton*
had noted a singular tendency for Mr Swayne to pay assiduous
court to Lady Walford but had dismissed this as a mere smoke-
screen erected by the gentleman with a view to being regarded
as fashionable; none could imagine the undeniably fashionable
Lady Walford having any serious interest in a man a good
half-head shorter than herself and distinctly less high in social
rank to boot. Martin had seen Hedley Swayne at numerous
gatherings, but this was the first time the fop had had the
temerity to approach Helen.

Long before he reached her side, Martin sensed Helen's
unease. Mr Swayne had picked his moment; there were none
but the more youthful of her cavaliers at present about her. As
he paused to dutifully exchange compliments with an ageing
dowager, a friend of his mother's, Martin saw Helen frown.

'I assure you, Mr Swayne, that I am not such a weakling
as to need to repair instantly to the terrace immediately a dance
is ended.' Helen tried not to sound waspish but Hedley
Swayne would try the patience of a saint.

'I merely wished to explain—'

'I don't believe I wish to hear any explanation, Mr Swayne.'
Helen wished it were permissible to glare. She came as close
as she could, viewing the pale face and long, pink-tipped nose
of the unfortunate Mr Swayne with every evidence of aversion. If the man had any sensibility at all, he would leave. Her
court had deserted her, prompted by his declared intention of
walking with her on the terrace. As if she would risk a terrace
in his company! But she knew from experience that Hedley
Swayne was all but irrepressible. She compressed her lips in
reluctant resignation as she watched him draw breath to put
forward his next suggestion. Why wouldn't he just leave her
alone?

'Mr Hedley Swayne, I presume?'

The languid tones surprised Hedley Swayne, making him
look rather like a startled rabbit. As his eyes rose to take in
the gentleman now by her side, the huge floppy bow at his
throat, hallmark of the well-dressed fop, all but quivered in

agitation. Swallowing a sudden urge to giggle, Helen turned slightly, putting out her hand to Martin. He took it and tucked it into his arm, but spared only a glance for her before returning his attention to her persecutor.

Under the grey gaze, Hedley Swayne blinked nervously. 'Ah—I don't believe we've been introduced, my lord.'

Martin noticed he did not say he did not know who he was. He smiled coldly. 'Not exactly. Your reputation goes before you, you see. I believe we just missed each other—in Somerset, some weeks ago?'

At the heavy meaning underlying the polite words, Hedley Swayne's pale eyes grew round. He blanched, then flushed. 'Er…ah…'

Martin's gaze grew steely. 'Just so.'

Helen watched in appreciation. It must have been Hedley behind her kidnapping after all. Then the musicians started playing the music for the next dance—a waltz.

Eyes still holding Hedley Swayne's, Martin smiled, letting dire warning show beneath his urbanity. 'My dance, I believe, my lady. Mr Swayne.' With a nod for the hapless Hedley, Martin drew his future wife firmly into his arms, a little shocked at how intensely possessive he felt.

Slightly surprised at being denied the opportunity to take proper leave of Mr Swayne, irritating though that gentleman was, Helen nevertheless could not find it in her to cavil. Waltzing with Martin was a heavenly delight—she had no intention of losing so much as a moment of her rapture over something as inconsequential as a fop called Hedley Swayne.

'Has he been bothering you?'

Helen glanced up to find a frown gathering in the grey eyes fixed on her face. Bother Hedley! She shrugged. 'He's totally innocuous, really.'

'Innocuous enough to have you kidnapped.'

This time, Helen sighed. 'There's no need to worry about him.'

'I assure you it's not Hedley Swayne I worry about.'

Helen looked up and was trapped in his grey gaze. Suddenly, she felt breathless, her pulse accelerating. 'You worry too much, my lord,' she whispered, dragging her eyes from his.

At her tone, Martin shut his lips on his retort. He was tempted to order her to avoid Hedley Swayne, but, as yet, his jurisdiction did not stretch that far. He placated his urge to ensure her safety with the reflection that, soon, he would be in a position to make sure she saw nothing more of Mr Swayne.

Despite his not having uttered his decree, Helen got the message quite clearly. She felt thoroughly disgruntled when the music ceased, denying her the chance to dwell further on the peculiarly addictive sensation of drifting, light as air, in Martin's arms. His discussion of Hedley had distracted her and now their waltz—the last one of the night, what was more—was over.

Nevertheless, she made the most of the rest of her evening, going into supper on the Earl of Merton's arm. She had given up trying to tell herself he was not serious. He was perfectly serious when he wished to be and on the subject of her future he was unshakeable. It was simply not possible to mistake the intentions of a gentleman who made it patently clear that he attended the *ton* parties purely to dance attendance on one woman. Being that woman made her more nervous than she had ever been in her life.

It was the first time she had been in love—the first time she had been the object of love. She comforted herself that it was only the novelty that sent her senses skittering in delicious disarray whenever she heard his voice. Doubtless, the effect would wane with time. A niggling suspicion that it would not, and that she had no real desire that it should, undermined her fragile confidence.

The truth was, she could not quite believe it was all real, that the rainbow that had appeared on her horizon would not simply vanish with the next dawn. Love was something she had convinced herself she would have to do without—to have it served up to her on a gilt-edged, solid-silver platter was well beyond her expectations. Helen Walford had never been so lucky.

Reconciling herself to her sudden change in fates was an uphill battle, her difficulties compounded by his persistent presence and the distraction of his grey eyes. As her carriage wheels rattled over the cobbles, taking her home to her lonely bed, Helen sat back with a sigh and sent a silent prayer winging heavenwards. Please God that this time would be truly different, that this time the fates could find it in them to be kind. That this time her dreams would not turn to dross, that happiness like Dorothea's would at long last be hers.

With a little shiver, Helen closed her eyes. And willed it to be so.

Damian Willesden returned to the capital the next day. Forced by the exigencies of financial commitments to endure a repairing lease with a friend in the country until quarter-day had brought relief, he sauntered into Manton's Shooting Gallery determined to find congenial company with which to make up for lost time. Instead, he found his brother.

The broad shoulders encased in a perfectly cut coat of the best superfine were quite unmistakable. Martin was shooting with a party of his friends.

Beyond informing him that Martin had indeed returned, hale and whole, and was busying himself taking up his inheritance, his mother had been unusually reticent on the subject of the new Earl. Damian had interpreted this as another display of her well-known indifference to Martin and all his exploits. Even more than she, he had lived in the confident expectation that his reckless older brother would have managed to get himself killed, leaving the title to him. Martin's continued existence had been a rude shock. To him and his creditors.

A further surprise had awaited him when he had applied to Martin for assistance. That interview, conducted within days of Martin's return, had left him convinced that he would see little of the Merton revenues while Martin lived. His memories of Martin had been hazy at best; ten years separated them—they had never been close. But he had vaguely supposed that his brother, having spent so many years in the backwaters of the colonies, would be easily enough persuaded to part with his blunt. Instead, the interview had proved *most* uncomfortable. Pulling the wool over his brother's sharp grey eyes was not something he would try again soon.

He comforted himself with the reflection that a man of Martin's known propensities could be counted on to die young. It could only be a matter of time.

Watching the steadiness of the hand that levelled one of Joseph Manton's famous pistols at the slimmest of wafers propped as target twenty paces down the gallery, Damian reflected that such skills were presumably required in order to support the rakehell status his brother enjoyed. The pistol discharged; the smoke cleared. A small charred hole had appeared in the very centre of the wafer. As Manton himself came forward with congratulations, Damian decided that any hope that an indignant husband might put a term to his brother's life was nothing more than wishful thinking.

Turning from Desborough and Fanshawe to lay aside his pistol, Martin saw Damian lounging just inside the door. He nodded and watched his brother reluctantly approach. He could not prevent his lips curving in a knowing smile as the fact that it was two days after quarter-day dawned. Damian saw the smile; his expression turned sulky. Martin felt his own expression harden. Studied critically, there was nothing in Damian's dress to disgust one—his coat was well-cut, although not of the finest quality; the same could be said of his breeches and boots. It was his demeanour that raised brows. At twenty-four, he should have attained the age of reason, together with a little maturity. But his petulant attitude coupled with his expectation that his family must necessarily support his wastrel ways convinced Martin that his brother still had considerable maturing to do.

He raised his brows as Damian halted before him. 'Returned to the delights of town?'

Damian shrugged. 'The country's too slow for my taste.' He considered asking for an advance on his allowance but rejected the idea. He was not that desperate yet. He nodded at the target. 'Pretty shooting. Learned in the colonies, did you?'

Martin laughed. 'No. That was a talent I'd polished long

before I departed these shores.' He paused, then suggested, 'Why not try your luck?'

For an instant, Damian wavered, drawn to the prospect of joining his magnificent brother in such a fashionable pursuit and in such august company. Then his eye fell on the gold signet on Martin's right hand and childish resentment clouded his reason. 'Heaven forbid,' he said, waving away the pistol Martin held out. 'Not my style. *I* ain't in any danger from irate husbands.'

A little stunned by his own gaucherie, and less than sure what reaction it might provoke, Damian abruptly turned on his heel and walked rapidly from the Gallery.

Tony Fanshawe, standing on Martin's other side, an unintentional auditor to the scene, threw Damian a curious glance. 'That pup wants training,' he said. 'Deuced bad manners, walking away from an invitation like that.'

Martin, his eyes on his brother's retreating back, nodded absent-mindedly. 'I'm afraid,' he said, 'that my brother's manners leave a lot to be desired. In fact, my brother himself falls rather short of the mark.' Making a mental note to the effect that some time he was going to have to do something about Damian, Martin turned back to his friends and their game of skills.

He loved her.

That refrain replayed in Helen's head as she revolved about Lady Broxford's ballroom firmly held in Martin Willesden's arms. There was no doubt in her mind of its truth; her heart soared as she finally allowed the prospect of spending the rest of her life under Martin's smoky grey gaze to take definite shape in her mind. The pot of gold at the end of the rainbow was to be hers at last.

She looked up to find the warm grey eyes upon her, a caress in their depths.

'A penny for your thoughts, my lady.'

The deep, slightly raspy voice sent a cascade of sensations tingling through her. Suppressing a shiver of pure delight, Helen narrowed her eyes in consideration. 'I don't know that telling you my thoughts would be at all wise, my lord. Certainly, all precepts dictate I should stay silent.'

'Oh? They can't be that scandalous.'

'*They're* not scandalous. You are,' Helen retorted. 'I'm sure it's written somewhere—in the *Handbook for Young Ladies* under the heading of "How to Deal with Rakes"—that it's *most* unwise to do anything to encourage them.'

The grey eyes opened wide. 'And knowing your thoughts would encourage me?'

Helen tried to return his intent look with one of the greatest blandness. Her partner was undeterred.

'My dear Helen, I suspect your education was somewhat circumscribed. You certainly never finished that chapter, or you would have read that it's even *more* unwise to whet a rake's appetite.'

At the unrestrained promise in the gravelly voice, Helen's eyes grew wide. To her relief, they had come to the end of the room and Martin had to give his attention to turning them around. His arm tightened about her, leaving her even more breathless than before. She felt like a lamb about to be devoured by a wolf. For some reason, the idea was quite attractive. Her wits had obviously scattered. With an effort, she sought to collect them.

Martin glanced down at Helen's face. The eau-de-Nil silk sheath she wore moulded to her ample curves, sliding and sussurating against his coat with every gliding step they took. With the shifting silk to distract her further he doubted her ability to reorientate her thoughts from the salacious direction he had given them. Thoroughly satisfied with her state, he forbore to press her to converse, giving his mind instead to the vexed question of when? When should he ask her to marry him?

He had planned to propose as soon as he was sure she had accepted the idea of being the Countess of Merton and had got over her apparent nervousness regarding a second marriage. His experienced assessment was that any doubts she had harboured were now things of the past. As the last bars of the waltz sounded, he made his decision. There was no reason to wait.

But the ballroom was crowded, the event a 'sad crush'. The ante-rooms, he knew, would be full of dowagers trying to escape the heat. He would have to reconnoitre.

The music ceased; they whirled to a halt amid the glittering throng. Breathless, wondering what came next, Helen raised her eyes to Martin's face. Their eyes met, their gazes locked, but before either had time to speak Lord Peterborough materialised from the crowd.

'There you are, Helen. I must speak to you about this bad habit of yours—letting this reprobate monopolise your time. Won't do, m'dear—not at all.'

'Gerry, how long has it been since someone told you you talk too much?' Martin released Helen to allow her to greet their old friend.

Peterborough slanted a shrewd look at Helen's radiant countenance. 'Don't seem to be having much effect in this case.' To Helen, he said, 'Aside from all the other dangers, I dare swear he's trodden all over your toes—been in the colonies for too long. Come and waltz with a man who knows how.'

With a flourish, he presented his arm to Helen. Laughing, she took it, throwing one last smile at Martin before consenting to be led back to the floor.

Free, Martin embarked on a perambulation designed to explore all potential sites for a declaration among the rooms made available to Lady Broxford's guests.

Helen was glad of the opportunity dancing with her usual court gave her to reassemble her treacherous wits and still the fluttering of her heart. She had lived in anticipation of Martin's declaration for the past week; a sense of acute expectation now had her in its grip. She laughed and smiled, teetering on the brink of the greatest happiness she had yet known.

After Peterborough, she danced with Alvanley, then Desborough and even trod a measure with Hazelmere, spared to her by a radiant Dorothea.

After the first few figures of the cotillion, Hazelmere raised a languid brow. 'I take it the pleasures of this Little Season met with your approval?'

Sensing a deeper meaning hidden beneath the urbane drawl, Helen threw him a suspicious glance but answered airily, 'Why, yes. It's all been most enjoyable.' Nothing could keep the sheer happiness from her voice.

Both black brows rose; the hazel eyes watching her were as sharp as ever. 'I wonder why,' Hazelmere mused. To Helen's heartfelt relief, her long-time protector forbore to tease her, although his hazel eyes suggested that her joy was transparently obvious.

As he raised her from her final curtsy, Hazelmere said, 'I fear I should draw Miss Berry to your notice. She's been trying to attract your attention for some time.'

Following his gaze to where small, bird-like Miss Berry perched on a sofa at the side of the room, Helen chuckled. 'Poor dear. I dare say she feels she's missing out on things, now she's so deaf.'

Hazelmere's lips quirked but he refrained from further comment. He escorted Helen across the room, leaving her ensconced on the sofa, lending a sympathetic ear to Miss Berry.

From the opposite side of the ballroom, partially screened by a potted palm, Damian Willesden eyed the voluptuous figure in eau-de-Nil silk. He frowned, chewing his lip in vexation. He had come to the Broxfords' without an invitation, knowing no hostess would turn him from her door. But doing the pretty by a lot of curst females was hardly his style. He had only come because of what his friend Percy Witherspoon had let fall, of the bets regarding his brother's impending marriage.

He had refused to believe Percy but the entries in Boodle's wagers book had been too numerous to ignore. He stared across the room at Lady Walford; disaster stared back at him. Supremely confident that he would eventually inherit the Merton estates together with the sizeable fortune his mother insisted on tying to the title, sublimely sure that Martin would never trade his free-wheeling rake's existence for one of dull matrimony, he had borrowed until he was ear-deep in debt.

Damian swallowed convulsively. It was a wonder the cent per-centers were not hounding him already.

No—not yet. They would wait until he was no longer Mar-tin's heir before they moved. Even then, they would start slowly, expecting him to be able to persuade his brother to fish him out of the River Tick. But when they found out Mar-tin had no intention of rescuing him... Never one to dwell on uncomfortable fact, Damian let that thought fade.

He hugged the shadow of the palm and cogitated on his fate—and how to escape it. Ever fertile in subterfuge, his brain fastened on the essential element of his discomfort. It was all quite simple, really. He would just have to see what he could do to prevent this ill-advised marriage.

Having evaded all Miss Berry's leading questions, Helen finally rose, leaving the old lady with a fond smile. She looked about the room, but could not spot Martin's dark head amid the throng. Knowing he would seek her with the Hazelmeres and Fanshawes, in whose company she had come to the ball, she headed in the direction of the chaise on which she had last seen Dorothea.

She had moved but mere feet into the crowd when a hand on her arm halted her.

'Lady Walford?'

Helen turned to see a youth—no, a man, she revised, ac-knowledging the unformed features that had led her astray. Pale blue eyes returned her regard. There was something vaguely familiar about the gentleman, something about the set and shape of his head, but she was sure she had never met him before. 'Sir?'

Damian summoned a smile. 'I'm Damian Willesden—Mar-tin's brother.'

'Oh.' Helen returned his smile readily. 'How do you do?' Did Martin know his brother was here?

Damian bowed over her hand. 'I haven't seen Martin yet. Is he here?' He knew it was imperative that no hint of the distance between Martin and himself should show.

'I saw him earlier in the evening.' Helen raised her head to glance around. 'I'm sure he's still about, somewhere, but it's so hard to find anyone in this crush.'

Damian fastened on the comment eagerly. 'Perhaps we could move to that alcove there.' He pointed to where a curved niche in the wall held a statuette. 'I'm most curious as to how Martin's been faring, getting back into the swim of things.'

Helen took his proffered arm, wondering why he was not addressing such queries to his brother direct.

'I've just returned from the country and haven't had a chance to speak to Martin yet. But,' said Damian, striving to infuse his light voice with meaning, 'I have heard certain rumours, linking my brother's name with that...of a certain lady.'

Helen blushed. 'Mr Willesden, I would suggest that rumour is an insubstantial entity and that you might be wise to wait for confirmation before you jump to conclusions.'

Damian looked grave, 'I can appreciate your feelings, Lady Walford, and if the case were straightforward I would share your reservations. However...' he paused, frowning '...I feel a certain degree of...affection for Martin and would be sorry to see him in difficulties once more.'

'Difficulties?' Helen was entirely at sea. What difficulties was Martin's brother alluding to—and why to her? 'Sir, I'm afraid you will have to be a great deal more direct if I'm to understand you.'

Bowing his head to hide an irrepressible smirk, Damian obliged. But when he spoke again, his voice and features were serious, as befitted his assumed role. 'As you doubtless know, Martin returned from the colonies to take up his inheritance. Naturally, what wealth he now has derives entirely from the Merton estates. And, due to past bad management, the Merton estates are kept afloat by my mother's funds.' Pausing to let the implications sink in, Damian gave thanks for his eldest brother's failings. Thanks to George's incompetence, he had the perfect threat to remove Lady Walford from Martin's scene. What woman would marry a man forced to hang on his mother's sleeve? A hostile mother, at that. And, once Lady Walford drew back from the well-publicised relationship, other ladies similarly disposed would, with any luck, have second thoughts. 'Unfortunately,' he continued, 'Martin and the Dowager have never been on good terms. My mother naturally demands that Martin marry as she dictates. Or else...'

Cold fingers had laid hold of Helen's heart, squeezing until it hurt, leaving nothing but numbness behind. But she had to hear all of it, understand the whole story. 'Or else what?'

Damian saw the stricken look in the large green eyes and was momentarily taken aback. Then his own future prospects arose in his mind, stiffening his resolve. 'Or else she'll withdraw her funds. The estate will collapse. Martin will be destitute, unable to support the lifestyle he's accustomed to, the lifestyle expected of the Earl of Merton.'

And he will lose all chance of restoring his home. Helen recalled all too vividly Martin's face, lit by enthusiasm as he had described the Hermitage and told her how it would be once he had finished refurbishing it. As it had been in the days of his father, he had said. In the past weeks, she had heard even more of his dreams and had come to realise how important they were to him. A bridge, a living link to the father he had lost. The destruction of those dreams was a blow he would feel most cruelly—if he married against his mother's wishes.

If he married her.

None knew better than she that few mothers would approve of an eligible son marrying the widow of a social outcast—a reprobate who had gone well beyond the invisible line and had subsequently taken his own life. She was, she knew, unsuitable.

It had never occurred to her to question Martin's right to choose his own wife. He had seemed so much in control, she had never thought of him as being in any way under another's sway. But his brother's tale rang chillingly true.

Dull emptiness and the cold taste of despair swamped her senses.

Chilled to the bone, deaf to the babel about them, she held out her hand to Martin's brother. 'Thank you for telling me.' Her voice didn't sound like her own—it was cold and distant, as if she were speaking from a long way away. She put up her chin. 'You may be sure I'll do nothing to encourage Martin to harm his future.'

Her voice threatened to break. She could say nothing more. Withdrawing her hand from Damian's, she turned and walked into the crowd, all but unaware of her direction, oblivious of the odd looks cast her way.

By the time she found Dorothea, on a chaise by the door, Helen had regained some semblance of composure. If she appeared before Hazelmere, or his equally intelligent wife, with her soul in her eyes, she would never escape explanations. Yet the very thought of Martin and her hopes of happiness, now all gone awry, was enough to bring her to the brink of tears. Resolutely, she shut her mind against the pain and forced herself to act normally.

'Is anything wrong?' was Dorothea's opening gambit.

Helen smiled weakly. 'Just a slight headache—no doubt due to all this noise.' She sank on to the chaise beside her friend.

'Well,' said Dorothea, correctly interpreting Helen's wish to have nothing made of her indisposition, 'I've determined to leave soon, so I can take you up with me.'

After a fractional hesitation, Helen nodded dully. 'Yes, that would be best, I expect.' Martin would expect to see her again that evening, but if she escaped with Dorothea, pleading a headache, then he would not worry. He would call at her home tomorrow, and then she would have to explain. But by then she would have had time to get herself in hand, enough, at least, to face him. For, despite the cold fogs shrouding her mind, there was one point that was crystal-clear. She could not, would not, marry Martin Willesden. She could not face the prospect of being the death of his dream. His interest in her was real—that she knew without reservation. His interest in other women of the *ton* was non-existent. If she was out of contention, he would no doubt allow his mother to find him a bride and so would achieve his ambition—an ambition entirely appropriate to his station.

Glumly, Helen stifled a sniff and struggled to force a smile to her lips. She would sit quietly by Dorothea's side until it was time to leave.

Unfortunately for her well-intentioned plans, Martin appeared by her side but minutes later. Helen's heart leapt in her breast at sight of him; she could not keep the welcoming smile from her face. But he instantly noted its tremulous quality. Drawing her to stand close beside him, he bent his dark head close to ask, 'What's the matter?'

With a calm she was far from feeling, Helen reiterated her story of a headache.

Martin frowned at the press of bodies about them. 'Hardly to be wondered at. Come for a stroll—some fresh air will help clear your head.'

Before she had time to protest—not, she suspected, that he would have listened—Helen found herself strolling by Martin's side along a suspiciously deserted corridor. Her heart started to beat rather faster.

Her suspicions were confirmed when they reached the door at the end of the corridor and Martin opened it to reveal a small walled garden, deserted and entirely private.

He led Helen to a stone seat worked into the rockery and waited while she settled her skirts on the thyme-cushion growing over it before sitting beside her. On his knees was the prescribed pose, but, given he was thirty-five and she a widow of twenty-six, he felt he did not need to do such violence to his feelings, or to his satin knee-breeches.

She turned to stare up at him. The moonlight gilded her features, features he had come to know very well over the past week. Her green eyes widened, her lips were slightly parted. Because it seemed the right thing to do, and because he had long ago ceased to stop himself doing whatever he wished to do, Martin drew her smoothly into his arms and kissed her.

Helen tried, really tried to hold firm against that kiss, against the invitation to melt into his arms. She had been gathering her strength to speak—to avert any possible declaration, when his dark head had bent and his lips had slanted over hers. But it was impossible to hold back the tide of longing that swept her. Yielding to the inevitable, she softened against him and felt his arms tighten about her.

It was scandalously wrong to sit in a deserted garden and

allow a gentleman she was not going to marry to kiss her. Particularly to kiss her like this.

The touch of his lips on hers was sheer bliss. She let her hands settle against his shoulders and leaned into his warm embrace.

Later. She would have to speak later. But for now she might as well enjoy the delicious sensations he stirred within her. He was unlikely to stop soon and at least while he was thus engaged he could not propose to her. Perhaps he did not intend to propose just yet—was merely indulging in a little dalliance further to enthral her? As the pressure of his lips increased, Helen gave up any attempt at thought.

When he finally raised his head, Martin looked down on glittering green eyes, wide and slightly stunned. She was quite speechless and, if experience was any guide, was probably having difficulty stringing two thoughts together. He smiled. It hardly mattered. She would not need to think to answer his question.

'Will you marry me, my dear?'

Helen's mind fell into place with a thud. She felt her eyes widen even further. She struggled to assemble the right words but none would leap to her tongue. When she saw the grey eyes sharpen and become intent, she swallowed. 'No.'

It was such a small sound, Martin thought he had misheard. But the expression in her eyes, the wordless pain, convinced him he had not been mistaken. Somehow, he had muffed it. When she drew her hands from his shoulders, he smiled and tried to make light of her problem, hoping to learn what it was. 'My dear Helen, I'll have you know it's not done to kiss a man and then refuse his suit.'

To his increasing unease, she hung her head. 'I know.'

Helen found she was wringing her hands, something she had never done in her life. 'Truly, my lord, I'm more than honoured by your proposal. But I…' Heavens—what was she to say? 'But I've not thought of remarrying.'

'Well, try thinking about it.' Martin strove to keep the edge from his tone. This was not how this interview was supposed to have gone. In fact, the more he thought of it, the whole business was deucedly odd. What had happened?

'My lord, I must make you understand—'

'No—it's I who must needs make you understand. I love you, Helen. And you love me. What more is there to it than that?'

Helen swallowed and forced her eyes to his. The moon shone from behind him, leaving his features in shadow and her with no real idea of his expression. She imagined it was forbidding. Suppressing a shiver, she tried to speak calmly. 'My lord, you know as well as I that there's a great deal more to it than that.'

Martin stiffened slightly, then remembered that he was atrociously rich. She must be referring to his past, but he had told her about that. Didn't she believe him? 'I'm very much afraid, my dear, that you'll have to be rather more specific if I'm to follow your thread.'

Helen's courage was fast deserting her. How to tell a man—an arrogant, proud man—that you knew he was his mother's pensioner? She shifted back on the seat and felt Martin's arms fall from about her. Instead of bringing her relief, the withdrawal of his protection left her feeling more lost than ever. She pressed her hands together and in a very small voice said, 'I was thinking of what your mother would say.'

His reaction was every bit as violent as she had anticipated.

'*My mother*?' Martin was dumbfounded. 'What the devil do you imagine my mother has to do with this?' He had almost forgotten his mother's plans. Had news of her machinations reached town? 'I'll marry who I damn well please! My mother doesn't have any say in the matter.' The idea that Helen thought him the sort of man who would allow anyone to interfere in such a matter made his tone even more steely.

Helen had winced at his questions; by the time he had finished his vehement denial she was more than flustered. Her nerves were jittery; she could not think straight. Her head throbbed in earnest. Of course he would deny it. What more could she say? How could she smooth things over and make him understand?

Martin saw her agitation. Immediately, he sought to cut through the morass they had somehow landed in and bring her to peace again. 'Helen, my dear, I love you. Even if my whole estate were in the balance, I'd still want to marry you.'

He spoke simply, from the heart. He was not prepared for her reaction. Wide eyes turned his way; her breath seemed to catch in her throat. Then her full lips trembled and the moonlight glistened on the tears hanging suspended from the tips of her long lashes.

'Oh, *Martin*!'

The whispered words caught on a sob.

Abruptly, Helen looked down, at her fingers tightly twined in her lap. She had never loved anyone as much as she loved him; she could not let him make such a sacrifice.

Becoming more worried with every passing second, every totally confusing minute, Martin frowned at Helen's bent head. He reached for her hand.

The door from the house opened.

'This way, m'dear.'

Helen would have leapt to her feet, but Martin's hand on hers restrained her. He moved slightly, so that his bulk shielded her from the intruders. As two guests emerged into the small walled court, Martin rose languidly then turned and helped Helen to rise.

'Oh!' said Hedley Swayne. 'My goodness! I'm afraid we didn't realise this area was occupied.'

One of Martin's brows rose. His gaze went from the frippery sight of Mr Swayne to the slight young thing wavering on his arm. 'No matter, I was just about to escort Lady Walford inside.'

He turned to offer his arm to Helen. She took it, trying to appear as unaffected as possible, with her nerves in knots and her heart in her shoes.

'Oh, Lady Walford,' the slight young thing warbled nervously. 'Would you mind if I came inside with you?' Without waiting for assent, the girl turned to Hedley Swayne. 'I really don't think I wish to view the gardens just at the moment, Mr Swayne.'

She bobbed a curtsy and hurried to Helen's side.

Swallowing his frustration, Martin was forced to escort Helen and her unexpected protégée back to the ballroom. Once under the light of the chandeliers, he saw how badly affected Helen was. Feeling very much as if his world had stopped turning, he resigned himself to letting the matter lapse until a more suitable opportunity to speak privately with her could be arranged. He left her with Dorothea, lifting her hand to his lips with a murmured, 'I'll call on you tomorrow,' before taking his leave.

Dorothea took one look at Helen's face, then, without comment, called for her carriage.

Dawn was streaking the skies before sleep finally closed Helen's eyes. The pillow beneath her cheek was damp, her lids decidedly puffy. But she had managed to make the decisions that had to be made. There was no hope of explaining things to Martin—he would not accept her refusal any more than she would accept his suit. So she would have to avoid him—make it plain by her behaviour that their association was at an end. It would cause talk, but nothing serious. The *ton* would wonder what she was thinking of, but there were too many waiting in the wings to claim his attention for the gossipmongers to dwell on her peculiar whims for long.

She would have to give him up, even though it would be easier to cut out her heart. Instead, she would have to live with it, a leaden weight in her breast, evermore. He would be hurt by her withdrawal and even more hurt by her lack of explanation. But if she tried to explain, he would refuse to accept her decision. She could not see him readily acquiescing; who knew to what lengths he might go to attain his goals? No—there was only one way forward.

As she snuggled her cheek deeper into the down, she sighed. She should have known how it would end—happiness of that kind was not for her—would never be hers.

The pot of gold at the end of the rainbow had always been beyond her reach.

CHAPTER EIGHT

'What will you have?'

Martin waved his hand in the direction of the well-stocked drinks tray reposing on the sideboard in his library.

'If memory serves,' said Hazelmere, sinking into the comfort of an armchair, 'your father was a particularly fine judge of Madeira.'

A grin twisted Martin's lips. 'Quite right. And George had no taste for the stuff. Apparently, there's three full racks in the cellar.'

He poured two glasses and carried one to his guest before settling in the armchair on the other side of the empty fireplace. A companionable silence fell. Hazelmere, well aware that Martin had asked him to his home for some purpose, was content to wait for his friend to open his budget. Martin, equally well aware of his friend's understanding, was in no hurry to do so.

The matter was a delicate one. He had called on Helen the morning after the débâcle of his first declaration, two nights ago. Hours of intense concentration had yielded no clue as to what it was that had made her balk at his proposal. Nevertheless, he had gone to her small house in Half Moon Street, confident of ironing out whatever wrinkles had insinuated themselves into the fabric of their relationship. That was when he had realised how serious her problem, now their problem, was.

She had refused to see him, sending her maid down with a story of indisposition. For the first time in his life, he had been totally nonplussed. Why?

There had to be a reason—she was not a dim-witted miss,

a flibbertigibbet. It had been his avowal of love that had thrown her, though why that should be so he could not imagine. Eventually, he had come to the conclusion that there had to be some hidden bogey in her past that his words, or the meaning behind them, had conjured up.

And the one person who knew enough of Helen's past to be of use was seated in the armchair opposite, a deceptively lazy look in his hazel eyes.

Martin grimaced. 'It's about Helen Walford.'

'Oh?' A look of reserve veiled Hazelmere's sharp gaze.

'Yes,' said Martin, ignoring it. 'I want to marry her.'

His friend's features relaxed in warm approval. 'Congratulations.' Hazelmere raised his glass in the gesture of a toast.

'Premature, I'm afraid. She won't have me.' Martin bit the words out, then sought solace in a hefty draught of finest quality Madeira.

A puzzled frown settled over Hazelmere's black brows. 'Why, for heaven's sake?'

'That's what I want you to tell me.' Martin settled back in his chair and looked pointedly at Hazelmere.

Hazelmere frowned back, an exasperated look in his eyes. 'She likes you. I know she does.'

'So do I—it's not that.'

Uncharacteristically at sea, Hazelmere threw Martin a thoroughly bemused look. 'What then?'

Martin sighed. 'When I told her how much I loved her...' He threw a warning glance at Hazelmere before continuing, 'She nearly broke down and wept.'

Hazelmere showed no sigh of treating the subject lightly. If anything, his frown deepened. Eventually, he said. 'That...is bad. Helen hardly ever cries. I've known her since she was three and she's far more likely to argue than weep.'

'Quite.' Martin paused, then added diffidently, 'I had wondered whether there was anything about her previous marriage that would account for it.'

Hazelmere's brows rose. Sitting back, he considered the point, absent-mindedly twirling the stem of his glass between his long fingers. Then, abruptly, as if having reached a decision, he looked at Martin. 'As you seem set on marrying her, and, even if *she* doesn't know it yet, *I* know that means she'll be the next Countess of Merton, I'll tell you what I know.' At sight of Martin's quick grin, he added, 'But I warn you, it's not much.'

His features impassive, the expression in his eyes much less so, Martin waited with what patience he could muster while Hazelmere fortified himself with a pensive sip of honey-gold liquor.

'I expect I'd better start at the beginning.' Hazelmere settled his shoulders against the back of the chair. 'Helen's parents presented her at sixteen—a mistake, for my money. She'd been a tomboy, a hoyden, for years and had yet to grow out of her adventures. But her parents had her life all arranged— a marriage to the son of an old friend, Lord Alfred Walford. The son, Arthur Walford, I think you knew?'

At Hazelmere's questioning glance, Martin nodded curtly. 'We met once or twice before I left for the West Indies. Hardly the sort of man careful parents would have in mind for a beautiful and wealthy sixteen-year-old.'

A fleeting smile lit Hazelmere's face. 'Ah—but you didn't know Helen then. I know it's hard to believe, seeing her now, but, take it from me, at sixteen she was a Long Meg—and a dreadfully scrawny one at that.' When Martin looked sceptical, Hazelmere waved the point aside. 'Not that it mattered. It wouldn't have made an ounce of difference if she'd been Cleopatra incarnate. The parents, both hers and old Walford, had settled on the alliance long before. It was intended as a dynastic marriage of the most calculated sort. Helen's parents were both ambitious in an odd sort of way. They never mixed much and lived in seclusion in the country, but they were determined to marry their daughter into one of the oldest families about.' Hazelmere paused, his gaze far away, remembering. 'There were many who tried to dissuade them, my parents among them, but they were fixated on the idea. Walford the elder was keen, because of Helen's dowry. Arthur Walford was amenable for much the same reason. So Helen was married to Walford a bare month after her come-out.'

'A *month*?' Incredulity sharpened Martin's tone.

'Precisely,' affirmed Hazelmere, equally sharp. 'The newly-weds repaired to Walford Hall. Less than a month after that, Walford reappeared in town. Helen stayed in Oxfordshire. That situation continued, apparently without change, for close on three years. During that time, all the senior players in the drama died—Walford the elder, and both Helen's parents. The crunch came when, against all odds, Walford succeeded in running through his funds. He had lost his own estates and those that had come to him through Helen. Only Walford Hall remained, as it was entailed. He returned there, not to take up residence but to see what more he could wring from the place. By then, Helen was nineteen. She had still not attained the stature she now has, but she had improved considerably on sixteen.'

Hazelmere paused, studying the glass in his hand. 'I don't know to this day what actually happened, but the upshot of it was that Walford struck Helen—during an argument, she said. For her part, she promptly broke a pot over his head and left.' Hazelmere drained his glass before glancing at Martin. 'She came to me. She had grown up with my sister Allison and we had always considered her one of the family. I sent her to my estate in Cumbria—well out of Walford's way should he try to find her. The story of his treatment of Helen got out—as such things do. It became something of a *cause célèbre*. The upshot was that Walford was hounded from the *ton* and comprehensively ruined. He took his own life rather than face Newgate.'

Hazelmere paused, considering the past, then shrugged. 'Later, many of those who had won stakes from Walford donated money to set up a fund for Helen. I manage it for her. It pays the rent on her house in Half Moon Street and keeps her in her current style—but little else. None of her estates was salvaged.'

Martin frowned, his chin sunk in one hand, his gaze fixed on the Turkey rug gracing the floor between them. Carefully, choosing his words, he asked, 'Is there anything in what you know of her that would lead you to suppose Helen feels any deep-seated revulsion towards marriage? An aversion to the physical side of matrimony?'

Hazelmere's lips thinned. His eyes on his glass, he shook his head. 'I couldn't say—but, conversely, I would not be at all surprised.' He lifted his gaze to Martin's face. 'You know what Walford was like.'

Slowly, Martin nodded. 'Could it have scarred her—so that she has difficulty bringing herself to contemplate marriage again?'

Hazelmere shrugged. 'Only Helen could answer that, but I would have thought it a distinct possibility.'

Almost imperceptibly, Martin's expression lightened. His eyes narrowed in consideration.

Hazelmere noticed. 'What is it?'

A crooked grin was Martin's answer. 'I was just thinking— who better to cure such a malady than I?' He shot Hazelmere a quizzical glance, then sat back, supremely confident, one brow rising arrogantly. 'All things considered, I would have to be the perfect candidate for the job of convincing Helen Walford of the earthy benefits of matrimony. If, with my extensive experience, I can't overcome that particular hurdle, I don't deserve the lady.'

For a long moment, Hazelmere's hazel eyes remained serious, while their owner pondered what was, after all, a distinctly scandalous threat to a lady whom many, including himself, regarded as under his protection. But, if he read things aright, Helen's future happiness was at stake. She had made her partiality plain. And he trusted Martin Willesden as a brother—Helen would come to no harm at his hands. Slowly, a grin twisted Hazelmere's lips. Inclining his head in tacit approval of Martin's avowed intention, he raised his glass in salute.

'Spoken like a true rake.'

Helen settled her skirts and waited for Martin to join her on the box seat of his curricle. The wind whipped loose tendrils of hair about her face and brought colour to her cheeks. As

Martin sat beside her and picked up the reins, she flashed a bright smile in answer to his. Then they were off.

With the raucous cries of the Piccadilly street vendors ringing about her, Helen sat, at peace and oddly content, and wondered that it could be so. It was remarkable, she reflected, that, given Martin's painful declaration just over a week before, they should be able to be together like this, companionably setting out for a drive in the Park. For her part, she would not have credited it. But, to her relief, Martin had behaved in the most honourable way.

He had claimed her for a waltz at the Havelocks' rout, the next major function they had both attended. Nothing in his manner had altered; he had behaved every bit as proprietorially as before. Only she had heard his whispered words, 'Trust me. Just relax—there's nothing to worry about.'

Strangely enough, she had. From beneath her chip bonnet, Helen glanced up at his profile, so harshly handsome. His eyes were fixed on the road ahead, his hands steady on the reins. A smile on her lips, Helen returned her gaze to their surroundings. Relaxing in Martin's company had been made a great deal easier by the fact that he no longer sought to befuddle her senses with his particular brand of wizardry. She was determined to keep her traitorous senses in line; his power over them was just as strong, but, if she was intent on her course, she could not afford to let them gain the upper hand. Thankfully, Martin seemed to understand. It was clear that, now she had brought the matter to his mind, he had, however reluctantly, accepted that, given his circumstances and hers, they could not marry. And, gentleman that he was, he was intent on keeping their situation from the world. All she was called on to do was respond to his lead, to make it appear as if there were no rupture between them. It was, she had realised, the sensible course. Now, as time passed, they would be able to draw apart without either being exposed to the avid interest of the scandalmongers.

The Park was reached without incident. They embarked on a slow circuit about the leafy avenues, stopping time and again to chat with their acquaintances. It was during one of these

halts that Ferdie Acheson-Smythe approached. His bland expression totally devoid of guile, he nodded to Martin then
reached up to shake hands with Helen.

'Hello, Ferdie. Is that a new coat?' Helen knew any question
of fashion was guaranteed to appeal to the immaculate Mr
Acheson-Smythe. She had known Ferdie, Hazelmere's cousin,
forever and was truly fond of the elegant dandy.

'Yes,' replied Ferdie, unwarrantably brief. 'But that wasn't
what I wanted to tell you.' His pale blue eyes flicked to Martin, engrossed with some friends on the other side of the curricle, then returned to her face, a slight frown in their depths.
Leaning closer, he said, 'I know you've made a damned habit
of this, but do you really think it's wise?'

With Ferdie, there was no point in pretending to misunder-
stand. Helen smiled affectionately at his brother-like concern.
She lowered her voice. 'You needn't worry. I'm perfectly
safe.'

'Humph!' Ferdie snorted, his gaze once more on Martin's
profile. 'That's what I thought about Dorothea and look how
wrong I was. Point is, rakes don't change. They're damned
dangerous in any circumstances.'

Helen laughed. 'I assure you this one's tame.'

The comment earned her a highly sceptical look, but Ferdie
said no more on the matter, turning his attention instead to
complimenting her on her new apricot merino pelisse. When
a short while later Martin looked around, ready to move on,
Ferdie bowed elegantly and stood back, contenting himself
with a warning look addressed to Helen's account.

Martin saw it. His brows rose superciliously, but by then
Ferdie Acheson-Smythe was already dwindling in the distance.
Then Martin's sharp ears caught the muffled giggle as his
companion tried to suppress her reaction. Martin relaxed. 'Tell
me, fair Juno, am I still considered "too dangerous", despite
my exemplary behaviour of recent times?'

Helen shot a startled glance up at him. Reassured by the
teasing glint in his grey eyes and the laughter bubbling through
his deep tones, she smiled and gave due attention to his question. Considering the matter dispassionately was a decidedly

tall order. Eventually, knowing he was waiting on her answer, she ventured, 'I fear, my lord, that there are some who see your "exemplary behaviour" as merely the wool beneath which a wolf is disguised.'

Martin's heavy sigh startled her anew.

'And here I was thinking none could discern the truth.'

Helen's eyes flew wide. His tone held equal parts of dejection and chagrin but the expression in his eyes was still gently teasing. She tried to read his meaning in their depths, but the subtle glint defeated her. Was he warning her that Ferdie was right. Or was he merely making light conversation, teasing her, knowing she was easy to twit on that score?

Uncertain, Helen spent the next ten minutes inwardly wrestling with the possibilities while outwardly playing the social game. They had finished their first circuit when Martin broke into her thoughts.

'I still haven't made the final decisions on the pieces for the parlour.'

'Oh?' Helen had heard about the redecoration of his London home, now in its terminal phase, in some detail. Discussions on the relative merits of damasks and chintzes and the impracticality of the current craze for white and gold décor had filled many of their hours together.

Martin was frowning thoughtfully. 'There's a piece of furniture on which I would greatly appreciate your opinion. It's at a house not far from here.' He glanced at Helen and raised an enquiring brow. 'Can you spare me a few moments of your time, my dear?'

Swallowing her instinctive response that such matters should be reserved for the consideration of his bride, Helen smiled her acquiescence. One subject she had no intention of mentioning was matrimony. 'I dare say I could manage a moment or two.'

Courteously inclining his head in acceptance of her boon, Martin headed his team for the gates, a slow smile of satisfaction curving his lips. They were wending their way through the traffic when Helen asked, 'What is this piece?'

'An occasional sofa.'

Seeing his attention was fixed on his horses, given to nervously jibbing in the crowded streets, Helen forbore to press him for details. Doubtless she would learn soon enough why there was any question about the suitability of this particular sofa.

To her surprise, Martin drew the horses to a halt in front of an imposing residence in Grosvenor Square. He turned to smile down at her. 'This is it.' Relinquishing the reins to Joshua who came running from his perch at the rear, Martin jumped to the pavement and turned to assist Helen. Once on his level, Helen eyed the elegant façade then realised the sofa in question must presently be in the possession of the owner of the mansion.

Surrendering to the subtle pressure of Martin's hand in the small of her back, Helen went up the steps before him. Martin paused before the door and glanced down, his eyes locking with hers, an unfathomable expression in the steely grey. Suddenly, Helen could not breathe. But before she could register more than a flush of unnerving excitement, Martin raised a gloved fist and beat a peremptory tattoo on the polished oak. The door was opened immediately by an imposing if portly butler, who bowed them into a spacious hall.

'M'lord.' The butler turned to her. 'My lady.' He reached for her coat. Uncertain, Helen raised an enquiring brow at Martin. When he nodded, she surrendered her pelisse and bonnet. Clearly, the Earl of Merton was well-known to this household.

'The room at the end of the hall.' At Martin's nod, Helen walked forward over the black and white tiles, towards the door that stood open at the far end of the hall. Martin started in her wake, then hesitated and turned back, handing his gloves to the butler. Hearing his footsteps falter, Helen glanced back. Martin smiled his encouragement. Reassured, Helen continued.

As she drew closer to the open door, she noticed a peculiar light glowing from within the room. Almost as if the curtains were drawn and the fire ablaze. Puzzled, Helen gained the threshold and looked in.

'We don't wish to be disturbed, Hillthorpe.'

Helen's gasp stuck in her throat. It did not need the butler's deferential 'Yes m'lord' to confirm her wild conjecture. The proof that, in the case of Martin Willesden, rake of the highest standing, she had been wrong and Ferdie perfectly right lay before her startled gaze. The heavy velvet curtains were indeed drawn, the fire fully stoked and crackling voraciously. A bottle of wine, uncorked, reposed in a silver bucket of ice on the sideboard. Automatically, irrelevantly, Helen searched the room for the sofa she had come to see—the occasional sofa. At first, she could not find it. Then her eyes widened in shock as they focused on the large piece of furniture standing squarely before the hearth. The most massive daybed she had ever seen.

Flee! was her first thought—immediately followed by, *How*? Martin's footsteps rang on the tiles; he was but feet behind her. If she turned and tried to escape, he would simply pick her up and carry her through the door. Certainly, his butler would be no help.

Helen drew a deep breath. Danger lay across the threshold. She tried to step back into the relative safety of the hall, only to find that she had hesitated too long. Martin, directly behind her, slipped an arm about her waist and she was swept, effortlessly, into the room.

'Martin!' Breathless, Helen swung to face him, to see him shut the door and turn the key. She was only slightly relieved to see that he left the key in the lock. It was him she had to escape; after that, escaping the room would be child's play. Summoning her defences, she took refuge in indignation. Drawing herself to her full height, in this case unfortunately insufficient to allow her to intimidate the reprobate before her, she fixed him with an affronted glare and prayed her voice would not betray her. 'You tricked me!'

A slow grin twisted Martin's mobile lips. ''Fraid so.' His gaze, heated grey, rested, intent, on her face. Slowly, he moved towards her.

He did not look the least bit contrite.

Helen tried to ignore her skittering pulse and let her temper

grow. It was the only thing that might save her. She narrowed
her eyes, shutting out as much of the potent male presence
approaching slowly but, as far as she was concerned, far too
fast, as she could. Forced to tilt her chin up as he drew nearer,
she struggled to overcome her suddenly breathless state. 'Your
behaviour over the past week has all been a sham, hasn't it?'
To her horror, it was all she could do not to squeak. What was
he about?

Stopping directly in front of her, Martin allowed his grin to
develop into the deepest of smiles, a smile of disturbing magnitude and unnerving intent. 'You've unmasked me, fair Juno.'
Eyes glinting, Martin spread his hands in supplication. 'What
can I say in my defence?'

Transfixed by the warmth in his gaze, Helen struggled to
collect enough wit to tell him.

Smoothly, confidently, Martin reached for the comb that
held her curls in a knot on the top of her head. With a deft
flick, he drew it free, sending golden tresses cascading over
her shoulders, down her back.

Helen gasped, instinctively putting up her hands to stem the
tide. But Martin caught them gently in his and drew them
down. Glinting, his eyes roamed the tumbled gold. 'You've
no idea how often I've considered doing that.'

The idea that he might have done that in the middle of some
fashionable ballroom suspended the few faculties Helen had
managed to reassemble. His hands released hers, long fingers
rising to slip in among the silken strands. The fingers played,
sampling the texture, removing loose pins and dropping them
like rain on to the floor, then they firmed about her chin, tilting
her head up until her eyes locked with his.

Held mesmerised by the smouldering heat in the cloudy
grey gaze, Helen felt all thought slipping from her. Martin's
hands left her face; he reached for her and drew her into his
arms.

Belatedly, self-preservation jolted Helen back to reality. She
braced her hands against Martin's chest. 'My lord—Martin!'
she amended, accurately reading the comment in his eyes.
'This is unseemly. Scandalous—and worse! If you wish to

atone for your behaviour—your deceit—you can escort me back to your curricle this instant!'

She tried to sound firm but her tone was weak and wavering, her diaphragm refusing to lend strength to her words. The smile on the dark face hovering closer and closer to hers only deepened. His arms, already about her, tightened.

'I've a much better idea of how to atone for my sins.'

Martin kissed her. And kept kissing her until every vestige of resistance was overcome, overwhelmed, drowned beneath their passion.

Trapped in his embrace, Helen reluctantly admitted that it was *their* passion—not his alone. That was what made Martin so very hard to resist. His scandalous advances drew an equally scandalous response from her. Caught on a crest of burgeoning desire, so sweet in its novelty that she was unable to resist, Helen gave up the unequal fight, softening against him. She felt his arms tighten further, crushing her to him. Then they shifted; his hands moved over her back, moulding her yielding form to his hard frame.

Helen struggled against the insidious invitation of his kiss, a blatant temptation to lose her wits and drown in a sea of sensuous sensation, striving instead against the steadily mounting odds to retain some fragment of lucidity.

Martin raised his head to glance down at her, his eyes glowing. 'Relax,' he breathed. His lips brushed her forehead. 'Don't worry—we'll take it *very slowly*.'

As his lips returned to hers, Helen wondered if he intended the deep, gravelly words as a threat or a promise. For a full minute, she considered the implications as her will sank slowly beneath the warm web of sensation evoked by Martin's sure hands. With a mental jerk, she called her wits to order. What was she to do? The way he was progressing, slow or not, she would only have a few more minutes in which to decide.

It was patently obvious to the meanest intelligence that Martin had reverted to form and intended to compromise her beyond all possible doubt, in fact as well as reputation. Helen had not the slightest doubt that he thought thus to force her acquiescence to their marriage, to overcome her refusal to ac-

cept his suit. But she was determined to give him his dream—
nothing, not even he, could shake her resolution.

However, she admitted, feeling the gentle tug of long fingers
at the buttons of her gown, any thought of escape from such
a masterful seducer was fantasy. What he had in mind was
undeniably scandalous. To her, it was undeniably attractive. If
she followed her heart, her truest impulse, she would do as he
had said and relax.

Fate had dealt against her, but that did not mean she could
not enjoy him, take the moment he offered—this once. This
was all the chance she would ever have. Her one touch at
happiness—her one chance to touch the pot of gold at the end
of the rainbow. She had never been there before, had never
known the joy she surmised must exist, wrapped in the clouds
of love. Martin's fingers skimmed her shoulders, easing her
carriage dress from her. With a little sigh, Helen drew her arms
from the long sleeves, letting her dress fall to the floor along
with her reservations. Glancing shyly up from beneath her
lowered lashes, she lifted her arms and draped them about his
neck in tacit acceptance of what was to come. Anticipation
throbbing its dizzying pulse through her veins, she waited to
see how he would manage her light stays.

Aware, as only one of his extensive experience could be,
of the import of Helen's tentative movement, Martin drew a
deep breath and fought to shackle a desire so strong, it threatened to addle his wits—a thoroughly undesirable outcome.
Juno needed to be wooed slowly, gently, seduced like the ver-
iest virgin, skittish and shy. He applied himself to the task
with devotion.

Soon, Helen's mind was whirling, giddy with pleasure. Her
past had held no clues to the passion that now engulfed her.
Her introduction to wifely duties had been mundane in the
extreme; her mother had told her what to expect—she had got
that and nothing more. The entire procedure had been so ba-
sically boring, she had been only too glad when her husband
had returned to his mistresses post haste. But, in the long
lonely years since then, she had come to the conclusion that
there had to be more to it than that, a positive side to the

undertaking she had never experienced—for surely it was that that brought the glow to Dorothea's pale complexion and the stars to her eyes.

She had thought she would never learn what it was. But fate had decided to hand her one chance—a consolation prize in the lottery of life. Who better to teach her of the delights of love then the man in whose strong arms she was trapped?

For he was a trap, to her senses at least. She would do well to acknowledge that, and remember it when the time for explanations arrived. He was going to be angry. Very angry. He would ask her to marry him, confidently expecting her, overwhelmed by his loving, to agree. And when she refused, he was not going to be particularly interested in her reasons. Which was just as well, for she had no idea how to make him understand and was in two minds whether it was safe to do so.

But right now two minds were two minds too many for her wits to cope with. He had stolen them, along with her stays—and she had not even noticed how he had accomplished the deed. All she knew was that she felt more enthralled, more consumed with desire than ever before in her life. Martin filled her mind, overwhelmed her senses—and took control completely.

There was nothing she could do to stem the tide of urgent need welling within and between them, engulfing them both in its heated embrace. Martin stopped and lifted her, carrying her to the daybed and laying her amid the silken covers. He hovered over her, his lips dipping to hers, his hands skilfully weaving webs of delight over her fevered flesh. Then his lips touched her eyelids, placing a kiss on each.

'Keep your eyes shut.'

Helen sensed he was about to undress. She wanted to watch. 'But—'

'No buts,' came the gravelly voice, even deeper and raspier than usual. 'Do as I say. Just lie there and relax and everything will be wonderful.'

The gentle persuasion in his tone had its effect. Helen lay still, feeling the warmth from the fire flickering over her skin,

contrasting with the shimmering touch of the silks and satin
on which she lay. Her lips curved slightly at the thought of
his lordship's scandalous taste in furniture. The rustle of
starched linen came to her ears. The temptation to peek from
beneath her lashes grew.

Helen opened her eyes a fraction. A heavily muscled back
filled her view. She watched as Martin divested himself of his
clothes, staring for as long as she could until, as he joined her
on the daybed, she let her lids fall before allowing them to
flicker innocently upwards.

Martin smiled gently, encouragingly. His shoulders were an-
gled over her once more, limiting her view of him. He studied
her expression but could detect no hint of panic. Yet. 'Good
girl,' he murmured, struggling to harness the passion that vibrated in his voice. He lowered his lips to hers and was relieved when her lids fluttered closed once more. In truth, he
had little idea what might scare her but, if she had had a
difficult time accommodating Walford, seeing him naked was
not going to help.

He released her lips to give more attention to the rest of
her, all the while soothing her with comforting, reassuring
words. It was not his habit to waste time with talk in such
situations but this case was different, unique. He kept watch
for any signs of withdrawal or distress, ready to backtrack at
the first hint that he was pushing her too fast.

Helen heard his words, letting them wash over her, unable
to concentrate on the sentences buried beneath his sensuous
rumble. She wished he would stop talking and give all his
attention to fulfilling her needs. Her hands itched to explore,
but, never having been visited by such a desire before, she
was unsure of the etiquette involved. In the end, when, driven
by her need, she tentatively spread her hands over the muscles
of his back, Martin moved and caught them, trapping them in
one of his and drawing them over her head.

'Not yet, sweetheart. We don't want to rush things.'

If she had been capable, Helen would have glared. Why
not? she wanted to know. She felt as if she wanted to devour

him whole and all he would say was 'Not yet'. Her body felt overheated but all she wanted was more heat.

'Martin—'

'Hush.' He silenced her with a kiss. 'Trust me. You'll enjoy it. This time will be different, I promise.'

Inwardly, Helen frowned. Of course this time would be different—she loved him. She had never loved anyone before. Her inward frown grew. She wished she could shake her head to rid herself of the niggle that there was something here that she was missing, something she did not understand.

'There's nothing to be frightened about. We'll take it slow and easy. No pain at all—only pleasure. Trust me this once and I'll show you how wonderful it can be.'

The gentleness in his voice, overlaying the suppressed desire, gave Helen the vital clue. Her eyes flew wide but Martin, busy kissing her, missed the shocked response. Quickly, realising her error, Helen shut her eyes again, willing her body to remain in the languid, floating state he had induced.

He thought she was sexually crippled—or, at least, had a broken bone or two. An aversion to lovemaking of some major degree. If he had not been kissing her, Helen would have shaken her head in amazement. How had he come to such a crazy conclusion? Arthur had never hurt her—he had simply failed to engage her passions. Now that she knew what passion between a man and woman was, she knew the truth. She was not the least averse to making love with Martin Willesden— but why had he thought she was?

This, however, was no time for imponderables.

Her wits were barely up to recognising facts, let alone dealing with their ramifications. As Martin deepened their kiss, Helen felt her conscious mind melt. Thought, in any form, became all but impossible. Sensation washed through her; joyfully, with abandon, she surrendered to the warm tide.

To Martin's gratification, not the slightest ripple of panic, not the smallest quiver of maidenly nerves, marred the response of the beauty in his arms. Nevertheless, he kept a tight rein on his passions, enforcing ruthless discipline in the face of extreme provocation. It was hard work, seducing a goddess—slowly. Painstakingly, he stoked the fever between them, blowing the embers to flame and pouring desire upon them until the conflagration had her firmly in its grip. It started to singe his control. Still, he held back, ensuring her pleasure beyond all doubt. When he finally brought her to the peak, and held her there for that most fleeting of instants, he felt the most intense surge of satisfaction, before his mind was swamped by his own delight.

The chimes of the elegant French carriage clock sitting on Martin's marble mantelpiece penetrated the pleasured fogs shrouding Helen's mind. Four o'clock.

Four o'clock! With a start, she opened her eyes. An expanse of tanned male chest, liberally sprinkled with curling back hair, met her bemused gaze. Her questing senses detected a heavy, muscled arm lying, relaxed, about her.

Stifling a moan, Helen closed her eyes. What now? Languid pleasure still had her in its grip, drugging her mind and body. It would be easy just to lie here, enjoying the warm intimacy, and let fate take its course. Then he would wake, and ask her to marry him, and she would have to refuse him, while lying naked in his arms.

Helen grimaced. She opened her eyes and slowly raised them to Martin's face. He was still sleeping. With a small sigh of relief, she set about carefully extricating herself from his loose embrace, untangling her legs from the silk sheets he had drawn over them, Luckily, she was lying on the outer edge of the daybed.

Once free, she dressed quickly. While she wrestled with her stays, she allowed her gaze to roam lovingly over the large frame lying sprawled amid the rumpled sheets. She smiled a trifle mistily. At least she now understood just what it was that lay at the end of the rainbow, what it was that gave rise to the glow of anticipation in Dorothea's eyes whenever she looked at Hazelmere. Martin had transported her to the end of the rainbow, had given her a moment of sheer delight beyond any she had ever experienced. She would hold the memory of that moment, enshrine it in her heart, to light the lonely years ahead.

Stifling a sigh, she stepped into her dress and eased it up over her petticoat. When he asked for her hand, how was she to answer him? Despite the passing of a week since her last attempt, no simple way of explaining her view to him had occurred. In fact, her cogitations had led her to conclude that explaining at all could itself prove dangerous. Martin was not the sort of man to accept her sacrifice tamely. He would argue, threaten, run the gamut of all means available to sway her. She was not going to be swayed; despite the glory of the past hours, or, perhaps, because of them, she was even more firmly determined to give him his dreams. She loved him—more deeply than she had realised, more completely than she had understood. Self-sacrifice was an undertaking of which she had considerable experience. Her girlish dreams had been jettisoned for her parents' ambitions, her pride for her husband's greed. Martin was more worthy of her sacrifice than any other; she would make it willingly, if sadly.

Calmly determined, Helen allowed her gaze to rest on the strong features only slightly gentled by sleep. She would never succeed in making him accept her view—it would be better not to try. If she offered no explanation, but simply held firm to her refusal, he would be exceedingly angry, but impotent to pressure her to change her mind.

He was not going to like it but it was for his own good.

The buttons down the back of her gown were proving refractory. Seeing her soft carriage boots on the floor, Helen slid her feet into them while glancing about at the elegantly furnished room. Each piece had been chosen with a judicious eye. The theme was simplicity of line and form, an austerity which balanced the stark black, blue and gold décor. In truth, the room suited its owner. She could not imagine him in less expensive surrounds; this was his milieu, this was where he rightly belonged. This, she was determined, was where he would stay.

Her eyes went once more to the handsome face. Helen smiled as she recalled his efforts to ease her imagined hurt.

Her smile faded. In refusing him, she was going to cause him even more hurt than anger. She was going to land a blow where it would hurt a great deal. Her refusal to succumb to his lovemaking was going to place a very large dent in his rake's pride.

Helen paled and felt suddenly chilled.

At sixteen, she had learned that her life was not destined to be easy. She had borne unhappiness and loneliness and put a brave face on her misery. But what she could not understand was why fate had singled her out for such continually harsh treatment. Why her?

Resolutely, Helen straightened, pushing her depression aside. Her fingers were still fumbling behind her, the small buttons sliding on the silk. Muttering a few choice curses, she attacked them with renewed vigour, only to find them slipping from her grasp.

Exasperated, she glanced up—straight into warm grey eyes, laced with lazy laughter. As she watched, Martin's smile grew.

'You should have woken me.' His voice was still several tones deeper than normal, a warm, raspy invitation to illicit delight.

Helen blinked, struggling to focus her wits. She had to keep calm. Trying for her usual brisk tone, she said, 'It's late and I need to get home. I suspected waking you before I got dressed would not necessarily be supportive of that aim.'

Thoroughly relaxed, Martin chuckled. 'You read me so well, fair Juno.' He beckoned. 'Come here.'

Helen eyed him suspiciously. 'Martin, I really *do* need to go.'

Martin's eyes flicked to the clock. His brows rose in resignation. 'I suppose you do.' He sighed. 'In which case, you had better let me do up your dress.' He sat up and swung his leg over the side of the bed, the sheet slipping down to his waist. When he waved her towards him, Helen reluctantly came to stand before him. Martin's strong hands closed about her waist. For one heart-stopping moment, their gazes locked. Mesmerised, her breath trapped in her throat, Helen watched as the slow smile she knew so well twisted his lips. Then he turned her about.

His strong fingers made short work of her buttons. But before she could move away, his hands fastened about her waist and he drew her down to sit on one sheet-swathed knee.

The feel of her warm body between his hands made Martin wish again that she had woken him earlier. He seriously considered pulling her back to the sheets and wrestling her out of her clothes. Who cared what the world thought? With a wry grin, he acknowledged that such wildness would no longer do, not if he intended to assume his social position as the Earl of Merton with his Countess at his side. Speaking of which...

He turned fair Juno about so that he could look into her face. He smiled devilishly, the complete rake. 'Did you like it?'

Helen's eyes flew wide. She blushed furiously.

Martin laughed, raising one finger to caress her cheek. 'Say you'll marry me and we can enjoy such delights every day—or at least every night.' His second proposal, he reflected, but in circumstances much more to his taste. He smiled confidently and waited for fair Juno's assent.

Helen could not meet his eyes. As the silence stretched, she felt Martin tense. Feeling a chill creep over her skin, she tried to ease from his hold. He let her go, his hands falling from her as she stood and moved to the fireplace before turning to face him.

Steeling herself, she raised her eyes to his. Cold grey stone would have held more warmth than the grey gaze steadily regarding her. His features were impassive, set like granite; his hands were fisted on his thighs. The light from the dying fire gilded the heavy musculature of his bare chest. He looked very powerful—and deeply angry.

'Martin, I cannot marry you.' Helen forced herself to enunciate the words clearly, calmly. Inside, she felt dead.

'I see.' The words came like a whiplash. Helen hung her head. 'You'll willingly share my bed but you won't *marry* me.' During the pause that ensued, she kept her eyes down, too frightened that she would weaken if she looked up and saw his disillusion.

'Why?'

The confusion and hurt in that single word nearly overset her. She pressed her palms together and forced her head up. 'I'm sorry. I can't explain.'

'*Sorry*?' Abruptly, Martin surged to his feet.

Startled, Helen glanced away, colour flaring in her pale cheeks. With a strangled curse, Martin stalked to where a silk robe had been left lying over the back of a chair. He shrugged into it, struggling to bring order to the chaotic and violent emotions seething through his brain. 'Let me just get one point clear,' he ground out, savagely yanking the sash tight. 'You were willing, were you not?'

'Yes.' Helen brought her head up, relieved to see him decently garbed. Her admission should have sunk her beyond reproach, shaken her to the core. Yet it was the truth; she admitted it without a blink, all her energies concentrated on the difficult task of persuading him to let her go. 'But that alters nothing. It is simply not possible for me to marry you.'

'Why?'

This time, the question held more demand. Martin stalked back and forth before her, a wounded beast. Helen stifled the instinctive urge to offer him comfort. She had to hold firm. 'I'm sorry, I can't explain.'

Eyes narrowed to steely slits, Martin stopped directly in front of her. 'Can't explain why you'd make a high-class harlot of yourself rather than marry me? I'm hardly surprised, madam!'

Inwardly flinching, Helen held herself proudly, refusing to quail under the glittering grey gaze. She felt sick. He was not impassive now; hurt pride was clearly etched in his forbidding features. But she could not regret their afternoon of delight; she did not intend to feel guilty over the greatest joy she had ever known.

Martin held her gaze, willing her to back down. When the clear green gaze remained steady, unwavering, he growled and flung away. He felt violent. He wanted to shake her—to take her back to the bed and reduce her to a state where she would do, and say, anything he wished. But that was no real solution. He threw a furious glance her way. She was still standing, with a calm he knew was assumed, before his fireplace—where he wanted to see her, but without the mantle he wished to place on her shoulders. He could push her to become his mistress, and she might just give way. But he wanted her as his wife.

With a growl of frustration, Martin turned and stalked back to her. 'If my honest proposal is repugnant to you, my lady, I would suggest you leave. Before my baser instincts drive me to make you a far more insulting offer.'

Helen's eyes widened. Martin's fingers closed, vice-like, about her arm. Stifling a gasp, she allowed him to march her, unresisting, to the door. It was better this way. If she had to depart of her own accord, leaving him hurt, wounded and without explanation, she might waver and fail. His furious rejection might break her heart but it might also save his.

In a muddled, befuddled fury, Martin strode into his hall, dragging Helen with him. 'Hillthorpe!'

Instantly, his butler emerged from behind the green baize door. At sight of them, his demeanour underwent a subtle change.

Martin ignored the evidence of Hillthorpe's surprise. 'Lady Walford is leaving. Get a hackney for her ladyship.' He released Helen and, with the curtest of nods, turned on his heel and strode back to the parlour.

When the door slammed behind him, Helen drew a ragged breath. She felt as if her world had crashed about her very ears. Her head was spinning; she felt queasy inside. But there was nothing to do but face the disaster with as much dignity as she could. Her hair was still down, but her pins were irretrievable; she would have to make the best of it. She refused to permit herself to break down and cry, much as she wished to, until she was safe in her chamber. Reaching that sanctuary with all possible haste was her immediate goal.

One glance at Martin's butler showed he was as stunned as she at Martin's rudeness but, unlike her, had no idea from where the uncharacteristic reaction sprang. 'If you would get my hat and coat?'

Her quiet question jolted Hillthorpe out of his state of shock. 'Yes, of course, my lady.' Never in his extensive experience of Mr Martin had Hillthorpe seen him in such a temper. Which, he thought, as he bowed to Lady Walford and hurried to do her bidding, was a damned shame. The servants had been particularly pleased when Mr Martin had inherited. Of the four sons of the house, he had always been their favourite. He was a hard but fair master; they were relieved that the estate was once more in capable hands. Not since the late master, his father, had they felt so secure. And, as servants did, they had kept abreast of his endeavours to secure his Countess. The news that he had chosen Lady Walford for the position had been greeted with considerable relief. Many were the instances when men such as his lordship married youthful misses who led everyone a dance and set the household by the ears. But Lady Walford was well spoken of, kind and generous, a lady in truth.

As he held her ladyship's coat for her, Hillthorpe frowned. She was upset, as she had no doubt every right to be. What was the master thinking of? A hackney? He would summon the unmarked carriage instead. As she turned to face him, buttoning up her coat, he bowed low. 'If you'll just take a seat in the drawing-room, ma'am, I'll summon the carriage directly.'

Grateful for the man's smooth handling of the matter, Helen followed him, battening down her emotions until it was safe to set them free.

From the bend in the spiral staircase two floors above, Damian Willesden watched her disappear down the hall. His eyes widened in surprise. Slowly, he slumped on to the stairs, the better to consider the implications of what he had just seen.

So—Martin had run true to form and seduced the beautiful Lady Walford? That thought pleased Damian no end. With a little crow of delight, he gave thanks for Martin's rakish tendencies. Lady Walford might be his brother's mistress but she would not be his wife. Her ladyship could be crossed off the list of potential candidates for the position of the Countess of Merton.

Or could she?

Damian sobered and gave the matter due thought. He could not imagine why a man such as his brother would marry a woman he could have as his mistress but the unpalatable truth was, such things had been known to occur. All too often. Particularly with unmarried peers.

The front door opened and shut. Lady Walford was gone.

But *he* was not yet safe. Damian frowned and drummed his fingers on his knee. He could not believe that Martin would want to marry the lady now, particularly after that abrupt dismissal, but that did not mean she might not try to entrap him later. Adrift in social straits he normally eschewed with a vengeance, Damian pondered deeply. In the end, he concluded that it would quite obviously be better all round, for Martin as well as for himself, if Lady Walford were not in a position to demand that Martin marry her.

And she could not do that if her reputation was already in shreds.

Aside from anything else, the Dowager would not stand for it. Damian had immense confidence in his mother. And her money.

With a smug smile, Damian rose and sauntered down the stairs. It would be easy, so easy, to ensure his peace of mind. He called for his hat and cane and, once supplied with these necessary items, issued forth from the house of his fathers, determined to make sure that it would one day be his. He turned his footsteps in the direction of St James.

CHAPTER NINE

The Barham House ball was to be held that night. Wearily, Helen acknowledged that it was impossible for her to miss the event—the Barhams had stood her friends for years. Hopefully, Martin, not so constrained, would not go.

With a dismal sniff, she hauled herself out of the comforting softness of her bed and gave her eyes one last pat with her sodden handkerchief. Janet would have to find some cucumber to take the swelling down. Her bout of tears had done no more than ease her immediate hurt; the deeper pain would linger, undimmed by any show of misery. With an effort, Helen stood and crossed the room to tug the bell-pull. Then she ventured to her wardrobe.

Black was what she felt like wearing, but in the circumstances, dark blue would have to do. The heavy silk was edged with gold ribbons; more ribbon cinched the high waist. In it, she knew she looked austere and a little remote. Perfect for tonight. With any luck, the solid colour would help disguise her paleness.

A bath restored some semblance of vitality. Janet fussed and fretted and coaxed her to eat some lightly broiled chicken. Her cook had tried, but the food might as well have been ashes.

And then she was in her carriage, bowling along to Barham House. What would she do if Martin did attend? Helen drew a long breath and buried that thought deep. In her present state, it was far too unnerving to contemplate.

The Barhams greeted her warmly. In the ballroom, she found Dorothea and Lady Merion already present. In the comfort of her familiar circle, she relaxed, allowed a mask of calm unconcern to cloak her bruised heart.

Midway through the evening, her mask slipped alarmingly. She was waltzing with Viscount Alvanley when she became aware that Martin had indeed attended the ball. He was standing by the side of the ballroom, powerful shoulders propped against the wall, a look of brooding intensity darkening his features. His gaze was fixed unwaveringly upon her.

Even Alvanley, genial chatterer that he was, noticed her start. 'What's up?' he asked, peering at her over the folds of his monstrous neckcloth.

'Er—nothing. What were you saying about Lady Havelock?'

Alvanley frowned at her. 'Not Havelock,' he said, piqued. 'Hatcham.'

'Oh, yes,' said Helen, praying that he would resume whatever anecdote he had been pouring into her ears. She kept her eyes on the Viscount's face, inwardly struggling to calm her panicky breathing and the erratic pounding of her heart. To her relief, Alvanley happily took up his tale.

Helen tried to ignore the grey gaze from across the room, tried to keep her mind engaged with all manner of distractions, afraid that if she allowed herself to meet Martin's eyes her fragile control would break. She could not let that happen—not in the middle of the Barhams' ballroom. Aside from anything else, Martin in his present mood was perfectly capable of taking advantage of such weakness to force her either to explain, or, if she was truly overcome, to accept his suit. Irrelevantly, Helen belatedly recalled Ferdie's warning. Her old friend had been right—rakes were dangerous in any circumstances.

Despite the sea of fashionable heads separating them, Martin's senses, finely tuned where Helen was concerned, detected her unease. Through the veils of rage that still clouded his reason, he realised she did not wish him to approach her. He was tempted to ignore her wishes and claim her for a waltz. Only his uncertainty over what might happen if he did, an unnerving occurrence in itself, kept him from doing so. He was not even sure why he was here, other than that there had been nothing else he had wanted to do. Seeing Helen every evening had become a habit—a habit he was damned if he could break—a habit he had no wish to break. The events of the afternoon had left him more than confused. Anger still rode him, a potent influence, effectively countering all efforts at rational thought. From experience, he knew his mind would not function properly until he had worked it out of his system. How to achieve that laudable goal had him presently at a loss.

He knew his continued staring at Helen was causing comment but he could not stop. His mind was totally consumed by her; his eyes simply followed his thoughts. He saw Hedley Swayne and spared a moment to scowl at him. The fop took fright and disappeared into the crowd.

'Martin! How pleasant to see you again.'

Martin looked down as a hand touched his arm. Seeing Serena Monckton—no, she was Lady Rochester now—smiling up at him, he repressed the urge to shake off her hand. He nodded casually and came away from the wall. 'Serena.'

Lady Rochester preened. It was the first time since he had reappeared as the Earl of Merton that she had managed to get Martin to use her first name. Perhaps there was hope for her yet?

Martin saw her reaction and inwardly cursed. He had studiously kept Serena at a distance, knowing how cloying her attention could be. He also trusted her not at all, a fact he felt was excusable. With his mind engrossed with Helen, he had forgotten to keep his defences up. Now he would have to repair the damage.

'I do *love* waltzing.' Coquettishly, Lady Rochester smiled up at him. 'So few of the men these days know how to do it properly. But you were with Wellington at Waterloo, weren't you?'

Stifling a curse, Martin reflected that no moss grew on Serena Monckton. She was shameless, propositioning him in such a way. Particularly him. He opened his mouth to put her in her place, when it suddenly occurred to him that perhaps here was an opportunity to demonstrate to another shameless woman just what it felt like to be rejected. The very same shameless woman who had spent the afternoon on his daybed and then rejected him. A single glance over the crowd showed that Helen was sitting out the dance, seated on a chaise by Dorothea's side. Martin's eyes dropped to Serena's eager face, his lips curved in a practised smile. 'I do believe that's a waltz starting up now. Shall we?'

He did not have to ask twice. But, immediately his feet started to circle, Martin wished he had thought twice. Dancing with Serena felt all wrong; she was not the woman he wanted in his arms. Gripped by a sudden sense of foreboding, Martin glanced over the heads of the dancers. Helen had not seen them yet. But many others had. He had made a habit of dancing with Helen Walford alone; his sudden appearance on the dance-floor with another woman in his arms, Serena Monckton at that, while Helen was in the room and unengaged, was, Martin belatedly realised, a somewhat obvious insult. The full enormity of his mistake hit him when he again looked Helen's way. They were much closer now. She had seen them; the expression in her large green eyes cut him to the core. Abruptly, she looked down and away, saying something to distract Dorothea, who was staring at him in undisguised fury.

Martin felt chilled. He waltzed automatically, paying no attention at all to Serena's chatter. When their revolutions took them past the chaise where Helen had been, he saw that it was empty. The third time around, and Dorothea was back, alone, staring daggers at him.

Helen had left the ball.

Because of him. He had hurt her and she had fled, not something she would readily do, having, as he knew, no liking for appearing in *on-dits*.

An odd numbness had closed about his heart; his mind refused to function at all. As soon as the dance ended, Martin bowed over Serena's hand and, leaving her standing by the side of the room, paid his respects to his by now curious hostess and left.

From the shadows of a potted palm decorating the side of the room, Damian watched Martin depart and rejoiced. Better and better. After that little scene, there was no chance of his brother and Lady Walford patching things up. Particularly not when the story he had spent the evening seeding into fertile soil took root. It would take a day or so, but after that he would be home and hosed, past the post, safe and sound.

He had decided that, in the circumstances, he would do well to attend a few of the *ton* assemblies, just until the danger of Lady Walford was past. Clearly, he would not have to suffer such boring gatherings for much longer. Virtually the entire ballroom had noticed the incident. Inwardly, Damian hugged himself. Whatever had possessed Martin to take such drastic action he could not imagine but he had to admit that, when his brother struck, he was effective. Lady Rochester was still standing a little way away, trying to pretend that Martin had truly been interested in her. Not that anyone would believe that. Feeling in unexpected charity with his brother, Damian decided to do him a favour.

He strolled to her ladyship's side and waited until the ageing roué who was currently bending her ear departed before nodding his greeting. 'Helpful of you to give Martin a hand.'

Serena scowled. 'Whatever do you mean, sir?'

Her peevish tone brought out the devil in Damian. 'Oh, I think you know.' He watched as Lady Rochester's face purpled. 'Who knows?' he continued smoothly before she could explode. 'Perhaps Martin might be grateful in a way you'd appreciate, now he's terminated his relationship with Lady Walford and will no longer be availing himself of her charms.'

Serena's eyes grew round, and then even rounder as the full implication of what he was saying sank in. 'You mean...?' Her voice was an incredulous whisper.

Damian looked surprised. 'Didn't you know? I thought everyone did. Ah well.' He shrugged. 'Just goes to show, don't it?' And with that he moved away, perfectly sure he had warned Lady Rochester off, too. For if Martin could seduce and ruin a woman of Lady Walford's calibre, it stood to reason that he would make short work of such as Lady Rochester.

Left alone, Serena took a long moment to sort out how what she had just heard could be used to greatest effect. She was perfectly well aware that Martin had only waltzed with her to hurt Helen Walford. The fiend had not so much as glanced properly at her—she was finished with trying to attract his notice. But she could not believe he was finished with the beautiful widow. From where she had stood, it had been blatantly obvious that he was still obsessed with Lady Walford. She had no quarrel with Helen Walford, just as long as she did not marry Martin Willesden. She herself held no illusion that she could ever fill that position—not now. But she drew the line at the thought of Martin enjoying his wife. Better anyone than Lady Walford. The rumour Damian was spreading, true or not, would surely cook Lady Walford's goose. And, if Martin was truly enamoured of Helen Walford, as Serena had every reason to suspect, then such an outcome would cause him grief.

Coolly, Lady Rochester smiled. None knew better than she that her long-ago claim of rape had been entirely without foundation. None knew better than she how furious Martin Willesden had made her by denying it and then accepting exile rather than marry her. Time had healed some of the wounds, but she saw no reason not to do what she could to spread Damian's delightful rumour.

Buoyed by a pleasant sense of mischief, she moved into the crowd to see what she could do.

His frown still black, Martin strode into his library. He shut the door with a decided click, then crossed to the sideboard and poured himself a generous quantity of brandy before slumping into the armchair by the fire.

Why? What had possessed him to make such an error of judgement? Never before had he made such a wrong-footed move. He had let his temper take control and it had led him off track. His equilibrium was out of kilter—he was dangerously adrift.

If this was what love did to a man, he was not sure he approved.

With a frustrated groan, he placed his glass on the table beside him and ran his hands over his face. He had hurt her. Dammit—all he wanted to do was make the wretched woman happy. Instead, he had succeeded in making them both miserable. The urge to go around to Half Moon Street and knock on her door until she let him in grew.

Reluctantly, Martin quashed the impulse and reached for his glass.

Enough of histrionics—they had landed him in a worse state than he had been in before. He was more than old enough to know better.

And, speaking of knowing better, did he really want to marry a woman who allowed herself to be seduced while having absolutely no intention of marrying her seducer? A difficult question, given that he had been the seducer and he had not married anyone before. Martin grimaced and took a long sip of brandy. Regardless of present appearance, regardless of her words, he knew, as only a rake could, that Helen Walford was not promiscuous. Why then her refusal?

For a long while, he stared at the fire while the long case clock in the corner ticked on. The sheer fury he had felt when he had understood her intention of refusing him again, when he had realised that the woman he wanted to place before his fireplace was the sort who could walk away from intimacy without a second thought, still seethed, scrambling his wits.

He shook his head in frustration. It was no good. He could not think straight with his mind in such turmoil. Best to get away, to get out of it, until his temper died and he could consider the matter more calmly. Right now, he was not even sure what he wanted any more, let alone how best to achieve it. His agent at Merton had written, begging his attendance. The decorators were there, making his dream a reality; he should see how they were progressing. He would go down for a few days. Perhaps the peace of the Hermitage would help him sort things out, decide where he stood, what he wanted to do.

Decision made, Martin rose and drained his glass. For a long moment, he stood stock-still, staring at the embers dying in the grate. Then, deliberately, he flung the glass into the fireplace. With a brittle tinkle, it shattered, sending crystal shards flying.

His jaw set, Martin swung on his heel and left the room.

* * *

The first intimation Helen had that anything at all was wrong came two days later, when she finally stirred herself from her lethargy to go driving in the Park with Cecily Fanshawe. It was her first outing since the disaster of the Barham House ball. Thankfully, Cecily had missed the ball through indisposition. As always bubbling with enthusiasm, she prattled on, giving Helen every opportunity to rest her weary mind.

She was worn out—depressed, hurt and heart-weary. The sight of Martin waltzing with Lady Rochester had caused her far more pain than she had been prepared for. She had thought she would be able to weather any such sight, knowing it would come some time. Her nerves had not been up to it that night. His action and her reaction would have caused comment, she knew. Consequently, when she detected the first few whispers, she made nothing of them.

But by the time she and Cecily had gone halfway around the circuit, Helen knew that something more serious was in the wind. There was a coolness in the air. A number of matrons with marriageable daughters drew back from her smile.

It was Ferdie who confirmed her suspicions. He waved to them from the side of the carriageway in the most popular section of the route. When the carriage came to a halt, he opened the door. 'Want to talk to you,' he said to Helen. He nodded to Cecily, with whom he was well-acquainted, then climbed into the carriage. 'Rather think it's time you dropped Helen home. I need to talk to her alone.'

Cecily frowned. 'But we've only just arrived.'

'Never mind. Plenty to keep you busy at home, I dare say.'

Cecily glared at Ferdie; Ferdie stared vacantly back. It was Cecily who gave way. 'Oh, very well!' she said, and leaned forward to give her coachman directions.

Helen had not thought her heart could have sunk lower than it already had, but, as Ferdie engaged them both in inconsequential patter, she felt the leaden weight in her chest descend to her slippers. But she refused to let herself worry—not until she had heard what Ferdie had to say.

Cecily dropped them off in Half Moon Street, airily declining an offer of refreshment. 'I hope I know when I'm not wanted,' she said, looking pointedly at Ferdie.

Ferdie grinned. 'Not up to snuff yet, I'm afraid. Being married don't make you older.'

Cecily put her nose in the air and, miffed, departed.

Inside her drawing-room, Helen found another visitor waiting. Dorothea was pacing before the unlighted fire. She looked up as they entered. 'Thank goodness!' she said. 'I hoped you wouldn't be long.'

Ferdie entered behind Helen. Dorothea greeted him with relief. 'You're just the person we need.'

Ferdie took the unusual welcome in his stride. 'Got rid of your sister, though. Didn't think she'd take it too well. Never know what she might dash off and do.'

'Very true,' Dorothea agreed feelingly.

'Do you mind,' said Helen, sinking into an armchair, 'telling me what all this is about?' She had a nasty suspicion but she wanted to hear it stated plainly.

The simple question succeeded in striking both her visitors dumb. They looked at her, then, rather uncomfortably, at each other.

Helen sighed. 'Is it about me and Martin Willesden?'

Dorothea sank on to the chaise. 'Yes.' She waited while Ferdie drew up another chair and sat down. 'There are rumours going the rounds. Perhaps one might expect it, after the Barham ball. But what I've heard this morning seems rather more than can be excused.' She raised her large green eyes to Helen's in a gently questioning glance.

Helen held Dorothea's gaze for a moment, then sighed and looked to Ferdie. 'You've heard them, too?'

Ferdie, unaccustomedly serious, nodded. 'At White's.'

Helen closed her eyes. White's. That meant it was all about town.

'The tales suggest,' Dorothea began, 'that you...have been... Martin Willesden's mistress.' She waited, but Helen did not open her eyes. 'Is it true?' she asked gently.

'Would it matter?' Helen returned, her weariness very evident in her tone. She opened her eyes, raising her brows in disdain.

It was Ferdie who answered. "Fraid not.' He paused, then continued, 'The thing we need to do now is decide how to quash 'em.'

'Yes,' agreed Dorothea. 'And I'm very much afraid, Helen, that you'll have to face it out. Marc's furious. After all, you first met Martin in our house. It was all I could do to persuade him to do nothing until I'd talked to you.'

Helen's eyes widened. Hazelmere after Martin? In truth, she could not predict who would be the victor in such a contest—they were both extraordinarily powerful men in every way. But Hazelmere had solid social acceptability on his side—and Dorothea. Abruptly, Helen sat up, reaching across to lay a supplicating hand on Dorothea's sleeve. 'You must promise me you'll make Marc promise not to do anything—anything at all—until he hears from me.' Helen stared at Dorothea earnestly. 'Promise?'

A worried frown in her eyes, Dorothea grimaced. 'I promise to *try*. But you know as well as I that on some issues Marc won't be led.'

That was indisputably true. Helen nodded her acceptance of Dorothea's limited offer. She sank back into her chair. 'I need to think.'

'Best thing to do is to carry on as usual,' said Ferdie. 'Merton'll have to play his part. If neither of you gets the wind up, it'll all blow over.'

Dully, Helen nodded. 'Yes. I suppose that's true.' With a visible effort, she put aside her depression to smile at her guests. 'With friends like you, I'm sure we'll get by.'

Dorothea rose, shaking out her skirts. 'I'll leave you to your thoughts. If you need any additional support, you know you can call on us for whatever you need. Meanwhile, we'll do what we can to dampen the interest.'

Helen nodded her thanks.

Ferdie rose, too. 'I'll come with you,' he said to Dorothea. 'Might help if I saw Hazelmere.'

Both Dorothea and Helen welcomed this magnanimous offer.

After seeing her guests out, Helen returned to her small drawing-room to slump, even more weary than before, into her armchair. She struggled to make sense of what had happened. How had the story of her afternoon with Martin got out? No one had seen her leave Martin's house—his careful butler had seen to that. And, against Martin's orders, he had sent her home in one of the Merton coaches, but an unmarked one, with no crest on the door to give her away.

Had Martin spread the tale—to hurt her? Given the fact that he had deliberately and so very publicly flayed her feelings by waltzing with Lady Rochester—of all women—under her nose, she felt reasonably sure that he was capable of anything. Knowing that her standing in society was one of the few assets she had left, had he set out to strip her of that, too? Helen bit her lip. A sickening sense of betrayal threatened to engulf her. Determined to see things clearly, she forced herself to think long and hard but, in the end, could not believe it of him. He might strike out at her in anger, as he had done at the Barhams', but to seek to pull her down by making public what they had shared that afternoon was not the action of a gentleman. And, beneath his rakehell exterior, Martin Willesden was every inch a gentleman.

The only proof she needed of that was her memory. He had taken great pains to keep her safe, from himself as well as all others, on their unorthodox journey to London. An unscrupulous rake would have taken advantage; she blushed as she recalled their night at Cholderton—he had certainly had opportunity enough.

No—whoever had spread the tale of their afternoon together, it was not, could not be, Martin. Nevertheless, the uncertainty added yet another bruise to her already battered heart.

After half an hour's painful cogitation, she succeeded in convincing herself that she would have to see Martin, to discuss what they should do. He must have heard the rumours by now.

Reluctantly, Helen rose and crossed to the small escritoire

which stood before the window. She sat and pulled a blank sheet of paper towards her. After mending her quill, she spent fifteen minutes staring fruitlessly into space. In the end, she shook herself in disgust. Without allowing herself any time to think further, she dashed off a note to the Earl of Merton.

The answer came back two hours later. The Earl of Merton, wrote his secretary, was presently in the country. It was not known when he would be back but her letter would be shown to him instantly on his return.

Helen stared at the plain note, reading the two sentences over and over. Ten minutes passed, then twenty. Finally, as the light started to wane, she stirred. Crumpling the note into a ball, she dropped it into the grate. Then, slowly, she went to the door and climbed the stairs to her chamber.

She lay on her bed and stared at the ceiling. She was alone. Not an unusual occurrence in her life, but it felt much worse this time. Insensibly, Martin had been with her ever since their first meeting in the woods. Now he had withdrawn, at the very moment when she most needed his strength.

What was she to do? That refrain played over and over in her head. The shadows lengthened. Outside, darkness fell. Inside her chamber, the outlook was bleak. In Martin's absence, she could not readily face down the rumours, scotch the scandal by simply denying its truth. Together, they could have pulled it off easily enough, even though, given their present situation, the effort would have cost both of them dearly. Without Martin, she did not have the strength to hold her head high until his return. Who knew when he might come back?

What were the alternatives? Helen bit her lower lip and frowned. If she retired from town for the rest of the Season, there was every likelihood that some other scandal would blow up to eclipse hers. Hazelmere, she knew, would not support such a course, tacitly admitting as it did that there was some substance to the rumours. But she was not a green girl. She was a widow of twenty-six. The *ton* was inclined to turn a blind eye to such matters, as long as the affair was not paraded before their collective eyes. As theirs had been. The cheapest price to secure her future acceptance seemed to be a sojourn

in the country. She had little doubt that next year she would
be able to return to town and join in the Season as if nothing
untoward had occurred.

So the country it would be. But where? Unseeing, Helen
stared into the gathering gloom. Hazelmere's estates were always open to her but, given that her absence from town would
be against his wishes, she did not feel at ease with such a
solution. There was Heliotrope Cottage, of course—her only
remaining land, all five acres of it, in west Cornwall. The
cottage was a tiny place, just big enough for Janet and herself.
Hazelmere had always been against her staying there, on the
grounds that she would be without male protection.

But Cornwall was a long way from London. Perhaps, in the
isolation of the country, her broken heart would mend faster?

With a sigh, Helen sat up and swung her feet to the floor.
There was no sense in thinking further—there was nowhere
else to think of. Heliotrope Cottage it would have to be. She
rose and crossed to the bell-pull. If Janet packed tonight, she
could close the house in the morning and hire a chaise to take
them down. Three days would see her far from the capital, far
from the grey eyes that haunted her dreams.

Late that night, with all her plans made and her orders
given, Helen sank into her bed and closed her eyes. She had
decided not to tell anyone of her decision. They would only
argue and, at the moment, she was not up to arguing back. No
one would worry, however, for, with the knocker off the door
and Janet gone, they would know she had shut up her house
and gone away. Her dearest friends, those whose approval she
valued, were all close enough to respect her wish for privacy.
After Christmas, perhaps, she could visit Dorothea once her
friend had returned to Hazelmere.

With a little sigh, Helen tried to relax, waiting for sleep to
claim her, wondering irrelevantly how long it would be before
slumber ceased to bring the image of grey eyes in its train.

CHAPTER TEN

Hammering still echoed throughout the ground floor of the Hermitage. Martin paced around the new conservatory, added at the back of the ballroom, admiring his new domain. It was all coming together much as he had planned.

The decorators would take another week to complete their work; the carpenters were expected to leave tomorrow. The sharp tang of new wood mixed with the smell of freshly mown grass. Not to be outdone by their house-bound rivals, the small army of gardeners he had hired to transform the wilderness back into landscaped grounds had taken full advantage of the fine weather. He had noticed the change immediately he had arrived. The drive had been cleared and newly gravelled, the huge wrought-iron gates that had hung for centuries at the main entrance to the estate had been cleaned and rehung. At the sight, Joshua's grumbles, all but constant since London, had abruptly ceased.

Martin leaned both hands on the sill of an open window and breathed deeply. Everywhere he looked, the evidence of his success leaped forward to greet him. Soon, his dream would be a reality; the Hermitage would be fit to take its rightful place as a centre of fashionable living once more, a suitable home for him—and his family.

At the thought, his mood clouded.

His success on one front had not been mirrored on the other. And now he was no longer sure which was the more important. Before he had met Helen Walford, restoring the Hermitage had been his principal goal. Now, with that goal in sight, he was looking far further ahead, beyond having his house, to fulfilling what he recognised as an even more basic need. He would soon have his house—he needed a family to fill it.

And, try as he might, there was only one woman he could picture in that all-important position before his fireplace. His mind was not capable of letting go of the image of Helen Walford, the flames gilding her glorious hair, with his son balanced on her hip.

From being merely an aim, marrying Helen Walford had become an obsession. He knew himself well enough to accept that if he did not marry her he would marry no one. His dream of a family inhabiting his home would never materialise.

He was determined that it would—every bit as determined as she seemed to be to fight shy of marrying him.

She was in for a shock.

He was not giving up.

Martin smiled a twisted smile. The life of a rake, a rich, well-born rake, was hardly conducive to teaching one self-sacrifice. He had no intention of giving up his dream. But how to convince Helen to go along with it was more than he had yet worked out.

Noticing the shadows lengthening, he shook free of his reverie. He would think more on the matter later. Right now, he was due for some light entertainment.

Quickly crossing the conservatory and striding through the refurbished ballroom, he paused to cast a critical eye over the now elegant dining-room before taking the stairs two at a time. He strode towards his mother's rooms, noting with deep satisfaction how different the atmosphere in the long corridors now was. Gone was the must and the damp. Newly painted woodwork gleamed, and the floor was well-buffed and covered with bright runners. Windows, long stuck, had been repaired and the fresh autumn air danced in. Slim tables stood along the walls, some overhung by paintings, others sporting vases filled with bright flowers. Martin stopped by one such and chose a pink for his buttonhole.

Tucking it into position, he fronted his mother's door. He knocked. When she called to him to enter, he grinned in wicked anticipation and obeyed.

Catherine Willesden looked up as he entered, unsurprised, for she knew his knock by now. To her amazement, Martin had taken to dropping by her room in the late afternoons, not to cause any furor but merely to chat. At first she had been stunned, then disarmed. He had a sharp eye and a ready wit, very reminiscent of his father. She had enjoyed his company far more than she would ever admit.

Regally, she nodded and watched as he appropriated one of her gnarled hands and bent to kiss it. Then he placed a dutiful kiss on her cheek and stood back.

'I've a surprise for you.' Martin smiled down at her.

Lady Catherine struggled to remain immune. 'Oh? What?'

'I can't possibly tell you, or it wouldn't be a surprise.' Martin watched his mother's eyes narrow.

'My dear sir, if you think I'm about to play guessing games with you, you're mistaken.'

'Naturally not,' Martin replied. He found his mother's acerbity refreshing and took the greatest delight in teasing her. 'I would never presume to play games with you, ma'am.'

'Huh!' was his mother's instant response.

'But you're distracting me from your surprise. You'll have to come downstairs to get it.'

Lady Catherine frowned at her son. 'I've not been downstairs for well nigh ten years—as you well know.'

'I know nothing of the sort. If you were well enough to look about the place six weeks ago, you must be well enough to see my surprise.' Martin watched as his mother's crabbed fingers picked at the edge of her shawl.

'Oh,' said the Dowager. 'You heard about that.'

'Yes,' Martin said, his tone several shades more gentle. 'But there was no need for you to see it like that.' He had learned that, when he'd left so abruptly after his first visit, she had insisted on being carried down to view the state she had by then guessed the house had disintegrated into.

'It was awful.' Lady Catherine shuddered. 'I couldn't even recognise some of the rooms.'

Her grief for her lost dreams, the images she had carried

for so many years destroyed when she had seen the decay of
her home, shadowed her voice.

'Enough of the past. It's all gone.' Martin stooped and
scooped her into his arms. Lady Catherine bit back a squeal
and clutched at him, then glared when he smiled at her. Reflecting that Helen was at least twice his mother's weight,
Martin swung towards the door. His eyes fell on Melissa's
bent head. 'Melissa—are you coming? Dinner will be downstairs tonight—come with us by all means, if you've a mind
to see the workings, or come to the drawing-room at six.'

Melissa gawked at him. Dismissing her from his mind, Martin strode towards the door.

'*Downstairs*?' Lady Catherine finally found her tongue. 'I
have my dinner up here. On a tray.'

Martin shook his head. 'Not any more. Now that we have
a habitable dining-room, while I'm in residence, you'll take
your proper place at the end of my table.' He made his voice
sound stern, as if he was issuing an order.

He glanced sidelong at his mother. She did not know what
to say. On the one hand, she did not like to accept what might
just be his charity; on the other, she longed to be seated at her
table again. Martin grinned and strode along the corridor to
the stairs.

Catherine Willesden barely noticed the bright new furnish-
ings through the veil of tears clouding her eyes. She had never,
ever valued Martin and his arrogant, impulsive ways as he
deserved. She knew quite well that it was because he had
never been tractable, as his brothers had always been. But,
while George had brought the place to ruin, Martin had set it
to rights. Her heart had been broken when she had finally
understood the full sum of the mess—Mr Matthews had been
distressingly blunt when she had asked. Now it was as if a
magic wand had been waved—it was even better than she
recalled.

Not that she could tell Martin that—the rogue would be
insufferable. As they reached the bottom of the stairs, she
blinked rapidly. Martin eased her into a chair which had been
set waiting. She settled her skirts as he stood back.

Suddenly, the chair started to move.

'Martin!' The Dowager awkwardly grabbed at the arms of the chair.

Her reprobate son chuckled—actually chuckled!

'It's all right. I've got hold of it.' Martin pushed the chair slowly forward. 'It's a wheelchair. Set on wheels so you can be moved about easily. See?' He stopped and showed her the wheels. 'I saw it in London. I thought you might find it useful.'

'I dare say,' said his mother, vainly trying to sound as forbidding as usual.

She failed. Martin pushed her on to the drawing-room, a smile of satisfaction on his face.

He took her through all the main rooms, explaining how those yet unfinished were to be decorated. To his surprise, she made no demur at any of his choices, going so far as to add some suggestions of her own. At five o'clock, totally in charity one with the other, they parted to dress for dinner.

The meal was the first they had shared in over thirteen years. Despite that fact, there was no constraint, beyond that provided by Melissa, who sat, dumb, throughout. Martin tried to include her in their conversation; in the end, his mother grimaced at him and shook her head.

But at the end of the evening, after tea taken in the comfort of the fashionable blue and white drawing-room, his mother declined his offer to carry her upstairs.

'Melissa can go,' she said, waving her ineffectual daughter-in-law away. She turned to look at Martin. 'Are you going to sit in the library?'

Martin eyed her suspiciously. 'Yes.'

'Good! You can wheel me in there. I want to talk to you.'

Reflecting that his mother had not changed all that much in thirteen years, Martin complied, a rueful smile hovering about his lips.

The library had been the first room rendered habitable by the efforts of his decorators. It had always been the room in which his father had sat. Simple but elegant furniture in the classic style Martin favoured was scattered in a deceptively ad hoc manner throughout the long room; warm wooden book-shelves, ceiling high, were packed with leather-bound tomes. Martin dutifully wheeled his mother in, wondering just what she had on her mind. But, when he had settled her before the fireplace, she did not seem to know where to begin.

The Dowager Countess tried to remind herself she was just that, and the mother of the gentleman lounging at his ease in the latest style of wing chair opposite her. She eyed the elegant figure, clad in a simple yet exquisitely tailored blue coat and black knee-breeches, with some hesitation. What she felt she had to say was sensitive—or at least likely to be, given her relationship with this unpredictable son. She drew a careful breath and began. 'As you know, I have always been kept informed of happenings in town by my friends. They write to me, telling me all the latest news and *on-dits*.'

Martin suppressed the impulse to put an immediate halt to the conversation. Instead, he raised one brow coldly. 'Indeed?'

The Dowager stiffened. 'You needn't be so defensive,' she said. Really, he was his father all over again. One only had to mention something he did not want to discuss and he with-drew. 'I merely wished to tell you,' she went on before he had a chance to hinder her, 'that it has come to my notice that you appear to have a great interest in Helen Walford. To wit, everyone expects you to offer for her. As you never were witless, I assume that means you do intend to marry her. My only aim in mentioning the matter is to assure you that I will not raise any objection—even though I'm perfectly aware you wouldn't pay any attention if I did,' she added ascerbically. 'I recall Lady Walford's story and was a little acquainted with her parents. From everything I've heard, she's eminently suit-able to be your countess.'

To Martin's astonishment, Lady Catherine paused, frown-ing, then added, 'I must say, I couldn't imagine you taking a bright little deb to wife—you'd probably strangle her before the honeymoon was over. Or, more likely, dump her on me.'

The Dowager raised her eyes to her son's, and beheld the amusement therein. Her eyes narrowed. 'Which brings me to my point. I don't know what state the Dower House is in, but if you would make arrangements to have it refurbished by this firm you're dealing with I'd be obliged.'

When Martin made no immediate comment, she added, 'I'll stand the nonsense, naturally.'

'Naturally be damned.' Martin put his glass of port down on a table beside his chair and leaned forward so that his mother could see his face clearly. 'You've lived in those rooms above stairs for…oh, yes—the past ten years. You've lived in this house for close on fifty. Neither I nor my wife would wish to see you leave.'

For a moment, his mother stared at him, wanting to accept his decree yet unwilling to be suffered out of pity.

'Don't be daft,' the Dowager eventually returned, although the phrase lacked strength. 'Your wife will hardly want me and Melissa cluttering up her house.'

Martin laughed and leaned back in his chair. 'I'd forgotten Melissa,' he admitted, his eyes twinkling. 'Who knows?' he said, his smile twisting. 'Perhaps Fair Juno will be able to get her to speak.'

'Who?'

With a quick smile for his parent's confusion, he brushed the question aside. 'Regardless of all else, I can assure you Helen will expect you to continue here. I suspect you'll deal famously. Aside from anything else, I imagine I'll be facing an unholy alliance every time I want to do anything the least unconventional. You never know, she might need your support.' When the Dowager still looked unconvinced, he added pensively, 'And then there's always the children to be looked after.'

'Children?' His mother's stunned expression suggested she had leaped rather further than he had intended.

Martin grinned. 'Not yet. Rake though I am, I suspect that they had better come after we are wed.'

His mother looked decidedly relieved.

'And now, if I've put all your worries to rest, I'll take you upstairs.' Martin rose. He scooped his mother, thoughtful and silent, into his arms. They were on the stairs when she asked, 'So you are going to marry Helen Walford?'

'Indubitably,' Martin replied. 'As the sun rises in the east, as one day follows another—you may count on it.'

Later, when he had returned to the library and his port, his words echoed in his mind. He had spoken the truth. The only question remaining was how to get his prospective bride to agree.

He lounged in his chair, stretching his long legs before him. Why she insisted on refusing his suit was still a mystery. But he felt certain, now, that he had misunderstood the nature of the hurdle which stood in his path. It was clearly not physical—which was something of a relief. Her reticence had to stem from some more simple problem—possibly a reluctance to place any faith in a man's avowed devotion? Martin raised his brows. Given her first husband's reputation, that was not hard to believe. Whatever the problem, he was confident of finding the answer. His anger at her apparent promiscuity had receded, draining away even as his need for her grew more acute. Rational thought now prevailed; he knew she was not promiscuous; her acts were driven by some deeper motive. He still faced a problem but it was not insurmountable. But he needed to solve it soon. With every passing day, he missed her more. There was nothing—*nothing*—that was more important to him.

With a gesture of decision, Martin drained his glass. There were no objections to be considered, no ramifications to be weighed. Tomorrow, he would return to town and see her.

He would woo her—he would win her. And then he would bring her home.

Two days later, at the fashionable hour of noon, Martin turned his bays into the familiar precinct of Half Moon Street. He drew them smartly to the kerb before Helen's narrow-fronted house. Joshua jumped down and ran to their heads. Martin threw him the reins. 'I don't know how long I'll be. Walk 'em if necessary.'

Martin strode purposefully up the steps. She was going to say yes this time. He was not going to leave until she did. He raised his hand to the knocker—and froze.

The knocker was off the door.

He stared at the empty hinge from which it normally hung—
a small brass weight in the shape of a bell. Only its outline
remained.

Helen had gone out of town.

Abruptly, Martin turned on his heel and strode back to his
curricle. Surprised by his master's sudden return, Joshua
glanced up and opened his mouth, then shut it again. Silently,
he handed his master the reins and scrambled up behind. From
long experience, he knew better than to ask questions when
Mr Martin looked like thunder.

Heading his team back into the traffic, Martin considered
the Park, then decided against it. The last thing he needed was
inconsequential chatter. He turned his horses towards Grosvenor Square mews. Soon, he was striding back and forth before the fireplace in his library, feeling caged and impotent.

Why? Why had she left?

The talk after the Barhams' ball could not have been that
bad. He might have committed a blunder under stress but he
knew his London. The tattlemongers would have twittered
over it for all of twenty-four hours, then forgotten it entirely.

So why had she gone?

To avoid him?

Martin thrust the thought aside, then, when no other explanation offered, reluctantly brought it back for examination.
Too restless to sit, he prowled the room. Could she have
thought he would repeat his performance—with Selina or
whoever—and make her life a misery? With a frustrated
growl, he shook his head. No—no he could not believe she
would imagine he would hurt her—well, not more than the
Barham effort. Given that they had developed a degree of understanding through the long hours they had spent together,
she would know he would calm down after that—after he had
seen her distress. Hell, he wanted to marry the woman—she
could not believe he would hurt her. Could she?

Sunk in semi-guilt, Martin prowled the room.

A sudden realisation brought him to a halt. He raised his
head and stared, unseeing, at his own reflection in the mirror

above the mantelpiece. She could not have gone off to escape
him—because he had taken himself off. With a sigh of relief,
he sank into a chair. She would have realised within a day or
so that he had left the capital. He doubted her friends would
have sanctioned a withdrawal before that. So…

So why had she left? Perhaps the reason had nothing to do
with their relationship? She had no immediate family; her
friends were a select few, all of whom were presently residing
in London. Perhaps Dorothea had taken ill and retired to the
country? Recalling the last sight he had had of Hazelmere's
lovely bride, Martin rejected that idea as unlikely.

Had Helen been forced to leave by something else entirely?
The thought jerked Martin upright. After a moment's cogitation, he rose and tugged the bell-pull, insensibly relieved to
have something concrete to do.

When Hillthorpe answered, he asked for Joshua.

Moments later, 'You wanted me, guv'nor?' broke across
Martin's thoughts. He raised his head and beckoned Joshua
closer.

'That gentleman I had you watch—Hedley Swayne. You
mentioned you'd struck up a relationship with his man?'

Joshua wriggled his shoulders. 'Not so much a relationship
as a drinking partnership, if you take my meaning?'

Martin did. He smiled, a touch grimly. 'That will do admirably. I want you to get over there now and find out what
you can of Mr Swayne's recent exploits. Particularly, if he's
had any unusual visitors—or if he's dressed down to attend
any meeting. I expect that's something his man would notice.'

'Oh, he'd notice right enough. Went on a treat over the
gent's new coloured silk neckerchiefs last time I saw him. The
way he tells it, the swell only thinks of the rags on his back.'

Martin raised a brow. 'That's certainly the way he appears—but I know for certain there's at least one other thing
Hedley Swayne exercises his wits over.' He fixed Joshua with
a commanding eye. 'I want to know what Hedley Swayne's
been up to this week—and I want to know as soon as possible.'

'Right-ho, guv'nor.'

With a cheery half-salute, Joshua left.

He was back far faster than Martin had anticipated.

'He's gone—bolted.'

'*What*?' Martin exploded out of the chair he had slumped into. 'When?'

'Seems like the gentleman's taken hisself and his man and his usual escort—whatever that might mean—off to his estates. In Cornwall, they be, so the housekeeper said. They left two days ago.'

'Two days,' Martin mused, pacing back and forth on the hearthrug. 'Any reason given?'

Joshua shook his head. He watched his master stalk the room, then, when no further orders came his way, he asked, 'D'ye want me to keep watch—to see when he returns?'

Martin stopped his pacing. He looked at Joshua, then slowly shook his head. 'I've a nasty suspicion that when he returns it'll be too late.' With a nod, he dismissed Joshua and renewed his striding. It helped him to think.

There was no necessary connection between Helen's leaving town and Hedley Swayne's departure. That did not mean there wasn't one. Martin swore. He wished he had followed up the peculiar Mr Swayne's abduction attempt. His preoccupation with making Helen Walford his wife—and thus safe from such as Hedley Swayne—had pushed that little incident to the back of his mind. His memories of it had been overlaid by far more interesting recollections of Helen herself.

Shaking such recollections aside, Martin acknowledged his worries. He wanted answers and the only way of finding them was to ask questions—of the right people. And, in this instance, the right people were undoubtedly the Hazelmeres.

When a rapid reconnoitre of the gentlemen's clubs drew a blank, Martin presented himself at Hazelmere House. To his surprise, although Mytton was as gracious as ever and went immediately to inform his master, ensconced in his library, of his arrival, he was kept kicking his heels in the black-and white-tiled hall for what seemed like an age. Eventually, the library door opened.

Dorothea emerged, the heir in her arms.

If she had looked daggers at him at the Barhams', this afternoon she had added spears and crossbows to her armoury. Bemused, Martin reflected that he should, by all accounts, be dead.

With a decidedly cool nod, Dorothea turned on her heel and climbed the stairs. The stiffness of her spine bespoke her disapproval.

Martin raised his brows slightly at the sight. He was not overly surprised that she should still be so starchy—he had yet to make his peace with Helen and Dorothea was, after all, Helen's closest friend. But there was a haughtiness in her disapproval that evoked memories of how the matrons had looked at him thirteen years earlier.

Mytton approached. 'His lordship will see you now, my lord.'

There was nothing, of course, to be learned from Mytton's impassive countenance. Martin followed him to the library.

Inside, he discovered that his pricking thumbs were justified. Hazelmere was standing by the long French windows, open to the afternoon breeze. His stance, rigid and unyielding, warned Martin that something indeed was up, even before he drew close enough to see the stony hazel gaze.

Martin stopped by a chair, laying one hand on its back. He raised a laconic brow and sighed. 'What am I supposed to have done now?'

There was an infinitesimal pause while Hazelmere assimilated the information underlying that question. Then his features eased. 'Don't you know?' he asked, his voice slightly strangled.

'Other than losing my head at the Barhams' the other night, I'm not aware that I've transgressed any of the immutable laws.'

'Not even *before* the Barhams' ball?'

At the quiet question, Martin's gaze locked with his friend's. After a long moment, Martin moved around the chair in front of him and slowly sank into it. 'Oh.'

'Precisely.' Slowly, Hazelmere came forward to sit in the

chair facing his guest. 'I take it I don't need to ask if it's true?'

Martin threw him a grimace. 'I did say I was going to cure her, didn't I?'

Hazelmere acknowledged that with a resigned nod. 'I hadn't, however, imagined you would allow such an item to become public property.'

'*Public property*?' Martin was on his feet and pacing. 'Bloody hell!' he growled. 'How the hell did that get out?'

Hazelmere viewed his friend's agitation with transparent satisfaction. 'I didn't think you knew anything about it.'

He spoke softly, but Martin caught the quiet comment. He swung about, brows knit in a furious frown. 'Of course I knew nothing of it! Why on earth…?' He stopped, struck, his face drained of expression. Slowly, he sank back into the chair. 'Dorothea—and everyone else—thinks I let the information slip?'

Succinctly, Hazelmere nodded. 'To Lady Rochester,' he added. 'She was spreading the tale shortly after you danced so briefly with her at the Barhams.'

Martin groaned and sank his head into his hands. How had Serena found out? A more worrying thought surfaced. He looked up. 'Helen can't believe that surely?'

A frown had invaded Hazelmere's face 'To be perfectly honest, I don't know what Helen thinks—I haven't had a chance to ask her. She's disappeared—gone out of town. I'd hoped you might know where she was, but obviously that's not the case.'

'I came to ask if you knew where she was.' Martin straightened, his worry overcoming his frown. 'I left town early on the morning after the ball. What exactly happened?'

Hazelmere told him, briefly, concisely. 'So Dorothea and Ferdie left her to think things through. The next morning, she left.'

'Damn!' Martin stood again, automatically falling to pacing before the hearth. With an effort, he forced himself to evaluate the situation coolly. 'Luckily, the position's not irretrievable. Once we marry, it'll cease to be news.'

Hazelmere inclined his head in agreement. 'True. But, if you don't mind my curiosity, when, exactly, is the wedding?'

The glance Martin shot him contained equal parts of frustration and sheer exasperation. 'The witless wanton wouldn't accept.'

For once, the hazel eyes opened wide in honest surprise. Black brows rising, Hazelmere considered his wayward charge. 'What on earth is she about?' he eventually asked.

'Damned if I know,' Martin muttered. 'But if I can lay hands on her, you can rely on me to shake some sense into her.' Tired of pacing, he returned to his chair. 'Have you any idea where she might have gone?'

Hazelmere frowned. 'There aren't all that many options. I know she hasn't gone to one of my estates—I'd have heard by now. I can't imagine her going to an inn or any such.'

Martin shook his head. 'Too risky by half.'

Nodding sagely, Hazelmere continued, 'Which leaves Heliotrope Cottage.'

Martin looked his question.

'As I recall, I told you that none of Helen's properties was saved from the collapse of the Walford estates?' At Martin's nod, Hazelmere said, 'As far as substance goes, that's true. But Heliotrope Cottage was considered beneath the dignity of any gambler. Consequently, it's the one part of Helen's patrimony that remains hers. It's a tiny place on barely five acres. In Cornwall.'

'Cornwall?'

At Martin's incredulous exclamation, Hazelmere blinked. 'Yes. Cornwall. You know—it's that bit beyond Devon.'

Martin brushed his levity aside. 'I know where the damned place is but, what's more to the point, so does Hedley Swayne. His estates are there, too.'

Hazelmere's hazel gaze was confused. 'Quite a few people have estates in Cornwall.'

'But,' said Martin grimly, getting to his feet once more, 'none of the others has tried to kidnap Helen.'

Hazelmere blinked. 'I beg your pardon?'

Pacing again, Martin threw his explanation over his shoulder. 'I first met Helen not here but in a wood in Somerset, not far from Ilchester. She'd been grabbed from a ball by two ruffians. They were waiting with her for their client to arrive. From everything I've learned, that client was Hedley Swayne. Helen thought it was at the time.'

Hazelmere met his glance, then fell to considering the facts. 'It doesn't make sense,' he eventually said.

'I know it doesn't make sense,' Martin growled.

'We've all seen Swayne dancing about Helen's skirts, but I wouldn't have thought he'd have any real inclination in that direction.'

Martin shook his head. 'He's definitely not one of us.' A moment later, he added, 'There must be some reason that we can't see. But whatever it is I'd much rather Helen was safe before I shake the answer from Hedley Swayne.'

With that, Hazelmere was in complete agreement. 'Will you go down or will I?'

'Oh, I'll go, if you'll give me her direction. I intend having a very long talk with your wife's dearest friend. After that, I rather think we'll return by way of Merton.' At the thought of taking Helen to the Hermitage, Martin's features eased for the first time that day.

Hazelmere nodded and stood. 'I'll write the route down—it's not exactly straightforward.'

Armed with a complicated set of directions which Hazelmere assured him would take him to the door of Heliotrope Cottage, Martin departed from Hazelmere House, pausing at the last to request Hazelmere to speak to his wife regarding her killing glances.

As soon as he crossed his threshold in Grosvenor Square, Martin issued a stream of orders, which culminated in his sending Joshua scurrying to harness the bays while he strode upstairs to throw a selection of clothes into a bag. Laying shirts and a supply of freshly laundered cravats in the base of the bag, Martin grimaced. He would have to get a valet if he was set on observing all the niceties. Men such as he were expected to have one, but he had managed well enough without throughout his eventful life. Nevertheless, if he was to settle down to socially acceptable wedded bliss, a valet seemed inevitable. The idea of marriage halted him mid-stride.

Who knew what situation he would face in Cornwall? Who knew to what lengths he might have to go to convince Helen to say yes? All in all, the insurance of being able to secure his prize the very instant she agreed to his proposal seemed advisable.

A wry grin twisted Martin's lips. He resumed his packing, mentally rehearsing his plea to the Bishop of Winchester, a connection of his father's who would doubtless be only too pleased to do what he could to entangle a rake past redemption in the sacred toils of matrimony.

The bed at the Four Swans was lumpy. Ruefully reflecting that easy living had exacted a toll from his tolerance, Martin stretched out and closed his eyes. The day had been unwarrantedly full.

First, his arrival in London, full of his plans for fair Juno, plans which were dashed by her absence. Then his interview with Hazelmere, and his preparations for his journey. As it had been his secretary's day off, he had decided to go through the pile of mail placed waiting on his desk before quitting his house for an indeterminate time. He had found Helen's brief note in the pile, with a scrawled message from his secretary appended. Initially, he had been downcast that she had appealed for his help and he had not been there to assist her. Then the implication of her appeal had struck him.

Despite the hurt he had inflicted, she had not balked from summoning him; she had clearly envisaged being able to play a part, with him by her side to conceal their illicit liaison. All in all, it would not have been hard, together. They would simply have pretended nothing was amiss—none, he was sure, would have pressed the point.

But the important feature of her call for help was that she had been prepared to see him again, to speak with him again. That was, Martin felt, definitely encouraging.

He sighed and settled his shoulders. Things were looking up. The drive from London to Winchester had been accomplished in time for him to be invited to sup at his Grace's board. His ageing relative had proved much as he had imagined, but more curious than censorious. A special licence had been duly provided. Thus armed, he was looking forward to the second day after the next with keen anticipation.

Even if he left early the next morning, it would still take him more than two days to reach Heliotrope Cottage. Two more days in which to polish his apologies and frame his proposal while keeping his cattle on the road. He had nearly landed them in a ditch this evening. He would have to make sure he kept sufficient wits functioning to drive; he could not bear any further delay.

He still could not fathom how the fact of their afternoon together had been broadcast to the *ton*. However, rake that he was, he recognised the added weapon the potential scandal gave him. It would have to be wielded with care, of course, and only if Helen still showed reluctance. No woman liked to feel jockeyed into any decision; none knew that better than he. Somehow, he would have to ensure that the idea of marrying him as the most socially acceptable course was subtly conveyed to his love.

No light had yet glowed on her reasons for refusing him; in truth, if she was simply too wary to try marriage again, the only way he could think of to convince her was to marry her and consequently demonstrate how wrong she was. A little gentle persuasion was surely excusable in such circumstances?

With a slight frown, Martin shook aside such quibbles and let his usual positive attitude resurface. He wanted Helen Walford to wife, therefore, however it came about, she would marry him. It was in her own best interests, after all.

The moonlight streamed in through the open window, a slight breeze wafted the net curtains. Martin felt sleep take hold. His dreams would doubtless be of the last inn bed he had slept in—and his fair companion in dreams.

CHAPTER ELEVEN

Was it two spoons of milk or only one? Helen rubbed a floury hand across her brow and struggled to remember Janet's instructions. She had sent her maid to the mill just outside the tiny village half a mile away, to buy more flour. Meanwhile, she had decided to use what was left and make some bread.

She had never cooked anything before—other than the pancakes she had assisted with during that night in the old barn. Even then, *he* had actually done the cooking. At the thought of him, whom she refused to acknowledge by name in the vain hope that that would assist her mind in forgetting him, Helen's eyes filled. Annoyed, she blinked rapidly. She sniffed. Damn! She had never been the sniffy sort but, ever since leaving London, she had hovered on the brink of tears. It would not do—she had to pull herself together and get on with her life. No matter how lacking in all enticement that life now seemed. For a while, he had filled her with hopes for the future. They had come to nought, but her life was not, in truth, any more drab than it had been before. She tried to reason with her emotions, to no avail. All they seemed capable of dwelling on was her misery at losing him.

Helen gritted her teeth and plunged both hands into her dough. Her sudden urge to action was simply an attempt to get some purpose, however inconsequential, into her life. The past five days had disappeared in a dull daze, the fine weather outside clouded by her misery. Heliotrope Cottage was comfortable enough but, without menservants, Janet had to do everything. Helen poked at the dough disparagingly and reflected that she would have to see about hiring a young girl to come in and help with the cleaning and cooking, and maybe find a gardener as well.

The kitchen was a sunny nook, part of the large room that made up the ground floor of the cottage. A window beside the table at which she stood looked out over the small kitchen garden. The plot was currently overgrown, choked with a full season's weeds, but reddish earth showed in one corner where Janet had made a start on clearing it. Helen breathed deeply of the tangy breeze wafting in through the open door of the cottage, to play with her curls before whisking out again through the back door. With a grimace, she regarded the floury mass in the copper basin. It must have been two spoonfuls.

She was replacing the milk jug on the dresser when the sound of horses' hooves and the sliding thump of heavy carriage wheels rolling down the rutted lane came to her ear. Helen froze. Then her heart started to pound, faster and faster as anticipation rose.

The cottage stood at the end of the lane; there was no passing traffic. Who was it who had come to visit her?

The likely answer addled her wits.

Then she heard a voice, a light voice, giving instructions, and knew it was not the Earl of Merton who had called.

Disappointment sent her back to despair.

Consequently, when a sharp rap came on the door-frame, she made no move to take her hands from the copper basin, but called out, 'Come in!' in as interested a tone as she could manage.

To her surprise, it was Hedley Swayne's slight figure that appeared in the doorway. 'Lady Walford?'

Helen stifled her sigh. Country hospitality demanded that she at least invite him in for refreshment. 'Come in, Mr Swayne.' She waited until her unexpected visitor had mincingly picked his way across her small front room, his features registering disapproval of her rustic surrounds, before commenting, 'I had hardly looked to see anyone from London hereabouts. To what do I owe the pleasure of your visit?'

'Dear lady.' Hedley Swayne bowed effusively. 'Just a neighbourly visit.' When Helen looked her confusion, he added, 'I own Creachley Manor.'

Creachley Manor? Helen blinked. If that was so, Hedley was, in fact, her nearest neighbour. The lands attached to the Manor all but enclosed hers; it was the largest single holding in the immediate area.

'I see,' she said. 'How very thoughtful of you.' She waved a whitened hand at a nearby chair and watched as Hedley disposed himself upon it, fussing about the arrangement of his coat-tails. Dismay was her predominant reaction—to his visit and to the news that he was so closely situated. She did not trust his airy excuse one bit. 'But how did you know I was here?'

For an instant, Hedley's pale eyes went perfectly blank. 'Er…ah, that is to say…heard about it. On the village grapevine, if you know what I mean.'

Helen inclined her head civilly. Having lived in the country for most of her life, she knew perfectly well what he meant, but, although it often amazed her with its speed, no village grapevine worked that fast. She and Janet had arrived late in the evening; their post-chaise and post-boys had immediately returned to the road for London. Today was the first day anyone in the village could know of their arrival and that only through Janet's appearance at the mill. Hedley Swayne was lying, but to what purpose?

'Could I offer you some tea, sir?'

Hedley looked slightly perturbed at the suggestion. His roving gaze alighted on a small decanter on the sideboard. Helen saw it and correctly divined that the fastidious Mr Swayne did not partake of tea. 'Or perhaps some cowslip wine would be more to your taste?'

To this, Hedley Swayne agreed readily. Sending silent thanks to her cook in London, who had slipped a bottle of her delicious wine into the provisions Janet had packed, Helen lifted her hands from her basin and looked in consternation at the gooey mess covering her fingers.

'Er…perhaps if you'd just tell me where the glasses are?'

Appeased by this show of neighbourly good sense, Helen directed Hedley to the cupboard beneath the sideboard. She watched as her visitor arose and helped himself, her brow creasing as she struggled to understand just what he was about this time. His visit was not driven by pure neighbourly concern, of that she was sure. But what did he hope to achieve? His dress was as finicky as ever, better suited to the Grand Strut than a small cottage in deepest Cornwall. The coat of puce cloth was offset by yellow pantaloons; a wide floppy yellow neckerchief tied in a bow proclaimed his allegiance to fashionable fripperies. As with most of the fops, he disdained the highly polished Hessians of the Corinthians, opting instead for heeled shoes, in this case sporting gold buckles. There was a gold pin in the neckerchief and a huge fob watch vied with a range of seals for prominence against a perfectly hideous purple embossed silk waistcoat. Considering the spectacle, Helen reflected that it was almost as if Hedley had dressed to impress. Unfortunately, in his present surroundings, he only succeeded in looking woefully out of place.

Her own dull olive gown, with its round neck and simple sleeves, was far more in keeping with the country atmosphere. Its colour did nothing for her complexion, drawn and sallow after days of weeping. Not that she cared. There was no reason to make the most of herself; she did not desire to impress her neighbours—not even be they Hedley Swayne.

Pouring himself a generous measure of cowslip wine, Hedley returned to his chair. 'I must say, dear Lady Walford, that it's a pleasure to see a woman such as yourself engaged in such a womanly pursuit.'

Helen eyed his smile warily. His attitude was one of a man well-pleased, almost smug, as if he had solved some fiendishly difficult problem and was looking forward to claiming his prize. Helen's unease grew, but she merely nodded, wondering what to say next. Luckily, Hedley had an inexhaustible flow of patter. He rambled on, and, at first, she thought his direction aimless. Then, as she followed his recitation of *ton* events, she started to perceive a pattern to his revelations. They were all concerned with recent scandals and how these had adversely affected the women involved. In particular, how the unfortunate proceedings had affected the subsequent marriageability of the women involved. She made the right noises at the right places, which was all Hedley required to keep him going while she wondered if she dared guess at his summation.

It was as she had suspected.

'Actually,' he said pausing to take a sip of his wine, 'I left the capital six days ago. So ennervating—the Season—don't you think?'

Helen murmured appropriately.

'And then, too,' said Hedley, examining his fingernails, 'there was a distressing rumour going the rounds.'

And that, thought Helen, is enough. 'Indeed?' She infused the single word with arctic iciness. To her dismay, the effect was not at all what she had hoped.

'My dear, dear Lady Walford!' Hedley Swayne was on his feet and approaching.

Helen's eyes grew round as she saw him place his glass on the table. She stood rooted to the spot in surprise as he advanced on her, arms spread wide as if intending to scoop her ample charms into his embrace. When one arm slipped about her, Helen came to her senses with a jolt. 'Mr Swayne!' She brought up her hands to ward him off. To her surprise, he jumped back, as if she had threatened him with a burning brand. Then she focused on her fingers and realised they were still liberally coated with dough.

When Hedley stared, nonplussed, at the threat to his immaculate suiting, Helen struggled to swallow her giggles. Determinedly, she replaced her hands in the dough. As long as her fingers constituted such deadly weapons, she was safe. 'Mr

Swayne,' she reiterated, striving for calm. 'I have no idea what rumours you have heard, but I assure you I do not wish to discuss them.'

Hedley Swayne frowned, clearly piqued at having his orchestrated performance cut short. 'All very well for you to say, m'dear lady,' he said peevishly. 'But people will talk, y'know.'

'I dare say,' Helen replied discouragingly. 'But whatever they might say is of no concern to me. Rumour is rumour and nothing more.'

'Ah, yes. But this rumour is rather more specific than usual,' Hedley continued, then, when he glanced up at his hostess and saw the wrath gathering in her clear eyes, he hurriedly expostulated, 'But that wasn't what I came here to say—dear me, no!'

'Mr Swayne,' said Helen, suddenly very weary of his company, 'I really don't think that you could have anything to say, on that subject or any other, that I wish to hear.'

'Now don't be too hasty, dear lady.' Hedley Swayne took a step back and, to Helen's wary gaze, seemed to reorganise his forces. 'I suggest you listen to my reasoning before you make any intemperate judgements.'

Helen's lips thinned. Her gaze as bleak as she could make it, she steeled herself to hear him out.

Encouraged by her silence, Hedley Swayne drew a portentous breath. 'I regret the need to speak plainly, m'dear lady, but your recent indiscretion with a peer—who shall remain nameless—is the talk of the town. We all understand, of course,' he went on, 'that this association is at an end.' He took several paces towards the door, then turned to look sternly at Helen. 'Naturally, the entire episode, and the consequent publicity, has left you in an unenviable position. That being so,' he stated, pacing back towards her again, 'you must be glad of any offer that will reinstate you in the eyes of society—the censorious eyes of society.'

Helen had no difficulty restraining her laughter at his mea-
sured periods; she could see where his arguments were headed.

'Thus, my dear Lady Walford, you see me here in the guise
of a knight in shining armour. I am come to offer you the
protection of my name.'

There was no help for it but to make her refusal as gracious
as she could. Helen suspected his motives were not nearly as
pure as he made out, but had no wish to antagonise the man
unnecessarily, a neighbour at that. 'Mr Swayne, I do most
sincerely value your proposal but I'm afraid I have no intention of marrying again.'

'Oh, there's no need to fear I'll claim any rights over the
marriage dear lady. A marriage in name only is what I propose. Why, you're a widow and I—I'm a man about town.
I'm sure we'll deal famously. No need for you to entertain
any worries on that head.'

Unbeknown to Hedley Swayne, his declaration, far from
easing Helen's fears, only added to the deadening misery
threatening to pull her down. Martin had offered her so much
more—and she had had to refuse him. How cruel of fate to
send Hedley Swayne with his mockery of a proposal in the
Earl of Merton's place. 'Mr Swayne, I truly—'

'No, no! Don't be hasty. Just think of the advantages. Why,
it'll put paid to all the rumours—you'll be able to return to
London immediately, rather than languish in this backwater.'

'I enjoy the country.'

'Ah…yes.' For a moment, Hedley's lights dimmed. Then
he brightened. 'Well if that's the case, you can take up residence at Creachley. No problem there. Can't abide the place
myself, but there's no need for you to come back to town if
you don't favour it.'

Helen drew herself up haughtily. 'Mr Swayne, I cannot—
will not—accept your proposal. Please,' she said, holding up
one dough-encased hand to halt his reaction, 'say no more on
the matter. I have no intention of remarrying. My decision is
final.'

Hedley's weak-featured face turned sulky. 'But you must marry me—stands to reason. Merton won't marry you. He's ruined you and now there's nothing left for it but that you must marry. You should marry me, indeed you should.'

What little reserve was left to Helen evaporated at his petulant tone. 'Mr Swayne, I am not constrained to marry anyone!'

Hedley returned her glare belligerently.

Just how long they would have remained so, locked in a contest of wills, Helen was destined never to learn, for at that moment the sounds of an arrival reached them. Another carriage, wonder of wonders. Her breathing oddly suspended, Helen waited, eyes glued to the door, to see who it was this time.

When a large, well-remembered broad-shouldered figure blocked out the light, she was not sure whether to feel relieved or apprehensive. She might have guessed Martin would come to find her.

The cool gaze swept the room, alighting on the occupants frozen in a most peculiar tableau. Martin instantly realised he had walked in on an altercation of sorts. As if on a stage, Helen stared at him from the other side of a deal table, her hands sunk in a copper basin, her golden curls rioting about her face. One glance was enough to tell him that she had not been taking care of herself as she should. Annoyance at her unwise bolt from the capital, which had developed over the long miles from London, grew. But his immediate concern was to relieve her of the obviously unwelcome presence of Hedley Swayne.

Martin nodded coolly to Helen and strolled into the room. Then he turned his attention to Hedley Swayne. 'Swayne.' With the curtest of nods, Martin acknowledged Hedley Swayne's flustered bow. The man's face was evidence enough that he had heard the rumours. Had he had the temerity to approach Helen with them? Martin decided that the sooner

Hedley Swayne left, the safer it would be—for Hedley
Swayne. 'But I believe you were about to leave, Mr Swayne?'

Hedley Swayne swallowed. He glanced nervously at Helen.

Helen sensed his glance but did not return it, too busy drinking in a sight she had convinced herself she would never see
again. It meant that she would have to argue with him again,
but, right now, she did not care. Just the sound of his deep,
raspy voice had sent tingles down her spine. She was alive
again. Her eyes roamed the large figure, noting the broad
shoulders stretching the blue material of his coat, and the long
sweep of muscled thighs encased in buckskin breeches. One
lock of thick dark hair had fallen across his brow. She had
forgotten the excitement his mere presence generated; for a
moment, at least, she would bask in the warmth.

'Actually—no.'

The tentative response concentrated Martin's attention
firmly on the flustered fop. 'What do you mean, no?'

Sheer aggression vibrated in Martin's growl. Helen blinked
and realised the danger. Good God—the last thing she needed
was to have to save Hedley Swayne from annihilation by
throwing herself into the breach! Knowing Martin, that was
what it would take, once he got started.

'What I mean, my lord,' said Hedley, screwing his courage
to its highest pitch, 'is that before you interrupted, her ladyship
and I were engaged in a delicate negotiation and I really don't
think it would be at all considerate of me to leave before we've
come to an agreement on the matter.'

A black scowl had invaded Martin's face. When the stormy
grey gaze flicked her way, Helen was no longer sure which
of her suitors it was safest to encourage. Martin radiated menace. He also looked very determined. His jaw was set, his eyes
were cold. Just how far he would go to gain her consent to
their marriage she did not feel qualified to judge. Hedley she
was sure she could manage; Martin she was sure she could
not.

Martin stalked the few paces to the other side of the table.

'Just what sort of "delicate negotiation" were you discussing?'

Helen wished she could have kicked Hedley but he was too far away. Predictably, the fool thrust his chin in the air and stated, 'As a matter of fact, we were discussing a topic I doubt you have any interest in, my lord. We were discussing marriage.'

Martin's black brows flew. 'I see. Whose?'

Helen closed her eyes.

Hedley blinked. 'Why—ours, naturally.' He bridled, but before he could say more Martin's deep voice, carefully controlled, cut him off.

'Contrary to your suppositions, I rather suspect I'm close to becoming an expert on marriage proposals.'

His grey gaze flicked Helen's way. Opening her eyes in time to catch it, she suppressed a wince.

'As it happens, I've already proposed to Lady Walford. I'm here to repeat that proposal and ask for her ladyship's...final answer.'

Hedley Swayne's jaw dropped.

Helen resisted the impulse to close her eyes and fake a faint. The subtle emphasis on the last two words did not escape her. Martin was telling her this was the last time—the last chance she would have to grab happiness. He had turned until he was facing her. The grey eyes were watchful, sharply acute. Then, as she watched, a slight smile twisted his long lips.

'Well, my dear?' The grey gaze became slightly mocking, distinctly untrustworthy. 'Now that our liaison is public property, it would seem the only respectable solution for you is marriage. It seems you have a choice. The Countess of Merton or Mrs Swayne. Which is it to be?'

Helen only just managed to swallow her gasp. *Outrageous!* He had jockeyed her into the position of accepting one of them, or appearing a reckless wanton, blind to society's rules. Her instinctive response to his manipulation was to reject them both summarily. Martin, at least, knew she did not have to

marry. He, damn his grey eyes, was merely using the situation
to further his ends. She opened her mouth but was forestalled
by his deep, gravelly voice.

'Think carefully, my dear, before you choose.'

The look in his eyes warned her that flat rejection of them
both would not work. Helen drew a tortured breath and struggled to think. Hedley Swayne was looking at her in fascinated
wonder. The fact that she had not immediately leaped to accept
Martin's proposal no doubt gave him heart. If she refused them
both, then she would face continued pressure, not just from
one, but from both. Martin might say it was her final chance—
she did not believe him. He was determined and she suspected
few had successfully gainsaid him—not in the past thirteen
years. Hedley, on the other hand, would hold out hope undi-
minished if she rejected Martin. He, too, would persist—he
had for the past twelve months, with even less encouragement.

Her gaze locked with the grey eyes across the table, Helen
felt all her strength drain. Frowning, she dragged her eyes
from Martin's and, automatically, put up her hand to push
back her curls. Both men moved to stop her. Startled, she
remembered the state of her hands and, just in time, used her
wrist instead. 'Give me a moment to think,' she pleaded.

Her tone twisted through Martin. He frowned. What the
devil did she have to think about? He loved her, she loved
him—there was no reason to cogitate. She looked so weary,
he was tempted to pick her up and put her to bed—to sleep.
Which said a great deal about the state to which love had
reduced him. Right now, all he wanted was a yes to his proposal, and after that Helen badly needed looking after—all else
took second place. The presence of Hedley Swayne was a
bonus. He knew Helen's instinctive dislike of the man—nothing overly strong but simply the natural antipathy of a beautiful woman for a man who had no use for beautiful women.
It was, he suspected, just the situation to break down her bar-
riers. He needed her to say yes—after that, he was prepared
to devote his life to ensuring that she never regretted it—in

fact, to ensuring that she enjoyed her second marriage as completely as she had disliked her first. He waited for her answer, supremely confident as to what it would be.

Helen wished the ground would open up and swallow her, that Janet would arrive and break the deadlock, anything at all to get out of making her choice. She did not want to marry Hedley Swayne. But, with every passing minute, that fate took firmer shape.

She had not expected to see Martin again, not after his brutal dismissal of her and his slap in the face at the Barhams' ball. That had all been reaction, of course, natural, no doubt, in a man of his temperament. But she had imagined that that would be the end of it; why, then, was he here? The answer was staring her in the face, stated plainly in his words. Her heart contracted painfully. He had come because of the scandal.

How could she have forgotten? Agonised as she imagined what his feelings must be, finding himself once more forced to make an offer by the weight of the *ton's* displeasure, she pressed her hands tightly together inside her dough. He was now the Earl of Merton and would be expected to play by society's rules. Thus, he would be expected to offer for her. But if she accepted, his mother would, she felt sure, have no compunction in disinheriting him. He would lose his dream. She could save him from both fates—social ignominy and maternal retribution—by the simple expedient of marrying Hedley Swayne. If she were already engaged to marry Hedley, Martin would be absolved from offering her his name in place of her reputation. He would then be free to marry a lady of whom his mother approved, and thus gain his most desired objective.

Martin shifted his weight. Helen noticed; her time was running out. She glanced up and met his gaze. Something of her decision must have shown in her eyes, for, as she watched, his brows descended and his eyes grew stormy.

'I've made up my mind,' she announced, afraid that if she

did not get it out quickly her courage would fail her. Her eyes remained on Martin's face an instant longer before she turned to Hedley Swayne. 'Mr Swayne, I accept your proposal.'

Hedley Swayne gawked at her. 'Oh. I mean—yes, of course! Delighted, m'dear.'

The silence from across the table was awful. Helen forced herself to look. Stunned astonishment held Martin's features immobile for a fleeting moment, then the hurt she had expected showed for the briefest of instants before a mask of impassivity put an end to all revelations. With dreadful civility, he bowed, his natural grace so much more polished than Hedley's flamboyant rendition.

'You've made your choice—I wish you happy, my dear.' He glanced up and met her gaze. His eyes were cold and stony, grey upon grey, his face a mask. 'I pray you'll not regret the bargain you've made this day.'

His eyes held hers for one last, agonised minute, then he turned on his heel and left.

Helen stood by the table, slowly extricating her hands from the mess of her dough. She was deaf to Hedley's garrulous self-congratulations, her ears straining to catch the sound of Martin's retreating carriage. When the rumble had finally died in the distance, she moved slowly to the chair by the end of the table and sank into it. Then, as the full measure of what she had lost, of what she had committed herself to, became clear, she leaned her arms on the table and, laying her forehead upon them, gave way to her tears.

The crackle of flames came from behind him but, although he felt chilled to the bone, Martin made no move to turn his chair to the fire. If he did, he would see the mantelpiece. Which in turn would remind him of the woman he had left to her fate that morning in Cornwall.

He could not believe she had accepted Hedley Swayne over him. His frown turned to a scowl. He took a long swig of the amber fluid in his glass. The most damning thought of all was the certain knowledge that by forcing his unholy ultimatum upon her he had driven her into Hedley Swayne's arms. That thought threatened to drive him mad. He felt like howling with rage. Instead, he drained his glass and reached for the decanter on the small table at his elbow.

Outside the uncurtained windows, the stars shone in a black sky. It had been full dark before he had reached the Hermitage, even driving in a frenzy as he had been. Joshua had been silent the entire way, a sure sign of dire disapproval. How long he had sat in the darkened library, drowning his sorrows in the time-honoured way, he did not know. Pentley, his new butler, had entered to suggest dinner but he had ordered him out. All he wanted to do was wallow in his misery—and drink himself into a stupor sufficiently deep to let him sleep.

He had lost her—irretrievably; nothing else mattered any more.

The doors to the hall opened. Martin glowered through the dark, preparing an acid rebuke for whoever had dared to disturb his despair. His eyes, adjusted to the gloom, detected no one until, awkwardly, a chair came hesitantly into the room. It stopped just inside the doors, then they shut behind it.

Stifling a curse, Martin rose to his feet. His mother had come down to him. Who the hell had told her he had arrived?

Drawing on considerable experience, he summoned the skills required to cross the long room to his mother's side. He kissed her hand, then her cheek. 'Mama. There was no need for you to come down—I would have called on you at a more fitting hour tomorrow.'

'Yes, I dare say you would prefer me to leave you in peace to drink yourself into oblivion, but, before you've entirely lost your wits, there's something I have to tell you.'

Through the dark, Martin frowned. 'I'm not in the mood to listen to homilies or any such, ma'am.'

Catherine Willesden's lips twisted. 'This is more in the nature of information. Information I think you would wish to hear sooner rather than later.' When her aggravating son made no effort to move, she grimaced. 'Do come to, Martin! You can't be *that* addled yet. Light a candle for goodness' sake; I'm not particularly fond of the dark. And, if you please, you can push me nearer the fire.'

With a deep sigh, Martin accepted the inevitable and did as he was told. He could not imagine what she had to tell him, but in his present befuddled state, he was not up to arguing with her. But once he had lighted a single candle and placed the candlestick on a table beside her chair, drawn up before the fire as requested, he retreated to his own chair, still engulfed in shadows, moving it back so that he could see his mother but still be largely screened from the mantelpiece.

As he sat, he noticed that her face was more drawn and pinched than he recalled. 'Have you been well?'

With a little start, she raised her eyes to his face. 'Oh, yes. Quite well. But,' she temporised, 'I've had rather a lot on my mind, of late.'

'Such as?'

She threw him a darkling glance. 'For a start, I suppose I should tell you that, as far as the question of Serena Monckton goes, I've known for some considerable time that her charge was without foundation.'

Silence stretched, then, 'Did my father know?'

Catherine Willesden shook her head. 'No, I only learned the truth from Damian some years after John died. But I gather most people now suspect the truth.'

For a long moment, she kept her gaze on her interlaced fingers, then, when no comment came, she glanced up through the shadows.

Martin shrugged. 'It doesn't matter any more. That's all history.'

Slowly, his mother nodded. 'I did consider sending for you, but, from everything I'd heard, it seemed you were enjoying yourself hugely and, very likely, wouldn't have heeded the summons anyway.'

A bark of laughter answered her. 'Very true.' Martin reached for his glass.

The Dowager caught the flash of the flames on the cut crystal and decided she would do well to make a long story short. 'Ever since you've returned and rejoined society, I've heard tell of you, from my friends' letters. What worried me was that, despite the fact he's been on the town for close to four years, I've never heard anything of Damian. That led me to ask some questions of my closest acquaintances. The answers were hardly conducive to a mother's peace of mind.' She paused to stare through the shadows at Martin. 'Is it true Damian is one of the louts who frequent such places as Tothill Fields, drinking gin and getting up to all manner of disgraceful exploits?'

There was a long pause before Martin answered. 'As far as I know, that's true.'

Catherine Willesden looked down at her hands and sighed. 'I suppose that explains some of what's happened. I just couldn't credit it that a son of mine could have behaved as he has, but clearly he's been off the tracks for some time.'

'In my esteemed brother's defence, I feel compelled to point out that he's had precious little guidance from any source. But what's he done now?'

The question flustered the Dowager. In her lap, her stiff fingers laced and unlaced awkwardly. 'I'm very much afraid that something I said put the whole business into his mind. You mustn't blame him entirely.'

Slowly, Martin sat up. 'Blame him for what?'

The Dowager winced at his tone. But she stuck to her guns, determined to present the matter in the most accurate way. If Martin wished to disown them all after hearing it, so be it. 'As you know,' she began, 'Damian was always my favourite—more than anything else because he was the last of you and so much younger. Also,' she added, determined to be truthful, 'because he was more ingratiating than the rest of you. You, certainly.'

'I know all this.'

'Yes, well what you may not know is that Damian has long imagined that he would eventually succeed to the title. If not to George, then to you. The catalogue of your past exploits reads like a deathwish. Furthermore, you'd shown not the smallest desire to wed. Naturally, Damian thought that, in time, the Hermitage would be his.' The Dowager paused to assemble her thoughts, then hurried on. 'However, more importantly, Damian has been in the habit of coming to see me on flying visits, and when he has done anything he feels is particularly clever he tells me about it.'

'Boasts about it, I suppose.'

The Dowager nodded. 'Yes. I must confess that, when I was making plans for you, before you arrived, I mentioned them to Damian.' She paused, then looked up. 'I dare say you recall what those plans were?'

'Marrying me to some dull frump, as I recall.'

'Yes. And forcing you to it with the threat of disinheritance.'

Martin nodded. 'So?'

The Dowager drew breath. 'So, when Damian saw you getting too close to Helen Walford, he repeated my threat against you to her. He didn't know it wasn't the truth.' She glanced up and swallowed. Martin was no longer lounging in his chair. The shadowy figure was tense and intent.

'Are you telling me that Damian led Helen to believe that if she married me I'd lose all my supposed wealth?'

The suppressed energy vibrating beneath the slowly enunciated words all but paralysed the Dowager. Feeling very like prey in the presence of an enraged predator, she nodded.

'Aaaaaagh!' Martin sprang from his chair and strode about the room, all feeling of indolence vanquished. Halfway down the room, he abruptly turned and came back to stand in front of his mother. 'Was Damian the agent who spread the tale of Helen's spending the afternoon at Merton House?'

The Dowager looked up into eyes like flint. All inclination

to defend her wretched fourth son evaporated. She nodded. 'Yes, he admitted that, too. However, it seems as if he believed he was doing you a favour at the time.'

Martin paused in his pacing to throw an incredulous glance her way. '*Favour*?'

'I gather he was certain you'd broken off with Lady Walford. He thought to protect you from any claim made by her ladyship by ensuring that her reputation was already destroyed.'

When Martin simply stared at her, Catherine Willesden nodded. 'I know. He's not really very clever at all. He doesn't seem to understand how people should behave.'

Martin groaned. 'Where is he?'

'At the Bascombes', near Dunster. He said he'd be back in a few days.'

Martin nodded. 'I'll deal with him later.'

For five minutes, he paced the room, his brow furrowed as he pieced together the tangled web of his proposals and Helen's refusals. The damn woman had put him through hell, believing she was saving him from financial ruin. With an inward groan, he recalled his comment of not caring for his fortune, only for her. He had tripped himself up with his passionate avowal. But he had it all clear at last. Damian, of course, would have to be licked into shape, but first he had to extricate Helen from the mess her penchant for self-sacrifice had landed her in. Now he understood her steadfast refusals. She had decided to save him and nothing he had been able to say had swayed her. Gratifying, that, even if it had proved frustrating.

With an exasperated snort, Martin halted before the mantelpiece. His raving about his plans for the Hermitage and Merton House had doubtless played their part—he had gone out of his way to share his dreams with her, to make her see she was part of his life. Couldn't she see that his dreams would not be complete without her, here, where she belonged, in front of his hearth? How could she have believed he would

value a house more than her—more than their love? Clearly,
fair Juno required intense instruction on the whys and where-
fores of a love match.

Glancing up, Martin noticed his mother's grey eyes, watching him in open concern. He smiled, for the first time that day.
Going to her, he turned her chair from the fire. 'Thank you
for your information, Mama. I'll take you to your rooms.'

'And then?' His mother twisted her head to look up at him.

'And then I'm for bed. At first light, I'm heading for Cornwall.'

'Cornwall?'

'Cornwall. I've a goddess to rescue from a fate worse than
death.'

When his mother looked her question, Martin added, 'Being
married to a fop.'

CHAPTER TWELVE

Wisps of fog wreathed outside the leaded panes of Helen's bedchamber window. She stood before it, listlessly brushing her hair, at one with the dismal chill of early morning. If she had had any sense, she would have stayed in bed. But she could not sleep; there had been no point in lying there, imagining what might have been. Trying to block out the future.

There was no escape. By her own choice, she had cast the die. Now she had to pay the price. She just had not expected the account to be presented quite so soon.

Hedley had a special licence. The man was a bundle of contradictions but could, apparently, organise himself well enough when sufficiently moved. And he had certainly been moved last night.

Helen bit her lip, her eyes fixed, unseeing, on the gloom outside. She had indulged in a rare exhibition of tears after Martin had left, sobbing for what had seemed like hours. Janet had returned and held her, rocking her like a child, soothing her with comforting nonsenses until, finally, she had been numb enough inside to stop. Only then had she become aware that Hedley Swayne was still there.

When he had explained the arrangements he had made, she had realised that he had left, but had returned to tell her of their wedding. The next day.

Today. This morning, in fact.

With a deep sigh, Helen moved listlessly to the window-seat and sank on to the simple cushions. She had spent half an hour arguing with Hedley, why she could not now recall.

Martin was gone; it did not really matter when she married Hedley. In fact, for her purposes, perhaps sooner was best, as he had said? Once the knot was tied, Martin would be forever safe.

Again, Helen sighed. She could barely summon the energy to stand, let alone think. Thinking was too painful. If permitted to roam, her errant thoughts showed a depressing tendency to dwell on the bounty she would have reaped as Martin's wife, throwing into stark contrast the dismal prospect of marriage to Hedley. He had made it plain, in a burst of quite remarkable candour, that he considered theirs to be a marriage of convenience, nothing more. She was coming to understand that he was truly indifferent to her but, for some unfathomable reason, was equally steadfast in his desire to marry her.

Shaking her head, she raised her brush once more to her tresses, which were tangling about her shoulders. Hedley was beyond her understanding. More definitely within her grasp was the realisation that, in just a few hours, she would say the words which would condemn her to purgatory a second time around. Like a wet grey cloak, despair sat her shoulders, dragging her down. She would have to put on a brave face at the church, although she doubted there would be many there. Janet, of course, and Hedley's servants, but she did not know anyone else in the village. She did not even know the vicar.

Her brush stilled. Tears filled her eyes, then slowly welled over to course down her cheeks and fall, unheeded, into her lap.

Minutes ticked by and the fog lifted, yet still the cloud of cold despair shrouded her heart.

Eventually, Janet came to her rescue. The maid fussed and prodded and poked and cajoled and at last she was ready—or as ready as she would ever be. Her bronze silk dress was the only one she had brought with her that was halfway suitable for the occasion, and even that was stretching tolerance a bit far. The low neckline and clinging skirts were intended for *ton* parties, not religious ceremonies. She had no bouquet but chose a small beaded purse to clutch. Her curls were set in the simple knot she preferred; she waved away the rouge pot, dismissing Janet's criticisms of her wan complexion.

Hedley had sent a carriage. Resigned to her fate, Helen allowed herself to be helped aboard.

The short journey to the village was accomplished far too fast. Descending before the lych-gate, Helen was surprised to find a small crowd gathered, country folk all, eager to view the unexpected happenings. She plastered a smile to her lips. As things were shaping, these people might well be her neighbours for the rest of her life.

Buxom farmers' wives bobbed their round faces in smiling greeting; their husbands, broad and brawny, grinned. Between the adults, children swarmed in a continuous stream. Suddenly, a freckle-faced miss bobbed up in Helen's path. Bright eyes, glowing with delight, looked up into Helen's face. A small hand held out a tightly packed bunch of flowers—daisies, lilies and assorted hedgerow blooms.

For an instant, Helen's determination faltered. She swayed slightly, but the necessity of taking the offering and suitably thanking the child took her past the dangerous moment. She would *not* think of what might have been—she could not afford his dreams and hers, too.

Relief swept through her when the cool dimness of the church porch engulfed her. Dragging in a deep breath, Helen saw that the tiny church was packed with locals, most likely Hedley's people from Creachley Manor, for they did not have the look of farmers, like those outside. Everyone had noticed her arrival. As she stood, frozen, at the entrance to the short nave, all heads turned slowly to view her.

With a last, desperate breath, Helen raised her head and walked forward.

Martin cracked his whip above the bays' ears, more to relieve his frustrations than to exhort his cattle to move faster. They were already rocketing along, the well-sprung curricle

swaying dangerously. Joshua had been silent ever since they
had passed out of the gates of the Hermitage just before sunrise.

Squinting against the glare, Martin took a blind curve at full
speed. Six hours of sleep had cleared his head; the brandy he
had consumed the evening before had been enough to ensure
his slumber free from worry. But immediately the effects had
worn off, he had woken—to a full realisation of the potential
for disaster. Just because he now knew Helen's reasons for
refusing him, it did not mean that he could afford to sit back
in comfort and plan how to best reassure her of his wealth and
the lack of necessity for her sacrifice. Not when he had left
her primed to make that sacrifice. Doubtless if he had been
less experienced in the ways of the world, he would accept
the wisdom that, having got Helen's agreement to marriage,
Hedley Swayne was unlikely to rush her to the altar. But he
had not amassed a sizeable fortune in commodities by taking
unnecessary risks—why should he take risks with his future?

Aside from anything else, a species of sheer terror rode him.
What if he had misjudged Hedley Swayne? What if the fop
really did desire Helen. What if he forced her to marry him
forthwith? What if, given she was promised to him, the blackguard sought a down payment on his husbandly rights?

The whip cracked again; Martin gritted his teeth. Reason
told him that, although pre-empting the marriage ceremony
was precisely the sort of behaviour he would contemplate
without a flicker of conscience, Hedley Swayne was not of
that ilk. Reason was not enough. He wanted to make sure of
Helen without delay.

As he checked his team for the turn into the narrower road
leading to the village of St Agnes, Martin reviewed his options
for getting rid of the redundant Mr Swayne. If necessary, he
would buy him off. At the thought, Martin's lips twitched in
a self-deprecatory smile. His father had paid a small fortune
to extricate him from Serena Monckton's clutches. Now he
was prepared to pay an even larger fortune to release Helen

from her misguided promise to Hedley Swayne. Doubtless, as
fair Juno herself had once observed, there was a moral in this
somewhere.

It was market day at St Agnes, which proved a severe trial
to Martin's temper. He carefully edged the curricle and his
high-bred horses through the mêlée, muttering curses at the
delay. Then they were through and heading out of the village
to the hamlet of Kelporth, beyond which Helen's little cottage
lay.

Joshua had not thought it possible to be glad to see such an
out-of-the-way place as Kelporth again. Yet, when they gained
the crest of the small hill before the village and went smartly
down the lane towards it, he heaved a decidedly heartfelt sigh
of relief. He glanced about at the neat little cottages, set back
from the road with their neat little gardens, tinged with autumn's colours, before them. Ahead, to their left, a gaggle of
children were playing about the back of a carriage drawn up
to the side of the road. As they drew nearer, Joshua made out
the dark mass of a lych-gate and surmised that a church must
lie beyond. He paled, then looked at the straight back of his
master, presently fully occupied with his fretting horses.
Joshua coughed. 'Master, I don't rightly know as how this is
important but take a look to the left.'

'What now?' Martin snapped but did as directed.

The horses plunged, hauled to a halt so abrupt that the curricle rocked perilously, nearly flinging Joshua from his perch.
He hung on grimly, then, as soon as it was safe, jumped to
the ground and ran as fast as his stiff legs would allow to the
horses' head. His master had already sprung down, throwing
the reins haphazardly towards him.

As Martin stared at the children playing in the dust behind
the carriage decked with white ribbons, his blood ran cold.
Slowly, he dragged his eyes from the horrifying sight and
raised them to the church door, just visible through the lych-
gate. What if she had married him already?

The thought jerked him into action. He ran up the path to

the church, all but skidding to a halt in the stone-flagged
porch. A few of the heads near the door turned his way, but
he ignored them, his eyes going to the sight which held most
of the congregation spellbound.

Was he too late? His heart was pounding so hard he could
not hear. Martin clenched his fists and forced himself to calm
down. Gradually, his hearing returning. He frowned. As he
was not familiar with the words of the marriage ceremony, it
was an agonising three minutes before he realised he had one
last chance remaining. Hard on the heels of relief came the
vicar's sonorous tones, 'Therefore if any man can show any
just cause, why they may not lawfully be joined together, let
him now speak, or else hereafter forever hold his peace—'

Martin waited for no further invitation. 'Yes!' he declared,
adding, 'I do,' just in case the vicar had misunderstood. He
strode forward, his boots echoing on the flags, his gaze fixed
on the object of his desire.

At the totally unexpected sound of that deep voice, a voice
she had convinced herself she would never hear again, Helen
froze. Abruptly, she lost all feeling, all sense of time and place.
Her breathing suspended, her eyes had grown round with disbelief even before she turned to find Martin all but upon her,
his grey eyes clear and bright and burning with determination.

To her amazement, he took her arm in a vice-like grip.

'I want to talk to you.'

He would have drawn her out of the church then and there
but for the combined expostulations of the vicar and the pu-
tative groom.

'I say, Merton, she agreed to marry me, y'know!'

'What *is* the meaning of this, sir?'

Martin looked at the vicar, a frown rapidly developing.

But the vicar, secure in his own house and thoroughly disapproving, was not readily cowed. 'This is a marriage ceremony. How dare you interrupt?'

Glancing up into Martin's arrogantly handsome face, Helen

saw the cynical gleam in his eyes. Her heart sank. Oh, God! He was going to be outrageous.

'But you asked for objectors to speak up,' Martin replied reasonably. 'I'm merely obliging.'

For one instant, as the truth dawned, the vicar looked blank. Then he looked thunderstruck. 'You're *objecting*?' His gaze took in Martin's austerely expensive dress, and his commanding visage. Then the vicar turned to gaze at Hedley Swayne. 'I knew I should never have agreed to such a hubble-bubble affair,' he said snapping his bible shut.

'No such thing!' Hedley had turned several shades of puce and was all but flapping in agitation. 'Ask him what his objection is—this is nothing more than some lark because he knows she agreed to marry *me*!'

Hedley glared at Martin. Helen felt ready to sink. But the grip on her arm eased not one whit.

The vicar glanced uneasily from Hedley to Martin. 'If you could, perhaps, tell me what your objection is?'

Without a blink, Martin said, 'Lady Walford agreed to marry me.'

Hedley gasped at what was, quite obviously, a brazen lie. Helen decided it was time for her to take a hand. Despite all, Martin could not be allowed to give up his dreams—not after all the mental agony she had been through to save them for him. 'I did not, nor have I ever, agreed to marry you, my lord.'

Martin looked down at her. As she watched, a glow of warm appreciation filled his eyes, shaking the grip she was endeavouring to keep on her senses. Her eyes widened as that look was superseded by an expression she could only describe as unholy. 'You did, you know,' he said with a slow smile. 'When you were in bed with me that afternoon.'

Helen felt her mouth fall open. Her cheeks were aflame. How *dared* he say such a thing? In church, with the entire congregation for witness?

The vicar threw up his hands in scandalised horror. 'I should have known better than to have anything to do with fashionable folk. London folk,' he added, glowering at Hedley. 'In the circumstances, I must ask you—all *three* of you—to leave the church immediately! And I most seriously advise you to look to your souls.' And with that parting shot the vicar turned and marched into the sacristy.

The congregation erupted. Under cover of the ensuing uproar, Martin dragged Helen through a side-door and into the graveyard. They were midway across the grassed expanse, dotted with worn headstones, before Helen found the strength to haul back, bringing them to a halt.

'My lord! This is ridic—'

The rest of her words disintegrated under the force of his kiss. Fiery passion seared her lips, then, when they surrendered, threatened to cinder what was left of her wits. She struggled, trying to escape a too well-desired fate, trying to deny the hunger that rose up to overwhelm her reason. In response to her ineffectual wriggling, Martin's arms tightened about her, pressing her more fully against his hard chest, until, at last, she admitted defeat and melted against him.

Only when all trace of resistance had been vanquished did Martin risk releasing her lips. She was a stubborn goddess, as he had every reason to know.

'Don't talk,' he said, laying one finger across her reddened lips to enjoin her obedience. 'Just listen.' Gazing down into her wide green orbs, he smiled and enunciated clearly, 'My fortune is mine. Not my mother's, not even vaguely dependent on her whim. I'm excessively wealthy in my own right and have every intention of choosing my own bride. Do you understand?'

The wide eyes widened even further. Helen could barely find the breath to speak. 'But your brother said…' was all she could manage.

'Regrettably,' said Martin, his jaw hardening, 'Damian was labouring under a misapprehension.'

Helen detected his anger but knew it was not directed at her. 'Oh,' she said, struggling to decide what it all meant.

'Which means I'm going to marry you.'

The decisive statement brought Helen's eyes up to Martin's grey ones. His stern, not to say forbidding expression gave her pause. 'Oh,' was all it seemed safe to say.

'Yes, "Oh",' Martin repeated. 'I've asked you three times already, which is more than enough. I've given up proposing. You're going to marry me regardless.'

Helen simply stared, too enthralled by the vision of the rainbow rising once more on her horizon.

When she said nothing, Martin went on, entirely serious, 'If necessary, I'm prepared to lock you in my apartments at the Hermitage and keep you there until you agree.' He paused, brows rising. 'In fact, that's a damned good idea—far more appealing than proposing.'

Helen blushed and looked down. Things were moving so fast; her head was spinning, her heart was beating an insistent but happy tattoo. She could barely formulate a thought, with her mind whirling with the giddy promise of happiness his words had implied. Could it really be true?

Martin examined her flushed countenance, conscious of a medley of emotions coursing his veins. Relief that she was once more in his arms was slowly giving way to pride that she had loved him so much she had been willing to accede to another meaningless marriage to save his dreams. An urgency to secure her hand, beyond all possible loss, was slowly growing. He was about to speak, to assure her that he now understood her odd behaviour, before showing her that he appreciated it as he should, when, from the corner of his eye, he saw Hedley Swayne, also leaving the church by the side-door. The fop saw them and turned away, disgruntlement visible in the slump of his shoulders as he made his way jerkily through the headstones.

Reluctantly, Martin released Helen. 'Wait here. And don't

move!' He enforced his command with a meaningful look, then strode after Hedley Swayne.

Mr Hedley Swayne had tried very hard to get Helen to marry him—why? Martin held no fears for his future wife—he intended to keep her safe from all danger. But the stone of Hedley Swayne's interest was too intriguing to leave unturned.

Hedley heard him and stopped, all but sulking with disappointment. 'What do you want now?' he asked as Martin drew near.

'One simple answer,' Martin said, coming to a halt directly before the slighter man. 'Why did you want to marry Lady Walford?'

Hedley scowled, then, after a pregnant pause, gave a petulant shrug. 'Oh, very well. You're bound to learn of it sooner than late, what with your business connections.' He eyed Martin with resignation. 'That little cottage of hers is on land bordering my estate. I own many of the tin mines around here. But the purest deposit my people have ever found lies under those five acres. Can't be accessed by any other route.'

For one long moment, Martin stared at the fop, now seen in a new light. Abruptly, he made up his mind. 'Here,' he said, pulling out his note-case, and extracting a card. 'Come and see me when we get back to town. We can discuss a lease then.'

'A lease?' Hedley took the card, speculation dawning in his pale eyes.

Martin shrugged. A crooked smile twisted his lips. 'I warn you you'll have to wait a few months but by then I think it very likely that both Helen and I will feel somewhat in your debt.'

With a nod, he left Hedley Swayne pondering over that cryptic utterance.

Helen was seated on the marble coping of a grave, trying to see her way forward. Could she safely agree to all Martin said—or was he making their situation appear more rosy than it, in reality, was? He wanted to marry her—that was beyond question. He was ruthless and determined and very used to getting his own way. Was it really in his best interests to marry her? And, most importantly, how could she find out? She looked up as he approached, a frown nagging at her fine brows.

Martin ignored it, holding out his hands to her. Dutifully, Helen put her hands in his and he pulled her to his feet. 'And now, fair Juno, it's time for us to depart.'

'But Martin—'

'I'll leave Joshua here to collect your maid and baggage. We can send a carriage for them from the Hermitage.' Martin paused to glance at her dress. 'Where's your coat?'

'In the carriage. But Martin—'

'Good. If we leave straight away, we should be able to reach the Hermitage by nightfall.' He guided her down the shallow steps to the roadway and fetched her coat from Hedley's carriage.

Taking her arm, Martin led her to his curricle. Beside him, Helen allowed her eyes to seek the heavens for one brief instant. If this was how he was going to behave, she would never learn anything to her purpose. With her own determination growing, she put her hands on his arms as he reached for her waist. 'My lord, I cannot simply go with you like this.'

Martin sighed. 'You can, you know. It's quite simple. But if it's all the same to you, my dear, while I'm perfectly ready to discuss our future together in whatever detail you desire, I'd rather not do so in such a public location.'

He stood back to allow Helen a clear view of the churchyard, now filled with a sea of curious faces. Her eyes grew round. 'Oh,' she said. She held her peace while Martin lifted her to the box seat, shifting across to give him room. He paused to give directions to his groom, before mounting beside her. Within two minutes, they had left Kelporth, and her past, behind them.

Helen took a moment to savour the fresh tang of the breeze on her face, to allow the feeling of having escaped a dismal prospect sink in. Ahead, the future beckoned, exciting and beguiling. But largely unknown. Drawing a deep breath, she turned to view the man beside her, noting the strong hands on the reins, the slight frown—was it of concentration?—tugging at the black brows. 'My lord—' she began.

'Martin,' promptly came back.

Despite her determination, Helen's lips twitched. 'Martin, then.' She raised her eyes to his face. 'Is it really true that marrying me will not alter your state?'

The smile Martin turned on her was dazzling. 'I very much hope it will alter my state.' At her confusion, his smile grew. 'But if you mean will it affect my financial state—no. Other than making suitable settlements on you, marriage to you will not seriously erode my fortune.' When she remained silent, he added, 'I did say so, you know.'

'You also said I'd agreed to marry you!' Helen countered, indignation at the way he had said it returning.

His grin was unrepentant. 'Ah, well. Needs must when the devil drives, I'm afraid.'

Helen swallowed a snort and looked away. He was impossible and, she was quite sure, would remain so, behaving outrageously whenever it suited him, making amends with a wicked smile in the sure expectation of being excused. For the space of a few miles, she let the steady swaying of the carriage soothe her ruffled sensibilities. 'I didn't want you to lose your home,' she eventually said, her voice rather small. Without that information, she was not sure what he might make of her own behaviour.

'My home—and my dreams of restoring it?' Martin asked gently.

Wordlessly, Helen nodded.

'Finally, despite the dust you and fate seemed intent on throwing into my eyes, I figured that much out. You'll be pleased to know that my dreams are all but reality, as far as the Hermitage goes. However, there's an even more important dream that I'm very keen to see transmuted to reality—one you can help me with.'

'Oh?' Helen glanced up at him, not sure any longer if he was serious or just trying to cheer her up. But the grey eyes were perfectly clear and intent, holding an expression which made her feel quite breathless.

'Yes,' said Martin, slowly smiling before giving his attention to the road again. 'It'll take some time to achieve, this dearest dream of mine, but I'm more than prepared to devote myself assiduously to its achievement.'

Helen puzzled for a moment before asking, 'What is this dream of yours?'

Martin considered long and hard before shaking his head. 'I don't think I should tell you just yet. Not until we're wed. In fact, possibly not even then.'

'How am I supposed to help you attain it if I don't know what it is?' Helen threw him an exasperated look, wondering again if he was merely trying to distract her. But his face remained serious.

'If I tell you what I want,' said Martin, frowning in earnest as he tried to unravel the tangle of his thoughts, 'then, with your propensity for giving me what I wish regardless of your own feelings in the matter, how will I ever know if you're helping me because you really wish to, rather than because you want to give me my heart's desire?'

Helen stared at him in total confusion. What on earth was this latest dream of his?

Seeing her confusion, Martin laughed. 'I promise to tell you if I need your—er—active assistance.' With an effort, he kept his face straight, despite the wild scenes his rampant imagination was fabricating. Thankfully, his horses gave him excuse enough to keep his eyes on the road.

As the miles fell beneath the powerful hooves, Helen brooded over Martin's disclosures, but could make all too little of them. His assurance about his home had relieved her mind of its most persistent worry, but there still remained one potential cloud hovering over his rainbow. 'Tell me about your mother,' she said. 'She lives at the Hermitage, doesn't she?'

Martin was only too ready to supply his bride-to-be with information on that subject, eliciting her ready sympathy for his ailing parent. 'And regardless of anything Damian may have said, she most definitely approves of my offering for you. In fact, it was she who told me of Damian's interference. Although she didn't say so, I have reason to suspect she was somewhat disappointed that I didn't leave to come after you last night.'

Privately, Helen considered that a reasonable reaction. Her thoughts must have shown in her eyes, for, when she glanced up and found Martin's gaze upon her, he smiled and added, 'I didn't because, quite apart from the state of the roads, I was—er...somewhat under the hatches. Your fault, I might add.'

Understanding this to mean he had been drinking rather more than usual because of her, Helen felt an odd inner glow warm her. As the curricle shot past a farmer's cart, she reflected that it was just as well Martin was not drunk now, for he was driving at a shocking pace.

Martin kept his horses well up to their bits, only easing them when absolutely necessary. They were a strong pair of Welsh thoroughbreds and made short work of the relatively level roads. Lunch was a hasty affair—some bread and cheese washed down with ale, taken in a small inn at Wadebridge. Even so, by the time they left Barnstaple, and Martin headed the horses on to the road to South Molton, the sun was sinking in the west, the way ahead lit by its slanting rays. Realising that they would not reach the Hermitage, just north of Wiveliscombe, until evening, Martin bethought himself of a pertinent point he would do well to inform fair Juno upon.

'We'll be married tomorrow.'

The bald statement jerked Helen's slumbering wits to life. Tomorrow? She looked up in time to catch Martin's glance. He was deadly serious. As she watched, one dark brow rose arrogantly. 'I've a special licence, supplied by the Bishop of Winchester.'

Helen straightened in her seat. 'Don't you think...?' she began lamely.

'No,' said Martin. 'I want to marry you as soon as possible and that's tomorrow.'

Seeing his jaw firm and the line of his lips narrow, Helen resigned herself to walking up the aisle at the earliest possible hour the next morning. But she was beginning to feel that her overbearing suitor was having things a great deal too much his own way. Consequently, she composed her features to calm and stated, 'That's as maybe. However, despite whatever outrageous claims you may choose to make to the contrary, I have not yet agreed to marry you, Martin.'

A worried frown, tending black, was thrown at her. For a moment, he said nothing. Then, 'All you have to do is say yes.'

The low growl suggested that was her only option. Helen put her head on one side, to consider his point. 'I would really feel much happier waiting until after I've met your mother.'

'You can meet her tonight and spend all tomorrow morning with her. We can be married in the afternoon.'

'But I've nothing to wear,' Helen said, appalled as she realised this was true. She had not thought anything of marrying Hedley Swayne in whatever was to hand, but the idea of becoming the Countess of Merton in a worn ballgown was too hideous to contemplate. 'No, Martin,' she said, her voice increasing in firmness. 'I'm very much afraid you'll have to wait at least until I get a suitable gown. I will not marry you otherwise.'

A groan of surpassing frustration fell on her ears. The horses were hauled to a halt; she was hauled into Martin's arms and ruthlessly kissed.

'Woman!' he growled when he eventually raised his head. 'What further tortures do you have planned for me?'

With an enormous effort, Helen focused her faculties.

Heaven preserve her, but if he realised she lost her wits every time he kissed her she would be in serious trouble. 'Is it torture?' she asked, quite fascinated.

That question got her kissed again. 'Dammit—I want you, don't you know that?'

She did, but Helen also wanted a wedding to remember. Her first, she had spent years trying to forget. And, despite the facts, a rushed wedding would be food for the gossip mills. Suppressing the shiver of delight that Martin's gravelly tone sent coursing through her, she set herself to the task of winning him over. 'It'll only take a few days—a week at the outside,' she offered.

Martin snorted disgustedly and released her. Helen watched as he took up the reins again and set the horses forward. The cast of his features suggested, at the least, disenchantment, at the worst, downright aggravation. She cast about for some gesture, some facet she could add to her plan, which would make the delay more appealing to him. Then she remembered his home and his hopes for it. She sat up straighter. 'You said your father used to entertain a great deal at the Hermitage and that you wanted to do the same.'

Martin shot her a glance from under lowered brows. 'So?'

'So why not make our marriage the first occasion you throw open your refurbished house?'

For a few moments, the horses' hoofbeats and the regular rattle of the wheels were the only sounds about them. Then Helen saw Martin purse his lips in consideration. When she saw his dejection lift, she inwardly hugged herself.

'Not a bad idea,' he eventually conceded. He glanced down at her. 'We could invite the Hazelmeres and Fanshawes and Acheson-Smythe and a few of the others.'

Helen smiled brilliantly, and slipped a small hand through his arm. 'I'm sure they'll come.'

The grey eyes glinted down at her. Then Martin humphed and gave his attention to the road. 'Just as long as you say yes at the appropriate time.'

CHAPTER THIRTEEN

The Hermitage was much bigger than Helen had expected. Even allowing for the deceptive perspective of twilight, the many-windowed two wings stretched deep into the formal gardens. They approached the house from the rear, Martin having driven the curricle around to the stables. The formal front façade, holding court before the sweep of manicured lawns leading to a lake on one side and a stand of majestic horse chestnuts on the other, had been impressive. The back of the mansion was even more appealing, with the pergola-like glassed conservatory positioned at the end of the ballroom in the centre of the main block. The conservatory steps led to a small fountain, centrepiece of the formal gardens enclosed within the wings. Beyond, Helen could just make out the outliers of a wood and the mellow brick wall of the kitchen garden.

Her hand firmly trapped on Martin's sleeve, she was led to a door at the end of one of the wings.

'I suppose I should take you around to the front door, but it's quite a long way.' Glancing down into her upturned face, Martin forbore to add that she was looking tired, which she was. Hardly surprising, for she had had a long day. But at least she was smiling and her eyes were alight. He patted her hand. 'You'll want to freshen up before we have dinner.'

Helen came to an abrupt halt, her eyes widening as she realised what he intended. Then her eyes went to her creased and crumpled bronze silk gown. 'Oh, Martin!' she all but wailed.

Swiftly, Martin pulled her to him and kissed her soundly.
'My mother would welcome you if you were dressed in rags.
Now don't fret.' He smiled down into her anguished eyes. 'I'll
take you to Bender, my housekeeper. I'm sure she'll be able
to help.'

Twenty minutes later, Helen gave thanks for Bender. The
large, round-faced woman, in country plaid rather than the
regulation bombazine, had immediately understood her wordless plea. While she washed her face and hands and brushed
her hair free of the dust of the road, her dress was ruthlessly
shaken, then quickly pressed. It would never be the same
again, of course, but at least it looked halfway respectable.
When Martin tapped on the door of the pleasant bedchamber
Bender had taken her to, Helen was ready to face what she
privately considered her final hurdle—the final hurdle before
she could reach for her rainbow.

Martin's presence by her side, large and infinitely reassuring, helped her hold her head high as she crossed the threshold
of the drawing-room, her eyes opening wide as she beheld
quite the most elegant room she had entered in years. At the
sudden thought that, if the fates were at last disposed to be
kind, she would soon be mistress here, Helen's confidence
faltered. But then Martin was speaking, introducing her. Helen
looked down into the grey eyes watching her, and blinked in
surprise.

How alike they were, was her first thought, superseded almost immediately by the recognition of subtle differences.
Martin's mother's dark brows were much finer than her son's,
though her features were equally arrogant in cast. Her chin
and lips were much softer in line, and the grey eyes, so startlingly similar, lacked the wicked glint often lurking in her
son's. Helen realised she was staring. With a little start, she
bobbed a curtsy.

'I'm most honoured to meet you, ma'am.'

Catherine Willesden eyed the golden-haired beauty before
her and was not displeased with what she saw. An unusually

tall woman and well-built with it—she could readily see just what in Helen Walford had excited her son's interest. And she looked the sort who could carry children well and would enjoy doing so, even more to the point. But what decided the Dowager in Helen's favour, beyond the slightest qualms, was the look of untold pride that lit her son's grey eyes whenever, as now, they rested on his bride-to-be. That, thought the Dowager, was what counted above all.

'Believe me when I say that it is I who am most thoroughly pleased to see you, my dear.' The Dowager threw a meaningful look at her son before, with an effort, she raised her hands to grasp Helen's cold fingers.

Realising the Dowager's difficulty, Helen immediately took hold of the frail claws and readily bent to place a kiss on the older woman's lined cheek.

From then on, it was fair weather and plain sailing between the Dowager and the soon-to-be Countess. Pleased with their ready acceptance of each other and not a little entertained, Martin drew back, leaving the two women to find their own way about each other. But when, after they had left the dining-table for the comfort of the drawing-room, and spent half an hour discussing the details of the wedding and planning the week-long house party, they turned their attention to the wedding feast, he had had enough.

'Mama, it's late. I'll take you upstairs.'

His mother's eyes widened. She opened her mouth to protest, then, catching his eye, closed it again. 'Very well,' she agreed. She turned to Helen, holding out one frail hand. 'Sleep well, my child.'

Martin wheeled his mother out before she could think of any more witticisms. He returned from the Dowager's rooms to find Helen wandering the hall, examining the landscapes on the wall.

'Come for a stroll. The light's not yet gone.'

Helen smiled and calmly placed her hand on his proffered sleeve. Inside, she felt anything but calm. Her heart was leaping about, turning cartwheels and somersaults with sheer happiness. The Dowager was no dragon and clearly well-disposed. The house—Martin's home—pleased her beyond her wildest dreams. She already felt drawn to it, at home within its spell, though whether the feeling owed anything to the house itself, rather than being a reflection of her all-encompassing love for Martin, she could not have said.

As they stepped from the terrace to stroll, arm in arm, along a gravelled path into a landscaped shrubbery, she felt contentment such as she had never known lay its hand upon her.

'We can send letters to the Hazelmeres and the rest tomorrow.'

Martin's murmur wafted the curls by her ear. Helen turned to smile her acquiescence, then, fleetingly, pressed her temple against his shoulder. With no need for words, they wended their way about the low clipped hedges of a miniature maze, to stand by the small fountain at its centre. Smoothly, Martin drew her around, so that the back of her shoulders brushed his chest. His arms slipped about her waist, steel bands holding her against him. He bent his head and his lips grazed her bare shoulder. Helen felt a giggle bubble in her throat. Only a very accomplished rake, she felt sure, would choose the middle of a maze to play at seduction. However, she was not in the mood to deny him. Obligingly, she tilted her head away, giving him access to the long column of her throat. She did not try to stifle the shiver of pure delight that ran through her at the intimate caress.

A crackling twig brought Martin's head up. His eyes scanned the bushes, then the grassed path leading around to the stables. Just discernible in the gloom was the figure of a man, temporarily immobile. With an oath, Martin released Helen and gave chase, leaping over the low hedges, making directly for the man who, after an instant's hesitation, had taken to his heels.

Martin's long legs gave him a telling advantage. He caught up with Damian before he had reached the wood. Catching hold of one padded shoulder, Martin spun his brother about before sending him to grass with a punishing right cross.

For an instant, Damian simply lay, eyes closed, stretched out on the turf. Then he groaned. Perfectly certain that he had not hit his brother with sufficient force to do permanent injury, Martin stood over him, hands on hips, and waited for him to get up. When it became clear that Damian was not going to get up without assistance, Martin's jaw hardened. He was reaching for his brother's coat when Helen erupted out of the darkness behind him and caught hold of his arm.

One glance at Damian, cringing on the ground, confirmed Helen's guess. 'Don't kill him,' she pleaded, gasping to catch her breath. Abruptly deserted by the fountain, she had spent no more than a minute staring in amazement. Then she had followed. But her escape from the maze had been a great deal slower than Martin's. She could not leap over the low hedges in her gown and, without Martin's assistance, she had not known how to get out of the maze. In the end, glancing about through the gathering gloom and deciding that the gardeners would long since have gone home, she had hiked her skirts to her thighs and clambered over the bushes.

Now, finding Martin looking as if he was preparing to thrash the life out of his brother, her only thought was to stop him.

To her relief, Martin promptly drew back, his hands coming to hold hers, his eyes searching her face in the last of the twilight, a curious expression in their grey depths. 'I wasn't about to,' he replied mildly. 'But I shouldn't have thought that, in the circumstances, you would mind.'

Still out of breath, Helen shook her head. She had learned the full sum of Damian's iniquity from the Dowager. 'If it were that simple, you could have at him with my goodwill. But if you kill him, you'll be tried for murder and where would that leave my rainbow?'

'Your what?' Martin's smile gleamed white in the dark.

Helen felt her cheeks burn with embarrassment.

Still smiling, Martin patted her hand. 'Never mind. You can explain it to me later.' He slipped an arm about his bride-to-be's waist and drew her to his side. Then he looked down at his brother, still sprawled at his feet. He shook his head. 'For God's sake, get up! I'm not going to hit you again, though, as God is my witness, you deserve to be horse-whipped.'

Damian half rose, but at the strengthening of his brother's tone he froze.

Martin looked down at him in exasperation. 'You may thank your soon-to-be sister-in-law for deliverance from any punishment I might otherwise have been inclined to mete out.' When Damian said nothing but simply stared, Martin snorted in disgust and turned away. 'Get to your room. I'll see you tomorrow.'

Drawing Helen with him, Martin started back towards the house, then bethought himself of one last warning. He turned to find Damian weaving on his feet. 'In case you're planning a sudden departure, I should warn you I've already given orders that, once here, you are not to be permitted to leave again. Not until tomorrow, when you'll depart under escort for Plymouth.'

'Plymouth?' Damian all but shuddered. 'I won't go,' he said, but to Helen his tone lacked strength.

'I rather think you will.' Martin's tone, on the other hand, radiated strength. 'Mama and I have decided a sojourn in the Indies might well be of as much benefit to you as it was to me.' He paused, then added in a more pensive tone, 'I rather think you'll find it a tad difficult, living in London, once it becomes known that both Mama and I have withdrawn our support.'

Even in the dim light, Helen could see how Damian paled. Obviously, Martin's threat was well-aimed. Martin did not wait to see how his brother reacted. He turned once more in the direction of the house, tucking her hand into the crook of his arm. Obediently, Helen paced by his side.

There was a storm brewing. Large ruffled clouds of deepest

grey were blowing up from the west. After a few minutes, Helen glanced up to find that Martin's forbidding expression had disappeared. In its place was a pensive look she rather thought she should distrust.

'Now, where were we?' he murmured, before flashing her a devilish smile. 'Wherever, I rather think we had better go indoors. The evening grows cold and you're without a shawl.'

Forbearing to point out that her lack of a shawl was entirely his fault, Helen happily permitted him to escort her within doors. He led her upstairs, picking up a candelabra from the table in the hall to light their way. In the long gallery, he showed her the portraits of past Willesdens, hanging between the long velvet-curtained windows.

Picking the most scandalous of the family's tales of yore as the most suitable for his purpose, Martin had Helen in stitches as they moved on through the long corridor that led to the west wing. Embellishing freely, he ensured that she was completely enthralled long enough for them to reach the door at the end of the wing.

It was only then that Helen, catching a sudden gleam in Martin's mesmerising grey eyes, looked about her and realised she was lost—in company with a thoroughly untrustworthy host. Far from feeling threatened, she revelled in the delicious anticipation that stirred in her breast. She looked at the door before her—a very large, well-polished oak door—and then looked at Martin, one brow rising in question.

All he did was smile, successfully scattering her wits, then leaned forward to set the door wide.

Feeling very much as if she was taking some irretrievable step, Helen crossed the threshold. The room was huge—and so was the four-poster bed that stood against the wall, long windows flanking it open to the balcony, their fine lace curtains streaming in with the freshening breeze. She watched as Martin closed the shutters. The only light came from the candelabra, which he had placed on a table by the bed. The glow centred on the bed, drawing Helen's awareness with it. A

heavy silk counterpane, embossed with what she recognised
as the Willesden arms, covered the expanse in deep blue-grey.
Silken tassels of the same colour hung from the cord holding
the bed curtains back. The oak headboard was heavily carved,
again incorporating the family arms, meshed within twining
vine leaves.

Nervousness crept up on her, but then Martin was there,
drawing her firmly into his arms. Before he could kiss her,
and render her witless, Helen placed her hands on his shoulders and smiled up into the stormy grey eyes. 'Is this where
I say yes?' she asked, and was surprised at the husky quality
of her own voice.

Martin smiled slowly, so slowly that Helen had plenty of
time to feel her heart somersault and her stomach contract.

'Actually,' he said, 'given the difficulty you seem to have
with that word, I've decided some practice would not go
astray.'

His tone feathered over her stretched senses, teasing and
tantalising. Helen opened her eyes wide. 'Practice?' she asked
in as innocent a voice as she could muster.

'Mmm,' Martin murmured, bending his head to brush his
lips across hers. 'I'd rather thought to make you say it a
great…many…times.' His last words were punctuated by light
kisses, firm enough to whet her appetite, insubstantial enough
to leave her hungry.

Helen felt her will slowly seep from her but she retained
sufficient curiosity to ask. 'How will you make me do that?'

Martin did not answer.

Instead, he showed her.

Much later, Martin reached out with one hand and snuffed
the candles by the bed. His other arm was occupied, cradling
Helen's warm body by his side. She was asleep, thoroughly
exhausted, having said the word he had wanted to hear a great
many times indeed. Martin smiled into the dark. She still
needed more practice—he was quite certain he would be able

to convince her of that later. With her head once more on his shoulder, her soft curls like silk at his throat, he listened to the storm passing overhead. Wind lashed the trees in the Home Wood, rain pelted down on the gravel walks. Helen had not even noticed the tempest without, being too much caught up in the tempest they had created within.

With a deep sigh, Martin closed his eyes. Contentment coursed his veins like a drug, bringing peace and satisfaction in its wake. His house was in order, fair Juno safe by his side. Tonight, with any luck, he would get some sleep. Maybe not much, but some. And, unlike the last stormy night he had spent with fair Juno, the torture between times would be much more to his taste. He closed his hand over one full breast. And fell asleep.

Helen awoke to rub her nose, then realised that the curly black hair tickling it was attached to Martin's chest. She stifled a giggle and pushed it aside, then glanced up to find lazy eyes watching her, a suspicious twinkle in their depths.

With a smile, Helen stretched, cat-like, and watched the twinkle intensify to a satisfying gleam. As she felt the arm about her tighten, she pressed her hands against his chest. Heavens! She needed at least two minutes to think! 'What is your latest dream, my lord?' she purred, hoping to distract him and appease her curiosity in one stroke.

Martin relaxed and laughed, the warmth in his eyes spreading like a languorous flame over her skin. 'Should I tell you?' he asked rhetorically. Then, 'Perhaps I should.' His eyes held hers, mock-serious. 'I don't think it'll be too hard for you to handle.' His smile grew. 'Well within your capacity, so to speak.'

Feeling the rumble of his laughter, Helen scowled. 'Martin!'

'Ah—yes. Well, having had an opportunity to assess your abilities, my love, and having ascertained that you really do enjoy our recent activities for their own delight, as it were, I feel secure in the knowledge that, once you hear of my dream, you'll not be called on to sacrifice any feelings of your own in its accomplishment.'

Helen glared at him. 'Martin! What is it?'

Martin eyed her a little warily. 'Promise not to laugh?'

Puzzled, Helen's glare turned to a stare. 'Why should I laugh?' she asked. When he said nothing further, she grimaced. 'All right. I promise not to laugh. Now, what is this dream of yours?'

'I have this vision of you standing before the mantelpiece— I think the one in the library at Merton House…' Martin paused, then went on in a rush, 'With my son balanced on your hip.'

Helen blinked. 'Oh,' she said, her voice non-committal. But she could not stop the smile that curved her lips, then deepened to light her eyes. Gazing deep into the grey eyes that held hers, and seeing the hesitant expression that lingered there, Helen decided that she had clearly reached the end of her rainbow and found her pot of gold. Rapidly blinking to clear her eyes of the tears of happiness that threatened, she swallowed and said, 'Oh, Martin!' before throwing her arms about his neck and burying her face in his shoulder.

His arms came up to close about her, holding her close. 'I take it that means you approve?'

A mumble which was clearly an assent answered him. Martin grinned and hugged her more tightly, conscious of the dampness of tears on his shoulder.

Once she had regained her composure, Helen could not resist asking, 'Is that a typical dream for a rake?'

'I assure you it's this rake's dream.' Martin moved to glance down at her. He smiled slowly. 'Now come and do your bit to make it real.'

Helen's smile answered him. 'Gladly, my lord.'

She reached up and drew his lips down to hers and, in truth, there was no dream in her mind beyond the attainment of his.